CHANCE

ENCOUNTERS

THE COLLECTION

L. MOONE

Published by eXplicitTales

ISBN-13: 9781913930141

CHANCE ENCOUNTERS

Chance Encounters is a series of stand-alone romances set in jolly old England, following a set of loosely connected people as they find love in unexpected places. Can love conquer all, from class differences to age gaps? Read on and find out.

Titles in this compilation include:

One Night Stand
Beautiful Stranger
Only a Taste

CONTENTS

ONE NIGHT

STAND

CHAPTER ONE

The meeting has left me exhausted and wired. Although it went well and I've landed the project, I don't feel too excited about it. The new customer is the sort of type whom you could give the equivalent of a perfect sunset and yet he'd be tweaking the colors until there would be no magic left in it.

Ordinarily I don't entertain such people, my web design company had grown successful enough that I didn't need to accept that kind of drain on my energy levels. However, lately things have been tough, and the project is too big and prestigious to pass up. Fingers crossed, with Akhil's support I can pull it off; it would turn things around for me.

Finding him to manage a team of freelancers in India had been a godsend on many previous occasions. I'm sure he will be equally valuable this time around.

If I ever deserved a drink, now is the time. I need to shake this knotted feeling in my chest, before it drives me nuts. It'll turn out fine, as always...

When I'm out by myself, rather than enjoying a fancy dinner, I usually opt for something simple, portable. A kebab or something from the chip shop. The rest of the evening will be spent whiling the hours away in the first decent-looking pub I can find.

And I've just found it.

As soon as I've found my seat of choice in the dimly lit establishment, I notice him. Sitting on a bar stool nursing a full pint while his two friends stand around waiting for their refills. They clearly arrived as a group, but while I observe them it quickly becomes clear that they are not planning to just sit at the bar together.

He's sporting a typical metal head ponytail, longer than my own hair and it really suits him. Too many guys can't get past their old faithful long hairstyle, even when their mane starts to thin. His hair is thick and full though and the first thing I noticed. I have always had a thing for men with long hair.

Chance brought me here tonight to the aptly named "Old Oak". Only a short walk from my hotel, its traditional wood paneled decor looks like the perfect environment to escape to.

It's the sort of place which you can imagine to have been here forever. Probably has done for hundreds of years, largely looking the same but growing ever brighter and shinier. I had planned to just sit here, have a couple of drinks and watch the normal goings-on unfold around me. But my initial plan of staying largely out of sight is starting to look like a bad idea.

From my corner by the window, in between sips of Baileys on ice, I keep eyeing him. Black jeans paired with sturdy biker boots and an untucked black shirt covering his broad frame on top. He looks like an imposing figure, even hunched over as he is at the bar. Like a giant.

ONE NIGHT STAND

I wish he'd turn around. I also wish I had bought my drink from this bar counter rather than the other one, at least I could have had a better look at him before finding my seat.

Like a reluctant predator, I'm just sitting here and staring at him from behind. If I hadn't chosen to sit in such a discreet location, it might have been the other way around.

My phone distracts, a message from Akhil, asking about the meeting and if we can talk. It can wait. I came here to forget about the irritating client with the project I couldn't refuse, not to talk about it. Stuffing the phone back into my handbag, I resume my earlier observations.

His friends are long gone by now, leaving an unoccupied stool beside him and my glass is getting empty quickly. Shall I? It feels so reassuring being unnoticed that I'm very reluctant to get up. I guess I'm just a coward when it comes down to making the first move, and my dark corner feels so safe.

He takes a big last sip from his glass and I panic. What if he's going to call it a night? If he leaves now I'll forever wonder what could've been!

Before I know it my feet carry me towards the bar, while I absent-mindedly smooth down my business-like grey skirt and waistcoat combo. Despite the buzz of the drunken conversations that fills the space, the clicking of my heels on the wooden floorboards is almost as deafening as my heart pounding in my chest.

He turns towards me as soon as I reach and I'm frozen in place. Concentrating on continuing to breathe,

I tuck my black wavy hair behind my ear and glance in his direction.

I take in his strong Nordic features, his full lips and steely blue eyes that stand in stark contrast against the dark brown of his hair and short beard. All I can manage is a shy smile before hurriedly looking away.

My instincts served me well, if I had stayed in my seat, I would've regretted it. I feel tiny standing next to him, which causes me to feel an even stronger attraction. And his eyes on me, I can almost feel them stabbing and probing.

His hands are huge as well, manly. I wonder how he'd touch me, if those hands could be gentle or if they only know how to be rough. There's no sign of a wedding ring: what a relief.

It has been decided, I want him at any cost.

"What can I get you, darling?" The bartender interrupts my thoughts.

"Oh I'll have a Baileys, thanks." Taking a deep breath I turn towards my mark. "Would you like anything, while I'm buying already?"

Surprised, it takes him a few seconds to respond. Or perhaps he's as distracted by our eye contact as I am.

"Ice?" the bartender asks. I nod in response before resuming to look at the giant's face again.

The short interruption appears to have helped him get his thoughts in line too.

"Another Guinness," he tells the bartender.

His deep voice matches his impressive stature and makes my heart jump a few beats. I put a tenner down on the bar, hoping that the goose bumps on my arms aren't too obvious.

"Mind if I take this seat?" I say, "You're not holding it for anyone, are you?"

"Sure, go ahead."

While I get onto the stool, our drinks appear in front of us.

"Cheers." I'm trying my best to sound a lot more confident than I feel.

"Cheers." His voice elicits another wave of chills to wash over me.

I desperately try to think of something to say. Apparently my brain thinks it's funny to only feed me utter clichés. I take another sip while trying to come up with something a bit less moronic than 'come here often?'

"You're here on your own?" I finally ask. Still pretty stupid but I can't do any better right now.

"Came with two mates of mine from work. They'll be around here somewhere, on the pull probably," he responds.

"And you've stayed behind? How so, got a girlfriend?" I blurt out the question before I'm able to stop myself. Still, the information is pertinent.

He blinks at me a few times, eyebrows pulled together possibly in surprise at my question.

"No girlfriend. And I opted to stay here because frankly I can do without the inevitable rejection."

"Understandable, I find it quite nerve-wracking to approach people myself."

He seems off, I wonder if I'm making him uncomfortable. But if there ever was an appropriate time and place to ask strangers prying questions, it certainly would be here and now; Friday night in a busy London pub.

He shakes his head slowly before lifting his pint to his lips. I follow suit but can't help wondering what he's thinking.

"I don't see how you'd have that problem. I'm sure you get plenty of attention without even trying," he says finally, almost mumbling the words into his glass.

I look him right in the eyes and helplessly give in to my urge to grin before answering.

"Perhaps the attention I tend to get without trying isn't the one I want."

We just stare at each other for what feels like ages. Neither of us seem in a hurry to look away. I leisurely let my mind wander, still curious what his hands might feel like against my skin. And those lips...

Objectively speaking, he looks like the sort of guy you'd avoid messing with if you can help it. I'm certain that when he walks down the street, people will instinctively part to make way. At the same time his mannerisms, his way of speaking have me convinced that behind the imposing facade, he's a really sweet guy. I wonder what makes me so sure, I don't even know him... yet.

"George, mate!" Two figures appear behind us, one giving him a supposedly jovial smack on his shoulder. The dark expression on his face tells me he's not overly pleased for the interruption.

"Lads..." he says.

"Made a friend, I see? What's your name, love?" The scrawny one who smacked George on the shoulder is leaning against him now and hungrily looking at me.

It doesn't help that he's had quite a bit more to drink than me and it's showing. Meanwhile, the other one is trying to get the bartender's attention.

"Lucy," I answer. My flight instinct becomes too strong to ignore. "Excuse me for a minute, guys."

I steady myself against George's arm while slipping off the bar stool. The apologetic expression on his face is quite endearing. I let go of him and start walking towards the facilities.

Hopefully by the time I'm done wasting some time checking my make-up, George will be by himself again. I suppose I can't blame him for staying at the bar while at least the creepy one of his so-called friends will make a fool of himself in front of every woman in the pub.

CHAPTER TWO

The Ladies' toilet is empty when I walk in, though had there been a queue it would've been a good enough excuse to take my time coming back to the bar.

While smoothing down my hair with my fingers in front of the mirror, I can't help wondering why he hangs out with those guys. When they came up to us, I really got the impression he dislikes both of them. I lean in closer, wiping off tiny bits of eyeliner that have made their way outside my lash line.

I'm relieved to find a condom dispenser on the wall next to the sinks and load it up with all the coins I have. It's best to be prepared, just in case.

The door opens and two girls stagger in, giggling and supporting each other by the arm. I catch the closing door as they pass me and sneak up to the corner from where I get a view of the bar. It seems that the coast is now clear. I guess creepy man and sidekick wandered off looking for more potential victims.

Luckily my seat is still unoccupied, or perhaps George held it for me. I feel a tad less nervous walking up to him and the unmistakable beat of my boots on wood is now more rousing than intimidating.

"So, where were we..." I say.

Climbing back onto my stool, I lean on one elbow

and face him. If this is me attempting to look laid back, I don't think it's working. With both feet dangling high above the floor like a toddler in a high chair, looking cool is an impossibility.

He looks over at me, the relief evident in his eyes.

"I'm sorry about that, especially Steve, he can be a bit of a knob at times."

"That's okay. Was it that obvious that I was running away?" My eyes are drawn to his lips, watching him reciprocate my smile.

"A bit, yeah, you had me worried for a bit that you weren't just avoiding him. Well, glad you came back anyway," he says.

"Of course I came back," I say, "just wanted to time it so I'd get you to myself again."

We're back to staring at each other. I wonder why he hasn't made a move, asked any personal questions. The way he's looking at me does suggest he is interested.

Finally I reach out for my glass which is still sitting there and start sliding it back and forth on the wooden counter causing the half-melted ice cubes in it to clink together.

"So, George... are you local?" I look up, catching his gaze once more.

It doesn't seem like he ever looked away.

"Sort of, just came in for a few drinks after work before heading home. I live near Heathrow. You?"

"Not really, I live in Reading and I'm only in town for one night, a business trip of sorts." I pause, wondering if I should clarify.

"I booked a hotel to save me the late journey home. It's only a short walk from here actually."

"Alright," he says.

Really, that's all? Subtle hints don't appear to be enough to convey my intentions for tonight.

Between the exchanged looks, the small talk continues for a little while longer. George is a programmer apparently, such a coincidence we both work in IT.

I give him my card with my contact details, scribbling on it to add my mobile number, but resist the temptation to go into more detail. After all, I came in here to escape work, not discuss it.

He studies the card, fidgeting with it for a short while before looking back at me.

"How about you, seeing anyone?" he asks.

Finally.

"Not for a while, no." I smile at him, waiting for a reaction.

He is interested, it's written all over his face. But why is he still making me work for it?

Inside my chest a confusing combined feeling of relief and nerves has built up. The tension between us feels strong, almost too intimidating.

I bite my lip and look down, underneath his half open shirt I can just about see a black Tee with a familiar looking band logo printed across the front.

"Say..." I lean towards him and push one side of his shirt out of the way. Just being so close to him and nearly touching his chest with my fingertips is making my heart skip way too many beats at once.

"Blind Guardian? What a coincidence, I love them!" I exclaim, nearly breathless.

It's impossible for me to contain my excitement and so I ramble on about my favorite songs and asking about his. Must be the nerves talking. He doesn't say much at all beyond naming a few titles and remarking how brilliant they were live.

Clearly preoccupied with staring at my fingers which are still holding onto his shirt, he stops talking again. I'm equally lost for words.

Time seems to move in slow motion when his hand finds my wrist, and pulls me closer towards him. Our faces move closer together until he finally looks up at me again.

His eyes look almost black in the subdued light and we're now so near that I can feel his breath tickling my face. His scent is pleasant, like a rather masculine sort of cologne with a hint of beer mixed in. The effects of the few drinks I've had already are making it hard for me to focus but I know what I want, and I desperately hope he does too.

"You're making it very difficult for me to resist..." he says.

I see the same nerves I feel mirrored in his eyes momentarily. But instead of acting on them, he continues to stare deep into my soul.

"That was the idea..." I breathe.

Both of us are ready to go where our instincts might take us, still my mind plays tricks on me by announcing his idiot friends' return. I can hear the creepy one even if I don't know or care what he's saying. It's making me want to run and hide again, away from all interruptions.

He releases my wrist so I can I run both hands up his shoulders and around his neck. I hardly need to make any effort to get him to come closer, he already stood up right in front of me.

George is quite a bit taller than he looked sitting down. With me still perched on my bar stool and him standing, I can reach him perfectly. I run my fingers through his ponytail while our lips meet.

His arms find their way naturally around my back. The world around us disappears, taking any unwelcome other people away with it. My legs part as far as they'll go in this skirt to allow him closer. If his lips are anything to go by, he is the gentler type definitely. Or perhaps he just likes to start off that way.

Meanwhile I crave more than the teasing kisses he is planting on my lips, I tilt my head slightly. My arm is firmly wrapped around his neck now, my whole body completely giving in to his embrace. Encouraged, his lips part, as do mine. His beard feels ticklish against my face, an extra stimulus to drive me insane.

A jolt passes through me when our tongues meet. I thought I'd had butterflies in my stomach before, but nothing I've felt before could prepare me for what he's doing to me now. Hungrily I accept him into my mouth; caressing, licking and tasting him. The room is spinning around me but his arms keep me steady.

He pulls back only slightly, upon opening my eyes I

ONE NIGHT STAND

see his, burning with lust.

"You taste divine," he whispers.

I rest my forehead against his and tug at his bottom lip with my teeth.

"Let's go..." I say.

CHAPTER THREE

Our moment of passion hasn't gone unnoticed, attracting quite a few stares. Ignoring his mates, who are just silently gawking at us, we stalk across the room towards the exit. Despite the substantial heels I'm wearing, he's still a good half foot taller than me.

The chill in the early spring air becomes more obvious as we rush across the street. His arm rests protectively around my shoulder and mine around his lower back. I feel like I'm on top of the world, like nothing could stop me from getting exactly what I want.

In the bright lights of the hotel lobby, I get a chance to admire our reflection in the polished elevator doors. The contrast between us is startling, it only turns me on more. The surrounding air feels warm but does nothing to subdue the goose bumps covering my entire body. I need him now, his touch, to make everything better. If only the lift doors would open...

After half an eternity, the bell chimes and doors jerk into action. We swiftly move into the lift and I'm aching to get my hands on him the moment we're alone and out of view. I press the button and wait. A quick look in his direction and sure enough, he's as focused on me, ready to continue our earlier affections.

The wicked smile on my lips vanishes when I see an

elderly couple approach, rushing to make it into the lift before the doors shut. Especially the lady looks disapproving of us, dampening my spirit slightly. All I manage is to squeeze his hand on my shoulder and press against him closely to allow them to join us in the tiny space until we reach the third floor.

The pause between the ding and the doors opening lasts forever, I'm that impatient.

We escape and the grumpy couple is now out of sight. I turn towards him for more kisses while fumbling with the key card outside my room.

We barely make it inside before items of clothing start to come off.

I rush to unzip my boots, kicking them across the room, and unbutton my waistcoat. George has stepped behind me now, leaning down to kiss the back of my neck. After wriggling out of my waistcoat I throw it over the sofa against the wall and face him again

His eyes burn into me, lit up by what I can only assume is an intense hunger matching my own. He looks down at my cleavage, which is still more or less covered by my white blouse.

"Tell me I'm not dreaming," he says.

I start to unbutton from the top down.

"I should hope not."

He wraps his hands around my sides, digging his fingertips into my skin. Having fully opened my blouse, I move on to ridding him of his shirt, pushing it off his broad shoulders struggling to reach.

"Wow, you're tiny..."

His hands rest on my sides for a moment, then travel around to gently stroke my back. Indeed now that I'm no longer wearing heels he's towering over me even more.

"That may be so," I say, slipping two fingers into his belt and firmly pulling him against me, "but I'm not fragile, you can be rough."

But he isn't. Instead he lets his hands travel back down softly, cupping the fullest part of my butt. It doesn't take long for him to find the zipper of my skirt.

Feeling his soft belly pressed against me drives me wild and the promise contained within the harder, pointier bulge underneath makes my juices flow readily by now.

Our kisses have become wild and rushed, only interrupted by the odd moan and gasp for air. I let my fingers explore his skin underneath his t-shirt, running up his side, feeling every curve and ripple of flesh. I try my best not to claw at him, instead caressing the hair on his chest and stomach. He is all man and I can't wait to discover more of him.

As I start to lift his t-shirt upwards, he stops and holds my hands in place.

"Wait," he says.

"Why?"

He doesn't respond, making me wonder if I did something wrong. But these thoughts fade away with the overload of kisses he lavishes on me; behind my ear and trailing down my neck.

"Ohhh!" I shake and twitch and he continues to

tickle me.

Overcome with desire, I dig my fingernails into his back. He doesn't seem to mind, if anything he pulls me towards him tighter.

I decide to let my hands roam once more, this time downwards. As soon as I slip my hand into his back pocket he suddenly pulls back. What have I done wrong?

The expression on his face doesn't give me any hint that he's uncomfortable, neither do his actions. He takes his time looking at me, slipping my blouse off my shoulders and stripping my skirt all the way down. I step out of it, thankful I went with bare legs today rather than unflattering pantyhose. He traces the outline of the black lacy thong with his fingertip.

"May I?" he asks, hooking his finger into the waistband, stretching it slightly.

"Please..." I say, watching him pulls down my knickers.

He takes a sharp breath while admiring the view.

Both hands on my hips, he falls to his knees in front of me. I'm taken by complete surprise. Rubbing my thighs with his hands, he kisses my lower abdomen softly, then around my hip bones, before settling himself down on the ground. His breath feels warm against my skin, softly teasing me.

A cry escapes my lips when I feel the first kiss. His fingers gently guiding my thighs apart, he moves in closer. Softly licking and teasing my clean-shaven skin, he makes me feel like a goddess. I tilt my hips to allow him better access and like a willing subject, he eagerly responds.

My hand grips tightly around his on my thigh. Our eyes meet and I just melt. Letting my other hand rest on his hair, I savor the moment. The flicking of his tongue against my clit causes jolts of pleasure to travel through my lower abdomen. How he skillfully changes style and licks me deeply at regular intervals is utter perfection.

"Enough, or I won't be able to last..." I breathe.

Immediately, he straightens himself and gets up. I reach for his face, drawing his lips into mine. I can taste myself on him. My interruption is quickly forgotten and his hands are back on me, unhooking my bra.

My hands meanwhile fumble with his belt buckle and then proceed to tug at his t-shirt again.

"Take this off for me," I say.

Barely able to look away from my now exposed breasts, he raises his eyebrows in response.

"I'm completely undressed and there you are, all covered up." I playfully put a hand on my cocked hip and grin at him.

"Unacceptable! Let me see you."

"Not much to see." He sounds reluctant.

"I'll be the judge of that." I take a step forward and slip my hand under his t-shirt, feeling his skin burn against my fingers. Soft, irresistible.

He closes his eyes and breathes in deeply under my touch. Focusing on his jeans again, I pull them down, revealing severely tented cotton boxers. While he steps out of them I quickly retrieve a condom from my handbag, before dropping the latter on the floor.

Who would've thought this impressive man would be so shy? I'm not going to let it discourage me. Something inside me tells me I must please him in any way I can, that's what I'm meant to do. Surely he'll come around once I show him just how much he turns me on.

Taking him by the hand, I walk over to the bed. At the edge, I turn to face him and slip one hand into his boxers. He starts to shiver when I wrap my fingers around his solid length. My other hand starts to pull his shorts down, to be discarded on the floor along with the rest of our stuff.

"Lie down... against these," I whisper.

I point at the plush pillows, yet still keep a firm grip on his cock. It's easy to get what you want when you've got someone's man parts in your hand.

His breathing has turned ragged and irregular, but he complies, eyeing me all the while. If he likes what he sees, I've no problem being on display. And I'm certain I'll get that t-shirt off him very shortly without any argument too.

I hand him the condom and kneel down on the bed, straddling his thigh. He fumbles about with it, his hands shaking slightly. Oh the anticipation is killing me!

Despite the distraction of me rubbing my moist sex against his leg, he somehow manages to put it on. Then I guide his hand down between my legs.

"You've made me so wet..." I spread, allowing his other thigh between mine too.

"Oh God!" he gasps as his fingers touch my lips.

I wasn't lying, they're nearly dripping. Moving up higher, I slowly tease him by rubbing myself against him. His balls and cock become slick with my juices and the direct contact gives me shivers.

He won't refuse me any longer.

Leaning down, I nibble on his neck, painfully aware of my tense nipples poking him in the chest. My hands find the skin on his sides once more, but rather than linger there, I start peeling his t-shirt up.

His hips jerk upwards, betraying what he really wants.

"Only if you take this off for me," I whisper in his ear while tugging at the fabric which I've now managed to get halfway up his stomach.

Flutters of excitement rush through me, watching him lean up and fulfill my demand. He does not disappoint, soft skin with just the right amount of hair trailing down from his chest. Flawless, except for the half dozen or so scars on his right side and a very detailed tattoo covering his shoulder and part of his chest. Fiery dragons amongst intricate patterns of smoke, it's breathtaking.

I lean forward with both hands against his chest, lifting myself over him until the tip of his manhood presses up against me. I'm throbbing with anticipation, but won't allow this first move to be over too quickly.

My lips find his for a deep kiss, while I ease down slowly but surely, my hips into his until he has filled me completely. The moment is perfect, I wish it would linger.

ONE NIGHT STAND

We moan in unison when our bodies are joined.

"You feel amazing..." I say, grinding my hips into him deeply to underline my point.

Every forward movement causes my tummy to press against his soft flesh and I love it.

His hands have a firm hold on my hips, guiding me into a faster rhythm. I run my fingers over his chest and kiss his neck and shoulders.

"Now I know I must be dreaming." His voice is strained, out of breath.

"I've never had a dream this good," I respond, equally breathless.

Bending down deeper, I let the tip of my tongue trail across his chest until I find his nipple. Sucking and licking it, watching him writhe beneath me.

I can't stop, wanting to push him further towards the inevitable. On knees and tiptoes I ride him harder and faster. His fingers dig into my flesh and his eyes shut. Ever since we first looked at each other, our lust has built up, begging to be released like this.

Despite the impersonal, slippery condom that separates us, I feel myself getting ready. A warm, gushing feeling is spreading through my insides, cheered on by the slight twitching of his cock.

He grunts with every push and squeezes my thighs. It's as if I can feel the pleasure building inside him, coursing through every vein and rearing to be freed. Sitting up straight on him now, I push harder and faster. I need to see his face, to know I made this happen. Lifting one of his hands off my leg, I push it up against my breast.

"I'm yours. Feel me!" I scream.

His eyes flick open and brows crinkle together and his other hand finds its way further back, grabbing my ass. He's ready and so am I, for the final push. I fuck him harder yet until he freezes and cries out something unintelligible. So very close myself, I enjoy the helpless look on his face and finish as well.

I collapse on top of him. Nothing left but a quivering mess, resting on his warm, inviting torso.

His arms wrap around me and there is nowhere I'd rather be.

I don't recall ever cuddling a stranger from a pub, but at this moment it feels right. The other unusual thing I'm noticing is that my desires have not been satisfied completely, despite the aftershocks of this intense orgasm still coursing through me. But I'm too tired to move, at least for now.

"I don't know what I did to deserve this..." he sighs.

CHAPTER FOUR

Snuggling deeper in his arms, I close my eyes and smile. Our moment of bliss doesn't last though, because I'm compelled to move by a sharp, sudden pain.

"Cramp! Let go!" I cry.

As soon as he releases me I manage to stretch out my aching muscles.

Much better, but I'm still feeling inexplicably clingy. Suddenly very nervous, I want his arms around me some more, but don't know if I could deal with refusal if the moment has already been ruined.

Rubbing the cramped part of my hip, I sit down and watch as he removes his condom and ties a knot in it. Carefully he places it on top of the empty wrapper on the bedside table.

My thigh is so close to his I can feel the warmth radiate off him. He's looking at me, as though he wants to say something but doesn't. Instead he lies back, his arm stretched out just far enough in my direction for it not to be coincidence.

I lie down as well, my head on his chest, relieved when he starts to hold me again. Although he appeared more relaxed only moments ago, he tenses up straight away when I rest my hand on him. I don't move, instead I listen to his heart racing underneath my ear. Gradually, he calms again, and I snuggle my face against him. He starts to caress my hair and shoulder.

"Mmm, that feels good," I whisper.

In a gesture that makes me feel so very special, he kisses my hair a few times.

No longer can I resist, and I let my fingertips roam over his body. Though his breathing turns irregular, he doesn't stop me and continues to do the same to me.

"This is some very nice artwork." I start tracing the outlines in his tattoo.

It's impossible to hold back on the one thing I know I shouldn't do: start an interrogation.

"Why so nervous earlier?"

He shrugs.

"Well don't be," I say.

Leaning up on my elbow, I kiss his chest where my head was resting until now. I'm finished exploring the patterns of his ink, and let my fingers run through his chest hair instead before heading down his side.

"What happened?" I ask, as my fingertips reach his scars.

"I used to work as a bouncer a few years ago. Ended up getting stabbed." His tone matches the length of his sentences. Clearly this isn't his favorite topic.

"I hope they got the guy," I whisper, before bending down and kissing every one of the five thin marks. He flinches at the first kiss but relaxes thereafter.

When I'm done, he pulls me back into his arms and starts playing with my hair. I respond by snuggling closer against him, one thigh over his, and caress his leg with my foot. Looking down, I'm pleased to find that he's still a bit hard.

"I haven't been with anyone since." His voice is a whisper, as if he's merely thinking out loud.

So that explains it. The lingering ticklishness in the pit of my stomach flares up again. In all likelihood I'll only have him for one night, but it should be one to remember for the both of us.

"In that case, one good turn deserves another," I chuckle, "And this time you're on top!"

Lifting my head, I grin at his bewildered expression and kiss his lips.

"No way, I'd crush you," he says finally.

"Try me," I dare, still grinning.

A glint appears in his eyes as he grins back at me. He grabs both my wrists and flips me off him and onto my back. Pinning both my wrists back onto the pillow, he leans over and just looks at me again. My eyes, lips and further down, before settling on my eyes again, there is a tenderness about him which I've not encountered before. He's something special.

"Let me know if it's too much..." he whispers.

I smile and shake my head.

"Kiss me some more!"

With both hands around his neck, I pull him into me. He lowers himself down until I'm sandwiched tightly between him and the mattress. Now that I'm finding myself in exactly the position I envisioned when I first laid eyes on him, I'm starting to feel feverish. Just one little detail is still off...

Reaching around, I carefully slip off the elastic holding his hair together allowing locks of brown hair to fall down framing his face.

"God yes, that's so hot!" Through the haze, I note that he's smiling again.

I'm not pretending, not wishing for something or someone else like what might happen during any other casual encounter. And it seems he has started to realize that I'm responding to him, not a dream or pretence.

Lost in further kisses, I'm cocooned between his strong arms either side of me. Both my hands roaming freely over his back, I can feel him starting to relax. I'm having a hard time pacing myself, having just found my favorite part of his anatomy.

Love handles.

How can something with such an enticing name be considered so undesirable? Running my fingertips over his sides softly at first, I can feel the goose bumps on his skin, though he does not say a word. Not too ticklish then, perhaps just a little.

But I want more, handfuls more!

As he finds a comfortable position on top of me, it is starkly obvious that not all about him is soft. I haven't touched his cock after getting off him the first time around, yet it is very prominently pressing against my thigh. I try to move underneath him but am unable until he lifts himself a bit, allowing me to spread.

I can think of nothing, but wanting him again and again. He leans on his knees between my legs, one hand resting to my left, the other reaching down. There is silence all around us, except our excited short breaths. All I can do is stare into his eyes, letting the anticipation build.

"Fuck," he interrupts and looks around to the night stand, "are there any more condoms?"

"Yes, my bag." I point to the floor.

He raises himself and stretches his arm to checks my handbag, retrieving several foil packets.

"Just in case," he grins. I like how he thinks.

Sat down on his knees between my spread legs again, he starts to put on the rubber. I lean up on my elbows, watching him. I try not to stare, for fear of making him uneasy but it's hard not to. Sure enough, he glances up at me through the strands of hair hanging in front of his face.

"Almost done."

I just smile in response and wait, trying not to be too impatient.

He seems in an equally big hurry, because he's back on top of me already, forcing my legs wide. With his hair loose and his eyes as passionate as I've ever seen on a man, he looks powerful. He enters me with new found energy and it's clear he has been completely transformed.

Gone is the shy IT guy whose character differed so much from his wild appearance. I'm being conquered by his inner Viking warrior. He plunges into me deeply and I cry out, squeezing my eyes shut involuntarily.

But I force myself to look again. I don't want to miss even a moment. Every movement of his, its sole purpose is seemingly to teach me that the tables are now turned. I had him where I wanted him when I was on top. Now it's his turn.

Helpless, legs wrapped around his thick waist. We must look like quite a pair, hair flying wildly around us, tickling my nose. I drag his face down towards me and feel my chin getting raw from the scratching of his beard. Still I demand more kisses.

And he's so good, so strong. I try to tell him, but it's all just coming out in strained fragmented sounds. The intense look in his eyes signals that he knows.

He fucks me harder and I feel my body reach new heights. Every muscle has a mind of its own, I spasm and contract and scream. But he keeps going and I've lost it.

When he thrusts into me finally, my cunt stings from the impact yet I'm fully satiated. Tears wet my face but I can't help smiling.

Little beads of sweat have formed on his brow and he looks down at me like he has just awoken from a dream. Carefully he lowers himself onto his elbows above me, just about managing to reach my streaked cheek with his fingers.

"Did I hurt you?"

"God, no," I say, "That was by far the best fuck I've ever had."

He takes a moment, scrutinizing my expression. If he's looking for a sign that I'm faking it, he's not going to get it.

Releasing him from the hold my legs had maintained

on him, I allow myself to relax rather than risk another irritating cramp. He puts his head down on my chest, but is mindful not to weigh me down too much.

I'm grateful for the moment of rest and not in any hurry to let him go. And this time around it's me playing with his locks. Shame on whoever decided men should have short hair. They shouldn't.

This is what a man should look like. It's also how one should fuck.

He lifts himself off me after a little while, seemingly as reluctant as I am. Once again I watch him and wait. The alarm clock next to the bed flips to 2:00 and I feel the long day catching up with me.

When he gets back into bed, he nudges me aside slightly and off the duvet. I have neither the will nor energy to move, and just wait while he pulls the covers over the both of us. With one big scooping movement of his arm, I'm drawn back.

His warm, reassuring presence surrounds me and I wouldn't change a thing about it. Not even the prickly hair of his still naked crotch pressed against my ass or the slight tickle on my neck caused by his every breath.

It has been a while since I slept with and not just fucked a man. The realization of how nice that kind of trust can be had been only a distant memory until now.

Relaxing utterly, for me there is no more fighting the inevitable.

CHAPTER FIVE

When I wake up, all is dark around us. I can hear his breathing next to me, deep and regular, but I'm completely restless. The night is ending and it hurts. It's not that I regret what happened, but I fear I may have gone about it all the wrong way.

This wasn't my first one night stand by far but it's certainly the first time I've felt this way after. Or during, for that matter. What's up with all this emotional crap?

My eyes are starting to adjust to the light, or lack thereof. The edge of the bed is starting to become visible, as well as the small couch at the far end of the spacious room which has some of our combined clothes piled over it.

Taking care not to wake him up, I lift up the sheets and slip out of bed. Suddenly I feel this incredible urge to cover up, to make myself just slightly less vulnerable. Luckily I had already laid out a nightie over the backrest of the couch, which I quickly put on.

Rummaging through my handbag, I locate my phone and earphones. Battery died, fucking great. I put it on charge but it'll some time to become usable again. Feeling in quite urgent need of some music, I decide to check his pockets for a more immediate solution.

I'm in luck, there's an iPod in his jeans and it has

plenty of battery life left. Hope he doesn't mind, but then again I'll probably never see him again after today anyway.

iPod in hand, I shove our clothes towards one side and sit down with my legs folded. Going into his playlists, I find the most played songs and start to listen. I close my eyes and let the music wash over me, calming me down.

Since I opted for the most listened-to songs, I'm again reminded of how similar our tastes are. I feel like I'm getting a glimpse of his personality through music. It's with a lot of difficulty that I remain quiet instead of tapping or humming along with the faster numbers.

I try to make sense of my thoughts, as I am, isolated from reality and surrounded by guitars and drums. I wasn't drinking particularly much and I don't think anything got slipped into my drink. But last night felt different than a normal casual hook-up would have. I noticed him by the bar, so far so good. I approached him, and then everything changed. The moment we made eye contact it was like a switch inside my head was flipped.

No longer did I want an anonymous bit of fun, but I wanted him. I wanted to know him, find out what makes him tick. Above all, I wanted to give him pleasure rather than fulfill my own needs.

I'm startled by a touch on my shoulder and open my eyes. Fuck, he's up. I look up at him briefly while turning off the iPod and handing it to him but can't bear to make eye contact.

"Sorry I borrowed this, hope you don't mind..." I say.

"No, not at all... Lucy...." he pauses.

"Yes?"

"Umm... I'm not sure how these things work, but I...."

I wish he'd just come out and say it. He wants to head home, obviously. Staring at the floor, I just wait for him to continue.

"Did you want me to leave? I mean, you were gone when I woke up, I thought perhaps I've made you uncomfortable by staying the night."

"Not on my account, stay as long as you like," I say, trying to not to sound as low as I feel. "I just couldn't sleep."

"How come?" he asks. "Hope I wasn't snoring!"

I let out a chuckle and look up at him. The concern on his face looks genuine, the situation would be quite comical if it wasn't for my confused emotional state.

"Don't worry, you weren't," I respond. "Actually, I couldn't sleep because... I didn't want this to end."

He remains quiet for a few seconds, then he leans over and picks up all the clothes and dumps them on the bed. As he sits down beside me, the warm sensation of his thigh pressing against mine is putting me on edge.

"And you thought I did want it to end?" he asks finally.

"I don't know, isn't that how it usually goes?" I say.

"So let me know if I understand this correctly..." he says, "you want me to stay?"

"Yes." My voice is a whisper.

"And then?" he asks.

I just shake my head. Being honest is such a struggle.

Rather than putting myself out there, it would've been so much easier if I had told him to just leave initially. Less risky, because surely I'm just being a silly, needy cow right now. Every guy's worst nightmare after a perfectly good fuck the night before.

Tears are burning in my eyes, suddenly it feels like I have everything to lose.

"Why don't you first tell me what you want?" I whisper.

He takes my hand and strokes it with his fingers. It tickles just a little and waves of delicious goose bumps travel up my spine.

"More," he says.

I'm taken aback by his answer. All this is getting a bit weird, not at all what I expected to hear and I wonder if I just misunderstood him.

"What do you mean, more?"

"I want more than just one night with you. But I worry that I can't have that."

"What if that's exactly what I want too?" I ask, stealthily exploring his very serious expression from the corner of my eye.

"You hardly know anything about me. Don't make up your mind just yet."

"So tell me about you," I say.

"I don't want to pretend, it wouldn't work." He takes a deep breath before continuing.

"You could say I'm a bit of a loner, mostly by choice. But lately, I've found heading to the pub every night a lot easier than facing an empty house."

Despite how sad his admission is, I have to suppress a smile. We really are not so different; if there's one thing I can relate to it's loneliness.

"I've done that," I say. "Sometimes hooking up with someone, sometimes staying until closing."

Surely now he'll be the one to change his mind, even if my actions last night may have already suggested that this wasn't my first casual encounter. I dare not look up, not even when he wraps his fingers around mine tighter.

I feel the need to justify myself, to voice observations that only now are becoming apparent to me.

"But I've never asked someone to come back with me, not once put myself in a position where I couldn't just escape without a trace."

He sighs. I wish I knew exactly what he's thinking. It's a lot easier to say you want to be honest than to actually follow through.

In the silence that follows, my heart skips a few beats when he lets go and raises his hand. He guides my face upwards by my chin until I can't help but look at him.

"What made you approach me last night?" he asks.

There isn't a hint of humor in his eyes, no sign that he's only playing with me.

"Because I didn't think you would've, even if you had turned around at some point and noticed me looking at you... Was I wrong?"

"No, I guess I wouldn't have," he admits. "As it was, I barely knew what to do when you sat down next to me."

"I can't quite explain what happened. When I saw you, I just had to talk to you. Of course I hardly knew what to say."

"And I thought I was the awkward one." He smiles at me and caresses my cheek, making me forget just how tense I felt only seconds ago.

"And what makes you different from all the guys who are all too happy to get something quick and easy with no strings attached?" I ask. "Why want more?"

He pauses before answering, but does not take his eyes off me.

"The way you looked at me last night, actually the way you're still looking at me now... Like I'm someone worth seeing," he says. "That's a rare thing, something worth keeping and taking a risk on."

"You know, check out isn't until eleven..." I get up from the couch and take his hand again. "What do you say?"

"I'm sure we can find a way to pass the time."

CHAPTER SIX

When we get back into bed it feels somehow different. On one hand there is more riding on this now, with both of us putting ourselves in a vulnerable position. But I'm actually more comfortable. There is no rush, the morning deadline no longer applies.

Lying sideways, facing each other, he takes me into his arms.

I know now what he meant when he described how I looked at him. It's the same way he explores my face now, lingering on certain features just that little bit longer before coming back for eye contact. I feel noticed, appreciated.

It's a strange thing, when you look at someone's face after you've developed some kind of feelings for them. We can look at a model on a billboard and appreciate their attractiveness on an objective level, but eventually you'll get bored and look at something else.

But when you like someone, there is so much more to see. You won't lose interest even if you stare at them for hours. Perhaps it's knowing that you'll miss them when you're apart and you want to memorize their face to keep with you at all times.

A glint appears in his eyes and before I can wonder what he's thinking he firmly grabs both my wrists. He turns onto his back and I've no choice but to be dragged along.

"You interrupted me last night, it'll not happen again." His deep voice is not one to argue with.

He lets go of my hands and instead lifts me up from under my armpits. My legs spread, surrounding him, but he's not satisfied with me yet.

"Sit on me," he says.

"I already am..."

He shakes his head, dragging me upwards by hooking his hands through the bend of my knees. A smile forms on his lips when I begin to understand and crawl further upwards, finally ending up covering his face.

It wasn't the drink that made this so amazing the first time around. He does know exactly what to do, but more than that it's obvious he enjoys this as much as I do.

The moment his tongue reaches my clit I am positive that whatever happens between us, it'll be a fun ride. I'm taken over by waves of pleasure, starting small like a little itch scratched in just the right manner, then growing in intensity.

His strong hands keep me in place by my hips, even when I involuntarily try to twitch and wiggle. Now that he has me right where he wants me, there is no way he'll let me go before seeing this through.

I feel my stomach tighten, breaths become deeper and louder. Upon looking down I find that he's staring at me. His blue eyes shine unnaturally brightly in the dimmed light of the table lamp next to us. His beard is slightly raspy against my sensitive skin but it does not detract from the magic of the moment.

His tongue is surprisingly long, reaching quite deeply inside.

"Oh God, you're killing me," I moan.

Then, with furious flicking of his tongue I can't take it any longer. I am taken over, crying out for him. Falling back when he finally leaves his powerful hold on my hips, and sliding off to the side of him, I'm completely spent.

He gets up, admiring his work with a smile. I close my eyes and concentrate on getting my breathing back under control and the world back into focus.

A moment later I feel him next to me, his hand cupping my cheek.

"Lucy," he says.

I open my eyes to find him sitting beside me, my phone in hand.

"Someone's calling."

Such terrible timing. I lean up and read the name on the display. Akhil. Dammit.

"I should take this, I'm sorry. It's work." I sit up and pick up the call.

"Hello, Akhil."

His voice sounds excited, or agitated on the other end while he starts to ramble. It's not at all about the project but about him.

"Wait, what do you mean you're getting married and leaving?" I can't believe my ears.

ONE NIGHT STAND

He continues to tell me about his parents finding him a match, in good old traditional fashion. Now he's getting married to some girl he used to know when they were little, but whose family moved to Canada two decades ago. The preparations are well underway to make his immigration possible.

"Fuck... I mean congrats on the happy news... How come you're only telling me this now?" I rest my head in my remaining hand while listening to his apologetic explanation that he was nervous about letting me down. That's why he didn't say anything until he really couldn't put it off any longer.

"Alright well, all the best to you, and I wish you a happy marriage. Canada is nice, I think you'll like it there." I sound defeated; I feel it too.

Without being able to count on his support, I'll not only have trouble with this new project, I'll also have to rethink how I run my business in general. In a daze, I disconnect the call.

"That didn't sound good," George says.

I shake my head but I haven't got the words yet to explain it all.

"My project manager..." In a somewhat symbolic gesture I discard the phone on the bed.

"When I land a big project, he would handle the outsourcing side of things: manage people, ensure deadlines are met. You can't fucking trust anyone, can you. If only he had thought to give some notice!"

Deep breaths! I didn't have Akhil when I started out, it's not all going to unravel now that he's gone either. I hope.

"I guess I'll manage without him, it'll just be a lot more work..." I force a smile.

Not his problem but mine. I would happily move on from this topic of conversation sooner rather than later. But he is giving me a rather serious, thoughtful look. It's the sort of expression men get when they enter troubleshooting mode.

"How about finding a replacement?" he suggests.

I shrug. That won't be easy.

"You just let me know if there is anything I could do to help, alright?" he continues.

I smile at him again. It's a kind offer, but it would be wrong to ask that much of him. I'm not in a hurry to make this into a business relationship, what I want from him is a lot more intimate.

"Thanks, I'll keep it in mind. But I think it'll be OK if I handled the work myself for now."

He seems to have given up on the idea, instead lying down and gesturing at me to join him. Good plan, I could use some cheering up.

I start to look at him again, resting my head on his shoulder. It feels familiar already, like we've known each other longer than just a few hours. But feelings can be so deceptive, he's mostly a mystery to me.

"I want to know everything about you," I say.

"Are you sure?" He grins.

"Absolutely. Everything. For starters, what else do you like to do? Except frequenting old fashioned pubs and having great taste in music of course."

ONE NIGHT STAND

He seems a bit distracted but eventually does answer.

"I've got a motorcycle. A classic Harley."

A biker as well? This is great news and very fitting too. He completely looks the part for a Harley rider, I should've known.

"How exciting," I say, "perhaps we can go for a ride sometimes? Assuming it runs..."

He immediately notes my teasing tone and goes on the defensive.

"Oh don't tell me you're into that newfangled Japanese crap yourself? Just because it's an old Harley, doesn't mean it'll break down."

"Fair enough. Mine's Japanese yes, but also a classic. A 1970s Honda CB750 which might as well live at the local bike garage."

"You are full of surprises, aren't you," he says.

"I do my best."

He's beautiful, even if saying that out loud would just make things awkward. But there's no need to talk anymore. He leans forward, guiding my chin upwards to meet him. We kiss, slowly.

Every inch of my body has woken up to his presence again. As long as the rest of the world doesn't intrude, this moment between the two of us is perfect. A perfect beginning.

We talk more, kiss more, caress one another and look into each other's eyes. Like two blind people who just started seeing for the first time. Time passes with little relevance, until we are forced into action around ten-thirty. The night is truly over now.

He programs his number and address into my phone. Everything of mine is already on the card I gave him.

"This weekend I'm going to have to sort out the mess left behind by the guy, Akhil, who just quit. But I need to see you again. Soon," I say.

No response, he's quiet while putting on his clothes. Then he helps me gather my things from around the room.

"Maybe we can do dinner anyway? I'm assuming you'll still eat at some point while working," he says finally.

This is probably the wrong time to explain that I have a habit of forgetting all about meal breaks when I get sucked into work.

"Let's see, I'll call or text you when I see some light at the end of this tunnel." I zip up my overnight bag and see him observe me from across the bed.

Dressed in the same clothes as last night, his presence still makes me weak. I don't want to leave or say goodbye.

"Before we go, would you like to join me for breakfast?" I ask.

CHAPTER SEVEN

What a complete turd of a day. The whole weekend actually. I've stared at my screen without interruption throughout. Not even a meal break. This client might just become the death of me, especially since Akhil has run off to Canada without warning, and left me in this mess all by myself. It's hard to swallow my resentment at his betrayal.

I sit back, rubbing my eyes which have started to burn. No doubt I'll work late into the night again, best to take a break now and recharge.

Perhaps I should've said 'no' on Friday. Of course I couldn't know that I'd be stranded handling this shit storm on my own, but still. My instincts were telling me to run, and I should've listened! To hell with the money, I could've spent this time drumming up business elsewhere.

Some tea will help, maybe a sandwich too. The dull ache in my right wrist is another sign I need some time away from the computer. Otherwise it won't be long before the shooting pains start making their way up into my elbow.

I get up and wrap my bathrobe around me tightly. There's a chill in the air which I hadn't noticed earlier.

I didn't even realize how dark it has become,

requiring me to switch on lights on my way downstairs to the kitchen. Until moments ago, I hadn't moved from my chair, not even looked out the window since this morning. I'm all stiff, tired, annoyed.

After getting home yesterday, the first thing I did was get rid of the uncomfortable business suit and throw on some pajamas, which I've been wearing ever since. The advantages of working from home are many, the disadvantage appears to be that it's easy to turn into a reclusive slob.

The second thing I did was switch off all those confusing thoughts that had muddled up my brain overnight on Friday. It hasn't even been forty-eight hours since I first laid eyes on George. But it took me quite a bit of effort to get rid of the thought of him. I almost managed it too.

Now that my focus has been broken, and I'm leaning against the kitchen counter, waiting for the kettle to boil, he's back though. As corny as it sounds, I do see him when I close my eyes. It's kind of nice as well as unwelcome. I don't have time for this.

A click tells me that the water is done, so I fill my mug, and watch almost in a trance how the contents turns progressively darker around the teabag in the centre. Swirls of brown escape through the fine paper mesh and spread throughout like writhing tentacles, until the color evens out. The spectacle brings back glimpses of memories from Friday night: George's hair, flying wildly while he was on top of me. His eyes, staring into mine, interested in *me,* as well as my body...

ONE NIGHT STAND

Lack of sleep must be getting to me.

Certainly on Friday there were more exciting things to do than sleep. And afterwards my own doubts and worries woke me way too early. Last night I went to bed at midnight but kept lying awake well beyond that.

Had Akhil not messed it all up, I may have had a moment to really absorb what happened on Friday. Instead it's one thing after another; needing to find a replacement, and reaching out to all the freelancers who normally answer to him to try to take over his role temporarily.

Plus I've had to make a start on the client's proposal.

Deep breaths. This isn't the first time I've been faced with a mountain of work and nobody to back me up. I'll be fine. I hope.

Goddammit, of all the times to have to deal with this sort of thing, the current timing is amazingly shit. If I mess up with this client, my reputation will most definitely take a battering. That's the sort of thing that's tough to recover from, with numerous competitors eager to take my place and the bank about ready to come knocking, should I miss my next repayment.

Every second geeky teenager is offering his web development skills on *Elance* at discount prices, so the industry isn't what it used to be. It takes a lot to survive nowadays.

Seeing the mug on the counter, still steaming, I am reminded to throw away the bag and realize I've left it in too long. Whatever, it'll have to do. The bread on the counter looks moldy, into the bin it goes. All I've got to eat right now is a pot of yoghurt from the fridge. Yoghurt and tea. Classy.

Right when I'm about to enjoy the first spoonful, I hear the familiar email ding on my phone. God, please let it be something other than further bad news. I try to finish eating first, but eventually cave and fish it out of the deep pocket of my robe. Apparently it's seven pm. Who would've known?

Dear Lucy , ... From George Townend? Who the hell is—oh crap, it's *George* George. It totally slipped my mind that I gave him my work email, and I never did find out his last name.

Seriously though? What man gets in touch right after a hook-up? Apparently George does. I'm not sure I can risk the distraction. Although part of me wants to close the email, leaving it for when I'll be more sociable, something makes me read on.

Dear Lucy,

From what I could tell, the call you took yesterday morning shook you up quite a bit. I understand you'll need time to figure out how to deal with all that extra work now. Just to let you know, I was serious; if there's anything I can do to help...
Seeing as you're undoubtedly very busy right now, I didn't want to intrude, so I chose to email rather than call. I've been thinking about you, all day, and yesterday too.

There is no logical explanation for this, but the connection I felt with you is very real, special. This is new territory for me, I don't have the best of track records when it comes to relationships. All I know is, I do want more; I want to make this work. If I fuck up in some way (which I probably will, if the past is anything to go by), I hope you'll tell me and give me a chance to fix it.

You said you want to know everything about me; well I'm not sure there's that much to know. But maybe in a small way this email will help.

Music plays an important part in my life, how it allows for escapism in just about any situation. It was obvious—when I found you sitting with your eyes closed, lost in thought after having borrowed my iPod—that you function in the same way. Perhaps music is the best medium of communication for us and I also hope this little soundtrack can help relieve some of the stress you must be feeling now.

I don't know if you listen to music while working, otherwise keep this for whenever you're taking a little break; I've put together a few songs that hold special meaning to me. Most of them have some kind of back story or they resonate with my moods at times, some I turn to again and again because they cheer me up. I'll let the music do the talking for now...

Hope to see you again soon,

George

There's a link to a <u>playlist on YouTube</u>[1] . Although I'm still skeptical, I decide to open it anyway and scroll through his selection. As much as I hate to admit it right now, he might be right. I need this.

I grab my tea and the half-eaten cup of yoghurt and head back to the office to find some tangled up earphones. My patience is wearing thin to the extent that I almost tear the buds off the wires trying to unravel them. Stupid, contrary pieces of shit that they are.

But then, the music fills me, not just my ears but all of me. In all my effort to get into business mode, I forgot this. I did a near perfect job of forgetting myself. With the tunes continuing on, I finish my food, sip the rest of my tea with my eyes closed, and am almost completely revitalized. Logic tells me the reason for that is mainly the sustenance, my heart tries to argue that it's the music and George's intentions behind sending me his selection.

When I'm done, I read his email again. And again. He thought of me all day. How sweet. He sent me this playlist to try to cheer me up; that's even sweeter. And to think that when his email came in just now, I actually felt annoyed about it. What the hell is wrong with me? It's no wonder I've been single for longer than I care to remember.

Right. After working my ass off for eleven hours,

------

[1] http://lmoone.com/fromgeorge

what's a few minutes to respond to him? It's actually nothing and I ought to be ashamed of myself for wanting to ignore him earlier.

Dear George,

Thanks so much for the email and the playlist. I've had a trying day and you seem to have shown up with impeccable timing to make it better.

Much like you, I also don't have the best history when it comes to relationships. Perhaps we can help each other in that respect. I can't promise much, except honesty.
Our night together feels like it happened so long ago already, and although I am absolutely swamped, I'm not sure it's healthy to go with my initial instinct of drowning in my work until the project is over. I'd like to see you again soon also. How about next weekend?

Lucy

I'm about ready to get stuck in again when my phone alerts me of his reply. I wonder if he's been waiting.

Dear Lucy,

I'm glad I was able to make a difference in a small way.

Next weekend would be great. How about we take our bikes out for a little ride, weather permitting? Lovely roads down near

Winchester, perfect for a day trip. I can be at your place at 9:30.

And honesty is all I can ask for.

George

That does sound lovely, a day trip down south. I can't resist one last response, to mark the end of my break, telling him I'm looking forward to it. And I really am.

CHAPTER EIGHT

The week flew by. Long nights, early mornings, CV after CV finding its way into my inbox, and out again after being discarded. I should've known: Akhil is irreplaceable.

It took until Wednesday to realize that this project truly would land in my lap alone, and so I put my recruitment drive on the back burner in favor of pouring more blood, sweat and tears into Nightmare Client's proposal. It's been a steep learning curve, talking directly to the freelancers, all of whom seem to relish giving me vague answers no matter what question I send their way.

Last night the resulting proposal passed my final check and off it went, just in time for me to be able to enjoy my weekend with a full night's rest and no outstanding work on my To Do list come Saturday morning.

A glance through the curtains reveals that finally things seem to be going my way. This morning, the sun is streaming down and lighting up droplets of dew on my lawn. It's only eight, but there's not a cloud in sight.

By the time George gets here after breakfast, it'll be simply perfect to head out for a lengthy ride. Contented and relaxed at last, I stretch the sleepiness out of my limbs one by one, only to be greeted by a nasty crack and one joint unable to free itself. This is a problem. A disaster, actually.

I hadn't been careful enough after the first warning signs popped up on Sunday: my right wrist has given up.

No way am I going to be able to ride for any length of time, with my accelerator hand out of action. Disappointment washes over me, but I refuse to be defeated just yet: I hope George's bike can carry two.

Juggling bike gear that has been sitting in the back of a closet for the best part of the winter, I head downstairs for much needed nourishment. Jeans should be sufficient for a spring day like today, especially if I'm riding pillion. Plus they look better than those big, all-weather trousers do.

The mug of tea feels heavy in my affected hand, it's uncomfortable enough for me to have to switch sides. No matter how often I stretch, flex and release my fingers, or attempt to rotate my wrist, it doesn't help. If anything, it's worse now than only moments ago when I first realized.

I decide to bandage it. And then I wait.

Checking the time, nine-twenty, I wait some more. By nine twenty-five, I'm unable to sit still anymore and pace about the kitchen, rearranging the odd cookbook here, and clearing away a stray breadcrumb on the counter.

And I wait.

At nine twenty-seven, I check my make-up in the shiny double-oven door. At nine twenty-seven-and-a-half, I brush my t-shirt down for what must be the tenth time, and force deep breaths.

This is ridiculous. I feel like a teenager waiting to be picked up for prom or something.

It occurs to me that I have about as much experience with dating as the average teenager. Perhaps less so. It's been a while... After spending the best part of my twenties building up my business leaving no time for socializing, once I hit thirty it seemed easier to just never allow anyone near enough to get to this stage. There have been a lot of lonely nights interspersed with the occasional stranger who never turned into anything more.

Weird, how these things happen. Little over a week ago, I couldn't have guessed I would find myself waiting for an actual second date, after picking up some guy who I initially only noticed from behind.

And yet...

He *is* going to turn up though, isn't he?

We've been emailing each other in the evenings, with him usually being a lot more prompt in his responses than me, suggesting he's still keen. But still, it's hard to ignore the niggling doubts that make their way into my overworked mind.

The bell rings, making me almost drop the cup I've decided to wash. *Shit, shit, shit!* He's here!

I rush to the door, nearly stumbling over my own feet in the process, take a deep breath and press the button on the security system.

"Hi!" My heart is hammering in my chest and I'm

breathless and faint. If this is what I'm going to be like before he even enters the house, how is the rest of the day going to go?

On the small black & white video screen, a leather-clad George is shuffling about uncomfortably before leaning forward towards the microphone again.

"Hey, Lucy?"

Shit, the gate is still closed. I press the button and the two large metal doors swing into action, allowing him space to enter.

"Please come in, park up anywhere and I'll be right out."

He hesitates a moment, then returns to his bike, just off screen, and the vaguely familiar rumble of an old V-twin engine filters through my windows. He's coming in.

I head outside, and greet him with an awkward smile. He responds, with an equal amount of awkwardness, reluctantly eyeing the driveway, with the heavy security gates slowly moving back into place, the carefully manicured lawn that leads around the side of the house, the gravel paths, shrubs, the garage and finally the Victorian style villa behind me.

"Nice house."

"Thanks." I shift from one foot to the other, and try to decide on my next move while he puts his Harley on its side stand on the block paved, broad drive.

The bike fits him. It's like a throwback to another era, unmistakable 70s style wide handles and a bright orange paint job with black pin-striping to match.

ONE NIGHT STAND

"Lovely machine," I say, noting with relief that it indeed has space for two.

We look at each other for a moment, not quite sure what to do. The time apart has made things a bit weird, despite keeping in touch this past week. I swallow my nerves and approach him to give him a hug. He's even taller than I recall, requiring me to tiptoe to reach.

I'm not wearing heels today, of course! That explains it.

It's such a relief, having his arms close around me. The effect seems to not be lost on him either because after a deep sighs, he draws me against him tighter. The cool leather of his jacket against my fingertips gives me goose bumps, yet I don't really feel like letting go. I do release him anyway though, before things get even weirder.

"I almost thought I'd come to the wrong place. Not quite what I expected." The deep bass of his voice makes the hairs on my arms stand up.

"It's..." I shrug, looking for the right words. "Well, it's home, whatever it is."

I can imagine it's a bit of a shock, for someone living in the city to be faced with a house of this scale. But at no point in the past week would it have been appropriate to tell him I live in what is practically a country mansion compared to most city dwellings.

Is that something people do? Compare pay checks and lifestyles at the very beginning of getting together? I don't really know, it's all new territory to me and the topic simply didn't come up.

"Let's go in. Would you like some tea or coffee?" Shockingly, I don't even know how he prefers to take his caffeine. Guess I'll soon find out.

"Yeah, tea would be great. No sugar."

"Cool. That's how I have it too." I shoot him a smile.

Perhaps it's just that initial touch which soothed my frazzled nerves, but things are surely going to be easier now. *Aren't they?*

We head inside, with him about a step behind me all the way, no doubt looking around some more. I'd never really thought about how my circumstances differ from others my age. Obviously I realize most people don't live in a freestanding house in the countryside, but I still find it hard to imagine what his place might be like. Hopefully I'll get to see it soon enough.

While I put the kettle on, I try to grab the second stool from the other side of the breakfast bar and immediately regret it.

"Ouch," I curse under my breath, rubbing my bandaged wrist.

"Need a hand?" George steps towards me and effortlessly moves the stool I just struggled with. "What happened?"

"I guess I'm a bit overworked." I continue rubbing my wrist and try to stretch my fingers just a bit. Pointless, it's locked.

"Right. Believe me, it pays to take care of ergonomics when you're stuck at the PC all day."

I smile bitterly, knowing he's right. Unfortunately all good intentions have a funny habit of flying out the window when you get fucked over by your most important team member at the start of a crucial project.

"Here, let me." He picks up the kettle, which has just boiled, and pours the steaming water into the two cups I'd already lined up on the counter.

"It only just started this morning, but I didn't want to cancel. I'd been looking forward to our little outing all week," I say, clambering up onto the stool nearest to me.

He nods, still looking down at the cups, adding splashes of milk and waiting for the color to turn right.

"Well, you're not riding your bike today, that's for sure."

"I was rather hoping I could ride with you. If that's OK." I accept the cup he offers me with both hands, enjoying the brush of his fingers as they slip out from around the mug.

"Certainly. If you're sure you're up for it." He sits down with his cup beside me.

"I wouldn't miss it for the world." We share a smile, before having our first sips of the relaxing hot liquid. His eyes somehow speak to me more clearly than any words could. We're good. Today is going to be just perfect.

CHAPTER NINE

There's something special about being on the back of a powerful machine, which effortlessly manages to zip along the narrow winding roads of the English countryside despite its size. More so, when it's operated by an equally powerful man, whom I trust despite not knowing him well at all.

My safety, my life is in his hands in a way. When he accelerates, I have no choice but to speed up along with him. If he misjudges a turn, we'll both go down together. And yet, I couldn't feel more safe than I do now, on the back of George's bike.

The spring sunshine has lit up the surrounding fields, their slight damp glistening in the morning light. It's an absolutely gorgeous day, featuring crisp, cool air which I know will warm up later. We're well prepared so we don't notice the chill.

After driving for about an hour, we're nearing Winchester, a name more famous for guns than the natural beauty we're enjoying today. He's keeping off the busy roads, preferring the smaller, country lanes where thankfully you still do get the chance to go at a decent clip.

"Almost there," George remarks when we slow for a particularly tight turn.

ONE NIGHT STAND

I smile, and wrap my arms around him tighter. If only I didn't have to wear this helmet, I could get even more comfortable behind him. Anyway, I'm determined to ensure I get that chance later today.

He pulls into a parking lot with only one other vehicle in it, the broad tires of the bike crush the dirty gravelly surface, making a distinctive crunching noise and we come to a standstill. We've arrived. The lot is adorned with the usual warnings and rules that apply to most nature reserves. Don't litter, dogs must be leashed, etc.

I initially didn't have much of an idea where we were going or what we would do there, but George had come prepared. His bike is outfitted with a pair of old fashioned leather saddlebags, which contain all the trappings needed for a good picnic. All I had to contribute was a thermos with yet more tea. It really is convenient that we take it the same way and the optimist in me wants to read some deeper meaning into that fact.

After locking up both our helmets to the sissy bar of the bike, he picks up most of the stuff, only permitting me to carry the picnic blanket with my good hand. Off we go, up the winding path through the hedgerows with all our supplies in tow.

"What a beautiful place," I remark, noting the gently sloping hills that surround the vantage point we're heading towards.

"Yeah, I love this area. But it's always a bit weird exploring these types of places on your own. People tend to look at you like you're a pervert if you go walking in the woods by yourself."

I giggle.

"I can imagine. Well, no such problem today."

"Nope. A perfectly wholesome day out and I've got the company to prove it." He turns to smile at me, then continues to climb the path ahead.

Once we reach the top of the little hillock and find a quiet corner in the sun, away from the breeze, I spread the blanket on the grass, allowing us to sit down. The sun has gained quite a bit of warmth, so we both take off our jackets to make the most of it.

George kneels beside me and unpacks various containers and wrapped parcels. I hadn't had time to realize how hungry I am, but as soon as the first items start coming out of their packaging, my stomach starts to growl.

"So, we've got some sandwiches, tea, obviously, various cold meats and cheese and of course, something sweet for after." He looks up from the spread he's laid out on the checkered blanket between us, somewhat shyly.

"Nothing too fancy..." he quickly adds.

"Looks perfect to me," I grin at him, grateful for what looks like an extreme amount of food for only two people. After the week I've had, I could eat a horse.

He hands me a paper plate and I'm having trouble deciding what to dive into first so I just take a little bit of everything when I note he's still observing me.

"Hungry?"

ONE NIGHT STAND

"Famished." I put the plate down in front of me and pour us some tea into the small metal cups that detach from the thermos.

"I was concerned, you know, that it wouldn't quite match up to your usual fare after seeing where you live." He brushes some strands of hair off his face, which had come loose from his ponytail, while taking off his helmet. Clearly he's not past the earlier awkwardness, he's still weirded out by what he perceives my lifestyle to be.

"It's not all foie gras and champagne, you know. I've been surviving largely on baked beans on toast for the past week." I don't add that with the way things have been going, I couldn't afford either champagne or foie gras anyway.

"Well then, I perhaps shouldn't have worried."

I raise my cup at him. "Cheers."

He responds with a similar gesture and we grin at each other for a moment.

I pick up my plate again, ready to take a big bite out of one of the sandwiches, but get distracted by the beautiful view. Pretty countryside as far as the eye can see, even the road and parking are hidden behind shrubbery, making it seem like we're in a different world. One without traffic jams, demanding jobs, and money worries.

His choice of destination is spot on. As are his efforts with the food. How incredibly sweet, a picnic for a second date. It certainly is quite the change from our first, which was a lot more one night stand than date.

Who could've guessed that we'd end up here? It's only been a week, and I don't know the guy sitting opposite me. Not really, anyway. But I will.

"What's funny?" George asks, making me realize I've been sitting here smiling to myself like a doofus for much too long.

"Oh, I'm just happy to be here. With you."

He offers me another sandwich, which I gladly accept.

"These are great, by the way." I take another bite. "I'm impressed."

"That was the idea. Plus I didn't have any clue what people generally do on a date."

"Same here."

"Refill?" he asks, gesturing at my empty cup.

I raise it towards him, allowing him to pour. He steadies my cup with his fingers brushing past mine, putting me on edge again. *This*. This is what I want.

"It's weird," George remarks while letting go of me and the cup, seemingly reluctantly.

"What is?"

"Just, meeting up again. New territory."

He looks away, focusing instead on the vistas stretched out before us. I understand completely, and he totally spoke my mind too.

"Soon enough, it'll be old and familiar," I joke.

He lets out a laugh, and turns in my direction again.

I lean forward, suppressing a wince when I accidentally put weight on my sore wrist. This occupational injury is really cramping my style. He reaches out for me, cupping my face in his hand, which I gratefully lean into.

"You're still into it though, aren't you?" he whispers.

"Absolutely. I've been thinking about you a lot this week." I smile, enjoying the slight shiver that travels my spine when I allow myself to really look at him.

He leans in, pausing just before our lips meet, making me impatient. But he continues to take his time, staring into my eyes, as if asking for permission to continue. I reach for him, wrapping my arm around his shoulder.

It was always going to be a bit of a risk, seeing someone again when the first connection only occurred a couple of drinks into a night out at the pub. Of course things will start off a bit weird, it's only natural.

I pull myself closer against him, and find myself supported by his arm, drawing me in tighter. Our lips touch, and I'm blown away again by the softness of his kisses. He is a paradox, the ultimate proof that appearances can deceive.

His gentle nature only makes me like him better. Plus I know there's raw passion in there, which only takes a bit of coaxing to come out.

He lowers me onto the plaid blanket, and follows, his other arm surrounding me as well. The kisses continue, sending my heartbeat into a frenzy. He tastes amazing, and his scent... It is only now that I realize how much I love the smell of leather on a man.

I wrap both arms around his neck and cling onto him. In the background, various food containers clang together, as we try to make sufficient space for us. Soft, careful kisses are replaced by deeper, more desperate ones. He sets me alight, making me forget any lingering professional worries, any concerns about how to make this connection last despite any as yet undiscovered differences between us.

"I'm really glad I gathered the nerve to talk to you on Friday," I whisper into his lips.

"Me too."

He pulls back, looking at my face again, before brushing the odd lock of hair out of the way and behind my ear.

"And I'm glad I emailed you, despite wondering if that one night together was just a fluke."

"It wasn't, was it? I still feel the same."

He flashes a quick grin, and answers with further kisses, behind my ear, down the side of my neck, before pushing aside the neckline of my t-shirt enough to reach my collarbone.

My eyes shut involuntarily, that's how intense the butterflies in my stomach are. I'm in quite a state, confused whether I'm still a bit nervous, or just overcome by the chemistry between us.

"Your wholesome day out is taking an unforeseen turn," I remark, in an attempt to cut the tension, while still refusing to let go of him. I need more kisses, more affection, more of a connection.

"Who says this is unwholesome, or unforeseen?" he says.

In an incredible moment of déjà vu, my phone rings

just as he starts to lavish the rest of my body with affections. I want to ignore it, but nobody ever calls me, except for my folks every other Sunday, or clients...

"You should probably get that," George whispers in my ear before releasing me.

"I don't want to," I respond, but I know he's right.

CHAPTER TEN

"Hello?" After recognizing the name on the display as the Nightmare Client, the tension I had managed to shed in the run up to today is back in full force. I had submitted the proposal on time and in full, what could he possibly want now, late morning on a Saturday?

"Thanks for sending over your estimate." Jack—Mr. Nightmare—Cleary manages to sound stern and humorless even through the phone.

"No problem, I trust it answered any lingering questions you may have had?" Despite my earlier disbelief, it seems we are really doing the follow-up now. This man has clearly never heard of work-life balance.

"Indeed, I'm about ready to move forward," Jack says, however his tone is inconclusive.

"That's wonderful."

George gives me a questioning look, clearly my own tone does not match my words either.

"But, before I'm ready to commit to such a big job, I'm going to need further reassurances that you and your team can handle the workload. Also, due to some other developments, my schedule for the new restaurant chain has moved up a bit, meaning I'll need the websites done sooner than the previously agreed date."

Bollocks . I suppress a groan. Of course he wants to

change the parameters of the project now, that's so typical.

"I completely understand. If you could inform me of the revised schedule in writing, I'll amend my proposal as necessary."

"Fair enough. And in the meantime, I think the importance of this project justifies another meeting to sign the contract in person, this time I'd like to meet your team as well. I need to know everyone is on the same page and equally motivated to make this a success. I'll be in touch with potential dates."

My team? It's an open secret that most successful web design businesses nowadays outsource a lot of their work overseas. Local talent is hard to find at competitive rates. Of course it's a fine balancing act, having an overseas workforce, while not coming across as an unprofessional one-man, or in this case, one-woman band.

Naturally in my efforts to secure the project, I had followed standard procedure and not laid out the finer points of my operation with him. It's just not done.

"Meet my team? Well, I'll see what I can do."

"I'm glad we understand each other. Good day."

And again, as I put down the phone, I find myself in another pickle. I should've known, nothing about this client is simple and straightforward.

"More trouble?" George asks finally, while I'm rubbing my temples, trying to focus on next steps.

"I'm going to have to pull out," I admit, after letting the swirling thoughts in my mind settle. It's the only logical thing I can do. And then, if I don't land another project pretty much immediately, I will be in deep financial shit. The job I was trying to use to pull myself out of this mess, might push me further into it.

"What's the problem, he wants another meeting?" George asks.

"Yeah, with my *team*."

"He doesn't know you farm out the work."

"Well, ordinarily I could have always arranged a video conference with Akhil. He's always been good at putting clients' minds at ease, even remotely. Obviously, that's no longer an option, and this guy is never going to move forward if it's just me. I recognize his type."

George leans over again, and wraps his arm around me, pulling me into his lap. I close my eyes, and try to focus on his soothing touch, but it's hopeless. I can't relax right now, not while I'm faced with the potential loss of my carefully built up professional reputation, as well as financial ruin.

"There may be another way out," George says.

I look up at him, unable to wipe the skeptical frown off my face.

"Only if you're comfortable, but if you'll allow me to help... I do have project management experience."

Surely I can't take him up on that? He offered pretty much immediately when the whole Akhil situation went down, but what guarantee do I have that he's suitable for the role? I barely know him.

"I imagine you'd be busy enough with your own work?"

He shrugs, and looks away.

"Don't you worry about that. I can make time."

I'm still unconvinced, although if he were to at least take on the role of Project Manager temporarily, it would solve a whole host of issues. Worst case scenario, I replenish the coffers, best case, Nightmare Client will bring in follow-up business. If George is good at his work, that is.

And the freelancers, my God, if only they accept him.

He looks down at me again, and rests his hand on my shoulder. If he really is happy to help out, it would give us a lot of time together, getting to know one another...

I really need to think about this. I don't know enough about his experience or skills to make an informed decision. Although, the way he talks does suggest he knows his stuff.

"Look, I get it. We've only just met. I don't expect you to entrust me with your business just because some guy with the worst timing ever went and let you down. Think about it. Believe me, I really just want to help."

"I know. It's just... weird, and sudden."

He smiles down at me and runs his thumb over my lower lip as if he can't wait to taste me again. The gesture as well as the look on his face make me want to throw all caution in the wind. I want to trust him, take his hand and jump in the deep end together, no matter what the consequences. But I've poured ten years of my life into this venture, and I'll be damned if I'm going to risk all now.

"How about, we just spend the rest of the day as if none of this has happened?" I suggest, severely distracted by his touch. I'll think about how to resolve the Nightmare Client situation when I get home. There's no point making rash decisions in the heat of the moment.

"Sounds like a plan."

I slip off his lap and back onto the blanket, beckoning at him to join me on top again.

"Where were we?" I ask, only to be muffled when our lips connect once more.

I wrap my arms around him, as we're overcome by a renewed hunger for one another. Although this isn't the first time by far that I've been with a man, it is the first time I've felt such a need for another human being. Something tells me that's a first for him too.

That's got to mean something, right? Perhaps I can consider the idea of accepting his help. Just this once...

I run my hands up his back, exploring the contours of his shoulder blades. I love how my arms struggle to reach all the way around him, how he is so much taller than me, yet the gentle nibbles of his lips on my earlobe remind me that he'd never hurt me, at least physically.

How far can we go, in this relatively public place?

"I want you." The words escape me before better sense prevails and I can censor myself. It's true though.

"Then I'd better not argue," he says.

This time, we're not disturbed by a phone call.

This time, we're able to rekindle that passion which

first surfaced last week Friday, and find that if anything, our desires are stronger than that first time even. At least mine are.

Although we do our best to keep things PG-13, just in case the odd fellow day tripper stumbles across us, I know today is going to be etched in my memory for a long time to come, hopefully forever. Picnics aren't just for family outings. They can be as romantic and sexy as anything, with the right company.

We spend the afternoon cuddled together soaking up the rays on that checkered blanket in the grass, until the incoming clouds signal it's time to move. After a thrilling ride through the same quaint country lanes, he drops me at my place well in time before dark. Neither of us want to say goodbye just yet, but I have no choice.

It's time to start work on Nightmare Proposal 2.0.

I lean closer to my monitor in disbelief. April 25th? Nightmare Client wants the project done, and live, by April 25th? That's only about... I flip over the page on my desktop calendar and count the weeks. Five-and-a-bit. Jesus Christ. And he suggests we meet on Tuesday.

With the way things have been going, I couldn't even get the developers to commit to an eight-week timeline, reducing it down to five is just crazy talk. I take a deep breath and open up a new email screen to give him a piece of my mind.

Dear Mr. Cleary,

I regret to inform you...

Pfft, this isn't going to be easy. He won't be happy, and neither am I. It's only seven o'clock, and since the man seems to not have any social life, I'm pretty sure he will phone me up to express his displeasure as soon as I hit *send* on this.

Before writing anything further, I pause, head in hands, and try to really think. The fifty per cent advance on this would really come in handy, fifty per cent more upon completion even more so. But he won't buy in if I mess up the meeting; I'm sure someone else has got a bid in too.

While I'm still deciding what to do, my inbox flashes in bold to alert me of a new email. I may as well check what it is.

The subject line, 'Restaurant project' instantly grabs my attention. But it's not from Nightmare Client, but instead a vaguely familiar other name: Callum Byrne. I could bet that I've heard this name somewhere, but I can't place him.

Dear Ms. Aldwell,

A dear friend of mine, Jack Cleary, has referred me to you for an upcoming project. Much like him, I'm also planning to launch a new chain of gourmet restaurants, to coincide with the new season of my show on Good Food TV — Fuck, so that's where I've heard that name before!

I sink back into my chair, reading the rest of the email. A project similar to the current one, only this guy seems a lot more sensible in his approach as well as timescale. A lot of the custom programming that would be required right now could be reused, and his tone, as well as specific requirements suggest he's not the micro-managing type, which is good. And the suggested budget... It would take the pressure off for months.

I knew Nightmare Client's project would be prestigious, and open up a whole new market to tap into, but I hadn't expected him to send other business my way without finalizing our contract!

Flipping back to the email in progress, I suddenly feel stuck. If I argue too much, or worse, withdraw my bid, I'll no doubt lose this new project as well. But Jack's phone call earlier today had made it painfully clear that I can't succeed on my own either. Enter George, who is so eager to help out and appears to be qualified as well.

Both these projects are a massive deal, big enough to warrant taking a risk. Once I've got the first one done, I'll be home safe with the bank. And who knows how many other people Cleary, as well as Byrne, could refer.

I decide to discard my half-written email to Jack Cleary and instead pick up my mobile to dial George's number. Let's see what he says when I explain how big this opportunity is for me.

CHAPTER ELEVEN

I've been careful, evaluated the situation and his qualifications like I would've done with anyone else. At least on paper, George is the perfect candidate. Still, I'm having trouble trusting someone else, when Akhil's betrayal still stings so sharply.

Looking over at him sitting at the spare PC, concentrating hard on whatever's on screen, I try to justify my actions further and swallow my apprehension. He seems dependable, and truly motivated. Fingers crossed this goes well, and I haven't made a massive mistake.

How many people would have been happy to come here on a Sunday morning, to potentially work through the day and into the evening, preparing for a presentation that isn't even their job, technically? Nobody would have, yet here he is. True, I did offer him compensation above industry standard, but that's hardly the point. He didn't even seem to be listening when I mentioned the money.

"So we're shooting for a four week development time, plus 1 week troubleshooting and testing?" George asks, looking up from the revised proposal I'd just shared with him.

"That's right. And we've got to have our ducks in a

row within the next two days, and present it to the client."

It's a very tight schedule, considering the amount of custom programming required to make his restaurant website one of the most cutting-edge in the industry. Cleary needs a fully integrated booking system of course, and a shiny user interface for customers and staff alike. This isn't just a matter of sticking a standard table reservation software in there. If that's what he wanted, he could've hired any old hack.

"It's ambitious, but not impossible. What system do you use to manage the development team?"

"Akhil used to be in charge of that, and he just sort of handled it all by email and Skype."

"Right. No problem." George scratches his beard, looking a bit unimpressed.

"How about I introduce you to the main players?" I suggest.

He nods and I get right to work, sending out emails to the senior freelancers. It had been a massive oversight on my part to give Akhil so much autonomy as project manager. Frankly, I don't really know how he managed everyone one-to-one while still having the time to report back to me.

I'd grown accustomed to instant and accurate responses, despite the time-difference between India and here. Yet when I tried to take over last week, it felt like I was getting bullshitted at every turn. It just hadn't worked quite the same. And now I've thrown George into this shit as well. Great. He's so going to hate me for this.

Glancing over again, I see he has logged on to Skype and is furiously typing away at something. I recognize the profile image in the chat window as one of the main programmers, Neeraj, who has been working for me for the past three years. Best to leave them to it, get to know one another.

"I'll make us some tea," I say, and George nods in approval.

On my way down the stairs, I can't shake the realization how strange this is, having another person in my office, which has often served as my refuge from the real world. I'm even wearing proper outside clothes today, rather than pajamas. It's making me anxious, handing over so much responsibility to another person again, right after being let down.

Once in the kitchen, I switch on the kettle and wait. We've got only a couple of days to figure out how this set up is going to work, and to present a united front with Nightmare Client. And all the while, I'm wavering between being grateful that George is here with me, and worried that things are going to go terribly wrong.

While I wait, I try to do a few simple hand exercises, in an attempt to free up my wrist. Bandages, joint rub and a bit of heat managed to improve it overnight, but as soon as I sat down in front of my workstation this morning, I got a painful reminder that I wouldn't be able to work at full capacity for a while at least.

Thankfully now that the proposal has been finished, my workload is slightly reduced until we get into the user interface design stage. Those are the two things I'm good at: drumming up business, and making things look good. But all the glue in between is going to be down to the guys in India and George. This truly is a team effort, and I feel helpless.

I lay out a tray, and a packet of biscuits, before adding the two mugs and heading back up.

"So, we should be fine as far as time is concerned," George announces as soon as I re-enter the office.

"Really?"

"Yeah, I had a good talk with Neeraj, and we managed to prepare a rough timeline. Here, take a look." George pulls my chair up next to him and points at the spreadsheet on his screen.

I'm speechless. After trying my best last week to get a feel for the time they'd need to finish off their part of the development process, I thought it impossible to get a straight answer out of any of them. I kept wondering if they were just telling me what I wanted to hear without really committing to anything.

"How did you manage that? And in what - five minutes?"

George smiles knowingly. "Programmers know how to talk to programmers. I also suggest that you implement some kind of project management system, like Basecamp. It would help keep everyone on track."

He gets up just enough to reach the tea and cookies I'd forgotten on the desk.

"I don't believe it."

George hands me my cup, and I continue to stare at

him in disbelief. Five minutes, and things are starting to come together.

"See, you've got to understand how these guys work. It's a cultural thing. There's a hierarchy to follow," George explains, before taking a sip.

"U-huh," I respond, but am not fully convinced yet.

"Tell the guy in charge what you want, and he'll say whether or not it's possible. Simple as. If you talk to the wrong person, someone lower down, he won't know what to say without running it past the senior guy first."

While George goes through the plan they've come up with, and shows me various bits of the spreadsheet they've done to organize it all, things fall into place. As he continues to explain, I start to feel relieved, mostly. By the end, I'm more optimistic about the project than I've ever been, and yet...

It's all going to work out, no thanks to me.

****

We sit back in the plush armchairs in my lounge, tired but at least I no longer feel like my world is about to implode. Today, with George's help the project has actually turned viable.

"Cheers," I say, holding up my glass of beer.

"To a job well begun," he responds, repeating my gesture.

Looking at him now, after having spent all day working together, my initial jealousy at how easily he managed to sort out my freelancer problem has waned.

Fine, I may not be brilliant at handling staff, but at least I've got help now.

And it strikes me again that said help is absolutely gorgeous. We've been in work mode all day, focused on the task at hand, but now we're off the clock and the relaxed mood is shifting my attention.

"I just wanted to thank you again for all you're doing for me. Things may just work out." I put down my glass on the teak wood side table between us.

"Not a problem, it's an interesting project. A bit different from the usual." He smiles at me, then looks around the half-lit room, until his eyes are invariably drawn to the large flat screen TV on the wall at the far end of the space. "That's... wow."

I follow his line of sight, and embarrassment washes over me. Everyone who has ever come in here, including my own parents, have commented on the TV.

"A bit big, but considering the size of the room..." I try to justify.

Perhaps I did go a bit overboard in the past five years when business was booming. It's mostly paid off, but I probably should have taken it easy. I was just too keen to settle in a place of my own that would remind me of the house I grew up in. To prove that this unconventional career of mine could be as successful as Dad's law practice.

What the hell, why should I be ashamed? I earned every penny that's gone into this place. And yet, I now worry I'm sending the wrong message.

"Anyway, shall we order in something for dinner?

Are you hungry?" I ask, trying to distract from the negativity that has crept back into my thoughts.

He shrugs. "Sure, what are the options?"

I get up to open the drawer of the coffee table, and retrieve a bunch of takeaway menus.

"The Chinese is particularly good, or there's always pizza."

While George picks through the leaflets, I wonder how long it will take for us to be more comfortable together. This weekend has seen a lot of firsts for both of us: the best picnic I've ever been to, me accepting someone else's offer of help rather than stubbornly struggling on my own. And finally, working together, which meant letting another person into my office. The latter was quite strange at first. I'm so used to living alone, that I'm not quite sure how people manage to relax with others around.

Despite being shattered after a hard day's work, still I'm restless. Like there's something I'm supposed to do tonight which has slipped my mind. I decide to check if I have other takeaway menus, perhaps in the kitchen drawer.

"Pizza sounds great," George greets me when I come back into the lounge empty-handed.

"Sure thing." I take the menu from him, as he mentions what he wants. Back in the hallway, I call to place the order.

As soon as I hang up, a realization hits me. *Shit.* It's Sunday evening, and my turn to phone Mum and Dad!

I stick my head around the doorway, cordless phone

still in hand, and find George flipping through channels.

"Just a sec, I've got make another call."

He gives me the thumbs up.

Before I get the chance to say much else, the phone rings on its own. They've beat me to it.

"Hello?"

"Hey, Lucy, darling. We hadn't heard from you so thought we'd phone up instead." Dad sounds as cheerful as always on the other line.

"Sorry about that, I got tied up with an urgent project." And considering the company still spilling over from said project, I'm anxious to get off the line soon. I probably sound like it too.

"How's business?" Dad asks.

"You work too hard," Mum chimes in from the background. They must have me on speaker.

"Yeah, not bad, Dad. Things are picking up."

"Anyway, sweetheart, we were just wondering if you were planning anything for your thirty-fifth," Mum continues.

"Uhh right, my birthday..." Time sure has flown by. Last time we talked about it, I had said I'd organize something, a family get-together perhaps, and it's completely slipped my mind ever since. "Well, I suppose there's still time."

"Don't tell me you forgot!" Mum exclaims.

"Uhh... No, Mum, just..."

"She forgot, can you believe it, Bernard?"

Dad responds with a grunt, signaling he can believe it all too well. I sigh in defeat. This particular anecdote is no doubt going to be repeated in front of anyone who will listen for years to come. Barely five weeks to go, and this big project, I don't know how I'll manage to organize a party as well.

"Anyway, I had an inkling this might happen, so I convinced your dad to make some enquiries at the club."

"Mum, you didn't have to!"

"Yes, darling, we did," Dad butts in.

"So, that's settled then. We'll let everyone know. You just turn up, all right, sweetie?" Mum says.

"Sure thing, Mum. Thanks so much."

"No problem. It will be nice to see everyone again. Otherwise we'll get to a stage where the only time we meet up as a family is at weddings and funerals."

"Indeed. Umm, mind if I call it a night-?" I'm about to say I've got company, but it seems wrong to announce that so early on, and will likely create questions. "I'm really beat after the week I've had."

"Of course, Lucy. We'll talk again next week. Take care of yourself, will you?"

"Bye, Mum, Dad," I say, before hanging up and finding George in front of me, empty glass in hand.

CHAPTER TWELVE

"Your folks?" he asks.

I nod and shoot him a sheepish smile.

"Shall I get us a refill while we wait for the food?" I ask.

He nods, and follows me to the kitchen, where he leans on a counter, while I get a couple more bottles out of the fridge.

"So... I couldn't help but overhear some of that. When is your birthday exactly? I can't believe I haven't asked yet."

"Oh, that. To be frank, I totally forgot about it. May first. Apparently Mum and Dad are throwing me a party and they're calling the whole family. I had told them I'd do it, but with everything that's been going on, it slipped my mind."

I pause for a moment, unsure whether to invite him or not. It's all a bit soon, isn't it? But then, he can always refuse.

"If you like, you're more than welcome to come... By then hopefully it'll be a double celebration. The project should be delivered." I focus on pouring his drink, avoiding eye contact. Great, now I'm nervous again, but I can't tell whether it's because I want him to say 'yes' or 'no'.

"It's going to be a big affair then?" he asks, nodding his thanks when I hand him the refilled pint glass.

"Sort of, they insisted that since it's kind of a milestone-"

George's raised eyebrows remind me that he hasn't got any clue what I'm on about.

"Sorry, it's my thirty-fifth. Ever since Dad's bypass, they feel any birthday should be celebrated, no exceptions. But those with a zero or a five in the end doubly so."

"Ah, right. Well, if you want me there, I'll come."

I look at him, trying to decipher his thoughts. He didn't sound all that keen, throwing the ball in my court, and yet, he looks his usual self, comfortable.

"I'll make sure you get an invite then," I say. "Cheers."

We walk back into the lounge where the TV is still on, showing a custom bike build mid-progress. It seems our tastes in television overlap nicely as well. Throw in an unhealthy compulsion to watch *Die Hard* every single time it's on, and we'll be golden.

"Umm... considering it's probably an hour's drive back for you, and the pizza is not going to come for at least another thirty minutes, would you like to stay?" I ask.

He sits down on the sofa right opposite the TV, and pats on the seat beside him.

"One condition," he says.

"What's that?"

"You come here and relax." He takes my glass while

ONE NIGHT STAND

I join him on the couch.

"You noticed that, huh?" I let out a deep sigh. "I'm just—well, I'm not used to having people over."

"I guessed as much." He hands me back my drink and puts his arm around me.

I look over at him, noting the amused glint in his eye.

"That's funny, is it? I thought it was kind of sad."

"It's funny, because I never get visitors either."

"And here I thought things were about to get awkward again. What with the oversized house, oversized TV and upcoming oversized birthday party." I put my glass down and lean back against him, closing my eyes.

"Well okay, all that is definitely a bit odd." He lets out a chuckle, which makes me smile too. "So tell me about your folks, what are they like?"

"Dad was a barrister, had his own firm right until his heart issues started some years back. Mum was at home with us. They still live a few villages over, in the same house where I grew up."

"So you have siblings?"

"Kind of. My cousin, Pete stayed with us from when he was ten. He's a few years older than me and always treated me like his little sister." Resting my hand on George's knee, I try hard to focus on the conversation, rather than our physical connection. "What about you? Tell me about your family."

He places his hand on top of mine, which makes me feel hot and cold at the same time, yet I dare not move.

"Grew up in Birmingham, my folks are still there. Dad worked at Longbridge, the car factory, all his life. Though he's a car guy, it's because of him that I got into motorcycles. The Harley, we built it together."

"That's really nice, to share something like that with your dad."

"I suppose. They weren't all that thrilled when I decided to get into IT though, and move down south."

"Mine weren't thrilled with my career choices either. Dad always wanted me to take over the firm from him. But law, it's just too dry for me."

George pulls me closer against him, and plants a kiss in my hair. How funny, the similarities between us, despite coming from vastly different backgrounds.

"Do you have any brothers or sisters?" I ask.

He shakes his head. "It's just me."

I turn to face him, and just look. It's funny, the more I get to know, the more familiar he becomes, the more time I could spend observing him.

"What?" he asks.

I have nothing more to say, so just smile.

"Stop staring at me." He tries to sound stern, but his eyes betray that he doesn't really mind.

"Make me."

No sooner do the words pass through my lips, than he jumps into action. He lifts me off the sofa, making me land astride him. Then he cups my face and guides it towards his. I try my best to stay alert, to not give in and instead drown in those blue eyes of his. But when our lips fuse, I have to admit defeat.

ONE NIGHT STAND

"Yep," I gasp.

"Mhm?"

"That'll do it."

It's infuriating, having to shut down so many of my emotions all day, then find a way to let them out after hours. A balancing act I'm not yet proficient at.

"What do you say we take this upstairs?" I suggest, just before diving into the crook of his neck.

"Too far," he says through gritted teeth while I start nibbling on his earlobe.

All day we've been together, his scent infiltrating my senses when I least expected it. In between the serious discussions about work, every so often his eyes would linger on me just enough to remind me that we're supposed to share more than work. But I had kept those emotions in check, as hard as it was.

And now, it's time to release everything, and yet I still hesitate. I need to stop playing boss or colleague or hostess and just be me.

"Why so tense?" George asks, his fingers exploring the rigid muscles on my shoulders.

I want to tell him everything that's been on my mind lately. From the mortgage payment reminders I've been trying to ignore, to my worries that us working together will hamper the more intimate nature of our relationship. Truthfully of course, I'd been tense way before I even met him, before Akhil left, ever since I haven't had a decent project in months. All of the rest is just adding to the mess.

"Work, you know. It never ends." I force a smile,

then shut my eyes as his hands work their magic on me.

Maybe one day I'll tell him everything that's been on my mind. But not today. I don't want to face it.

Opening my eyes again, I lean down for a kiss, only to find him as intensely hungry for me as I am for him. He peels off my t-shirt, letting my hair cascade down over the naked skin on my shoulders and cleavage. I look back up at him, and hook my finger under his shirt as well.

Your turn.

He hesitates just a bit, so little that a casual observer might not have noticed, but I do. My fingers start work on his buttons, revealing more tempting skin as I progress upwards. Seeing the dragon tattoo on his shoulder again makes me want one of my own. I wonder if he likes girls with tattoos as well.

I dive down, kissing, licking, nibbling my way down his torso. Soft, warm skin, burning into my lips. Lust surges within me, making it hard to be gentle, when what I really want to do is claw, bite, suck and tear. It's hard to explain, to analyze why when you're engrossed in someone, you feel a need to own them, sometimes even to hurt them, because it's the only way to release the tension inside.

Of course I don't hurt him, not much anyway, looking at the feverish expression on his face. He's ready, he wants this as much as me.

His fingers dig into my ass, his teeth gently surround the nipple he has just freed from my bra. Items of clothing, discarded on the ground one by one, until we're both naked.

He's brought condoms, of course he has, and puts one on in a rush so we can progress. Soon we may not need them, it's the ultimate sign of trust to forgo all barriers.

When I lower myself onto him, I imagine what he'll feel like unsheathed, how much better it will be. If that's even possible. Had he not made the first move, I may have let things progress without the rubber already. I want him. Closer, skin against skin, deeper as well as harder.

The leather of the sofa sticks against our skin, causing a hot prickling sensation whenever we move. Funny how the things that are annoying while watching TV can be such a turn on during sex. Pain and pleasure are related like incestuous cousins.

He lifts me with every thrust, causing me to bounce up and down on him higher and faster than I could manage on my own. The tension that has been building all day, in between the chats, emails, spreadsheets and briefings is trying its best to claw its way out of my chest. His too, his eyes seem to burn with a lust more intense than words could express.

"Cum for me, Lucy," he groans. "I love to see the pleasure written all over your face."

I'm done holding back, done being proper or professional. For him, I want to be it all, a saint in the day, slut at night. I fuck him with renewed energy, to make it so he's unable to talk, just like me. Our means of communication is limited to thrusts, groans, moans and screams.

He bucks his hips, his brow furrowed and lips slightly parted. More kisses, more caresses. I grab hold of his neck, anchoring myself down with every movement. Until I lose it, and die a thousand deaths in his arms, only to be reborn, sweaty and exhausted, as well as sated.

Just at the moment when my thighs threaten to give way, he tenses up, making me continue on, fighting to keep moving, to push him over the edge with me. His cock seems to grow and pulsate inside me. His pleasure infects me again, making me shiver from the inside out, and I cry out again, taking his full length inside me until everything subsides for the second time.

Not just my thighs, but all of me gives up and all the sound left in this room is a roar of an engine behind us. The bike builders on TV finally managed to get their creation started it seems.

"Did you just..." George asks, while panting for air. His arms wrap around me again, gentler this time.

"Twice," I whisper, unable or unwilling to move.

"Wow."

CHAPTER THIRTEEN

The sound of my phone alarm wakes me, but I struggle to emerge from the fog straightaway. Across me, tucking me safely into my duvet, George's arm serves as protection against the inconvenient outside world. He stayed over, and unlike the first time we fell asleep in the same bed, last night wasn't interrupted by sleepless doubts on my part.

"Morning," he whispers in my ear, making the prospect of getting up even less tempting than it already was.

I blink against the light filtering through the gaps in the curtains, and wait for reality to come into focus.

"Morning."

The peace and quiet is now ruined by my alarm clock, which is set to come on mere minutes after the phone, just in case the former doesn't rouse me. Another day lies ahead, but one which is set to start just a bit differently.

"Back to the grind, eh?" George stretches, letting go of me in the process.

Suddenly overly aware of my nakedness underneath the sheets, I wrap them tighter around myself.

"Unfortunately. Staying in bed would have been much more fun."

I turn around, resting my hand on the dragon tattoo on his shoulder which I've spent a lot of last night familiarizing myself with. What is it with men and tattoos, that makes them infinitely sexier than men without tattoos? And long-haired, big men with tattoos... My mind instantly shows me a replay of some of last night's more poignant moments. Sweaty, sticky, delicious moments that they were.

The phone goes off again, as it will do every minute until I shut down the alarm completely.

"Sorry about that." I struggle with the touch screen in my half-dazed state, wondering if perhaps it would be best to throw it against a wall if it doesn't stop screaming straightaway.

"Needs must." George starts to get up, and I stay back and watch as he picks up his t-shirt and boxers off the floor.

"Bathroom's this one, right?" He points at the door on the left, next to the one leading to the walk-in closet.

"That's right."

"This house is too damn big and confusing," he mumbles, as he steps inside.

"I can draw you a map if you want," I joke behind him just before he shuts the door.

Whew, that was... amazing, different, out of character, and a bit scary. It's also coming up on the most time I've ever spent with another human being not directly related to me.

***

"So..." I look up from my screen, and struggle not to let my voice crack while making light of the shit storm that's about to unfold. "I've got good news and bad news."

"Start with the good."

"The prep work for the presentation is going to finish a lot sooner than expected."

"What's the bad part?" George asks.

"He wants to meet today, at one. Apparently he's been called away for the rest of the week and wants to settle things before then."

He looks at me, I look at him. "I'm beginning to understand why you keep referring to him as the Nightmare Client."

"Right. Is it even possible? We're so not ready yet."

"Four hours," George mumbles, while checking the clock on the wall behind me. "Where?"

"Pretty close to where we first met, Waterloo."

"Fuck." He runs his hand over his hair. "Sorry."

"I know."

"And how far exactly would that be from here?"

"Little over an hour by train, plus about forty-five minutes total to get to Reading Station from here, and walk to his restaurant from Waterloo."

"I am so glad I already had a shower."

"Tell me about it." My shoulders slump down, and I rest my face on my fists. Perhaps it's time to admit defeat.

"Please tell me you have two laptops hidden away in

this place somewhere?" George pushes his chair back and walks the few steps towards me, leaning over and resting his hand on my back. "If we can keep working on the train, we may be able to wing it."

I raise my head, to find him looking down at me. His lips pressed together in determination, and a thoughtful frown to match.

"Do you really think so?" I ask.

"You don't suppose he would give us a little leeway, considering he moved up the meeting?"

I shrug. "Maybe, though as far as he knows we've been working as a team for ages."

"True. Well then, we'll just have to act confident enough together to convince him."

George smiles down at me, causing all kinds of warm, fuzzy feelings. If he really thinks we can do it, perhaps it's worth a shot. There's a lot at stake for me, but if we don't try at least, all is already lost.

"There's a sample follow-up presentation Akhil made in the Documents folder, perhaps it helps. I'll see about those laptops."

I get up and head straight towards the large filing cabinet by the window. I don't like working on a laptop, especially when doing graphics, but sometimes you do need something more portable than a workstation with a twenty-three-inch screen. It doesn't take long for me to find the new one, but my back-up is proving more difficult to locate.

"I've got an older one too, but I think it may be in the attic. Give me a moment?" I ask.

ONE NIGHT STAND

George nods without looking up from his work. "Take your time, I'm going to make a start on this."

It takes me a solid fifteen minutes of rummaging through old boxes full of documents and other business stuff in the attic to locate the other laptop. Fifteen minutes that I wasn't able to spend preparing and left George to his own devices downstairs.

Another fifteen minutes get wasted trying to upgrade Office so at least we can share the same documents between us.

This second meeting will be the one to convince a control-freak micro-manager that we can indeed deliver to his highly accelerated time frame. People often say once they call you back, that's most of the battle won. For our sake, and for the sake of my bank balance, I hope that's the case.

We keep our heads down, working away with no breaks until it's time to leave. George is forced to wear whatever he was wearing yesterday, which thankfully did feature a button-up shirt of sorts, even if it is denim. How lucky he keeps a beard, so the issue of shaving doesn't come up. I opt for a trouser suit, so at least one of us looks the part.

Before we know it, most of our prep time is over, and we find ourselves on a train zipping through fields and villages, on our way into the capital. It's the same journey I made for the first meeting, before George and I had even met.

Although there is a significant chance we're not ready, we're unwilling to give up either. Our backs are against the wall—at least mine is—and we have no choice anymore but to move forward. The adrenaline has kicked in, and not even the shrieking teenage girls in the row of seats behind us can break our focus.

As our train pulls into Waterloo, we rush to pack up our things and start walking, with me leading the way while still rehearsing parts of the presentation. We arrive at Cleary's with ten minutes to spare, and the front door opens the second we arrive.

"Lovely to see you," Jack Cleary greets me with a handshake, while scrutinizing George, who's towering over the both of us more like a bodyguard than anything else.

"This is George, my project manager." I'm still trying to catch my breath after the brisk walk from the station, as is he.

"I see. Please do come in." Cleary turns on his heel after shaking George's hand briefly.

George gives me a quick look, and a shrug. While I've thrown on a business suit as usual, of course George doesn't quite project the same image. I like to think that's okay, considering he's a techie. It's all about attitude from here on.

As soon as we move into Cleary's office, some glasses of water appear and we're on the clock. He hasn't got much time, and neither do I wish to drag out this already stressful and uncomfortable situation. We get right down to business, explaining the revised timeline, and suggested milestones along the way. George takes over, running through the PowerPoint like a total pro, allowing me to fall back and just observe.

I'm impressed.

By the end, so is Cleary.

I hand over the paperwork, which he signs without hesitation, then he hands me a check and we're escorted out of the office, and restaurant, before getting the chance to say or think anything else.

"Whoa..." George lets out a sigh, as we find ourselves, rather helplessly, on the pavement outside just when the clouds threaten to burst open with the first droplets of rain. In all this rush, neither of us thought to carry a decent coat or umbrella.

"That went well." I straighten myself, stretching achy back muscles; a reminder of just how stressed I have been for weeks. "Thank you so much."

I rest my hand on his arm, and am rewarded with heavier raindrops landing square in my face.

"Screw this. Let's have lunch somewhere, celebrate. I think we deserve a bit of a break after all that. From tomorrow, the real work starts."

He nods, but doesn't say anything more. The rain speeds up, forcing a quick decision.

"How about this place?" I point at an inviting glass frontage, with rustic looking wooden tables and chairs inside. It's not very busy, but there are enough people inside to suggest the food may be edible.

"Sure. Hey, you go ahead, I'll be just behind you," George says, his hand stuck firmly in his pocket.

I shrug and head inside, getting a table for the two of us halfway towards the back of the little bistro. After casting off my jacket, and attempting to shake off most of the water from it, I sit, facing the windows. It's significantly darker outside than only a moment ago. In good old British fashion, the weather has made a U-turn for the worse in mere minutes.

"Can I take your order?" a very cheerful female voice with a hint of a Mediterranean accent asks beside me.

"I'm waiting for someone. Just a coffee for now, thanks."

In an attempt to pass the time, I decide to respond to Callum Byrne, asking him when he would like to meet to discuss the project. Meanwhile, my coffee arrives, allowing me to warm up a little.

What's taking George so long?

It's only by the time I'm done with the email, as well as most of my coffee, when he enters, stuffing his phone back into his pocket. Good. I'm starving, as I imagine he is too.

CHAPTER FOURTEEN

Another day, another boatload of work. We may have convinced Cleary to hand over his advance, but that's only the beginning. Now the real job starts.

George arrived early, after staying the night at his place. The roar of his Harley no doubt woke the entire neighborhood, it certainly made me take notice. I was slightly disappointed he didn't want to stay with me after lunch yesterday, but I can't really expect him to stop going home altogether.

I still have to broach the topic of his job somehow. How is he managing the time off? I can't imagine your average employer would be pleased to find out that their staff has started taking days without notice just so they can work with someone else in the same industry. Then again, he assured me it's fine, perhaps I ought to trust him.

There's not much time for idle chat now. We have to put the timeline he had prepared with Neeraj earlier into action. Everyone has a job to do, so now they have to be informed, and managed, so everything remains on schedule.

It's been a very long time since I worked in an actual office environment, but I imagine it's something similar to the set-up we have now, just with more people. At the spare desk, George is briefing Neeraj and a couple of the other guys by Skype, while I'm catching up on a bit of admin work. Within days, he's been able to fill the gap Akhil left, and more.

I'm actually starting to relax a little, which is unusual at the beginning of a new job. Normally, I don't allow myself to become too comfortable until the end is in sight.

The phone rings, a London number, which I decide to take in the other room to get away from George's chatter in the background. It's Callum Byrne. Ordinarily I'd be tense, having two such important jobs overlap slightly but George's involvement has made me confident the current project will be on track. As a result, I'm pleased Byrne called back so soon after my email.

Now, we agree that I work on a proposal for him, to be presented in person when he's back from some sourcing trip to Italy a few weeks from now. Things sound extremely promising, and I can't wait to share the good news.

When I return to the office, George isn't at his seat, his briefing must have finished. I decide to wait, answering a few emails, after which I begin to sketch a few rough ideas for the Cleary website. After around five minutes, impatience starts to grow in me.

Deep breaths, you can't expect him to be glued to his chair twelve hours a day! He's not me, after all.

I know I'm being unreasonable, and yet...

When he comes back, mobile phone in hand, he

seems a lot less cheerful than I just was after the chat with Byrne.

"You alright?" I ask.

"Yeah, fine. Hey, if you don't have anything else for me to do right now, do you mind if I duck out for a bit?"

Wonder what that's about.

"The guys are on task?"

"Yeah, just a matter of them doing the work now, I should probably check in with them for daily updates though."

"Good idea. Well, why not take the day? I feel kind of bad for taking up all your time lately."

"Thanks, Lucy. See you tomorrow," George says, the relief evident in his eyes.

Wonder what all that was about. I watch him as he packs up his things, and get up myself to see him out. He's rather quiet, all the way down the stairs. I don't ask what's the matter, because I don't want to pry. This whole dynamic, him asking for time and me suggesting he ' *take the day'*, is all very cold to me. We're working together now, so technically he's an employee at least for the time being.

But he's not, really, is he?

"Later," I say, unsure of whether to kiss him goodbye, or what else to do.

He nods, then puts on his helmet before starting his bike and speeding out of the gate.

When I get back upstairs and sit down to continue working, the silence of my now empty office is deafening.

***

"Hey, just wondering whether you'd like to have dinner tonight," I speak into the phone.

The crackle on the other end of the line is distracting, while I wait for his response.

Now that work on the back-end development of the website project is in full swing, I've needed less and less of George's time. So much so, that I insisted he stop sitting around my place every day, and go back to his regular job. Despite his protests, I couldn't imagine how anyone would be able to get that much time off without consequences.

And so, for the past two weeks, he's been handling the daily briefings and updates mostly from home.

Things are rolling along nicely, and I've assured him it won't change his share of the profits. But it has meant we've seen less and less of each other, while I've been neck deep in my part of the project, as well as prep work for the next one. Those times we did meet up, he seemed distant. No matter what we started talking about, our conversations always ended up being about work in the end.

Things just haven't been the same. And I couldn't help noticing that he always seemed to keep one eye on his phone when we were together.

ONE NIGHT STAND

"Dinner? Out or in?" George asks.

I hadn't considered that yet, but the answer presents itself in the paperwork on my desk.

"Well, how about we go somewhere nice? The new client, Byrne, has a restaurant in Henley. We could check it out, and I'll write it off as research, what do you say?"

The line is quiet for a bit, except for the continuous interference.

"Come on, it's a nice ride to get there too. We could take both the bikes this time."

"Alright then. I'll be at your place at seven."

With a click, even the persistent crackle in the line goes silent.

Is it just my imagination or did he seem less than thrilled by the prospect of going out tonight? Or perhaps I'm just projecting my own doubts and worries onto him?

After the intense early days we spent together, picking up the pieces Akhil left behind, all the business stuff is getting in the way of *us*. It has been hard to pick things up where we left them, romantically. Even our emails back and forth have changed drastically in tone. It's all business, no play, and it's been getting me down.

I need to turn things around and tonight could be the time to do it. And perhaps we'll do better once we can focus on us as a couple, rather than this impromptu working relationship we've found ourselves in. Things are going well, we've been on target for all the milestones set in the initial schedule for the Cleary project, including getting him to sign off my design.

There's only one thing I can think to do to fix this: I'm going to draw a line under it all. I'll cut a check and see if George and I can find our way back to how it all started. Just two regular people, who found each other by chance. Time to take the business nonsense out of the equation. I'm sure I can take over now that most of the work is done.

Despite planning to go for a ride this evening, I decide to dress up a bit. Skinny jeans and a nice top with a plunging neckline, to remind him of what we shared before work got in the way. Just enough make-up to show I've made an effort, and even some jewelry. I don't recall the last time I even wore earrings since all of this began.

It's been weeks since we've truly been ourselves, or so it seems. Like we've both forgotten how much we share, other than one silly project that's going to be over before we know it.

I wonder if he's even still interested in me? Could it be that we just didn't click as well as I thought? Perhaps our connection was one-sided from the start, and I just didn't realize it?

I try to shake these unhelpful thoughts, and while away the time until seven o'clock. But no matter what I do to distract myself, the doubts keep on returning.

By the time he turns up, I've been ready for half an hour, pacing about the place just like the first time we were going to go on a ride together. Although we know each other better now, it still feels like I've barely scratched the surface and I just can't tell where his head is at mostly.

"Hey, I'll be right out," I tell George over the intercom when he reaches the gate.

He gives me the thumbs-up and returns to his bike.

I gather up my helmet and gloves, and head out to warm up my bike. The Honda's engine doesn't roar like George's Harley, rather it shrieks, especially at higher revs. *Like a banshee,* the thought makes me smile. It goes like one too, I have no doubts that I'll not only be able to keep up with George, but outrun him. They're different beasts, much like him and me, even if they're both bikes of a similar age.

After a couple of minutes, I can't wait any longer and get in the saddle, joining George outside the gate. With a nod, I speed off the drive and onto the road, with him hot on my heels.

This time of day is just right for a little ride. Most of the office rush fizzles out by about six-thirty, leaving the way through Reading quiet enough to make it enjoyable. Then, once the countryside opens up, it's like entering a different world.

I let him know where to go with the odd hand signal, but the road signs are self-explanatory. We take turns leading, overtaking one another with either a growl or a scream from our exhausts. By the time we reach, I can't wipe my smile off my face. Although he had seemed unenthusiastic at first on the phone, when we park up at Byrne's restaurant, his eyes have lit up as well.

We weren't meant to sit in an office together. This—

riding through winding rural roads together—is what we were meant to do!

"Hungry?" I ask.

"Famished," he responds, while trying to get his wild, long mane under control after taking off his helmet.

CHAPTER FIFTEEN

I can't take my eyes off him as we sit down. Earlier worries, forgotten while on the road together, come creeping back into my thoughts. The check is in my pocket, I just have to find the right time to bring it up, and to make it so there is no misunderstanding my intentions.

This is the right call, isn't it? I just want things to work out somehow, he must realize that.

He's studying the offerings, while I pretend to look at the specials board behind him. Actually, I keep glancing down, taking in every detail of his features. Even though we're sitting down, he still looks tall. And broad. And irresistible.

His blue eyes, so focused on the menu, I can't look at them without remembering the first moment we truly seemed to connect. That was not long ago at all, only a few weeks, and yet everything is so different now.

I remember that night so clearly, how we'd started flirting almost reluctantly, how surprisingly shy he turned out to be once we were alone. And then, all of a sudden, all hesitation vanished, when our beings came together spectacularly. It was as if subconsciously we both decided to ignore all sense and reason, and just give in to pleasure.

For years I've been alone and not really felt like I was missing out. Now I know I have been. I want more of this in my life. Someone to spend time with. To make it seem worthwhile to sit down in a nice place together, whiling the hours away with good food and better conversation.

I want to feel wanted, and needed. And... loved. Surely, that's what everyone wants? He would too?

"Have you decided?" George looks up, snapping me out of my wishful thinking.

"Umm, steak. I could murder a good steak." It's the first thing that popped into my head, probably because part of my research on Callum Byrne involved watching a few snippets of his TV show, one of which about steak.

"Sounds good. I'll have the same thing." George shuts the leather binder containing the menu, and leans back, checking out our surroundings. "I don't think I've ever been at a TV chef's restaurant before."

I smile, and follow his gaze towards a photograph of the man in question, hanging above the bar counter. With his carefully styled hair and blindingly white teeth, Callum Byrne's picture looks like a TV still, not at all like a real person.

"I'm sure whatever they're serving, it's just food."

He shrugs. "At least they wrote down the weight of the steak, so they can't get away with plating up half a bite of meat, while charging all that money for *presentation*."

I let out a chuckle, and allow myself to relax. Might

as well broach the subject.

"Say, George," I start, waiting for his attention to move away from the various certificates and awards lined up on the wall beside us, and back to me.

"Yeah?"

"I've been thinking about us, working together." No matter how hard I try to convince myself it's all for the best, still my heart starts to pound. What if he takes it the wrong way?

"It's been rather stressful, and intense, hasn't it?" I ask.

"Not too bad."

"Well I just feel like we've just been talking about work and nothing else."

George leans back in his seat, his eyes only on me now. I have his full attention, and still, I can't read him at all.

"How about we start over? Just you and me. No work, no clients, no distractions?" My voice cracks slightly, betraying my nerves. It's the moment of truth, this can either go the way I want it to, or completely to hell.

"I'm not sure I understand."

I find the check in my pocket, extracting it carefully and place it on the table right in between us.

"The amount is what we agreed. You know how people say not to bring money into relationships? Well, I wanted to get it out of the way."

He picks it up, and frowns.

"I thought things were going well with the project?"

"Yeah, they are. Everything is going perfectly. But I don't like thinking of you as an employee, you know? And as long as this job is hanging over our heads..." I explain, but the look on his face tells me he's not on the same page. Rather than an attempt to save our relationship, he's seeing it as a judgment of his work.

"George, you have been absolutely invaluable." I reach over to touch his hand, which twitches slightly when my fingers connect with his. "I want something more intimate with you than a working relationship. Lately, I've been wondering if perhaps I can't have both."

"I see." He removes his hand from underneath mine, to fold the check in half and put it in his shirt pocket. "Well, I guess you've made your choice."

I try to look him in the eye, to figure out just how he feels, but he's avoiding my gaze. My heart sinks, but I don't let it scare me off. I need to make him understand somehow.

"All I'm saying is, I want you in my life. Not just in my office." My eyes are getting moist, causing me to blink a few times. "I really like you, George."

He nods, then just sits there, quietly. I want to press him for a reaction, to find out whether he feels the same, but part of me is too afraid to ask. Instead, I just hold my breath, forcing my emotions back in check.

"Your order, please?" An impeccably dressed waiter has appeared out of nowhere, clutching one of those electronic machines that sends the order straight to the kitchen.

ONE NIGHT STAND

I wait for George to take the lead, just in case he wants to forget about dinner and leave. The few seconds of silence make my heart skip a whole lot of beats, but then, he collects himself.

"Two steak platters, please. A coke for me, and you?" He gestures at me.

"Same. A coke."

The waiter disappears almost as quickly as he had shown up earlier.

"I was worried you'd want to leave," I whisper.

"Nah, I'm not going anywhere until I try this guy's steak." George shoots me a wry smile.

I've hurt him, but the fact that he's still here means he's trying to see things my way. Perhaps we can move on from here after all. Onwards and upwards.

Throughout dinner, and the mind-blowing dessert that follows, we don't talk much. I ask him a few necessary questions about work, the last ones I hope, just so I can take over from tomorrow. Beyond that, suddenly it seems like we have nothing to say.

It's only temporary, I try to convince myself, *we're transitioning and then everything will be fine.*

But when we get ready to leave, and I ask if he wants to have a coffee at mine, things are not yet fine. He refuses. I ask when I'll see him again, and he doesn't commit either way.

Perhaps I need to give him some time to digest this new situation. Yes, that's it. I'll give him some space, and time. If we are meant to be, things will work themselves out.

***

"So it's all set then," I say, waiting for Callum Byrne's reaction on the other end of the phone.

"Indeed. Monday, nine am. Will your project manager be joining us?"

His question makes me pause. Dammit, why does he have to bring up George now?

"It'll just be me."

"Oh, that's too bad. Jack was very impressed by him."

Cleary told him, of course! The two of them do seem to be very close, it's only obvious that they'd discuss the project, and our meetings, in detail, even if I now wish they hadn't.

"George is actually focusing on Jack Cleary's project at the moment, making sure everything is completed on time. Hence he won't be attending the meeting." It's the best justification I could come up with, though in truth I have no idea what George is up to. Our contact since dinner last week has been strained at best. If I had time to let my imagination get the better of me, I would say he was avoiding me.

"Oh well, maybe next time, eh?" Byrne says.

"Indeed. Looking forward to meeting you on Monday."

"Likewise." With that, Byrne hangs up, leaving me lost in thoughts.

I should reach out to George, see how he's doing.

Surely a week should be enough time to think things through and realize I decided what I did to help us, not make things worse between us? Then again, I have been incredibly busy myself, so I shouldn't just blame him for not keeping in touch.

It's early Friday evening, perhaps he's just leaving the office now. Let's see if he's free to talk, or willing to meet up tonight.

I dial his number, and wait. Switched off. Maybe he's still at work then, oh well.

Instead of obsessing about George, I decide to finish off some emails. The Byrne proposal is as good as done, and the Cleary project is racing towards the finish line. Thanks to George's help with the freelancers, things have been going relatively smoothly.

I shoot off an email to Neeraj, asking him to confirm the proposed timeline for the Byrne project, the last piece of the puzzle, before the proposal can be sent off in preparation for Monday's meeting. It's quite late in India, so I don't expect a response until the morning. However, just when I'm about to try George's number again, a response does come in. It's just a single sentence from Neeraj:

Where is George?

Goddammit!

When I took over last week, I did explain that George had work of his own to go back to, so I'd handle things myself again. His reaction had been skeptical at first, but then he dropped the issue. Now, it seems his curiosity is getting the better of him again.

There's only one problem: it's none of his business. It's none of anyone's business. From the start, I'd made it clear that George was helping out temporarily, so why can't people just drop it? If Byrne's question wasn't already irritating enough, now this. This is my company, has been from the start, and yet it seems like I'm the fucking third wheel. How is that fair, after all the years I've killed myself to grow this business?

Jesus Christ.

I'm dangerously close to losing my cool, but decide to pound out a quick response to Neeraj anyway.

Never mind George, what about the schedule I asked about?

He'd been quick enough to reply last time, so I sit there, my heart still pounding in my throat, and cheeks burning up. No matter how hard I stare at the screen, nothing else comes in. No confirmation, not even a repeat of the same question.

I'm about to lose it and send another, harsher email, when my phone interrupts me.

"Hello," I all but bark into the phone.

"Hey, George here. You called?"

Deep breaths, don't say anything you'll regret later.

"Oh, yeah, sorry. I just wanted to ask what's going on. If perhaps you're free to talk, or meet up or something?" I want to sound genuine, agreeable, but it's hard to get over my earlier frustration.

There's a pause, filled with the familiar crackle I always seem to get when calling George's mobile number. Keeping the phone wedged between my ear and shoulder, I rub my temples and focus on calm, slow breaths.

"Lucy..." George starts, his voice breaking up slightly with interference.

"Yeah?"

"I don't think this is going to work."

His words hit me like a blow to the gut. Is everything destined to go to shit within one day?

"What do you mean?" I ask.

"My folks, you know they've never been happy about me living so far away, plus they're not getting any younger. It's time I moved closer to them. Just thought I should let you know."

"You're leaving? When?"

"Next week."

I'm speechless, and still riled up after the emails earlier, but now I'm starting to see red. *What the fuck?*

"And you thought you should let me know, now, after *I* called *you*. That's fucking great."

"I'm sorry, Lucy. I never meant to hurt you."

"This is not happening. You don't get to do this over the phone. Are you home?"

"Yes."

"I'm coming over." I hang up and throw the phone onto my desk in disgust.

CHAPTER SIXTEEN

Throughout the drive to George's place, I'm reeling with conflicting emotions. Sure, things were complicated lately, but I still hoped we could get past it. But instead of making an effort, he drops a bomb of epic proportions on me. Finally, here's a guy I could imagine having a relationship with, who seemed reliable at least at first, but in the end, you can't depend on anyone but yourself. I should've known.

Despite the rush hour traffic, which for some reason is so much worse on Fridays, my bike makes it into town in record time. Anger does that to a person: it makes you speed up when the most rational thing would be to slow down. I'm not entirely sure where I'm going, so I'm relying entirely on the SatNav to take me there.

Broad A-roads make way for smaller streets, turning off into a quieter residential area. The identical looking boxy houses are crammed together, window after window covered with net curtains, blocking their inhabitants from my view. I guess George's place must look something like this, since apparently I'm about to reach.

In a hundred yards, turn right.

On the corner, a group of teenagers stand around their scooters and smoke, while observing me. They can't tell from here of course, but I truly feel the outsider in what can only be described as a rougher part of town. Like if they'll figure it out, they'll pounce on me to punish my intrusion.

Your destination is on your left.

I look up from the SatNav, and check behind me to make sure the youths aren't following, before turning the key to switch off the engine. The house number, 23B, greets me on the concrete grey wall. There's a wonky *To Let* sign planted in the grassy bit next to the pavement. Inside, all looks dark and there is no movement. He'd better be here like he said!

Scanning the surroundings, I spy what looks like a two-wheeler, his I assume, protected by a grey waterproof cover, and a paper stuck on the front: *For Sale, call for more details.* Weird.

Just when I take off my helmet, letting my hair fall down over my shoulders, and stuff my gloves into my pocket, the dark curtain on the first floor twitches slightly. Shortly after, the click of a lock and creak of a door follows, putting me back on task. I will have my answers, soon, I will know what the hell is going on!

"So you found it all right," George remarks from the top of the exposed staircase, leading to the first floor. His tense expression makes all the muscles in my body turn rigid, preparing for a fight.

"Can I come in?" I say, while trying to keep my breathing under control. My cheeks are turning flushed, my blood truly is boiling.

He steps aside as I climb the stairs, and leads me

inside, closing the door behind us. Despite the half-dark in his cramped hallway, I can make out the silhouettes of cardboard boxes. He's almost completely packed, I can't fucking believe it! The only items left out are a small side table with a phone and a big stack of torn open envelopes, plus their contents.

"Now tell me what you have to tell me." I put my hands on my hips and glare upwards. He's towering over me but I couldn't be less intimidated.

"Look." He sighs and avoids my angry stare. "It's been nice and all, but you and I both know this wasn't going to work out anyway."

"Bullshit. From where I'm standing, we had something special, at least before we started working together. I was trying to get that back, was giving you space to see things my way, except you suddenly decide to leave. If your parents do need you to move back up north, that's fine, we could have worked something out. But to just give up now..." I'm starting to sweat, despite the chill in his apartment. It's a good thing he doesn't have his heating on, or I'd really boil over. "And to not even let me know in advance, Jesus Christ, I expected more from you!"

"Well, maybe you shouldn't have."

"Clearly!" I take a deep breath, before allowing myself to voice what I really want to know. "Who is she?"

"What?"

"Don't even. You think I didn't notice? When we just landed the Cleary project, you were glued to your phone, checking messages or whatever, typing things when you thought I wasn't looking, hiding yourself away to take mysterious calls. And now you just want to end things without giving us a chance, it's the only logical explanation!"

Throughout the drive here, I kept analyzing every moment we had spent together, and I couldn't pinpoint exactly where things went bad. Sure, working together had made things weird, and last week's dinner was uncomfortable, but those can't be the only reasons, can they? We'd also spent a lot of happy moments together.

"That..." He runs his hand through his hair, and just stands there with his mouth half-open, but no explanation is forthcoming.

"Just tell me this. Was it already going on when we first met?"

"No... I..."

"Because if so, I really have to get my head examined. I can't believe how easily I fell for your lies." Tears prickle in my eyes, making my vision hazy.

I rest my hand against the wall, flexing my fingers, which ache after being balled into a tight fist for the past five minutes. I try my best not to punch something or someone. Him.

I don't even know when I've last been so angry, so hurt. Betrayed. The whole Akhil incident has nothing on this.

"There is no one."

"Bullshit."

"Look, I understand you're angry, and not likely to

believe a word I say. Look at me." George reaches over and guides my chin upwards, but I close my eyes to hide the accumulating tears.

I shake him off, and try to blink the wetness away, which sadly has the opposite effect. "Then why?"

He steps through the doorway, into the darkened living area, gesturing at me to follow. Inside, yet more cardboard boxes await us, and random clothes, strewn over the only item of furniture left: a shabby sofa.

I enter behind him, and sit down, without bothering to move any of the mess aside. What do I care? I came here for an explanation, not to be his fucking housekeeper.

George, meanwhile, leans against a tall stack of boxes across from the sofa, where one would have expected a TV to be. I check the room once more, noting the outlines of what might have been picture frames, faded into the wall. This place really could do with a lick of paint. No wonder he's never invited me over.

"Why, George? It couldn't have been what I said at dinner last week, could it? Nobody decides to move in less than a week! I know the Cleary project started out a total cluster fuck, but then, you offered to help yourself." My earlier rage is starting to dissipate, with desperation appearing in its place. Am I really that clueless that I can't tell whether a guy is even interested in me? Am I that hopeless? Perhaps I am better off alone.

"I haven't been entirely honest with you. From the

start." His words pierce me like a knife. Here it comes, the confession.

I press my lips together, fearing what he'll say next. Whatever it is, I'll endure it. I can't let this break me.

"That night, when we first met, it was sort of my farewell from the job."

Wait, what?

"Go on," I say, confused whether this is yet more bullshit or the beginning of an actual explanation.

"I was let go, made redundant. It was my last day, so afterwards I went to the pub, feeling sorry for myself. I had planned to just drink, to forget the fact that my asshole of a manager had kept Steve, who is an incompetent twat, while choosing to fire me."

I'm speechless. This is the big reveal? He could've just said something, I would've understood. People are losing their jobs all over the place nowadays.

"And then, you came along, and I felt like maybe things would work out somehow, that the only reason I even lost the job was so I'd go to that particular pub on that particular night, you know?"

I'm not sure that I do know, but I choose to keep quiet.

"So instead of moping around, I decided I'd pull myself together, apply for whatever job I could, to find something as soon as possible—hence the phone calls."

Now that my eyes are more used to the darkness, I can see George staring at me from across the room. Even though I don't want to let him affect me, it's still giving me goose bumps to know he's looking right at me.

"But then, as I found out more about you, I just didn't see a way it would ever work out. Sure, we get on, we share some interests, but I could never measure up. Towards the end, I was sort of hoping you'd keep me on, but that's no basis for a relationship."

"None of this makes any sense," I mumble to myself.

He's breaking up with me because he doesn't have work? How stupid does he think I am?

He shrugs, and crosses his arms.

"You expect me to believe that you would choose to leave, just because you haven't found a job yet?"

"It's not *just* that."

"And what do you mean 'measure up'? I don't understand."

"We live in different worlds, you and I. You're a nice middle class girl, living in a nice middle class neighborhood in the countryside, surrounded by lawyers and bankers. Meanwhile, I've had to give notice on this shit hole because I won't be able to pay the rent anymore. You deserve so much more."

Holy shit. That explains the 'for sale' sign on his bike. How did I not put two and two together? But then, there's still one problem.

"So why didn't you cash the fucking check?" I exclaim. "And why not just be honest? What the hell, George! We were supposed to be honest with each other." That last bit almost makes me bite my tongue. How can I accuse him of dishonesty when I haven't been totally straight with him either?

"Because I didn't help you for the money. It felt... wrong."

Anger, made way for sadness, now I'm well on my way towards denial. I'm about to lose my mind, and yet a part of me still wants to believe.

What if...

"Okay. Tell me one thing. And if you say 'no', I'll drop the whole thing and let you get on with-" I gesture around the haphazardly stacked boxes. "Whatever. The move."

"Fair enough. What's that?" Right now, with his shoulders hanging down, he looks about as small as I've ever seen him, even if he's still impossibly tall. I'm reminded of the first time we met, how I somehow felt he was trustworthy, kind, and I wonder if perhaps I wasn't wrong about him after all.

"Deep down, and please be honest this time: if I lived down the road from you, same person, same interests, same everything, except the business. Different circumstances. Would that change anything? Would you still be breaking up with me?"

He looks down at his shoes and hesitates. Meanwhile I hold my breath and my heartbeat is going into overdrive. If his answer is negative, I'm certain I'll lose my composure entirely and cry my eyes out, right here in his living room.

"I guess not. But that's just hypothetical."

I let out a partial sigh of relief, hoping my next question gets a similar reaction.

"And what if, I was still the nice middle class girl that

I am, living in the nice middle class neighborhood with the bankers and lawyers, who—before you rescued her restaurant project—was looking at having her nice middle class house repossessed by the bank?" I hadn't allowed myself to voice this terrifying possibility, ever since the reminders started coming a couple of months ago, it had been too painful. But now I must admit, it's a relief to have it out in the open.

"What?" George whispers, unable to hide the shock at my admission.

"Cleary's project. I didn't want to take it because he seemed so difficult from the start, but I had no choice. Business has been really slow for *months*. I've been behind on my mortgage since December."

"You're joking." George slowly rubs his chin, yet does not take his eyes off me.

"Everything isn't always how it seems. And the kicker is, I'm up to speed now, but if I don't stay on track with the Byrne project and whatever else comes my way afterwards..." I shrug. "The truth is, if I've learnt anything this past month, it's that I can't do this on my own. Never could."

"That's not true, you just have to adapt."

"I'm a terrible manager, I know that now. Neeraj has been asking about you. Forget that, even *Byrne,* when I set up a meeting for Monday wanted to know if you'd be there. Cleary told him about you. Before, when I had Akhil, I didn't appreciate this fact, everything just worked out. But it became painfully obvious after I failed to take over and you agreed to help. Meetings, presentations, getting contracts signed, and the design side of things are all fine. But I can't for the life of me manage a group of stubborn programmers." I wipe my eyes with the back of my hand. "I wish things were different, really. All I've ever wanted was to be independent, to prove that I could be a success without Dad launching my career. But I just can't. I've failed."

The silence resulting from my outburst and confession grows until it threatens to swallow me and the entire room whole.

"I can't believe you're broke." George shakes his head.

After minutes of silence, a smile forms on his lips and he starts to chuckle.

Then that chuckle turns louder, into a laugh, until he can't contain himself anymore and infects me too.

He walks over, sits down beside me and rests his face in his hands and we both laugh uncontrollably, until tears stream down my face again.

"And I thought-" He turns towards me, allowing our eyes to meet. "Oh God. This is tragic."

We burst out laughing again.

"I didn't want to tell you about the bank because I was worried about what you'd think!" I confess, in between further giggles.

Funny, how sometimes the saddest things can tickle you the most. Minutes pass before either of us calm down enough to break the cycle.

"Now what?" He looks over at me with those steely eyes that have haunted my imagination since the first time we met.

"You tell me. What do you want?" I ask. "Do you think we can get past this?"

He doesn't answer, instead just continues to stare into my eyes, silencing me as well. After what feels like forever, he leans towards me, his arm outstretched. I gladly accept the gesture, falling into his embrace and resting my face on his shoulder. I don't know what will happen between us now, I just know I want to feel him close to me. His touch on my skin, his lips against mine, all of which make me choke up again.

I need him now, even if it's the last time. And especially if it's the first of a new beginning.

CHAPTER SEVENTEEN

As it turns out, we could get past it.

Of course, relationships aren't always a smooth ride. We both knew that going into it, even if we lacked a lot of practical experience. And honesty really does need to come first.

It's been a few weeks since our big fight and reconciliation, and after a long day working on Callum Byrne's website project, we find ourselves having to do something other than ordering takeout.

The date of my birthday party crept up on me almost without warning, but tonight is the night.

A few days after we both came clean, George did move out of his old place, and used the profit share from the Cleary deal on a deposit for a place in Reading itself, greatly reducing the daily commute to come here. In truth though, he stays over quite a lot, and over the weekends, we've been taking a break from the computer by doing up his new place together, spending the initial night together on a mattress on the floor.

It felt like such an adventure, camping in his new flat. The beginning of a new chapter for either of us.

He still thinks my house is too big, and he may have a point there. Although he has gotten used to the big TV, he is a man after all, who likes his toys.

"Luce, just exactly how formal is this birthday thing going to be?" George asks, while unpacking an overnight bag with fresh laundry he's brought from home.

"Just wear whatever you want, I know I will."

With a bit of luck, the weather will hold up, meaning we will get access to the club lawn as well. For the first time in quite a while, I'm actually looking forward to a birthday party.

In between picking out shoes to match my dress, I send a quick message to Dad, making sure he's bringing what I asked him for. The response is almost instant; he's got it, I need not worry.

"Still, if I'm going to meet your parents, I should at least make a bit of an effort, don't you think?" George wonders.

"Relax, they'll love you once they get to know you." I put the phone away again, smiling to myself.

"You think so?"

"I know so. I know I do." It slips out before I can analyze what I'm saying, but George catches it straightaway and leaves the bag, the clothes, whatever he's doing and walks over.

"You what?" He guides my face upwards, staring straight down into my eyes.

It still overwhelms me, the beautiful tension, that can only be broken with the right kind of physical contact. I blink a few times, trying to find the nerve to truly open up.

"I love you," I whisper, while my knees threaten to

buckle.

This look of his, when he's so close to me, so close that we both find it hard to focus on anything other than our most primal instincts, this is what I crave. A look that truly sees me for me. He doesn't see a bit of fun for Friday night. He doesn't see the workaholic who felt her business was more important than making a true connection in life.

Me. *His.*

He runs his thumb over my chin, and I fight with everything I've got to keep my eyes open and prolong the moment. As long as I really pay attention to what's there, in his eyes, I'll always feel safe.

"I love you too." His voice sounds rough, making me wonder what he's thinking. If he's ever said this to someone else, and gotten hurt. But it doesn't matter, because I won't hurt him, not anymore.

Finally, I can't keep my composure anymore, and am forced to blink.

He places his hands on my hips, and bends down until I'm able to reach his lips with mine. That first kiss always does the trick, driving me crazy, making me want infinitely more.

I start to float, literally, as he lifts me, allowing me to wrap both legs and arms around him tightly.

"You know, if you do want to impress my folks, perhaps we shouldn't be late..."

"I hate it when you're all practical."

"And right?"

He nods, staring into my eyes deeply, which once

again gives me shivers. I don't want to release him, instead I want to see where this will go, but we really do have to get dressed if we want to make it.

When he releases me, I almost want to scream at him for listening. But I don't, instead I focus on putting on a pair of stockings and then the dress I'd picked out earlier. Behind me, he's most definitely watching, which puts me on edge. Patience... we'll get our chance, later. We always do.

Tonight will definitely start off a little weird, when I introduce George to my folks, but they'll come around soon enough. It's not every day that I turn up with a plus-one, in fact I don't remember the last time it's happened at all.

***

As it turned out, things were a lot less awkward than I'd anticipated. After scrutinizing him only for a couple of seconds, Mum accepted George for the sweet, kind soul that he is inside. Dad took just a little longer, insisting on asking professional questions, which he aced, of course. I'd gotten a little taste of George dealing with difficult people during the Cleary presentation, and Dad was much easier to win over.

After the initial surprise, Mum especially couldn't contain her excitement that I'd finally met someone special. She literally told George as much, leaving me embarrassed and blushing in the background.

Then Dad took me aside, and after I reassured him I

know what I'm doing, handed me what I'd asked him for. A large brown envelope, containing the one thing which I know will ensure things stay perfect between George and me. I tucked it away safely in my bag, now I've just got to find the right time to give it to him.

We mingle for a bit, and sample the food. If there's one thing Mum and Dad know how to do, it's organize a get-together. I'd feel guilty for not helping out at all, if I didn't know deep down Mum loves being in charge of parties. She's always been the perfect hostess.

After introducing George to cousin after cousin, and aunts and uncles, one member of our family remains absent. Perhaps Peter couldn't make it after all. Or Stephanie, his wife might have thrown a spanner in the works. Despite his absence, it's still a nice party.

"I suppose it would be rude to skip out on everyone now, wouldn't it?" George asks, bringing me back to reality.

I let out a laugh. "Definitely. But I suppose we could hide out in that pavilion over there for a while, until people take notice."

He follows my gaze across the lush green lawn of the club. The old-fashioned gazebo, surrounded by large rhododendron shrubs in full bloom, looks like a setting taken right out of a romance movie. Despite still being overlooked—it has open sides after all—it's more private than where we are right now, next to the buffet table, so off we go.

"I know you said you didn't want a gift, but I got you a little something anyway. Happy birthday, Lucy."

George wraps his arm around me, as soon as we step up into the pavilion.

"Oh?" I turn to face him, unable to hide my excitement. I didn't expect a gift, actually the fact that we managed to talk things through and decided to try again was more than enough of a gift to me.

"Well, it's more something for the both of us to enjoy together..." He hands me an envelope, which I accept with a slight tremble in my fingers.

I open the flap, and pull out a black, shiny slip of paper. It's a ticket to a music festival. It takes me a while to scan through the various logos on the back, but there it is: Blind Guardian. It was one of the first things we discovered about one another, that we share the same favorite band.

"Perhaps we can make a ride out of it?" George suggests.

I knew he'd seen them live before, I hadn't. There isn't much fun in going to a music concert on your own, but now I've got both the necessary ticket and the perfect company.

"Thank you," I whisper, shooting him a smile, before examining the ticket again.

The concert may be a couple of months away, but that's not what catches my attention. Rather, it's the booking date... It's dated the day of the Cleary presentation. My eyes moisten at the realization.

"You've been keeping this a while, eh?" I ask.

"I may have been broke, but I couldn't very well ignore your birthday once I found out about it."

"What if it hadn't worked out? What if you'd actually left like you said you would?"

He shrugs, and avoids eye contact, almost making me regret bringing up that painful memory.

"I was going to post it to you along with my ticket. I wouldn't have wanted to go on my own."

That admission pushes me over the edge, causing a lone tear to drip down from my lashes, and roll down my cheek.

"I wouldn't have wanted to either," I whisper.

"Hey! Don't cry now, you're supposed to be happy, celebrating." George cups my face with his hands, and wipes the tear away with his thumb.

"I've got something for you too," I say.

"That's funny, seeing as my birthday isn't for another three months," George jokes, releasing me.

I retrieve the A4-sized envelope Dad had given me earlier from my bag and hand it to him.

"Here." I wait, my heart once again beating in my throat, even though this time I'm pretty sure I'm on the right track. There is no way this particular decision will misfire. *I hope.*

"Well, this sure doesn't look like gig tickets." George gives me a questioning look, before tearing open the envelope and pulling out a thick stack of papers, held together with a paper clip.

I give him a moment to read the front.

"This is..." He pauses, reading it again.

"A partnership agreement."

"Why?" He looks up, the surprise still evident in his

face.

"Like we talked about, you being my employee is hardly a good basis for a relationship. And I can't do this alone, so..."

"You would do this? Make me a partner in your business? After you worked so hard to build it up from scratch?"

"Everything, including the business, is so much better when you're a part of it. So, yes. If you want."

George puts the contract down on top of the circular bench lining the edge of the gazebo, and takes me into his arms.

"You're quite something, Lucy, I don't know what to say."

I hang on to him, tightly. This closeness with him, this newfound honesty, is making me feel safer than I've ever felt, even while taking what could be seen as a massive risk.

"Then say yes," I whisper, before leaning back just enough to be able to look him in the eye. "Will you be my partner? In this as well as in life?"

"Of course."

We embrace again, neither of us in a hurry to let go.

"I love you," George whispers, his deep voice tickling me to my core.

"I love you too."

***

AUTHOR'S NOTE

Firstly, thanks so much for reading One Night Stand!

This novella has been quite a long time coming. You see, it all started in March 2013 when I released a short story called Just for One Night. That little story, which I intended to be a stand-alone snapshot of two people finding each other in a pub, has now grown to 3 times its original length. I always knew Lucy and George's story wouldn't end after their one night stand, but I didn't get the chance to write about it until now, the beginning of 2015.

Much like my other work, One Night Stand also deals with regular people, whose love life is often less than perfect. In this case, everything started out well enough when Lucy and George first meet. But after a fantastic, almost surreal and passionate night together, real life inevitably kicks in. What we're left with is control freak Lucy, who has never needed anyone in her life, suddenly coming to terms with the idea that perhaps life is better when you're not on your own. And George, who may look tough and imposing on the outside, struggling with a whole host of his own issues, not least of which the perceived imbalance between his own (professional) worth compared to Lucy's.

Although it's romantic to think that money (especially when one person has way more than the other) should not affect relationships, the opposite is often true. Even the most enlightened, forward-thinking man can feel inferior when faced with a woman who is seemingly so much more successful than he is. He may admire her, even love her, but it's hard to completely break free of the societal norms which expect that a man should take on the role of breadwinner in a household. It can be emasculating. And to then start working together, not as a team, but as boss and employee can really amp up the conflict.

Luckily, Lucy and George are able to save what they have because they adjust. Lucy accepts that she didn't just need George's help temporarily, before taking back control of her business and her life for herself. And when she confesses her dire financial situation to him, he realizes she's not as perfect as he thought she was, which actually makes her more lovable. She not only lets him in on her secret, but creates a situation where both of them can help each other, not as boss and employee, but as partners.

ONE NIGHT STAND

Anyway, I hope you got some pleasure out of this story. Feel free to connect or get in touch via email or social media; I do my best to answer every message I get as soon as possible!

x, Lorelei

- ❖ LMoone.com
- ❖ Lorelei Moone on Facebook

BEAUTIFUL

STRANGER

CHAPTER ONE

I've been dreading my drive home all day. In fact, that is an understatement. After a long day at work, the last thing I need is to be reminded that I've decided to live in that beautiful, mostly serene part of the world called Ascot, Berkshire. Which of course during this week of the year turns into a hellhole, overrun by obscenely rich people clogging up the roads in their Bentleys, Rollers and whatnot. Actually the Bentleys and Rolls Royces don't bother me so much, it's the hordes of not-so-rich people who think it's classy to hire a Hummer limo that I can really do without.

Such is my aversion that I've even started to avoid newspapers this week, the one week in June that the Royal Ascot races take place. If I wanted to see photos of ridiculous hats and passed out drunk people on the lawn, I could've just bought a ticket and gone myself. But I don't really care about horse racing, or showing off. I would much rather attend a music festival, if I had to brave the Great British Weather in inappropriate clothing anyway.

My neighbors tend to flee around this time of year, but unfortunately I can't afford a holiday. With the way things have been at work, I'd better put every spare penny away for a rainy day. At least tonight will be the last time this year I'll have to deal with this mess, tomorrow is my day off and I don't intend to venture out onto the roads at all until next week when normality has returned.

I'm already looking forward to my quiet long weekend, focusing on nothing but my paintings. All I have to do is get there.

Slowly I make my way through the various traffic control measures set up seemingly to hinder the flow of traffic rather than improve it. I suppose it all makes sense to someone. It takes me an hour to get onto Blacknest Road, which in ordinary circumstances would be about five minutes from home. But these are not ordinary circumstances.

As my car creeps along in its spot within the tedious metal conga line that has formed around me, all I have for company are my radio and my grumpy thoughts. And the occasional sympathetic smile from someone in much the same situation in the opposite lane.

I occupy myself by looking at the flash cars that slowly pass by. Nothing too unusual in this part of the world, various Ferraris, Lambos and of course the already mentioned Bentleys and Rolls Royces of all ages. I almost give up on seeing much variety when something small and dark blue catches my eye parked up on the verge ahead. Twin white racing stripes accentuating its curvaceous body, top down to reveal its cream leather interior. Absolutely beautiful. I wonder if it's a real AC Cobra or just a good replica. And more importantly, what is it doing sitting in the muck next to this busy road?

ONE NIGHT STAND

Traffic creeps ahead and I get closer, there's a man in the driver's seat, arms folded and head resting against them on the steering wheel. He is sporting the accepted race-going uniform; grey waistcoat with a matching hat and coat on the passenger seat beside him.

I don't know what possesses me, but I leave my coveted place in the traffic queue and pull up behind him. Just to see if he's okay—I tell myself—or at least to get a better look at his magnificent car.

Stepping out has me cursing under my breath immediately. Of course I managed to position my exit right in the middle of a patch of sticky mud left behind by this morning's early summer showers.

"Excuse me, are you having car trouble?" I ask. He lifts his head off his forearm which is still resting on the steering wheel. "I was wondering if you need help..."

His pale blue eyes stand out against his face and particularly against his dark hair which is starting to grey around the temples. If I had to guess I'd say he was in his late thirties or early forties, and the salt and pepper look is really working for him. Something seems off, though. I remind myself he's probably just had a few too many glasses of champagne or whatever it is they drink at the races.

"I wanted to leave, but thought I probably shouldn't be driving. So I pulled over." His voice sounds friendly, if a tad uncertain. Everything about him suggests money, from his accent to his clothes. Perhaps the car isn't a replica after all.

"You're probably right, I suppose you shouldn't be

driving. Where were you headed?" I ask.

He averts his eyes downwards before answering. "I don't know."

"Right. Where do you live?" I try.

"I can't go there." There's an awkward silence after his response, and he grips the steering wheel with both hands and rests his forehead against his knuckles.

I think for a little while and look around. The traffic jam heading away is still going strong, but traffic moving in my direction has started to thin. If pulling over wasn't already weird enough, what I say next actually stuns the rational part of my brain completely. The impulsive surge inside of me is simply impossible to fight, causing my lips to utter certain words before better sense prevails.

"What do you say, you come with me and we'll figure out where you should be going after reaching my place?"

When he looks back up at me, there is not a hint of suspicion in his eyes. It doesn't seem to register with him that only a reckless lunatic would invite a drunk stranger home. *What the hell am I thinking?*

"That would be nice. Thanks." He tries to smile but instead his face twists. "Oh God, I feel ill." I hurry around the car and open the car door to pull him out by his arm.

"Believe me, tomorrow you'll really regret it if you throw up in that nice car of yours!" I warn him.

He walks a few steps away from the road and leans against a tree. I can't help but stare. He looks fit, about six feet tall, broad shoulders. Any other observations would be pure speculation though, plus it would be difficult for anyone not to look good in formal wear.

I still can't believe I'm doing this. There's something special about him, tempting even. Something that makes him appear trustworthy and harmless. Still, I'm sort of aware of the possibility that it may all be a clever act on his part and I'm about to let an axe murderer into my house.

Walking towards him now, I can see he has his eyes closed and is just breathing in the fresh air away from all the traffic.

"Never mind, I guess it was a false alarm," he mutters.

"Well then, let's go," I say, "I don't think your car would be safe here, though."

"Mine, on the other hand, nobody would touch if I abandoned it here for weeks. And since you're not fit to drive just now..." I continue.

He doesn't say a word, simply places the car keys into my outstretched hand and opens the passenger door for himself. Looking at the gorgeous car, I decide then that even if I end up hacked into bits and buried in my own garden tonight, it will have all been worth it.

After grabbing my handbag and locking my own vehicle, I sit down next to him. His expression has hardly changed, he shows no sign of concern that he's letting a complete stranger drive his car. I have to conclude he's not all there. I turn the key and the engine purrs to life with a deep, thundering rumble which can only mean one thing: under the shiny, curved bonnet, there lives a huge beast of an engine.

"Why so distracted, did you lose big at the races today?" I ask while checking over my shoulder for a gap in the traffic. It occurs to me that my attempt at small talk is making me sound like a cabbie.

"I don't gamble. But yes, in a way." He sighs.

I'm intrigued but don't want to probe too much. The car behind me flashes its lights, allowing me to merge. After a moment's silence, he takes a few deep breaths.

"My wife..." His voice trembles ever so slightly while he speaks, "and someone I'd considered a friend..."

My question unintentionally cut right to the core of the matter, it sounds as if he lost hope rather than money.

"Wow, I'm sorry. That's terrible." I'm not sure I want further detail but I can't take the question back now.

He shakes his head. "I should've seen it. But I guess I wasn't around enough, working long hours, sometimes Saturdays too..." He turns towards me and when the traffic stops again, I get the chance to study his face. Perfectly symmetrical, high cheekbones and a sharp jaw line. He is gorgeous, perhaps even more so because he looks so lost.

"But it was all for her! I wanted to give her the life she deserved. Why didn't she see that?" Tears are starting to blur those magnificent eyes of his. "Instead, she fucking replaces me."

Well, that's one mystery solved. I guess posh

people *do* swear.

"You're right, she should've understood," I say.

The traffic starts moving again and we get just a little bit closer to our destination.

"It was all for nothing." He looks out at the trees and houses passing by, lost in thought again.

Nothing more is said for the rest of the drive; fifteen minutes or so. I pull up into the cul-de-sac on the hill where I live, the three surrounding houses are unoccupied while the neighbors are on holiday. The setting is secluded, idyllic but the actual house is modest by most standards. It makes me wonder what his home would look like, the exact opposite I bet. The gravel makes a crunchy sound underneath the tires as I park the car under the rustic wooden carport which is always smothered in pink clematis blooms at this time of year.

Right at this moment the clouds break apart, letting through the pleasantly warm evening sun. I hand him the keys and we both get out of the car. Rather than head for the door, he distractedly takes a few steps towards the fence that surrounds the driveway.

"Beautiful." He's right, but it's been a while since I really appreciated the view myself.

Perhaps I should try my hand at painting a landscape this weekend.

Tall trees line the fields that cover most of the hill below. The lush green leaves on the trees as well as the long grass glisten in the golden light, giving everything a warm glow.

Meanwhile I open the low gate and enter into the

garden that runs along the side of the house. There's a large wooden table and bench set up against the wall, overlooking the same downhill aspect. He follows a few steps behind me.

"Make yourself at home, I'll just go inside and get some cushions." I turn the key and enter the cozy living room through the patio door.

While I'm inside already, I might as well cobble together a meal of sorts. Rushing to pop some pre-baked bread in the oven, I raid the fridge for cold meat and cheese.

I vaguely wonder why I'm bothering to hide the Aldi packaging, or arrange everything on a nice plate. After all, my bluff is pretty much called already, the classiest bottle of wine I have probably wouldn't have cost more than five pounds. Must've been a gift that's been languishing in my kitchen for much too long.

It annoys me that I even care, I never pretend to be something I'm not, why start now?

CHAPTER TWO

"Excuse me, where's your bathroom?" I hear him call from the back door.

"Oh, please come in, it's just over there..." When he enters, I point out the right door in the hallway.

The contrast between us is even more obvious to me now, he looks like everything I am not in his formal wear which probably cost more than my car is worth. At the same time I—at twenty-four—still dress like I did as a teenager, faded jeans and t-shirts with inappropriate prints. The only 'fancy' clothes I own are worn exclusively to job interviews and then too they're Primark or at a stretch, Next. You could mistake me for a simple idealist, not moved by worldly possessions, when in fact I am just a bit stingy and lazy.

Plus, I've never really understood fashion.

Strangely, he looks quite at home, walking over the terracotta tiles and towards the door I've just shown him. He shoots a few glances at the eclectic mix of paintings and photographs on my walls on his way. Like he's meant to be here, in my house. I try and shake off that thought. He's just some stranger and I'm an idiot for doing this.

The ping of the oven timer brings me back to reality and I pile all the food, plates and cutlery high onto a tray, and head back out. After I've arranged everything on the garden table and made another trip for the cushions, a water jug and the aforementioned cheap wine, he comes back out as well.

"You didn't need to..." he says with a smile.

Looking at him now, much more at ease than before, I feel like I'm getting a hint of his usual demeanor. Charismatic is probably the best word for it, but still he seems genuine.

"I sort of did, I'm starving," I respond, "and Domino's doesn't deliver here."

He lets out a laugh while sitting down on the bench beside me.

"I wasn't sure what you'd like," I point at the food, wine and water, "unless you want coffee or tea, I can do that too."

"Yeah, I don't tend to drink much, is it that obvious?" He smiles again. My heart is pounding all the way up in my throat. I can't get over how handsome he is, the change in body language has made that even more obvious.

"Well, whatever you need, just ask." My eyes are drawn to his, they seem more turquoise than blue now but that might just be the light. He holds my gaze just a little longer than strictly necessary before picking up the wine and corkscrew.

"I suppose one glass won't hurt. I promise I don't feel ill anymore." He doesn't look it either, must be the fresh air.

"Don't be so sure, you haven't tried it yet. It's probably nowhere near the quality you're used to," I say, still mesmerized by his eyes.

He grins at me. "Everything is only as good as the company it's enjoyed in."

I feel the corners of my mouth respond immediately, this is a game I can play. "Well, and what do you know about current company other than that I was overly keen to get my hands on your car keys?"

"Firstly, you took a huge risk trying to help out a complete stranger." Winking at me, he adds, "Car keys or no car keys."

I accept the glass of wine he has poured for me.

"Furthermore, I don't recall the last time anyone has made an effort putting together a meal for me..." His gaze wanders out over the field again.

"Fine, if you say so," I say, "but for all you know I could be a psychopath, only pretending to be friendly."

He looks back at me again, the amused glint in his eyes reappearing. "So could I."

"Cheers," I say, raising my glass towards him. "To us, pretending to be friendly."

We both take a sip, stealing little looks at each other in turn.

He's putting on a brilliant performance, like what he said in the car never happened. Perhaps it's his way of dealing with things. Who am I to argue with such a tempting façade?

I offer him the bread basket and platter of cold cuts. He eats eagerly, like he's famished.

"You know, had I known, I would've prepared something a little nicer than this," I joke.

"I'll keep that in mind. To warn you in advance before randomly meeting at the side of the road," he responds.

I eat a few bites myself.

"What's your name?" I ask.

"Peter. Peter Layton."

"Well, it's nice to meet you, Peter. I'm Claudia de Wit."

"The pleasure is all mine. Dutch, eh? I wouldn't have been able to guess," Peter says.

"Well, only by name. I've always lived here." I take a big bite of bread and cheese, realizing that I'm clearly kidding myself.

We eat in silence until the food is nearly finished. Taking small breaks in between bites for a sip of wine and a few covert glances back and forth.

Peter straightens himself and leans back against the bench, arms folded behind his head. It's still so bright, it would be quite impossible to correctly guess the time.

He clears his throat and looks at me. "That was lovely, thank you."

I blush, *how undeserved.* "Oh, stop it."

I look at him from the corner of my eye, wondering if my growing attraction towards him has at least in part to do with the slight wine buzz I've developed. But whatever the cause, the feeling seems mutual, because he's now blatantly staring back at me.

"Claudia." The way he says my name makes me weak inside.

"Yes?" I respond.

ONE NIGHT STAND

"After all this..." He motions over at the empty bottle. "I think it would be even less appropriate for me to drive anywhere."

"You know, you're quite right."

I lean over towards him slightly, seeing him do the same wreaks havoc with my heartbeat. *It's only the wine*, I tell myself. But I'm drawn to him, lips parted slightly, as he is to me.

His face just inches away, I hold my breath and slip my hand over his shoulder, around his neck and keep drowning in the blue depth of his eyes as our lips meet. His eyes close when I press my lips against his. I'm overcome by how soft they are. I want to taste him, feel him closer.

His arms wrap around me, pulling me in. The tip of my tongue finds his lips open just enough. He returns my kiss with a need so infectious it causes my own to surge dramatically. With our tongues entwined, his hands explore the contours of my back. Through my t-shirt at first, but quickly progressing underneath. They're warm and determined, rubbing my tense muscles as if I still need further persuasion. I don't. My own hands are fumbling with the buttons of his shirt, aiming to rid him of it entirely. As soon as I've got it wide open, he pulls back and gives me a devilish look before stripping my t-shirt off me in one swift upward tug.

An appreciative smile appears on his face as he looks down at what he has just uncovered. I'm glad that by some sort of cosmic coincidence I actually wore pretty underwear today and not my everyday rags. My cleavage is practically spilling out of the bright red push-up bra, I know my jeans hide the counterpart frilly thong.

I get up from the bench, eager to move somewhere more comfortable, more intimate. But he has other ideas. As he stands up next to me, his eyes would've been enough to hypnotize me to stay. To emphasize his point further, he slips two fingers into the waistband of my jeans and with a jerk I am pulled tightly against him, his other hand squeezing firmly into my waist.

"Oh no, you don't!" His voice is determined as his hands, I am frozen in place, still looking up at his face.

He starts to unbutton my jeans, I can't wait to feel his hands on my bare skin all over. My fingers meanwhile are running up his lean chest. I have no doubt that he must work out regularly to maintain his physique. He isn't overly buff, but I can clearly feel his abs under my fingers. There isn't a hint of fat on his perfectly V-shaped frame. His perfection begs to be captured in a sketch at the very least, something I'm certain I'll attempt from memory if I have to.

Meanwhile he has peeled my skin tight jeans halfway down my ample hips and is letting his fingers work through my curvaceous ass. I can't match up to his level of physical perfection by quite a stretch, but my soft femininity seems to excite him further. One of his hands has come up to explore what is still hidden beyond my bra.

I continue to study him by touch, down the curvature of his muscular back, leading to his ass. A fine specimen indeed, amazingly firm. As I grab him, hard, he presses forward, encouraging further exploration. I want to devour him, kissing and sucking on his silky smooth skin, running my nose through the little patch of curly dark hair that sits in the centre of his athletic chest. I'm glad he's not one of those guys who gets rid of it all; this to me is the ultimate symbol of masculinity.

His right hand loosens on my ass cheek before travelling upwards, leaving a trail of fire burning along my spine before gently nudging my head upwards from the back of my neck. His breath against my face again, I am overwhelmed by him and his hungry kisses once more. But I don't just want his tongue, I also want what's pressed up against my thigh. His cock as hard and strong as the rest of him through the fabric of his trousers. I'm just about to open his fly and slip my hand inside when abruptly he stops and pushes me down.

He leans with me and slides the dirty dishes and tray swiftly aside before laying me down on the garden table. His right hand pulls my jeans off me completely, leaving them piled up on the ground. His other undoes his trousers and strokes himself, allowing me a glimpse of his perfectly straight, huge manhood which is standing proudly just for me.

I lift my feet up onto the bench either side of him, and slip off my bra straps before opening it and flinging it onto the ground as well. He cannot take his eyes off my hard dark pink nipples which are now aching to be kissed and caressed. So much so I decide to show him exactly how, cupping my breasts in my hands, rolling my nipples between thumb and forefinger. He shows little patience and dives down, taking both nipples into his mouth one after the other, licking them and circling around them with his tongue. It tickles me and heats me to my core.

While one of my hands claws at the smooth skin on his back, the other travels down my length and into my panties. I can feel pearls of moisture already accumulated on my labia, my fingertips softly spreading it over my silky, hairless skin. I am throbbing, engorged with anticipation and lust, any moment now my perfect stranger will take me in this vulnerable position on the wooden table.

He lifts up to observe what I'm doing to myself, keeping a firm grasp on his impressively proportioned member, groaning with the same desire that is reverberating through my veins.

"Shit, do you have a condom?" he asks, the cool façade he had so carefully constructed crumbling suddenly.

"No. But I'm clean, are you?" Clearly, this must be the wine talking. I may be on the pill but I only just found out his name a short while ago. If he has any sense, he'll refuse but I am way too far gone to care about the consequences.

"Yes. Are you sure about this?" His voice is trembling with built up tension, aching for release. Even so, I get the impression that he would respect it if I said no.

Lifting my butt off the table slightly, I wiggle off the last bit of frilly red mesh which had been covering the remainder of my modesty.

Giving him my most seductive look, I breathe: "Yes, absolutely!"

The naughty grin from before makes a reappearance on his face. Looks like he's ready to be reckless together.

Both hands locked around my hips, he lifts me and slides me down to the very edge of the table. The rough wood scrapes my back in a sensation that feels appropriately bittersweet.

His huge cock is pressing at my entrance, making me moan in anticipation. He enters me with grace, pressing his hips into my widely spread thighs in a swift motion that takes my breath away.

My insides are set alight and I scream with pleasure every time he enters me, our combined sounds of delight not held back by shame or worry. I feel liberated by his every move; he's playing me like I'm a musical instrument. His hips continue to move energetically, filling me to my core with each deep thrust. The slight upward tilt he adopts as he enters makes his head scrape deliciously against my G-spot, causing it to tingle and burn at the same time.

I run my hands over his torso, feeling his muscles harden in ripples as he moves. He continues to look at me throughout, eyelids half closed but not fully hiding the deep blue sea that lies beneath. I've never been fucked quite how he takes me, his hands kneading my thighs, hips and waist in turn, in between fondling my breasts, none of these unusual by themselves but his touch feels special. Just the right amount of pressure, teasing, heightening my pleasure further and further.

His focus unfaltering, not broken by any worry of being overheard, he is truly in the moment, with an expression so serene he could have been meditating. And his timing is immaculate, fast and sure as he continues to speed up and fuck me as hard as my body needs it. He is so aware of every noise and movement I make, there is no need to speak, he understands me perfectly. I continue to ache for more, panting heavily and raising my hips to meet him in his frenzied rhythm.

"Oh God, yes, I'm so close!" I cry out, feeling the

walls of my pussy contract suddenly as I tense up, fingers dug deep into his hips as he pushes deep and hard a few more times, before letting go of my thigh and rubbing his thumb on my clitoris through the shudders and loud screams of my orgasm.

"You're so beautiful," he whispers at me. The tense focus he has shown all along is still obvious while he tenderly caresses my spent body. I know he must still seek release and I'm desperate to give it to him.

I force myself upright and to his surprise push him back and out of me.

"Your turn, baby," I say, while dropping down on my knees in front of him. The cold gritty surface of the brick paving presses hard into my knees, but the pain feels surreal to me.

I grasp his balls and base of his shaft with one hand and lick along the bottom length of his cock. His taste mixed with my own, I softly open my mouth to let him in, testing my limits as I suck him clean. He looks down at me, his eyes widening and closing in turn every time I take him deep into my mouth, now firmly gripping his thighs to steady myself.

It is so obvious now that I'm concentrating purely on his pleasure that he has been holding back for quite a while. A real gentleman all the way, taking care of me before himself. But there is no more reason for that now.

One hand travels around his hip and starts kneading through his ass cheek, the other focusing on his balls which have started to firm up. I increase my tempo slightly, pressing my tongue against his shaft as I take it deep. A gasp escapes his lips, he clearly loves to watch me look up at him with my mouth full.

He is very well hung indeed but with a bit of practice I can get the angle just right to allow him inside me further. I speed up slightly, encouraged by his hand which is running through my hair now. Still the gentleman, he lets me set the pace without pushing. His shallow short breaths act as my guide.

I suck on his head and tease the tip of his cock with my tongue. He shudders and his hips press towards me. I take the cue and continue my deeper, faster rhythm from before, the deep guttural groans he lets out with every movement a sure indicator that I'm on the right track.

Speeding up faster and faster, as I bump the head as far back into my throat as I can, he goes rigid. First his muscles in his ass turn to rock under my hand, then his thighs refuse to flex like they had done before. Finally his hand in my hair clamps into a fist and he is completely still while I suck hard. His balls shrink and his whole length pulsates violently while he gushes into my throat.

I draw back, rubbing my tongue against his shaft and over his head before letting go, swallowing all he had to give. He stumbles back while letting go of my hair and gasps for air, leaning against the backrest of the bench.

"Bloody hell," he pants.

I get up and try my best to brush the dirt off my knees before straightening myself. From behind the long streaks of hair falling into my face I still can't keep my eyes off him. A calm has washed over him, his face relaxing into post-orgasmic bliss. Leaning in and slipping one arm around my waist, he brushes my hair out of my face before another, more tender kiss. When he lets go, he starts to gather my clothes off the ground.

I accept them with a smile, but have no intention of covering up.

"Excuse me for a minute," I say, before turning towards the house. The evening sun is still strong and warms my naked skin, soothing the scrapes on my back left behind by the rough wood of the table. But I'm still riding the high he gave me, knowing it was exactly what I needed so I'll wear these scars with pride.

I turn my head slightly to glance back at him as I open the door, pleased to note that he's still watching me walk up the garden path in a state of full undress.

Inside I make my way to the bathroom, discarding my clothes in the laundry hamper and finding a pair of slippers.

Considering it's not very late yet, I check the fridge before going back out. Fresh strawberries and cream are supposedly an early summer classic; it seems fitting. Through the window I can see that he's sitting down now, arms draped over the backrest and equally unconcerned by his lack of attire. Not that he has any reason to be, as far as the eye can see there's not a soul in sight, just greenery.

Balancing the bowl of strawberries and another filled with cream on my arm and holding onto the neck of another full wine bottle, I struggle through the door and greet his expectant expression with a wide grin.

"Dessert?"

"Why not." He quickly rescues the bottle and puts it on the table while I sit down next to him.

After putting down the strawberries I make a half-hearted attempt to stack up the used dishes from dinner. A buzzing noise starts coming from his waistcoat which is by now hung neatly over the side of the bench. Leaning over, he starts to check the pockets.

"Oh, bollocks," he curses under his breath when he finds his iPhone.

"I'll give you some privacy..." I start to get up but he stops me, shaking his head.

"No," he says, putting the phone face down on the table, "I've nothing to say to her, neither of them actually."

The next minute or so of silence passes in slow motion.

"What are you going to do?" I finally ask, despite realizing it's none of my business.

Luckily my question doesn't appear to offend him. "I don't really know... But I'm not going to forgive her and pretend this never happened."

He leans over and helps himself to strawberries. Feeling a slight chill in the air, I put my feet up on the bench and wrap my arms around them.

"What exactly happened? If you don't mind me asking..." It's not just that I am nosy by nature, but I wish I could get a glimpse of what's going on in Peter's head.

"I saw them, my wife and Chris. After the races finished, the three of us and some more friends went to a nearby pub on the High Street, planning to just stay for a little while before our dinner reservation. By then everyone had had a few, except me because I was driving. On my way back from the men's room I saw them, hands all over each other. So humiliating."

"I can imagine," I respond softly, taking his hand and weaving my fingers in between his.

He turns towards me, the uncertainty in his eyes reminding me of earlier in the car. "Do you really want to hear all this, I mean...?"

"Whatever you want to tell me, yes." My index finger brush against his, hoping to emphasize my point. I do care, even if we've only just met. I just wish I could help somehow.

"Alright, well, God knows how long it's been going on between them. All these years I was clueless and preoccupied, trying to earn enough to maintain the lifestyle she had been craving. Every demand of hers I tried to fulfill. Thinking about it, I can't remember if there was ever a spark between us. When I saw them together it hit me that she wasn't cold like I had come to accept, except around me...

"Had a few drinks at the bar to try and calm down and decided to leave them to it, I was too angry and hurt to face them. I had no idea where I was going to go, and after getting the car I somehow ended up parked alongside that road. And then you magically appeared."

His fingers wrap around mine tightly and he looks at our hands woven together. The tense frown on his face is starting to melt away once more.

"I never strayed once in fifteen years."

"Until today," I whisper.

"Yes, until today." He lifts up my hand and kisses my knuckles.

"No regrets?" I ask.

The same infectious smile he has been using to win me over with has returned. "None."

He takes me into his arms. We kiss tenderly, rekindling earlier desires, but now there is also a new closeness between us. He may have come into my life completely by chance, but I'm really starting to like this mysterious and beautiful stranger.

"Maybe it's not such a bad thing..." I say in between kisses, "getting a second chance, to reconsider what you want out of life. Do you have kids?"

"She never wanted any. You're right, this is a second chance, isn't it?" As soon as he finishes the sentence his smile turns into a naughty grin. Before I know it he scoops me up in his arms. The shock of it all causes me to start giggling uncontrollably.

"Now, where to, my-lady?"

Unable to speak through my giggle fit, I just point at the door which he manages to negotiate relatively easily even with his arms full. Once inside I direct him straight down the hall and to the bedroom, feeling very grateful that there are no stairs in our way.

CHAPTER FOUR

He lays me down on the large wooden bed, the sheets are smooth and cool against my skin. I roll over onto my stomach, with both feet pointing playfully in the air.

"Insatiable, are we?" I wink at him.

"You make that very easy..." He kneels on the bed next to me, his manhood well on its way to grow to its former glory.

Leaning on one elbow, I reach for him, feeling his cock in my hand once more. The touch of my hand against the velvety skin on his shaft causes an immediate reaction, he shifts forward, moaning eagerly. His hands run over my back towards my ass, massaging me. His fingertips trace the fold between butt cheek and thigh. I let out a moan myself, lifting my hips up to guide his fingers where I want them.

He takes his time, caressing my inner thighs right up to my outer labia but no further. After running his hands over my ass cheeks and thighs a few more times, he holds on to my hips and lifts me up on my knees.

"Spread, baby," he instructs me.

I do as he says, spreading my legs apart as far as possible while still kneeling, upper body pressed against the bed and ass up in the air. He positions himself right behind me and grabs my thighs, and the uncertainty of what comes next has me pulsating and dripping with anticipation.

Unexpectedly he plunges his tongue into my slit, deep. It feels so good I cry out into the pillow. His lips close around my labia while he flicks his tongue inside me, making me quiver. I am well on my way to bursting with hardly any effort on his part. He seems not to want to rush it, moving out a little bit, licking my inner labia and planting soft teasing kisses all around. The mattress moves behind me but I'm frozen and unwilling to check what's happening, both my hands are clawing at the sheet beside me.

His hands wrap around my thighs now from the other side, pulling me down on top of his face, kissing the delicate skin around my clit and giving it soft teasing licks with his tongue. Every time he touches me there, I feel like an electric current hits me, causing me to spasm and twitch. But his strong hands hold me in place and within his reach.

"Oh my, you're so good!" I breathe.

He responds by diving into my pussy again, licking me deeper than before. I shudder and gasp for air, feeling the tension inside my lower abdomen build up more and more. Then he stops and lifts me up to get out from underneath me.

"I need to be in you." There's no arguing with his tone. He firmly grabs hold of my hips again and adjusts my position to his liking.

With the tip of his cock he circles me, teasing me.

"Oh take me!" I cry. The wait is almost too much for me to bear.

He thrusts inside of me and it lights my skin on fire. He finds his same controlled rhythm from earlier, pushing into me with determination and focus not to give up until I'm done. But I crave for him to lose it, just like I have.

"I'm so close," I gasp, "promise you won't hold back this time. I want all you have to give!"

His manhood twitches in response and he lets out a low groan. If he likes for me to talk, I aim to please.

"You're the best I've ever had!" I tense up my arms and shoulders, pushing back into him with every stroke, it's my turn to be focused. "Fuck me harder!"

As I will my pussy to contract around him, keeping him in a stranglehold, his fingers bury deeper into the soft flesh around my hips and he speeds up.

"You're driving me crazy!" His voice sounds choked, still holding back.

"I want you! Out of control!" I scream, squeezing him tighter inside me. It's as if a switch flips inside his mind, because he starts panting heavily, bruising my hips with his fingers that had still tried to be gentle earlier. He slams into me so quickly and forcefully that I can feel the skin on my ass zing after every impact.

I cry out, loudly, so close to orgasm it's killing me. He joins in, still pounding me at a breath-taking speed. Then he tenses with a primal groan, I look around to see his eyes are closed in a gorgeous frown as he's pressed deep into me. It is the most glorious sight I've ever laid eyes on. I squeeze hard, rubbing back against his hot, pulsating cock. He fights his urge to stay still, his forced short thrusts send me over the edge with him. Involuntarily my back curves and head tilts upwards, I let out a loud scream as my body is being shaken by the most intense orgasm I have experienced so far. I feel tears burning in my eyes and my muscles one by one turn into jelly. Peter stops shuddering from his own climax behind me and lets go of my hips. However hard he may have held me, I can feel no pain.

He leans forward on one arm and I feel the other slip around my waist, cradling me. We lie down on our sides just as we are, he doesn't pull out and neither do I want him to.

With his head pressed into my hair and arm wrapped around me, I feel not just satisfied but safe. Lazily I wonder whether this is more than just sex.

Just as I decide I'm better off not overcomplicating things, he interrupts my thoughts.

"Best you've ever had, eh?" The sound of his voice tells me he's smiling, and so am I.

"By a mile," I sigh, tugging at his arm to get it around me even tighter.

"Likewise."

"Don't sneak off while I'm asleep," I mumble, suddenly starting to feel overcome by tiredness.

"You wouldn't get rid of me that easily." He kisses my ear.

"You know, you're simply amazing." I say, while drifting off. His face pressed against my neck and shoulder, right now feels utterly perfect.

ONE NIGHT STAND

***

A quick glance at the alarm clock reveals that it's only eight am. My body clock seems unaware that it's my day off, in any case the pressing need I'm feeling is one I cannot ignore for long.

I get up and sleepily wander to the bathroom, my head still fuzzy from last night's wine excesses but at least I don't have a hangover. *Where is Peter anyway?* The sheets next to me were cold when I awoke but I never noticed him leaving.

The back of the bathroom door hides a satin dressing gown which I decide to put on. One can never be sure whether the postman or someone else will turn up early. When I'm done washing my hands and splashing water in my face, I head to the kitchen. His car is still prominently parked outside and I'm relieved that he's still around just like he said he would be.

I can hear his voice outside now, a quick check through the living room window shows that he's sitting on the same bench overlooking the view, phone to his ear. He is naked from the waist up and bathed in crisp morning sunshine

Observing him for another minute, I note he has a mug and teapot sat in front of him on the table. *Good idea, I could use the caffeine as well.* After a quick trip back into the kitchen, I step outside, mug in hand.

"Morning," he smiles, while putting the phone down next to him.

"Hey," I respond, "you're up early."

"Oh, I guess I'm used to getting up at five every day. Such habits are hard to break." He notices the mug in my hand and reaches out for it. "Tea?"

"Yes, please. How lovely, waking up and then not having to make my own." I sigh and sit down next to him.

"I see you found yourself something to wear," I chuckle, noticing that he is sporting a pair of ultra-girly pink pajama bottoms.

"Well, I was improvising. Didn't want to wake you."

"That's very sweet of you," I grin before lifting the mug up to my lips to take a sip.

We sit quietly for a few minutes before his phone rings again.

"I'm sorry, that'll be the office," he says, "I'm not there one day and you'd think the world was coming to an end."

"Well, I guess it's good to be needed," I respond.

Gazing out over the garden, I try to occupy my mind with other things rather than focus on the one-sided conversation going on next to me. The call finishes quite quickly.

"What about you, going to work?" he asks after putting the phone back on the table.

"I have today off." I stretch lazily and lean back, conscious of his arm on the backrest behind me. "I don't think I want to go anywhere at all today."

He doesn't flinch, in fact it seems as though he's getting closer to me with every movement. He definitely isn't the one-night-stand type, instead he's dragging this out. I wonder if, no, *I hope* he'll want to stay today as well.

"So what do you like to do, when you have the day off?" He gives me a coy smile.

"That all depends on whether I have company," I respond.

"It would appear that you're in no hurry to get rid of me then." His smile has turned slightly naughty.

"Whatever makes you say that?" I make a very poor attempt at innocently batting my eyelids before grinning back at him. He pulls me close to him and gives me another of his mind-blowingly passionate kisses I remember so clearly from last night. I can't think, breathe, only reciprocate. How has he in such a short time managed to make me so weak? I couldn't resist if I wanted to.

But something else rudely interrupts us.

CHAPTER FIVE

"Claudia? You there?" mom! What is she doing here?!

My eyes open wide in shock and he lets go of me instantly.

"Shit. I had no idea she was coming over," I whisper.

"Umm, Mom? I'm here," I call out, giving him an apologetic smile.

Immediately she saunters through the gate and in our direction. Noting that she's immaculately dressed as always, every time I see her I am more convinced that I received the vast majority of genes from my dad's side of the family, not hers.

"You weren't answering the door, and your car wasn't... Hey, Claudia, whose car is that?"

She's hardly aware of us until she's halfway up the garden path.

"Oh." She gives Peter the visual once-over in a critical fashion which only a mother can get away with. "I see."

He isn't fazed at all and as soon as she's near enough he gets up to shake her hand with a warm smile on his face.

"Mrs. De Wit, it's a pleasure to meet you. I'm Peter."

She is quite flustered, shaking his hand and staring at him too long for comfort.

Meanwhile I'm seventeen again, sat with my head

resting in my hands, preparing myself for the inevitable embarrassment which is coming my way.

"Oh call me Liesbeth, please... nice to meet you too, Peter." She recovers herself quickly and gives me a special mother-daughter glance.

"I didn't think that you'd have company, Claudia. Don't let me interrupt anything..."

I helplessly get up to give her a quick hug.

"We were just having a cup of tea, why don't you join us?" Peter asks.

Grateful for the chance for a quick escape, however short-lived, I agree. "Indeed, let me get you a cup."

I go in to grab another mug and some blueberry muffins that happen to be lying on the counter. Meanwhile my Mom has settled in nicely, chatting to Peter who looks equally at ease.

As I open the door I can just about overhear enough of the conversation to make me cringe.

"...about time she found a nice man." *Oh dear God.* Peter winks at me, obviously he thinks all of this is just hilarious.

I put the mug down in front of her and try to change the subject.

"So, Mom, what brings you here today?"

"Oh I thought it's such a beautiful morning, and you have the day off work anyway, I thought I'd see what my little girl was up to." *Ugh, could she lay it on any thicker?*

"Umm, right," I Momble.

"Anyway as I was saying, Claudia..." *Clearly there is no hope of steering her away from this topic,* "I'm happy for you both. Peter, you won't believe some of the guys she's brought home in the past!"

I stop chewing my muffin and try to shut her up with my stare alone, but she's purposefully avoiding eye contact.

Peter, meanwhile, is intent on encouraging her. "Really, I'm intrigued, Liesbeth."

"The last one was probably the worst of the lot, Mark, big scruffy fellow. Too many tattoos."

"Mom!" I yell out.

I can feel the blood rushing into my cheeks and ears. This has to be one of the most awkward situations I've ever found myself in. Possibly even worse than when she gave a teenage boy the 'don't knock up my daughter' lecture before our very first date when I was sixteen.

"Sweetheart, don't worry about it. Peter doesn't mind, do you?" she chirps.

"Not at all." He's still grinning at me.

My flight instinct is well and truly awake now and I can't fight it any longer.

"I need a shower," I say while getting up to rush inside.

"Excuse us, Liesbeth." Peter is up at nearly the same moment, overtaking me to hold the door open.

Once inside I can feel that my cheeks are still burning up. I turn to face him, but can't bring myself to make eye contact, I'm still just mortified.

"Damn, I'm really sorry. I really didn't know she was coming over."

Peter cups my face in his hands, making me look up at him.

"If you'd ever met my mother-in-law, you wouldn't be this concerned." He smiles at me and gives me a quick kiss on my forehead.

"I think I should get dressed and head home. There is so much I need to sort out. You have a lovely day with your Mom." He looks down at me and caresses my cheek while I lose myself in his eyes.

Although I don't want him to leave, I really don't want a re-run of the conversation Mom just initiated outside either so I don't argue.

"Thanks for rescuing me last night." He gives me a quick wink before his tone and expression turns serious. "I don't know where I would've ended up, if you hadn't come along."

I wrap my arms around his gorgeously toned body and press myself against him, drinking in his irresistible scent.

"Will I see you again?" I whisper, before lifting my head off his chest.

"Definitely. I promise," he says and kisses my lips gently. His smile looks sincere, making me wonder if he feels the same magnetism I do. Deeper somehow than just physical attraction.

"Well, in that case, see you later," I say, with a cautious smile. "Take care of yourself."

"Sure. See you soon," he responds, giving my cheek one final stroke with his index finger.

We let go of each other and he gathers up his clothes

from the armchair next to us before heading into the bedroom to change.

I go outside again, and pour myself another tea.

"Peter already had plans for today, he's getting ready to leave. So what do you want to do?" I ask Mom.

"What do you say we do a bit of shopping, have a nice lunch somewhere? A proper girls' day out?" she responds.

"Sure, that would be nice." I take a sip of my tea, vaguely overhearing doors opening and closing before Peter's car starts with the same deep rumble I remember from last night.

I'm not sure if I should be sad he's going, but I'm not. I smile to myself, realizing now even more than last night, I trust him. *This isn't goodbye.*

"Mom, mind if we go pick up my car before heading out shopping? It'll only take a few minutes."

CHAPTER SIX : PETER

It's almost over. I check my watch, comparing it to the clock hanging on the wall, as if it will make time pass more quickly on this dreary Friday afternoon. Even a quick glance at the weather outside confirms it's a gloomy October day. It can't even be described as cloudy, just white.

A few months ago, everything changed for me; my expectations, my future plans wiped clean. I like to think it's a change for the better; a fresh start and a chance to follow what I truly want in life rather than just do what I'm supposed to. At five sharp, I'll take my belongings and leave this building and soul-destroying job for good.

Stephanie cheating on me had been the wake-up call I so badly needed. I don't blame her anymore, even though it irks me that she didn't just speak her mind first. In any case, the split was as smooth as could be expected. We agreed to put the house on the market while each of us have made alternate arrangements. It's strange to be on my own again. Some days it's liberating, others not so much.

Checking the time again reveals no progress whatsoever. Stretching my arms and folding them behind my head, I stare at nothing while my thoughts revert back to a more comfortable memory from the same day; Claudia. The crazy, impulsive evening spent together which made me see not the despair, but the opportunity ahead of me. I've been thinking about her a lot, even if I doubt I've had an even remotely similar impact on her.

"Hey, Pete. Thought I'd just come in for a little chat..." Chris closes the door behind him and sits down across the desk.

"Sure, have a seat," I say. It's surprising that his affair with Stephanie hasn't made me hate him more. At first I was obviously furious, but now all that's left is detachment. Plus he's always been a bit of a prick, so really I shouldn't have been surprised."

He leans back and looks around the blank canvas that used to be my office, before folding his hands together and focusing on me. Strange, how nearly a decade of my working life fits into one cardboard box; yet without these little things the place looks barren.

"Well, it's certainly been quite a ride, hasn't it? Seems like only yesterday, when we both started off on the floor and look at us now," he says.

"Yes, indeed." I nod, betraying my real feelings that actually it all feels like a lifetime ago.

"Say, how about you join us for one more little get together; Ascot, Saturday next week for the Champions Day meet? Just wouldn't be the same without you there." It's obviously just polite small talk, not sure if he expects me to accept. But, Ascot? I wonder if...

"Yeah, sure. It'll be good fun," I hear myself say.

"Wonderful, I'll have your name added to the guest list."

ONE NIGHT STAND

I nod absentmindedly while he gets up and leaves my office again. It's a bit short notice and I haven't been in touch with her after that day, the morning I left her place.

Would it be odd, contacting her after almost four months? Pretty young girl like that, surely she wouldn't have been sitting around waiting? While my life has felt on hold—waiting for today—hers will have continued as normal, as if our little encounter didn't even happen.

But it did happen. It still does, vividly, whenever I allow myself a moment to recollect it all. From the first kiss—no, the first flirtatious glance—she reminded me of everything I'd been missing. By the time I had her on her back on that wooden table in her garden, I was consumed by a need to prove to her as well as myself that I wasn't just a suit and a pay check. I could tell that she saw it, felt it.

Her dark blonde hair was fanned out over the rough wood, eyes alternating between shut and wide open. I thrust into her with just one purpose; to give her pleasure. Any sound she made served both as a reward and further encouragement.

The image of her naked body has been forever scorched into my memory. She looked beautiful, sensual and primal all at once. Her skin was flawless as silk, irresistibly soft under my touch. Similarly she had difficulty keeping her hands off me.

At the point of no return, her voice pierced through the surrounding countryside; it must have carried for miles. It makes me smile now, that it seemed to not make a difference to either of us whether anyone would hear.

It's impossible to pick a favorite moment of that night. Once the ice was broken between us, our passion showed no signs of slowing. She fell to her knees in front of me, gazing up almost throughout. She knew exactly how to please, but it was the view that nearly killed me. Her eyes seemed to smolder through her long lashes, her hair cascaded down her back and swept back and forth with every movement. I can't remember the last time I'd had a blow job before that; it must've been years. The way her lips stretched wide around my cock drove me insane with lust.

I'd never done anything as rash, and that after only just finding out her name minutes before. That night was in an entirely different league of spontaneity as I'd shown for as long as I could remember. Although she showed all the signs that she was feeling the heat as intensely as I, still I wondered if I had injected the whole experience with more meaning than it deserved.

Sure, we had an intense physical connection. For me that alone made it special. And she was easy to talk to and seemed genuinely interested in me. Something about her made me want to share my darkest moments from earlier that day.

It's hard to pinpoint when I fell for her, as stupid as that seems. I think it happened before we even kissed; it's what made me want to kiss her. Or was that just lust? I'm going to have to see her again and find out.

I spend the rest of my afternoon trying to look her

up online. Earlier I'd refrained from doing so because it seemed inappropriate. But the prospect of coming down to her neck of the woods again next weekend surely justifies it now. With a bit of searching, I locate her house on Google Maps. Her name is unusual enough that she should be relatively easy to track down elsewhere..

Her LinkedIn profile looks empty, as if she only registered because someone told her to. Then I realize I'm an idiot, Chris is on there, with his five hundred plus connections and dozens of rubbish endorsements. If someone asked him, he'd name networking as one of his hobbies. Of course someone like Claudia wouldn't use bloody LinkedIn!

I decide to sign up on Facebook, something I'd resisted for years. Maybe the new me can get to like it. This is what I tell myself anyway, the real reason is simply that maybe that's the sort of thing she uses. *She does.*

Her profile pictures are stunning, every single one of them. Even the one where she's covered in paint splatters; her face, hands, even her clothes. Actually that's the best one. There are a fair few of her in what looks like somewhere in the Far East. I admire her for seemingly living life on her own terms. I let the cursor hover over the 'Add Friend' button. Would she even remember me?

No, this feels wrong. I close the page down again and reopen the map. With the phone already in my hand, I open another window and search for something a lot more appropriate. Firstly I owe her an apology for the long wait; secondly, well, Facebook just isn't my style, yet.

"Helen's Flowers, hello?" says a female voice on the other end of the line.

"Hi yes, do you deliver?" I ask and she answers in the affirmative.

"Well, I'd like you to put together something nice with a card. This is a little unusual but I know the delivery location, just not the exact house number. I hope you can accommodate such a request?" After that I explain the exact location with the help of the map, give her Claudia's name and describe the house to avoid any confusion. I also think of something suitable to have written on the card.

Red roses would've been a bit too loaded with symbolism, so I opt for a mixed arrangement instead. I give—let's call her Helen—free rein on picking out something nice.

When I hang up the phone, I can't help but wonder if I'll hear back from Claudia, or if that ship has long since sailed.

CHAPTER SEVEN

"Mom? Have you seen my keys?" I frantically dig through my purse and look around the bedroom in case I've left them on a shelf somewhere.

"Claudia, sweetheart, how *do* you manage on your own...?" Mom walks in with the keys dangling from her index finger.

"Yeah, yeah, alright. Let's go then," I say.

It's been a busy few weeks and I'm actually really looking forward to having lunch together, just the two of us catching up.

We take her car and head to a charming little gastro-pub nearby. Upon sitting down, I scan the menu and firstly opt for some wine. I could really use a drink after the month I've been having. The place is busy, as it usually is on a Saturday, but we'd booked a table in advance. Of course, Mom insisted on it.

"So, what's been going on with you lately, you look a bit pale," she says, leaning over and brushing a few stray locks of hair out of my face.

"Yeah, just work really. It's been crazy ever since they let a bunch of people go in August," I respond with a bleak smile.

"You're safe though?" she asks.

"I should hope so." *But honestly, I'm not so sure.*

The waiter comes to take our order and soon after

places the drinks down in front of us. Lovely.

"Oh, isn't this nice, lunch together after such a long time. I can hardly remember the last time we caught up like this..." Mom leans back in her chair and crosses one leg over the other.

I can remember it all too well. Last time her visit was pretty much unplanned, just like a lot of things were. The memories of that day, or mainly the evening prior have been in the back of my mind for months now. I'd tried not to obsess about it, but they never quite went away. Then yesterday, all of it forced itself back into the forefront.

"What's so funny?" Mom asks.

"Oh, nothing..." I try to deflect by taking a sip of wine.

"Say, you never told me the whole story about that guy, what was his name? Are you still seeing him?"

I have a feeling she's not going to let this topic go.

"No, not really had the time for dating you know," I try, hoping this answer will be sufficient.

"Mhm, not had the time. Claudia, you really are strange. And last time you barely talked about him, as if... He's not your boss, is he?" Mom's frowning, scrutinizing me.

"No, no, nothing like that."

"Good." She takes a sip and then focuses on me again.

"So? You seemed to get along. Granted he was a bit old for you maybe, but so charming. What happened?" she continues.

I shrug, feeling yet another smile form on my lips. *God, this is awkward.*

"I... well actually if you must know, we weren't *dating.*"

She stares at me, waiting.

"We, you know... Just hooked up the night before."

A deep sigh and a roll of her eyes later, she leans forward with that expression she gets when I've done something idiotic; lips pressed into a thin line, one eyebrow just slightly raised.

"You hooked up. What, you just took a stranger home from a bar or whatever? Jesus, Claudia, when I saw him at your place I honestly thought you were starting to grow up."

I can't help grinning now, she does have a way of getting out my rebellious side.

"You did say he seemed nice, mature. I thought I'd done pretty well, considering," I tease her.

She shakes her head.

"And after that, you didn't keep in touch? I mean, it seemed like there was something more going on, beyond one night," she says.

I take a deep breath, ready to just burst out giggling.

"Well, he was technically still married. So, no." I eye Mom for her reaction and am not disappointed.

She throws her hands in the air as if to say 'where have I gone wrong with this one'. "Married. Really, Claudia?"

"Well sort of, at the time. Not anymore." I dismiss her implied criticism.

"So you *have* kept in touch?"

"Well, I came home yesterday to find a bunch of flowers on my doorstep and a card..." I smile again. "He invited me to join him at some race on Saturday. Apparently he's divorced now."

Mom sits back, both eyebrows raised and arms folded in front of her.

"I thought I'd never see the day, you watching the races... Are you going to go?" she asks.

I shrug and take a moment to mull it over. It might be weird, I don't know what he's expecting from me. But I *have* been thinking about him, a lot.

"Maybe, I guess. As you say, it seemed like there was something there..."

Our food turns up and her attentions are diverted away from Peter and his invitation. I thought it was rather sweet, clearly an expensive bouquet which dare I say isn't really my style. But it's a nice gesture. And the card... It's actually in my handbag, where I kept it so I wouldn't lose his contact details.

'Dear Claudia,

I know I've left this too long, even so I've been thinking about you a lot these past months. Know that I'm deeply sorry; I'd like to make it up to you on Saturday, office lunch at the racecourse. Will you join me?

Peter'

Underneath were a mobile number and an email address.

ONE NIGHT STAND

I know he didn't write it himself, recognizing the logo on the ribbon as that of a local florist. But reading the note gave me a warm feeling inside. He seemed like a good guy back then. I hope the real deal will match up to my memory of him.

Mom doesn't bring up Peter until we're back in the car after our meal.

"Whatever you decide, be careful, okay. He seemed nice, but a man who would step out on his wife... I'm not sure about this," she says, resting her hand on my arm.

"It wasn't quite so simple, though. Technically it was the wife that did it first. When we met he had just found out and was quite upset by it all..." I mumble, deep in thought and replaying the events of that evening in my mind.

"Oh?"

"Yeah, so in a way, the marriage had already ended before anything ever happened between us," I say.

"I guess that sort of changes things. Still, be on guard, after a thing like that he might be a bit—well, being cheated on changes a person," she says.

I wonder... . I guess I'm going to find out soon enough because I've made up my mind to accept his invitation.

***

Later in the afternoon once I'm on my own again, I find the card in my purse and settle down on the sofa. To call or to email?

It's actually making me nervous. I may have been thinking about him too, but I sort of put the idea that anything would come out of this out of my head. For all I knew he could've reconciled with his wife and forgotten all about what happened between us. His invitation opens up a whole range of possibilities I hadn't dared to consider before.

I decide to respond by email.

'Dear Peter,
'So nice to hear from you! I'd love to join you on Saturday. Just one thing, I've never attended such a thing before, please do let me know if there's a dress code to follow... '

I sign with my name and phone number and sit back. For the first time in four months, I allow myself free rein to relive all those buried memories. Alright, perhaps not the first time, but finally I need not feel silly about it.

Googling his name reveals something which I actually could've guessed; he's successful and loaded. A prestigious position in an investment bank which I'd never heard of, not that that means anything. The address in central London and the fact that it has its own Wikipedia page suggests it's one of those which doesn't make the mainstream news often, but is probably influential in the right circles.

Crap, he wrote office lunch, didn't he...

The situation is starting to make me anxious. Mental note: don't drink too much bubbly and do not get political in front of his colleagues. Or cuss, or generally be myself. Oh God. On the bright side, at least I know my way around a full table setting.

I decide to try and put it out of my mind while waiting for a response, which as it turns out doesn't take long at all. His answer is slightly puzzling, but I decide not to question it. He will pick me up at noon on Saturday and says not to worry about the dress code, he'll 'sort something out'. Well, let's just see what that means.

By Tuesday, I've just about forgotten about most of this. Work is a nightmare, and actually the best part of each day is the drive home in the evening. The snaking, narrow roads are a great place to unwind when they're quiet. It helps that I've always enjoyed driving.

But then I'm interrupted by the phone and my heart skips a few beats. Who would call me at this hour, could it be him? I barely even remember what his voice sounds like. I pull over into the nearest parking space and check, a local number.

"Hello?" I say, "Yes, speaking?"

The posh sounding lady introduces herself as working for a clothing shop on the High Street. Apparently she is meant to deliver some dresses to me this week and would like to know my size.

So that's what he meant. I'm taken aback, but do give her my details and answer some basic questions about what colors and styles I like. She's going to send someone to my house in an hour.

I didn't quite know how to react, so I just went with

it. Thinking about it now, it's all a bit uncomfortable. The way she said certain things made me wonder how all this must look. *The gentleman kindly requested that something appropriate be sent to your home.'* Appropriate, right.

When I told her my dress size, she responded with, *'Oh, well. I'll see what I can do.'* As if to suggest that I'm making her job difficult by not being a thin waif. The nerve!

Anyway, I suppose he must not agree with her assessment, otherwise why invite me? He seemed to very much enjoy those curves a few months back.

.

CHAPTER EIGHT

Once home, I tidy up a bit and make myself something quick to eat. No sooner am I done eating, than the doorbell rings. That'll be the dresses. Weird, I've never had someone visit my house to show me clothes before.

"Hi," I say, opening the door.

The girl outside looks a bit flustered, with a large selection of gowns wrapped in plastic in her arms. She just about makes it inside the house without dropping any of them and I decide to help before she has a mishap.

"I'm sorry, we should really have a clothes rail or something for these kind of visits. But it doesn't happen all that often," she says, eyeing me curiously.

I realize I must look quite different to her usual clientele. Though I may live in the local area, my house is fairly modest, as is my wardrobe. I don't fit in with the average Range Rover-driving, fake tan-sporting trophy wives or mistresses who would seem like more likely customers. In fact I hate those people.

This is starting to seem like a worse and worse idea.

She checks me out from head to toe and starts going through some of the dresses, keeping around four or so to one side, and the remainder draped over my sofa. I can't make out yet which one is the 'reject' pile, but I do hope it's the smaller one or this visit may not turn out to be a success.

"You're so lucky, he must be quite a catch. When he phoned the boutique earlier, I thought my boss was about ready to faint. She was practically hyperventilating on the phone," she says.

I'm not sure I still feel lucky, awkward is more like it.

"Yeah, he's great..." I mutter.

Finally she seems to have everything sorted out how she wanted and picks up the first dress and rids it of its protective covering. Deep blue satin, a straight pencil shape which seems roughly knee-length. Not impressed by the weird ruffle on top and asymmetric neckline, but I don't want to be rude so I don't say anything.

She gives me one look and puts it aside in favor of something else. A pink, flowing dress with an empire waist. I nod, *yes, this one could work*. Rummaging through the rest of the stuff, there are more blues, purples and pinks following the rough preferences I'd mentioned on the phone.

Thinking maybe the pink one is going to be the one, I get distracted while she continues to show me more dresses. Instead I wonder how much the damn thing costs; whether it's more or less than my monthly salary. Less, surely—*hopefully*...

But the last option brings me back to reality. Red— not subtly red, but in-your-face red. From the nearly off-the-shoulder, rounded neckline to the form-fitting shape. It's actually quite a sensible design; three-quarter sleeves and only just over the knee. Very classy and yet, *red*.

ONE NIGHT STAND

The girl—totally forgot to ask her name—observes me carefully. She already knows this is the one, it's written on my face. All I can think of is how it exactly matches the underwear I wore last time. I wonder if he'd remember that.

I take the dress from her, feeling the soft fabric against my fingers. It's gorgeous. Trying it on confirms this notion; this is the one. A head turner. She remarks that it's very close to some dress someone or other from the TV wore at Royal Ascot. I barely pay attention to her but am pretty much in love, if that's possible.

Taking care not to get it dirty, I hang it up again and put the plastic back over it. Meanwhile she puts all the others back in the car and comes back with some much needed accessories; shoes, bags, the lot. Since I tend to be rubbish at such things, I let her pick out whatever goes the best. Apparently nude pumps and a matching clutch bag are the way to go.

She advises the classy thing would be to wear pearls with it. I suppose I can just about manage that on my own without spending even more of Peter's money.

It's hard not to stare at all of the stuff she's grouped together.

"Don't worry, he'll be speechless when he sees you!" she tries to reassure me.

Yeah, or he'll be speechless when he gets the bill for it all. Is the color too bold though?

"I feel kind of bad accepting all these gifts," I say.

"From the way the boss lady acted, I don't think it'll make a dent in his bank balance. I wouldn't worry about it." She winks at me.

This does not make me feel any better. But instead of arguing, I thank her for all her help and watch as she finishes packing up her car and leaves.

Should I call him to say thanks? It's kind of late, I decide to just send a quick email. Not that it helps make things feel right.

If anything, past relationships tended to be the other way around; I'd be the one holding down a job, whereas the guys I dated were of the starving artist variety. No wonder Mom has been on my case about what she perceived as entering into a grown up relationship.

Let's not get ahead of ourselves, I don't even know the guy.

***

By Saturday morning, I'm starting to get excited as well as nervous. I have no clue what he expects from this. I don't even know if my memories are right anymore or if I've subconsciously managed to embellish them. Was he really that hot, as well as gentlemanly, charming as well as kind? I suppose I'll find out soon enough.

The long, hot shower doesn't do much to relax me, so I decide to pour all my energy into dressing up. At eleven, I'm pretty much done except for some last finishing touches to hair and make-up. I decide to keep it classy, downplayed. The dress is loud enough on its own.

Then I wait, sitting on the sofa with a freshly brewed

cup of tea and a clean towel over my lap to avoid any spillages. Deep breaths, *he's just a guy*. Who happens to be taking me as his date to a fancy lunch with a bunch of other normal people. *Except they're most likely filthy rich and powerful.*

I grab the remote and turn on the TV to pass the time. It doesn't work and my tea finishes too quickly as well.

If I have another, I'll be heading for the bathroom the moment we get there. That's not classy, is it?

Finally it's getting close to time and I slip into the elegant nude colored heels which until now were just sitting underneath the coffee table, taunting me. I really want to feel optimistic, but I can't help wonder how badly I'll stick out.

Sure enough, with ten minutes to spare, I hear gravel crunch outside, making me jump up and head for the window. Damn, I do love that car of his; as much as I hate myself for thinking it, it looks like sex on wheels. Even with the soft top on.

When he steps out, I realize my memory did not play tricks on me. Knowing exactly what hides underneath that smart, slim cut grey suit only heightens my excitement. He closes the car door and adjusts the bright red tie he's worn for the occasion. Coincidence?

I open the door and greet him with a big smile.

"Oh my, look at you!" he says, stepping forward and giving me a hug and a kiss on the cheek. I'm not quite sure how to respond so I just go with it.

"Hello, gorgeous," he whispers in my ear, before

letting go too soon.

"You're not so bad yourself. Hi," I say.

I'm still nervous, yet not really. Similar to last time, something about him is slowly putting me at ease. Yet I haven't a clue what to talk about now. The time that's passed has made me retreat; the fact that almost everything about today has put me out of my comfort zone doesn't help.

"You had me worried for a bit, whether or not you'd be free today and give me this chance," he says.

I could drown in those deep blue eyes of his all over again...

"Why wouldn't I? And what chance?" I mumble.

"I shouldn't have left it this long. But I didn't want to contact you while still being married. It seemed disrespectful," he explains.

Who says chivalry is dead?

"That's understandable, she was still your wife even if things had gone bad between you." He starts to shake his head while I speak.

"You misunderstand. My concern was with you, it would be wrong to leave you hanging while needing to focus on getting my home life sorted out."

He is too smooth and yet, could he be genuine? I hope so; his words have made the hairs on my arm stand up, in a good way.

"And everything's sorted now?" I ask.

His smile says it all.

"Ready?" he asks. I take a quick look around, grab my bag and pull the door shut behind me.

ONE NIGHT STAND

Walking across the gravel in heels without damaging the shoes or myself is harder than expected.

Opening the car door for me, he waits while I sit down and get settled in. It's times like these that I'm glad Mom forced me to learn essential skills like getting in and out of cars in dresses. He shuts the door behind me and walks around to his side.

I take a moment to appreciate the walnut console between the two seats and the dash which is covered in sumptuous cream leather. To think he actually let me drive last time is still beyond me.

CHAPTER NINE

"So it's an office lunch thing?" I ask.

He pulls the door shut and turns the key before answering.

"Yes, we—they've got a regular hospitality contract for all the major events."

"Oh that's nice." *If you like that sort of thing.*

His laugh tells me he caught on to my tone; I really should watch my sarcasm.

"I'm sorry if this is prying too much, but what have you told them about me; who I am, how we met, that sort of thing?" I am starting to get fidgety but I catch myself and instead try to just hold onto the grab handle on the door and look out the window at the trees passing us by. The dense greenery has turned an autumnal mixture of reds and browns. I've unintentionally managed to dress accordingly, how funny.

"Frankly, I haven't told anyone anything. But I suppose that'll soon enough have to change. So, who would you say you are?" He sounds amused and I'm beginning to wonder if he thought this through at all.

"Well, obviously you already know my name and where I live, also, I'm twenty-four and work in a call centre in Egham." This situation is beyond ridiculous and I can't help but poke fun at it. "Other than that, I enjoy long walks on the beach and have occasionally been known to invite handsome strangers home with me."

His laugh is infectious. Could it be that he hasn't thought this through because he's not too concerned about what anyone would say?

"So, what about you? My own research only tells me you're a banker and drive a very nice car..."

"Former banker, actually." He pulls up at the mini-roundabout and indicates right to head into the village. "Other than that, I'm forty-one, also enjoy long walks on the beach and have indeed once found myself being invited home by a pretty lady, but I try not to make a habit of it."

I chuckle, remembering a similar dynamic happening last time.

"Why former?" I finally ask.

"Ah, I guess I failed to mention this earlier, Friday last week was my last day. They invited me today as a formality and I realized it would be the perfect chance to see you again. And here we are." The car creeps through the busy traffic on Ascot High Street, reminding me why I try not to go out on race weekends.

He left his job? Surely had he been let go, they wouldn't have invited him at all.

"Well, I suppose you can fill me in on all the details later. First though, what if anyone asks how we met?" I say.

He shrugs.

"Might as well stay close to the truth; we met in

June, purely by chance, we got on well and after that I invited you to join me today." The traffic starts to move again and we creep into a car park, following the huge grey Jaguar ahead of us. Perhaps it only looks huge from this perspective.

After showing the attendant his badge, we pull into a space and he rushes around to open the door for me. I doubt this will ever get old.

I take his arm and we make our way out and along the crowded High Street. The sky is grey, but it's surprisingly warm for late October. Wonder if we'll be indoors, wherever we're going.

The shops thin out towards the end of the High Street, but the crowds do not. It never fails to hit me how small and quaint the village actually is, right until you get within view of the new racecourse entrance. This is the first time I'm walking right up to it, normally I'd just see from the car, driving past.

The view of the glass and steel structure towering above the entry stiles is breath-taking. I remember the controversy surrounding this new design when they built it, but now that I'm seeing it close up, its grandeur seems appropriate. The crowds of people everywhere merge together into a multi-colored, moving mass which seems to have a collective conscience. Pulsating and shifting forward in the corner of my eye, while I continue to admire the building in front of me.

"You know, I've never been inside?" I say.

"Funny, how it takes a visitor to bring a local to the racecourse," he responds. *Right he is.*

ONE NIGHT STAND

He leads me off to a separate entrance where he steps forward, showing his badge again. After checking the guest list, they let us inside, pointing out where we're meant to be going. Not that they needed to, Peter knows exactly what to do and I just follow.

Past the busy lawn, straight towards the big, shiny construction dominating the view ahead; its most prominent feature from this angle are the banners; 'British Champions Series' and similar. Inside and up a few floors we go, greeted by a few more 'gatekeepers', some of whom recognize Peter and quickly move aside to let us through.

Once we've made it into the inner sanctum of the spacious corporate sponsors' box, I start scanning the room. The demographic is largely male, graying and as yet sober. For a moment I feel reassured that I'm not standing out as much as I thought I would, hardly anyone gives me a second look. The obvious exception consists of around half a dozen women who are grouped together by the window. Checking out the competition is what it feels like, but I'm not certain what we're competing for.

A few steps forward and I hear a familiar, thundering yet cheerful voice, the owner of which soon comes into view. I put my hand on Peter's arm, causing him to pause and turn towards me.

"Oh my God, that's...?" I whisper, keeping my gaze fixated forward at the man with the unmistakable freshly-out-of-bed white-blond hair, who still seems to be very much engaged in loud banter with the two bystanders. In proper old boys' club fashion, all three are wearing identical dark ties with light blue diagonal stripes.

"The Mayor, yes." Peter laughs and asks if I'd like him to introduce me.

I shake my head, *let's not do that*. He places his hand on the small of my back and excuses himself to get me some champagne. I'm frozen in place, trying not to stare but failing miserably when the man with the wild, blond hair steps towards me, introducing himself.

"Oh, hi," I say, for lack of something better to say when he shakes my hand.

"I do hope I can count on your vote in the upcoming campaign?" He sounds just like on the TV. Of course he does.

"I can't, I'm afraid," I say.

This is not what he was expecting to hear in this crowd, his crowd.

"Oh?"

"I don't live in London, so I doubt they'd let me vote..." I mumble.

"Ah yes, right you are," he responds, "Can't have everything, eh?"

He flashes a grin at me, places his hand on my arm and nods once before heading past me. That was surreal. Turning around to observe him continue his cheerful spiel with the next little cluster of people, I wonder how he manages to stay 'on' all the time.

"Here you go." Peter turns up at my right, offering me a champagne flute.

"Thanks," I smile.

He throws a quick glance and nod in the mayor's direction before offering me his arm and leading me out and onto the balcony. Lucky for this time of year, it's pleasant outside and dry. Unlike the rest of the week.

As we start making our way towards the railing overlooking the track, he greets a few more people. I just try my best to look respectable and not stumble over my own feet.

"Pete, you made it!" Another guy steps forward and gives him a pat on his upper arm.

"I said I would," Peter responds. His tone doesn't quite match the other guy's enthusiasm.

He turns towards me and introduces us. Apparently the guy's name is Chris, he puts a lot of emphasis on the word 'colleague'. Oh hang on, *that's* Chris?

The advantage and disadvantage of having just one shared memory is that I've often replayed every moment of it in my head even though I tried not to. I'm pretty sure the guy his wife was banging was called Chris. Shit, I hope she isn't here too; that would be way too awkward!

I hope I do a decent job hiding this realization, covering it with a smile and offering my hand to greet him. He takes it and gives it an old-school kiss. *Icky*.

"It's a pleasure to meet you," he says, to which I give him a nod and respond likewise.

He turns towards Peter again and starts chatting about horses and odds. I tune him out but take a moment to casually get more of an impression of whom

I suspect is half of the indirect reason I'm even here today.

Roughly similar in age; in his forties definitely, another dark blue suit, white shirt and another striped school tie, this one blue with a double white stripe. His hair is a little longer, greyer as well as thinner and he's kind of shiny and red-faced. I don't like him; wonder if that's due to intuition or bias...

I decide to leave them to their conversation; if Peter wants to get out, he can excuse himself and join me. The balcony overlooks crowds of spectators a few floors below and of course the track a little way ahead of us. There aren't many people outside so I take a moment to catch my breath and enjoy the view. Earlier it had seemed like the sun tried to break through the cloud cover, but this is looking less and less likely now.

I wonder what time the actual racing will start, and if I can bring myself to care about it. As I take the last sip of champagne, someone actually turns up almost immediately to take the empty glass away.

From the corner of my eye I see two of the same women approach who were looking at me earlier.

"Hello, I don't think we've met before," one of them says, her hand stretched out towards me, "I'm Caroline and this is Alison."

"Oh, indeed. Nice to meet you. Claudia," I respond with a smile.

"Do you work at the company as well?" Alison asks, while now offering me her hand to shake.

I shake my head. "No, just a guest. How about you?"

ONE NIGHT STAND

They explain they're here with their husbands. Something about them makes me uneasy, even if I can't identify anything specific in their words or tone which is putting me off.

The questions keep coming though and I do my best to answer. No, this is my first time at the races and yes, it's all very exciting. They comment on my dress, ask what designer it is and I'm finding myself unable to respond. In the end I explain that it was a gift so I'm not really sure, and excuse myself to go freshen up.

As I walk off, both of them are giving each other knowing looks. The gossip has started.

I find Peter still unable to rid himself of Chris, give him a sympathetic smile and continue on towards the facilities. Funny how he stands out to me. In this crowd of stuffy suits in boring old school ties, he seems to shine.

In the ladies' room, I take a moment to check my makeup and hair. All seems in order. Really, I mainly wanted to get away from the interrogation squad before things got too weird. I hope they'll serve lunch soon. Or at least Peter and I can have some time alone to chat and catch up.

CHAPTER TEN

On my way back after wasting what I assume is a suitable amount of time, I hear some familiar voices talking, mentioning my name. I pause. Sounds like Chris has joined forces with the evil twins.

"Really, I'm not sure this is wise. Don't get drawn in by the first pretty young thing that looks your way, Pete," I hear Chris say. "I mean you've only just finalized the divorce..."

What the...

"Absolutely, I'm sorry to say, but she's just after your money, I can guarantee it," says a shrill female voice. *You should know, bitch!*

I wait and listen to more of the conversation, but my heart has sunk already. My biggest worries about today had focused around what to say if the conversation shifted to something I knew nothing about. Or perhaps if I were to slip up and go all liberal on someone. I hadn't considered this sort of scenario at all.

With arms crossed, I step forward and into view. The two trophy witches exchange glances and slip away towards the bar. What I'm left with is Chris, who has his back turned towards me and Peter, whose expression tells me that he knows the shit has hit the fan.

"Mate, I know it's easy to get carried away. My advice would be, have your fun with her, but then find someone—" Chris gets distracted by Peter's head-shaking and gesture to 'kill the conversation'. "What? You need someone more suitable, so at least you won't have to pay for her wardrobe and God knows what else."

Enough, I don't need this. In one swift move, I turn and nearly knock over a waiter carrying a tray of champagne flutes. With that mishap narrowly averted, I head for the door, head swimming with rage. Who do these people think they are?

In the background I vaguely hear Peter's voice: "Chris, you're such a twat—Claudia, wait!"

But I don't wait, instead I stomp through the door that is opened for me and down the corridor to the stairs. When I've reached the bottom, I just about manage to slip by a large crowd pushing into the building. The exit comes into view and my formerly long strides turn into an awkward jog.

It seems not only the company, but the world as a whole has turned on me, demonstrated by the heavy drops which are starting to fall. What starts as a sporadic and almost hesitant shower, turns more intense by the time I'm through the turnstiles. I stop beside the now-closed ticket office and take off my shoes. I can't walk in these fucking things!

As I start making good progress towards the shops, a car pulls up alongside me.

"Love, can I drop you somewhere?" I throw a quick glance at the guy, a taxi driver, and shake my head.

He gives up pretty quickly when I speed up, with my

arms wrapped around myself. I'm too pissed off still to really feel the cold, but the rain is definitely starting to soak through. Also, the pavement is quite rough and small puddles have formed in places, making my feet not just wet but numb as well.

All of the High Street passes me by in a blur, before I know it I've turned off and am just a little bit closer to home. Unfortunately that's where the pavement stops being of much use and a quick look down at my feet reveals that my formerly flawless tights have turned a muddy, soggy brown.

Today sucks. All of this is a complete nightmare. Nothing went how I hoped, and I can't believe I was such a dumb shit that I actually had hopes of some kind. And why the fuck didn't I get into that damn taxi? I'm nowhere near home, filthy and it's still pissing down. And the cold is getting to me. Another car pulls up beside me and slows to a crawl. If it's a taxi, I'm taking it.

"Claudia." *Oh fuck.*

"Just... don't." I try to speed up, not that it'll help. How the hell am I going to outrun a sports car?!

"You're all wet. Get in," Peter says.

I stop, arms crossed, and look at him. This is so fucking humiliating and I don't even know why I'm resisting anymore. I bite my lip, hoping it'll somehow contain all this rage and confusion I feel. It doesn't, of course, and tears start to stream down my face; angry tears.

He leans over and opens the passenger door.

"Please."

"But, I've got mud all over me." I sound choked, still holding back because I worry if I don't I might just scream my head off.

"I don't give a fuck. Get in the car." His tone isn't one to mess with.

A quick glance at his face confirms I'd be better off complying, so I open the door wider and carefully get in and perch on the edge of the seat in an effort not to drip all over the immaculate leather.

The moment I shut the door, he speeds up and the soggy brown scenery zips past us as I am forced against the backrest. Retracing the route taken barely an hour earlier, the drive doesn't take long. Neither of us speaks a word. I suspect he's furious, whereas by now I'm just drained and empty. I just want to reach home.

Getting out and closing the door behind me, I rummage around for my keys and head straight for the door. The gravel pokes uncomfortably into my feet. I don't check behind me, frankly I don't care whether he follows me in or not. This whole thing has been an incredibly stupid idea. I don't know him, he doesn't know me. There is literally nothing I can think to say to him.

I place the shoes on the hallway floor and proceed towards the bedroom to grab something dry to wear, when his hand closes around my arm, holding me back.

"Let go," I say. He doesn't.

Rationally, I know I should be concerned now. A stranger, in my house, holding on to my arm in anger.

Instead I'm still too pissed off myself, fear doesn't even come into it. So I face him, chin thrust forward and face his tense stare. His jaw is clenched and nostrils slightly flared.

"Claudia, I'm sorry about what they said."

I can feel my lip starting to shake, together with the rest of me.

"You don't fucking get it, do you? Why did you even come back, why invite me there? What did you think, everyone would just get along?"

He continues to stare. I should feel threatened but I don't.

"You just fucking stood there and let that dickhead run his mouth after he fucked your wife behind your back—sorry, ex. You get the point! Jesus, what the hell is wrong with you!"

"I thought... hoped that once they'd said whatever they had to say, they'd give up and let us be."

I shake him off and at last he does let go, allowing me to enter the bedroom and slam the door behind me. After listening for a few seconds, I figure he's not going to come after me. Quickly I take the dress off and put it back on its original hanger. Then I rid myself of the muddy tights and wet underwear, both of which I dump on the floor.

It's definitely cold now and I start to shiver. I grab the first warm thing I can find in the wardrobe and a fresh towel for my hair. Did I just mean what I said to him? Had I overreacted about him not defending me in front of those people? Does he perhaps share their view and I'm just a little entertainment to distract from his failed marriage? And why do I even give a shit? Why did I expect more from someone I hardly know? Someone I actually ended up fucking barely ten minutes after finding out his name. I've brought this all on myself.

I sit down on the foot end of the bed and start to cry properly when I see the pathetic looking wet dress hanging a few feet away. Yep, I feel exactly how that looks.

The door creaks but he doesn't come in. Just stands there, observing me.

"I'm really sorry," he says.

Just let me be, damn. I get up and pick up a box of tissues from the bedside table, attempting to dry my face with one. It's useless, though, because new tears just keep coming as soon as I wipe the old ones away.

"I never expected things to turn out this way." The anger he showed earlier has vanished and he looks helpless.

No shit. I throw him a nasty glance.

"May I come in?" he asks.

I shrug and he takes a few steps forward. Leaning against the chest of drawers, he squeezes the bridge of his nose with forefinger and thumb.

"Today seemed like the perfect chance to see you again."

Anger flares up in me again, though I still don't know why I even care.

"Why? Please explain what you were trying to achieve with all this. Dress me up in expensive clothes à la *Pretty Woman* and show off to your rich and powerful friends? Because if that was your strategy to impress me, you're more clueless than I thought."

"I..." he stammers.

"Honestly, if you wanted to see me again, you could've just gotten in touch. All this..." I gesture at the dress. "It's just fluff. I don't get it."

"Okay, yes." He raises both hands in a sort of defensive gesture. "I was trying to impress you. Didn't think just turning up out of the blue would do the job. I couldn't be sure what I was up against. The truth is I haven't been able to stop thinking about you and felt I had to give this a damn good go."

That last bit softens me, if only for a moment.

"I guess it didn't come across that way, but it took all my restraint not to punch Chris in the head right then and there. He was bang out of order."

"Damn right," I say.

"The only reason I didn't was because I had hoped to salvage the situation and at least enjoy the rest of the day with you. Also, after today I'll never have to see his face again, which was a calming prospect."

I think for a moment, trying to decide what of everything he's just told me is worth taking seriously.

"You honestly thought you needed to bribe me with gifts and promises of fancy lunches, or I wouldn't be interested?" I blink away some of the tears and look at him, hands in his pockets and staring down at his shoes.

"What do I know? As you so kindly reminded me, my wife of fifteen years seemed to prefer Chris over me."

I see where he's coming from. Despite trying so hard to be self-assured, he's probably been having quite a shit time lately. Wouldn't all of this have been much easier without the games? *Men!*

"Shall we start over? Just us, no smoke and mirrors," I say.

He looks up and the moment he lays eyes on my hair and face, he lets out a small chuckle.

"All day it was dry, until you walked out without an umbrella. How unlucky was that."

I get up and check my face in the mirror and it makes me laugh as well. It looks as though my eyes have melted and started dribbling down my face. While I start to wipe off the blackness and other assorted makeup from my skin, he offers to make some tea, which I gladly accept.

CHAPTER ELEVEN

As soon as I'm done cleaning myself up, I join him in the kitchen. He's leaning against the counter and staring out the window, taking small sips from his mug. With his jacket off, tie loosened and shirt sleeves rolled up, he is quite a sight to behold. *Was he really just trying to impress me? What an outlandish idea.*

"I'm sorry I overreacted earlier," I say, placing my hand on his arm.

He turns and hands me the other mug.

"No, you were absolutely correct. I'm sorry." When he raises his hand to brush a lock of damp hair out of my face, I am frozen in place.

So captivated am I y his blue eyes, I forget to hold on to the tea properly, before being forced back into reality by the burning sensation in my hand. *Ouch.*

"Shall we sit?" I nod my head in the direction of the living room.

He follows me and we sit beside each other on the soft leather sofa. With my still ice cold legs folded underneath me, I turn to face him and place a woolen throw over my lap.

Mug in hand, carefully, to avoid further burns, I try my best to think of a way to break the ice again.

"I just want to make it clear that I don't care how

much money you have." I take a sip of tea and look over, waiting for his reaction.

He smiles subtly before leaning into the backrest and resting his free hand on his thigh. It's frustrating how my eyes are drawn to his hand and as a result linger just a bit too long on the entire surrounding area.

"Well, there goes my entire strategy then," he says.

"How about—and I know this is weird and unnatural—just telling me more about yourself? You quit your job, why?" The mood has largely lifted, and although I really would like to know more about him, I'm also reminded of why I managed so little restraint last time. The wine will have helped, but mainly there's this magnetism I can feel pulling me towards him, it's hard to stay on track.

He sighs and puts his mug down on the table before folding both his hands together. Initially I find it hard to concentrate on what he's telling me, but soon I realize that I actually do care about what he's been up to lately. I really want to hear all of it. Even if he is distractingly handsome.

Starting at the beginning, he tells me about confronting his wife and how easily she agreed to just call it quits. How he then started to think about what I told him: that this would mean a fresh start and a chance to do things he hasn't been able to so far. Shortly after, he decided that what he wanted most was a career change. Money had never meant all that much to him, it was free time and happiness he was after. Sadly his demanding job meant he had a long notice period to work through.

"So what would you like to do now?" I ask. My question causes an awkward smile and a shrug.

"I was rather hoping to take a little time to figure that out."

Still lost in eye contact, I can't help wonder about the massive risk he's taking. Drawing a line under everything he's known for the better part of his adult life with no real plan, that's drastic. Admirable, though; it's the kind of crazy idea I might come up with if I had the opportunity.

Leaning over to keep my mug on the table as well, I feel his eyes on me. It's a nice sensation, albeit a little strange because I don't feel particularly appealing in my fleecy lounge wear and damp hair. He must be seeing something I can't.

Then he asks about me, how I've been lately, to which I briefly mention the mass redundancies at work and resulting added load on the few that remain. My answer is met with a stare and a pause. *My personal life? Oh, no news there.*

This seems to please him and there is another moment of silence though which he briefly touches his chin before running his hand through his hair.

"I don't want to be presumptuous. Whatever happened last time was obviously mostly the heat of the moment. But I've struggled with this dilemma throughout today... I would very much like to kiss you." The very obvious shyness in him makes me want to squeal, but I don't, instead I just grin.

"Sometimes such dilemmas are easily resolved." I lean forward and indeed any anger I felt towards him earlier has vanished.

He's gorgeous and I want my lips to remember his. Our last meeting was too brief, but perhaps the same need not be the case now.

Pushing himself away from the backrest of the sofa, he comes closer and I'm thrilled. Despite everything, there is something so special about him. It makes me want to forget that we're possibly incompatible in many ways. His hand slips behind my neck and into my hair, the roots of which seem to zing with excitement.

I'm drawn to him, unable and unwilling to resist. His kisses burn into me, warming me to the core. I wrap both arms around his impressively toned shoulders. The cotton of his shirt is so soft, it does nothing to disguise the temptation underneath.

"I'm sorry," I whisper in between kisses.

He responds with more determination as if to tell me I have nothing to be sorry about. Forgetting any semblance of restraint, I crawl closer, straddling him as our lips and tongues continue their little dance. His fingers run down my back and both hands end up firmly on my hips; he seems to enjoy holding me there. He leans into the backrest again, and I join him, leaving just enough room to get at his chest. My memories were spot on, and he hasn't changed.

"Claudia," Peter whispers.

"Mhm?"

"Wait," he says.

I sit back, worried about where his interruption is going.

"Before we do anything else, I just want to clarify my intentions." He runs his hand through his hair and looks at me with a slightly uneasy smile.

"Okay, well what are they exactly?" I ask.

"Despite all the rubbish Chris talked earlier, for me this isn't just about sex. Though don't get me wrong, I've had an impossible time trying not to constantly think about everything..."

I smile at him and wait for him to continue.

"I need you to know I want..." His eyes wander while I adjust my top which had gone all twisted.

"Yes?" I say.

"That too." He grins, still watching my attempts at getting sort of decent.

"But I felt an inexplicable connection with you, it started almost straightaway. Beyond the physical. I need to know if you did, do."

"You realize we might not have much in common?"

"I'm not convinced, and in any case I love that you challenge me. I no longer want to be this boring..."

"Posh guy with the nice car and stuffy friends?" I grin at him.

He laughs.

"Yeah, something like that, though I do quite like that car."

"Fair enough," I say.

"I guess what I'm trying to say is, I really like you. And I'd like to see where this goes."

ONE NIGHT STAND

I put my arms around his neck again, attempting to find the truth in the deep blue of his eyes. He's serious. Though I do have my doubts about whether we're compatible, he seems to want to reinvent himself. I don't think I could resist if I tried, I too felt that instant connection and the four months apart or even a big emotional blowout haven't been able to kill it.

"Well then, let's see where *this* goes…" I lean in and brush my lips past his, teasing him with a soft near-kiss. His reaction is instant.

He grabs hold of my sides, just below my underarms and raises me off him. Within the blink of an eye, I'm on my back on the sofa and he's hovering above me, leaning on his hands placed either side of my head. After a moment spent just looking at me, he gets down on his elbows with his face only inches off my chest.

"You're special, Claudia. Let me show you how special…" He peels my top off slowly, kissing any skin as soon as it's exposed.

I smile at him, a little more reassured about our situation than before and completely ready for a good, hard reconciliation. When he makes me feel the way I do right now, how can I worry about what may or may not happen in future? Here and now, everything feels right.

With one hand in his hair, I try to guide him towards my nipple which so far he is carefully avoiding; kissing and teasing only the surrounding skin. I impatiently start unbuttoning his shirt before lifting myself and quickly taking my own top off completely.

"In a hurry?" He grins, I just give him a look that says it all.

He leans on one arm and takes my wrist with his other hand. Before I know it, he pins first one arm back against the armrest of the sofa, and then the other. I'm helplessly spread and his appreciative gaze tells me he likes it this way.

"I want to touch you..." I beg.

He shakes his head and kisses me firmly, gathering both my hands together before I have the chance to regain my composure. His lips make me weak. I can't take my eyes off his face but quickly get distracted when his free hand finds its way down between us, massaging my thighs from the outside in. Getting ever closer to where I really want to be touched.

I let out a moan and he leans in for a further taste. His tongue slips into my mouth the very moment his hand moves past the waistband of my pants.

"How wet you are," he groans against my lips.

Bucking my hips upwards, I feel a rush of pleasure come over me as his finger enters me. He's good, gentle yet firm. He's also rock solid and straining against my thigh. I try to move around, rubbing my leg against his erection in an attempt to break down his control. It's working because he pauses mid-kiss and his eyes close.

"I want you," I whisper.

He presses his cock against me hard but then retreats. My hands are free again when he leans back and sits on his knees between my legs, opening his belt and fly. I quickly rid myself of any remaining clothes and watch him do the same. We're both naked, except for his red tie. He stares at me, eyes dark and unfocused as he grips his length and strokes himself a few times.

My own hand has travelled down as well, circling my clit and coating it in my own juices. This image appears too much for him and he is on me again, biting and sucking on the soft skin of my neck and guiding his cock inside.

I let out a sharp cry once he's in. He fills me completely and utterly and I think I'm sold on the idea of us. I want to tell him but can't speak through the deep, rhythmic strokes. He is focused on me, like a predator on his prey, or perhaps in this case we're both predators in competition with each other, taking turns to please.

My stomach feels taut on the inside, so much tension, anger transformed into passion. I could cry and laugh at the same time, but most of all I just want to keep moving. I run my fingers down his back and he responds by speeding up.

Once again he takes my wrists and holds them firmly above my head. His movements are determined and mostly regular, except the odd twitch and microscopic pause. He wants to be in control but he's failing. I feel pressure building inside me; waves of pleasure increasing in intensity until I'm ready to be ripped open. Moans and gasps fill the room, which I know are mostly mine.

He continues to fuck me faster, harder. The sofa shudders back and forth and I'm done for. My whole body tenses, and I cry—no, I scream.

"Come with me, I need you!" My fingers cringe but have nothing to hold on to. His hands grip me tighter, not letting me move my arms even a little. I look down and see his beautiful body, muscles contracting and relaxing in quick succession; it's hypnotic and altogether too much. How did I get to be with this man? How come he seems to want plain old me and not someone equally perfect?

He pounds into me, releasing my tension and as soon as I'm clearly done for, he freezes with his eyes closed. I know that frown from last time. I also remember the shuddered breathing, the last twitches. I remember the sweet scent of our combined arousal.

When he lowers himself onto me, finally I have my arms back and straightaway wrap them around him. We're both a bit clammy, but it makes no difference. I let my fingers follow the contours of his back muscles which are starting to relax. He breathes deeply and finds my other hand to wrap his fingers through.

"I feel it as well, you know," I say, "not just lust, but something more..."

"It's strange, isn't it? All of this is totally irrational and yet it seems to make perfect sense." He sighs.

"I know. We're practically still strangers, but I can't fight the urge of wanting to know you so much better. I do like you a lot too."

He raises himself off my chest and gives me a peck on the lips. His eyes linger on my face.

"You should cover up, you've already been rained on

today. Being naked and sweaty would almost guarantee that you catch a cold," he says.

"I have a better idea." I sit up and stretch while watching him get off the sofa, gathering our clothes.

"Oh yeah?" he says.

I take his hand and lead him into the bedroom en-suite. He gets the picture straightaway and leaves the clothes in the hamper next to the shower. I open the door and turn on the water while he just observes.

"Join me?" I ask and he does.

Before long we're once more only inches apart, letting our hands do the talking. Caressing, exploring, washing, rinsing. He insists on washing my hair for me, which is sweet. Our shower is prolonged by lengthy, lazy kisses which somehow feel that much better while surrounded by hot flowing water.

When we get out, he wraps me into a towel and dries me off without even entertaining the idea of taking care of himself until I'm done.

"You know I'm not that fragile," I giggle.

"Still, I wouldn't want you getting sick," he insists, and wipes some droplets off my face.

"Alright, alright. Hey, are you hungry? It just occurred to me that we missed lunch."

"Sure," he responds.

CHAPTER TWELVE

Once again I find myself in the kitchen, trying to improvise an unexpected meal. Peter has meanwhile dried himself and is standing by the counter, watching me, wearing one of my bathrobes with, I'm assuming, nothing underneath.

"So where are you staying now?" I ask, while tossing some cooked chicken and greenery together into a large bowl. *Hope he likes salads...*

"When Stephanie and I separated we put the house on the market and I rented a flat closer to work. But I suppose it's time to move now, there's no more reason for me to be in the City," he explains.

"Are they still, you know…"

"What, Stephanie and Chris? I think so, frankly I don't really care. They deserve each other," he responds. I regret asking but a quick glance in his direction suggests he didn't really mind the question.

"I'd been meaning to ask you actually, this seems like a weird place to stay for someone like you," he says.

"Someone like me can't live in a bungalow in Ascot?" I chuckle, "It's okay, I know what you mean."

"This is the house Dad moved into after my folks got divorced. When he passed away two years later, he left this place to me and I just couldn't bring myself to sell it."

"Oh, I'm sorry." He places his hand on my shoulder.

"That's cool, shit happens, eh." I turn around, bowl in hand.

"Could you take this inside? I'll come with the rest of the stuff," I say.

As soon as I've collected plates, cutlery and some bread rolls together on a tray, I follow Peter into the small dining area inside the living room. He's standing at the other end of the room, looking at the dresser.

"Did you draw this?" he asks, picking up a sketch I had mindlessly left on a shelf. I turn bright red, caught in the act. I had tried to sketch him after our first encounter. Actually, the one he picked up was one of countless attempts over the past months.

"Err, yeah." I'm not quite sure where to look, such is my embarrassment.

He chuckles and walks over.

"Don't be shy, it's really good." He looks at the sketch again, it's unmistakably him, sitting on the garden bench with his shirt off in much the same position as I'd found him that morning four months ago. I suppose things could be worse, he could've found one of the even more revealing ones. Hopefully I've hidden those better.

We sit down to eat and he keeps stealing glances at the sketch and at me but doesn't say anything else. It's awkward.

"I noticed you have quite a few photographs hung up on the wall, mostly exotic looking ones," he says, in between bites of food which of course he has already complimented. Polite as ever.

"Yeah, I took some time out backpacking after Dad passed..."

"I've never travelled much, beyond the obligatory beach or city breaks twice a year," he says.

"Ah well, that was then. I don't get the chance for much of that anymore."

"We could go somewhere together, if you like?" He looks at me expectantly, making me smile. God knows he does try.

"Sure, that would be great," I respond.

We continue eating our food, talking about this and that but nothing very meaningful. When we're done, we settle down on the couch again which still seems to have that distinctive scent surrounding it, reminding me of our intense acrobatics earlier.

He tells me he's been considering Windsor as a possible new home base and I am quick to support the idea. It's a charming city if you ignore the tourists, and only a short drive away. I decide to help him find potential options online, which takes up the best part of the afternoon.

"Oh my, I need a break." Peter stretches himself and leans back into the sofa.

Meanwhile I'm in a similar state, rubbing my eyes while closing the lid of the laptop.

"We've made good progress, though," I say. "With a bit of luck one of these could be your new home."

He takes my hand and pulls me close. The warmth of his arm around me has an immediate effect.

ONE NIGHT STAND

In between subtle but increasingly naughty kisses we decide he should stay the night today, and tomorrow. On Monday while I'm at work he can continue the house hunt from here rather than driving back and forth from central London.

"But no more work today, I've got a much better idea." I turn towards him, grabbing hold of the collar of the fleecy robe he's wearing.

After a hurried kiss, I get up and gently tug at his hand to follow. The bedroom will be the perfect place for an evening of lazy lovemaking and even lazier pillow talk.

Let's just see where this thing between us will go; I've decided to keep an open mind. And indeed I really do like him, a lot. Every time I look into his eyes, the feeling increases. With every kiss, it seems I am drifting away further and further out to sea and away from steady ground. But for some reason that doesn't scare me.

We started off without care for the consequences, as strangers by the side of the road. Now isn't the time to back down. I expect after Monday, the wait to see Peter again will be a lot shorter than four months, and I'm really looking forward to it.

I grip the steering so tightly my knuckles show white. *Of all times, don't you do this to me now!* Sadly the car doesn't listen to me, there is still this terrible screeching sound coming from the engine when I turn the key, but nothing further. It won't bloody start.

After the shit day I've had, with yet further positions hanging in the balance at work, the last thing I need is a big repair bill. I check my watch, quarter past six. Damn, at this rate, I'll be late as well.

Peter has been doing his best to vacate his London flat, selling off most of his stuff and storing the rest of it in my garage. A *life makeover*, he calls it. He wants to rid himself of reminders of his old life, in order to make room for the new. Tonight he's finally coming back with the last load of books or whatnot, ready to move everything into the first suitable place he's able to find in Windsor.

And now I won't even be at home to receive him when he gets there. Goddammit.

Just looking at the to-let ads with him last weekend had made me uneasy. If I didn't have Dad's old house here, I'd never be able to afford to live anywhere one third as nice as what he's considering. Of course I didn't say anything, he can decide for himself how much he's willing to spend. But some of the rents did make me wonder how long he could afford to live around here while he figures out what it is he wants to do next. Surely his resources can't be endless.

I dig around in my handbag, looking for my phone. Of course my breakdown coverage has expired, so I can't even call anyone to fix this issue right now. I'll have to leave the car here over the weekend and find another way home.

Just call a cab, Peter would say. I know he would. *Call a cab, don't worry about the cost, I'll cover it.*

Looking around the parking, I barely recognize any of the cars still left here. Most of the people I get along with have already gone home. It's only then that I see Diane, our team leader, exit the front doors of the office building. I decide to make a run for it, trying to catch her before she escapes too.

"Hey, wait up!" I shout, while trying to collect my bag, the car keys, as well as my coat, trying not to let the wind close the car door in my face.

Diane looks around for a moment as if trying to place the sound of my voice, then pauses when she notices me hurrying towards her.

"Thanks. Hey, my car won't start. Would you mind giving me a lift?" I ask, out of breath, after almost dropping half my stuff on the way from the car.

"Sure thing, but I do need to head into town for a bit first, buy some groceries." Diane checks her watch, then watches me as I try to put on my coat, my hands already shaking in the sharp November wind.

"Okay, thanks a million. I need a few things myself."

As we head into Egham town centre on foot, I send a quick message to Peter, letting him know where I am and where I've hidden the spare key. He doesn't respond, suggesting he's driving. I hope he won't end up waiting for me for too long.

***

When I walk up the gravel drive past Peter's car, my worries of how very late I am are interrupted by the abrupt opening of my own front door.

"Claudia!" Peter greets me with an enthusiastic hug, and takes the bag of groceries from me, allowing me to kick off my muddy shoes before stepping all the way inside. I don't even know why I was nervous at all, considering how pleased he looks to see me.

"Hey you!" I smile at him, thrilled to bits even though we've only spent a few days apart. Somehow every moment away from one another feels like an eternity. I take a moment to just check him out top to bottom, how different he looks in jeans compared to formal clothes.

"So, what happened?" He puts the groceries down on the side table and helps me out of my warm coat, while I start telling him about my ordeal with the car.

"It's never done this before, I don't understand," I complain.

He just looks at me for a moment, as if he knows something I don't.

"These things happen. It's an old car."

ONE NIGHT STAND

I'm about to protest when I realize that in normal people's terms, yes, fifteen years is pretty old for a beat up little hatchback. But I've always had it, and as such am mostly blind to these things.

"It just needs a little TLC. That's all."

I take off my scarf and woolly hat and enjoy the feel of the warm indoor air against my cold skin. I have always had a love-hate relationship with winter. On the one hand there's nothing prettier than a frosty sunrise, when even the tiniest blade of grass seems to shimmer in the sunlight. But it's just too damn cold for my liking, and it tends to take me ages to warm up after a day in a badly designed, insufficiently heated office.

Peter watches me as I rub my hands together and blow some warm air into them.

"Shall I light a fire?" he asks. My smile says it all.

I follow him into the living room, and try my utmost to shed the remaining tension that's deposited itself right in the pit of my stomach, after today's announcements at work. More redundancies are coming, they are going to downsize considerably within the next months.

"What's wrong?" Peter asks, as soon as he's finished with the fireplace and notices my tense expression.

"Just work stuff," I try to brush away his question.

"That doesn't sound good."

All I want is for all that stuff to go away, for the two of us to have a nice evening together, even if all I've brought as nourishment is frozen pizza. The last thing I need is to talk about work crap, so I just shrug. Luckily he backs off the work questions and just takes my hand.

"So it's all done. I've given the keys back this afternoon." Peter runs his fingers over my knuckles, making my heart surge with excitement. "Looks like we'll be seeing a lot more of each other now."

The prospect makes me smile. We've agreed that it's too early to move in together, but while he continues to look for a new place, I'm more than happy for him to stick around.

"Have you found anything promising yet?" I ask.

He nods. "A few flats, yes. The agency is sending someone this weekend for viewings. Perhaps you'd like to come along?" His intense stare burns into me, and I know he's only half thinking about flats and lettings agents. Most of his attention is firmly on me and I love it.

"Since I got back so late, all I've got for dinner is pizza… I hope you don't mind."

"Not at all." Peter takes a step forward and wraps his arms around me until I gladly surrender. "I know just the thing to build up an appetite."

"Oh yeah?" I grin just when he tries to plant a kiss on my lips, which again makes him smile.

"Sexercise. Perhaps you've heard of it?"

I let out a chuckle and pull him tighter against me.

"Sounds familiar, why don't you show me how it works?"

Before I get the chance to do anything further, he scoops me up into his arms and deposits me right on top of the sofa facing the open fire. He makes it seem effortless, even though I'm not that light. We don't get the chance to sample the frozen supermarket pizza until much later in the evening, but neither of us mind the delay.

***

"Say, would you feel weird if I had a bunch of friends over Sunday night?" I ask, while checking the various messages on my phone. Some of my school friends are going to be in the neighborhood shortly, and it would be unfortunate to miss the chance for a reunion. It would also be a great chance for me to reminisce and relive some of the good old days when life seemed a lot simpler.

"Not at all," Peter says, while finishing up an email on the laptop. "There, all done. Once they check my references, I should be getting the keys shortly."

The past week has been all about compromise and adjustment. Although the situation with Peter is only temporary, we've made great progress towards establishing a harmonious living environment. Sure, he's just a house guest, but it's impossible to keep things so casual when you're in a relationship together. The closet in my bedroom has changed from a dumping ground for all my crap, to being almost equally shared between the two of us. There are two toothbrushes in the glass by the sink, and we've even picked sides in bed.

We've also been sharing the chores, which has been quite a relief for me because I hate cleaning at the best of times. Despite all that, it's still weird having him drive me to and from work, now that my car is still in the shop. He hasn't complained even once, but sometimes the way he looks at me when I give him updates about the car repairs suggests there's something he's dying to say but holding back on.

"Great, I'll let them know. I think you'll get along very well." Although I am mostly trying to convince myself rather than him, I'm not all that certain that my crazy friends will mingle well with Peter. The problem certainly won't be at his end, he's always charming in company. No, it's my friends I worry about, they all have very distinct ideas about life and love.

He looks up and winks at me.

"These friends, any chance I'll recognize some of them?" He motions over at some of the pictures scattered around the living room.

"Actually, yes," I say, before getting up and grabbing one group shot from the mantel. "This one has everyone." I point out the various people in the shot to him; Caroline, Jean, Alice… "It was taken in Vietnam." Running my finger over the frame, I can't suppress a smile. We did have a good old time backpacking, the four of us.

Peter leans over and inspects the picture, then puts his arm around me.

"Maybe one day we'll have our own photos to add to your collection."

Yes, maybe, hopefully. Though the car is well on its way towards wiping out what little savings I had, making an exotic holiday seem completely beyond reach.

"I have an idea, how about once I get settled in my new place, we plan a little road trip? Find a nice little country inn somewhere, Kent maybe…" Peter pauses and looks over at me. "Only if you want, of course."

I realize my face must be betraying the conflict going on inside my head. Kent sounds nice, but I'm well on my way towards being desperately broke. I hate it when my savings fall below a certain level so simply the idea of going on a trip is making me panic.

"Sounds great, but I'm not sure I can afford a trip just now…" I explain. Hopefully he doesn't think I'm dissing his idea, it's just that the timing isn't brilliant.

"My treat. Don't worry about a thing."

I smile bitterly at him. He means well, but I'm not sure I want to accept the offer. Best to let the topic lie until later, so I just nod quickly and put the Vietnam photograph back where it belongs.

The rest of the evening is spent for the most part with both of us working on our own separate plans. He's looking at van rentals to move his things into the new place, while I'm planning what to serve for Sunday's get-together. It's already eleven by the time we end up in bed. Although we're too tired to make love, we never do miss the chance to fall asleep in each other's arms.

CHAPTER FOURTEEN

As foreseen, Peter's references check out and come Saturday afternoon, his phone rings. Overhearing only half the conversation suggests it's the lettings agent about collecting the keys. Peter is visibly excited while setting the meeting, but I'm suddenly overcome with a bit of melancholy.

"Would you like to come along?" he asks, after hanging up the phone.

"Sure." I smile, even though I can't shake the sadness at the prospect of him moving out again. It has been nice having someone around, especially someone as surprisingly easy going as Peter. It's been a while since I've been in a proper relationship, and although everything moved way too quickly, I felt like this thing between the two of us could actually work out.

"I promise you'll love it, you can even see the castle from one of the windows."

Ah yes, castle view. That will have pushed the rent up considerably.

"What time are you getting the keys?" I ask.

"Whenever I get there."

There's a moment of silence as I think of something appropriate to say.

"I guess it's time to start thinking about a house

warming gift then," I remark.

Peter steps forward and takes me into his arms. "Don't you have a whole shed full of potential house warming gifts already?"

He has a point. I've been painting and sketching for the better part of my life, and have collected quite a few finished pieces.

"I didn't realize you've been in the shed," I say.

He smiles mysteriously. "I had to do something to amuse myself while you were at work. And anyway, it's a shame to leave them in there unseen and unappreciated."

"You think so? I mean you would want a painting, of all things?" For a short while growing up, I had entertained the idea of following in Dad's footsteps, becoming an artist just like him, but the charm of that quickly wore off when I saw how his choices affected Mom, and caused them to drift apart. Plus, I never believed that people would actually pay to see my work.

Peter cups my face and plants a kiss on my lips.

"Why not? You're extremely talented."

I know he's just saying that because he likes me, but his compliments make me smile anyway.

"In that case, you can have any canvas you like."

He shakes his head while still staring deeply into my soul.

"You pick. That way it'll mean more," he says.

I can't wipe the smile off my face. He sure knows what to say, the smooth talker, but he does have a point. I'll see his place this afternoon, and then I'll choose a painting to give him. He'll be the first person, other than family, to hang an original *Claudia de Wit* in his house. The prospect is both exciting as well as a little nerve-wracking. I hope he likes what I'll come up with.

"Sure." I force a smile. "Let's go whenever you're ready."

He nods and puts on a coat, smiling widely at me. "Ready when you are."

I follow suit and before we know it, we're zipping along familiar roads until we reach the edge of Windsor, where traffic starts to slow us down.

"It's been a while since I've last been to Windsor," I remark.

Peter lets out a short laugh. "Don't tell me that in all the time you've lived in the area, you haven't been to the castle, though? Like how you hadn't been inside the race course before I invited you."

"Don't be ridiculous," I say with a grin. "Everyone has been to the bloody castle." *Even if it was just for a school trip.*

"Okay then." A quick look in his direction reveals that he's still grinning.

The traffic ahead starts to clear up and he pulls away, navigating through the various narrow streets like a local. He must have gotten quite familiar with the route, viewing the various flats that caught his eye online. We zigzag through the older part of town for another five minutes, before coming to a halt.

"Here we are." Peter parks neatly inside a bay marked 'residents only'. The lettings agent—clad in the obligatory blue suit, ridiculous tie and brown leather shoes—is already waiting by the main door of the apartment complex.

"Here you go, Mr. Layton," he says, while handing Peter a bunch of keys and a completed rental contract.

"Just a couple of signatures needed and I'll let you get settled in."

I keep looking around, taking mental note of the various luxury cars parked around the area, as well as the squeaky-clean, glass-clad façade of what is going to be Peter's new home. Looks posh, expensive. Best not ask how expensive.

Once the paperwork is done, the lettings agent says his goodbyes and leaves us alone.

"You first," Peter says, unlocking the main door and holding it open for me.

I step inside and am again overwhelmed by how clean and shiny everything is. It looks nothing like other apartment buildings I've been inside, visiting friends.

"Fourth floor." He presses the button and the lift doors open, guiding me inside to select the correct floor.

Once we reach it he uses another key to unlock the front door, and a vast living area opens up ahead of us. The wooden floor looks like it might actually be real, not laminate, and indeed there is a wonderful view through the large French windows leading to the small balcony outside. Perhaps it only looks huge because there's no furniture yet, I try to convince myself, but I already know I'm deceiving myself. It's massive.

Peter's new place is the exact opposite to my house, which looks dark and pokey in comparison. But I like it that way, this open bright space makes me feel exposed and vulnerable.

"Nice, so airy," I remark, while moving through the living room and into the spacious kitchen, with its granite worktop and white glossy cabinets.

"Glad you like it." Peter puts his hand on my shoulder and gently gives it a squeeze, making me feel all warm and fuzzy inside. I guess I could get to like it, in time. Then again, I'm not going to live here so it doesn't really matter what I think.

Though it's not quite what I'm used to, looking around some more at the views, including the one of the castle from the bedroom window, does inspire me. I can't wait to get home and start working on a little something to brighten up these blank, white walls. An already existing painting just won't do.

"If you wait here for a minute, I'll be right back," I say, without giving Peter much of a chance to react, leaving him with a puzzled expression on his face.

I rush out the door, down the elevator and all the way out and quickly make my way towards the small supermarket I'd noticed opposite the parking lot. Though I haven't moved in a while, my friends and I have always had a little tradition, one I'm keen to carry on with Peter now. I make the necessary purchases and rush back to his new flat, where he's already waiting in the doorway.

"Here. Now we can celebrate," I say, while handing

him the small chocolate cake and paper napkins I'd bought.

"Excellent." He accepts my rather simple offering with a wide grin, and starts opening up the box, while I take off my coat, spreading it on the floor so that we have somewhere to sit.

"Hope this place turns out to be everything you want it to be. To your new life." I hold up a chunk of cake, as though making a toast, and he does the same.

"It already is all I want it to be," Peter says, eating his bite and leaning over to give me a kiss on my lips as soon as I've finished mine. I wrap my arms around him with a giggle, and within a split second I'm on my back, and he's on top of me, kissing me deeply. Our hands are sticky, leaving little smudges of chocolate on each other's faces, but none of that bothers us. All we can focus on is our lips connecting, tongues as well as limbs entwined until we've found our release. The only time we pause our lovemaking is to feed each other further little mouthfuls of chocolate, the richness and sweetness adding to our pleasure.

Yes, visiting Peter's new flat for the first time definitely does inspire me on multiple levels.

✳✳✳

Later Saturday evening, I'm back at home, and on my own for the first time in a couple of weeks. Peter is sorting out a few things, taking the obligatory trip to one of the big do-it-yourself stores in the area, and I decide to make a start on his housewarming gift.

His place was light, the view was vast, endless, a lot of sky, a lot of space. Sitting on the paint-stained stool in the middle of my modest shed, I close my eyes and let the mental images flow. I can see waves, clouds, mysterious distant lands. Blues, purples, greens fill my mind, until I'm ready to begin.

I pick up the palette and start with broad strokes until the beginnings of shapes cover the formerly empty canvas. With every passing movement of my brush, the image builds up further, until hours later, I'm exhausted, yet fulfilled. It's been a while since I've done any painting, and I hadn't realized how much I missed it.

Creating, seeing something appear where there was nothing before, that's always been my outlet. When you get busy with life, spend most of your time with another person, it's easy to forget about what makes us tick deep inside.

The months we'd spent apart, after the first time Peter and I met, I'd whiled away many hours in here, sketching his face, his body, along with random shapes and colors that reminded me of how I'd felt when I was with him. Now that I actually had him, it seemed a lot less necessary to hide myself away in here.

But it was necessary. Painting is a part of me, always will be.

I squint and look at the painting. It's unmistakably the sea, with the suggestion of islands in the background. There are also shapes in the waves, as well as the clouds, that remind me of bodies, engaged in a passionate dance.

Someone with a different outlook could easily see something else in it, that's the whole point. Art isn't objective, its meaning changes from person to person. That's the funny thing, I could paint something with one meaning in mind, but it takes on a life of its own after it's laid down on paper or canvas.

I wipe my hands somewhat clean, although most of the stains on my hands are going to remain for at least a week, and head back into the house.

Things may have started off weird, but today has been a great success. Perhaps with Peter moving into his new place, we can find a balance between our new relationship and us as individuals.

He needs to figure out what he's going to do with his life now, and I'm going to need my alone time to paint.

CHAPTER FIFTEEN

Sunday passes in a blur. After presenting Peter with his gift over breakfast, and a quick trip to the shops for the necessary supplies, party preparations take up most of my afternoon.

It's just after six when the doorbell rings and I can see Caroline and Alice walk up past the kitchen window, straight towards the door. Shortly after, Jean follows from the rear of the car.

Shit, they're here!

"Shall I get it?" Peter asks.

I turn around, my hands still covered in meat marinade and give him a grateful nod. "If you could."

Taking a deep breath, I continue to transfer the chicken kebabs one by one from their plastic tray into the grill. Oh well, I may not be the best hostess, as demonstrated by the fact that I'm still messing about with food when my guests are at the door, but at least I've got help.

"Come in, Claudia is just in the kitchen." Peter greets everyone, their voices slightly more muffled than his.

They must be surprised to see him—or anyone other than me—answering the door upon their arrival.

Just when I'm washing my hands, all three of my friends wander into the hallway leading to the kitchen, giving me all sorts of looks when they notice me.

"Hey! How are you guys? Been a long time," I say, while doing my best to give everyone hugs without dripping water from my freshly washed hands on their backs.

"Not bad. Looks like we have some catching up to do, eh?" Alice remarks, while stealing glances in Peter's direction.

"How about something to drink?" he asks, causing everyone to once again turn and look at him. All three of them are having trouble disguising how taken aback they are. I suppose I could've taken the time to mention this recent change in my love life to them, but in the short back-and-forth setting up tonight's get-together, it just didn't come up. Plus, what was I supposed to do, send a memo? *No longer single, party will include one male guest.* That's ridiculous.

"A drink would be great, wouldn't it, Caroline?" Jean answers, while prodding her in the side with her elbow.

"Uhh, yeah. Thanks…" Caroline straightens herself and tries to stop staring.

"Peter. That's Peter. And this is Caroline, Alice and Jean," I quickly remember to introduce them.

"Nice to meet you," Alice says, holding out her hand much more coyly than generally fits her outgoing character.

"Where did Claudia find you, and do you have any single brothers?" Jean says with a wink, causing giggle fits in the other two girls. *Good Lord, here we go.*

One look in Peter's direction makes me forget my embarrassment. Of course, he's being a very good sport about it all.

"Well, it all began on a rather moist evening back in June," Peter begins, while he starts pouring wine for everyone. He tells the story in broad strokes almost as it happened, but without making it sound as stupid and irresponsible as it really was.

"Cheers," everyone erupts, as soon as the filled glasses have made it around the room. "To Claudia, finally having a social life," someone remarks.

"To all of you people for finally showing your faces around here," I butt in.

Peter remains quiet, with a hint of a smile on his face as he takes the first sip. I can't remember the last time I introduced a boyfriend to this lot. All things considered, it's going pretty well.

"Okay, so who's hungry?" I ask, and am immediately met with applause. Everyone, apparently.

The chicken kebabs will take another five minutes, but I invite them all into the kitchen to help themselves to the bread rolls, salads and various cold snacks. Once everyone has taken what they want, I serve the chicken and we head into the living room together. Conversation flows easily from then on, however Jean does spend an inordinate amount of time interrogating Peter about all sorts, mainly his job, which at the moment is non-existent.

Meanwhile, I chat to Alice about how her writing is going. Apparently she's built up quite the blog following since the last time we've met.

The more the wine flows, the more our chatter

comes back to stories of our travels when we decided to take a gap year together, before figuring out what we were going to do with our lives. Every so often, I sit back and just listen in to everyone talking, telling little anecdotes, only half of which I can actually remember, and realize how lucky I was to have such awesome friends. I certainly wouldn't have gone backpacking on my own, I was so nervous about everything back then.

As I lean back in my chair, enjoying the last couple of sips of my third glass, my eyes are drawn to Peter, who is quietly listening in to our conversations. There's a certain wistfulness in his eyes, he seems to be drinking in the story of the hotel owner in Hanoi, trying to put us up in his overpriced cockroach-infested hovel of a room, assuming we wouldn't know any better. Or the time we thought the bus conductor had run off with our luggage…

Although panic-inducing at the time, all these things did make for funny stories now, years later.

"We should do it again," Alice says, while fidgeting with a few peanuts left in the small bowl on the table in between us.

"Yeah. Definitely," I say, while still observing Peter. He's staring right at me now, I know what he's thinking. He wants the same thing. The two of us, exploring the world together. *Maybe one day.*

As soon as everyone is done eating, we leave the dining area in favor of the more comfortable living room. Squeezed together on the couches, we share newer stories, of work, horrible bosses, worse boyfriends and difficult parents. I can't help myself and tell everyone about when Peter and I had just met and Mom turned up out of the blue. Funny how what was once super-embarrassing and awkward has become hilarious in retrospect. Peter jumps in with Mom's remark about the type of guys I would bring home, much to everyone's enjoyment.

We sit around the now lit fireplace—thanks to Peter—for hours, until night threatens to turn to morning. Shortly after three we decide to call it a night, after all, everyone has work in the morning and Alice especially has quite a drive ahead of her to get home.

"Thanks for coming by, I had a lovely time," I say while giving all three of them hugs.

"Same here," Caroline says before heading out to Alice's car.

"You know, he's not bad," Alice whispers in my ear as she's about to go outside too. "At first I thought oh God, Claudia's gone and got herself a sugar daddy. But he's okay."

Glancing quickly in Peter's direction, who is helping Jean into her coat and oblivious to our little moment of gossip, I can't help smiling.

"Yeah, he's a good guy."

"I'm happy for you anyway." Alice gives me a couple of pats on my back before stepping out, and Jean follows behind her.

"Let's do this again sometime." I wave them goodbye, and lean into Peter, who puts his arm around my shoulder.

ONE NIGHT STAND

"Bye!" All three of them wave back at me and soon after, the car pulls out of the drive.

I turn towards Peter, and give him a peck on the cheek. "I'm sorry if that was awkward."

"Not at all. They're quite a lively bunch, aren't they?" He smiles at me and I let out a chuckle.

"You have no idea. The three of them could get a saint in trouble."

I decide I'm in no mood to clean up, so I leave it for another time.

"What time are you getting the van tomorrow?" I ask.

Peter shrugs. "Whenever I want. Perhaps I'll have a lie in to recover from tonight and then make up my mind," he jokes.

A good idea. Wish I didn't have to leave for work so early in the morning…

***

Ironically, last night's wish is sort of granted come Monday morning.

With tears still prickling in my eyes, I stare down at the half-crumpled letter in my pale hands. It's way too cold to be standing outside in the drizzle without a proper coat on, but I simply couldn't stand being inside the office any longer. As far as Mondays go, today has got to be the worst one ever.

"Hey, Claudia, are you okay?" Diane rushes up to me, putting her hand on my shoulder.

I know she got a letter too, but with better news than mine. For now. We're supposed to all be in the same boat, but it doesn't quite feel that way right now.

Rather than respond, I just sniffle and shrug.

"It sucks, hey. I hope they're at least paying you decently." Diane looks concerned, but I feel like her sympathy is mainly superficial. She'll be relieved that she's safe at the moment. I can't blame her, that was how I felt when I was spared during the last round of cost cutting.

"I just don't know what I'm going to do now, you know? I suck at interviews," I complain.

She pats me on the back and gives me a wry smile. "It'll work out. At least you've got that man of yours to support you while you're looking."

Though I know she's just trying to make me feel better, her remark rubs me the wrong way.

"It's not like that, Diane," I grumble, wiping the remnants of tears away from the corner of my eye.

"Fine. I just meant at least you're not all on your own, you know?"

I shrug and decide to leave the topic before I say something I'll regret. Being told by the powers that be that my services are no longer required has really affected me. I'd underestimated how shit it would feel to no longer be needed.

Just when I turn away from Diane and start walking towards my regular spot, I realize that of course, the stupid car is still not fixed so I can't even go home on my own. Hopefully Peter is around and not yet in the middle of moving his things out of my garage.

With shaking fingers, I fish my phone out of my jeans pocket and dial his number. He answers almost immediately.

"Hi. Yeah, I'm really sorry to disturb, but could you come get me?" My voice trembles uncontrollably, and as soon as he says he's coming and cuts the phone, I'm crying again.

What a fucking mess.

I decide to hurry back inside to grab my coat which I'd left behind in my rush earlier, all the while doing my best not to look anyone in the eye. *With immediate effect,* they said. *Your services are no longer required with immediate effect.*

How worthless am I that they don't even need me to finish up my work, or do anything else? They've just discarded me in a meeting lasting about fifteen minutes. Bastards.

By the time I make my way back outside to wait for Peter, my anger and hurt has been largely replaced by detachment.

I don't even know how long I loiter around in the cold car until Peter arrives, but it must be quite a while because my fingernails have started turning purplish.

"Are you alright?" His voice makes an attempt at soothing me when he opens the passenger door for me, but I'm entirely too cold to warm up to him straight away.

"I'll survive," I snap as I sit down and shut the door.

"It doesn't take a genius to guess what's happened."

I shrug. It still hurts.

"Claudia," Peter says, resting his hand on my shoulder. "Look at me."

Despite not really wanting to, preferring to keep staring at my feet, I do finally turn my head to look in his direction. Almost immediately, the waterworks are back on and I start blubbering like crazy.

"With immediate effect. Can you believe that?" I cry.

He guides me into his arms, awkwardly, with the gear shift blocking the space between our seats. I rest my face on his shoulder and continue to complain. About the meeting, the HR woman who seemed to enjoy the whole thing, and mostly about how they couldn't wait to get me out of there.

"This is does not reflect on you, your abilities. You know that, right? These things aren't to be taken personally. It's all numbers. Profit and loss."

I want to believe his words, but my heart can't accept it right now, so the tears just keep on coming.

"But I've got to pay the car bill, and there's a leak in the roof, and…" I'm so overwhelmed, the words escape me. How am I going to manage?

I had wanted to save more, to be more organized, but something always happened that needed immediate attention. And it's not like my salary was all that much to begin with. But it was better than nothing at all.

"I'll understand if you don't want to share, but what package did they offer you?" he asks.

I shrug again, during the meeting they'd explained it all, but everything had just gone in one ear and come out the other. I remember it must be in the letter, so I hand him the moist sheet of paper I've been clutching ever since coming out of the meeting.

He takes a moment to read through it, then gives it back to me.

"It's more than what they had to pay by law, that's decent of them. The way they've gone about it though..." Peter closes his other arm around me and kisses my hair. "They had no right to spring this on you without warning. Without giving you the chance to get used to the idea. You may have a case to sue them for not following proper procedure, if you want."

I shake my head, not suing anybody. It's best to just forget about it.

With his arms still around me, I close my eyes and try to focus on his touch, his soothing voice, but my throat feels like it's closing up and my chest is ready to explode. I don't know what I'm going to do now. While I've certainly made my fair share of mistakes in the past, I've always worked, never been in debt. I don't even know how one applies for benefits or what I'd be entitled to. What if I can't find another job soon enough and can't afford the upkeep on my house—Dad's house?

Frozen in place, with all these fears swirling in my mind, I don't know how much time passes. Neither am I in any state to keep track of where we are or where we're going. When Peter's car finally comes to a halt outside my house, I'm still in a state of shock.

"Let's get you inside," he says, but I don't move,

until he walks around the car and opens the door for me, gesturing at me to get up. I follow him inside, largely on auto-pilot.

CHAPTER SIXTEEN

For the best part of Tuesday, I've been moping around the house with no real clue of what to do. I'd sat down with the laptop for a while, trying to update my CV, but just looking at it made me want to pull my hair out so I gave up. Looking at the Job Centre website didn't help any either.

I know I should do better, to get on track and start looking for a job as soon as possible, but somehow, everything still feels too raw, too painful. Part of me can't believe that this has actually happened to me.

"Any luck?" Peter asks, when he sees that I've put the laptop away again.

"Meh." I know I am being a complete bore, and terrible company, but I'm not ready to get out of my funk yet.

He's being a pretty good sport, holding off on his move in order to spend time with me while I'm down. And in return, I'm making things as difficult as I possibly can.

"You remember what you told me when we first met?" Peter sits down next to me and takes my hand. Despite this dark cloud hanging over my head, I still feel a hint of butterflies in my stomach at his touch.

"What's that?"

"That finding out about Stephanie and Chris was in a

way a second chance. The same is the case for you now. A second chance to find out what you want to do in life."

The way he's caressing my hand is making me weak, as is the genuine look of concern on his face. I know I can be frustrating to be around, and when I get in a mood it's extremely hard for me to get back to normal, so I'm trying my best to let his words sink in.

"I guess so."

"Think about it. When you were little, did you dream of working in a call centre? Probably not. What *did* you want to do?"

I shrug. I know what I wanted to do, for as long as I can remember, but there's no way that will turn out well. Just look how Dad ended up.

"Paint, I guess."

"So paint. The money they gave you is tax free, the whole point is that you use it to cover costs while you figure out your next move."

"Yeah, but why take risks with it, when I already know I'll need a job by the end of it all anyway?"

"Says who? I've seen your work, that seascape you gave me for my new place is nothing short of a masterpiece."

Although I should feel flattered, hearing such big words thrown around for something I cobbled together in a few hours grates me the wrong way. He's bullshitting me. I take my hand out from under his grasp and fold my arms.

"Show me one guidance counselor who will advise

someone to pursue painting as a career. One. One responsible parent, who thinks their child should play with acrylics and oil all day, instead of study something sensible like accounting." I'm trying hard not to let my annoyance shine through in my tone, but I'm failing miserably. My heart is hammering in my throat and I can't help but go on the defensive. He's delusional if he thinks becoming an artist is a good career choice. Where else did the term 'starving artist' originate from, if not the cold, hard reality? Even if you don't end up broke, you'll end up alone.

"All I'm saying is, there's no harm in trying it out. I could pick up the phone right now and get you a few sales immediately, based on just that painting you gave me. You could exhibit, or even do commissioned work."

I shake my head, what does it prove that he knows people with more money than sense who would buy some unknown person's paintings, just on his say-so? Nothing. It proves absolutely nothing.

"Fine. Let's not argue."

"Think about it."

Despite still being grumpy about the turn our conversation has taken, I decide to keep quiet and let him have the last word. Just at that moment, my phone rings and I jump up to get it.

"Hello?"

"Hi, Bob here. About your car," the voice on the other end says. The chat that follows does absolutely nothing to improve my mood. After waiting for some part for over a week, they've now figured out that it doesn't actually fix the problem. They're going to have to open up the engine.

"I don't think it's cost-effective, to be honest," Bob finally says. "You'd be better off looking at something newer."

"Alright." I take a deep breath in an attempt to get my frustration under control. "I'll think about it and call you back later."

"Not a problem. Have a good weekend." The line goes dead and yet I'm still standing there, clutching the phone. It never rains but it pours.

"What's wrong?" Peter asks.

"Apparently the work is going to cost a lot more than expected. More than the car is worth."

I feel defeated and sink back into the sofa, covering my face with my hands. *Great.* I guess it's time to start looking at classified ads for a new car. There goes most of my redundancy payment.

"Tell you what, why don't we go for a drive?" Peter suggests.

I shrug. Why not? Staying here sure isn't going to improve matters.

"Where to?"

"Does it matter, no matter where you go, it's nice around here. And it looks like the rain has stopped too."

He makes an excellent point.

***

ONE NIGHT STAND

I stare blankly out of the passenger window, watching the shrubs, trees and fields zip past while Peter navigates around the quaint country lanes. Everything is glistening in the hazy sunlight that is trying to break through the clouds. Usually, drives make me happy, because there's always something to see. City life has never appealed to me, too much concrete tends to make me feel claustrophobic.

Today though, even the rich colors of autumn do nothing to inspire me or cheer me up. We continue on in silence, until I notice we're leaving the scenic countryside and entering a town. I'm about to ask where we're going, when Peter pulls up outside a big, sprawling used car dealership.

Oh God, he's not actually doing this now?

"Just go with it," he says, noticing my horrified expression.

"U-huh."

He gets out, then walks around and opens the door for me like the gentleman he is, and guides me towards the main entrance of the showroom. The large parking area is full of cars of varying sizes, colors and brands.

"Don't you think I should do some research first?" I whisper, while pulling at his arm to convince him to turn back before the slick salesman notices us.

"Why? Anything you need to know is right here." Peter pats his pocket where he keeps his smart phone.

I take a look around at the small cars parked towards the left of the lot, and quickly notice they haven't got anything over five years old. Great. Not only am I completely unprepared, I'm also in no position to even consider any of these cars.

"How can I help you?" The salesman rushes up to us, and shakes Peter's hand.

"We're looking for a hatchback, low miles, good fuel efficiency. Rest is up to her."

"Very good, sir. How about this Ford Fiesta?" We are led up to a lime green car parked right outside the office. Seeing the price tag makes me want to turn and run immediately.

"That looks quite nice, doesn't it, Claudia? It's practically new." Peter leans over to read the information card on the windscreen more carefully, while I try to tug him in the opposite direction.

All I can do is shake my head.

"Can we have a moment, please?" I ask the sales guy, who holds up his hands in sort of a defeated gesture and nods.

As soon as he's out of earshot, I turn to Peter. "You've seen how much they paid me. I can't afford any of these cars!"

"You don't have to. Let me help out."

His answer is exactly what I was afraid of. This is not fucking happening.

"I'm not letting you buy it for me!"

"And why not?"

"Because…" My breath has started going ragged, despite the drive to get there, and all my attempts to get my negativity under control, I'm pissed off all over again. "It feels icky."

ONE NIGHT STAND

"Me doing something nice for you, so you can focus on whatever it is you want to do—whether that's painting or finding a new job—without worrying about maintaining an unreliable, not to mention unsafe old car, feels *icky?*"

Part of me realizes how stupid that sounds, but it's the honest truth. The thought of having Peter spend thousands of pounds on a car for me does feel wrong. I can't accept it. I wouldn't know how to ever repay him, except actually returning the money. The niggle is, I would not spend so much on a vehicle. He's forcing me into something I would never do myself even if I did have enough money in the bank.

"At least you could have asked me before just bringing me here. I just found out about the bloody car an hour ago!"

"It wasn't exactly pre-planned. While driving around, I kept thinking about how to cheer you up and thought maybe solving at least one of your problems might do the job."

"Well, it's not working." I fold my arms and glare at him. The fact that he still looks amused, as though I'm the unreasonable one, is making my annoyance turn to anger.

"At least you won't have to worry about transport."

"Instead I'd be worrying about you spending all that money on me. Seriously. Buying me an expensive outfit was pushing it, but a car crosses way too many boundaries. I'm just not comfortable with this. You throwing money around is not going to cheer me up."

And especially not while he also doesn't have a job either. It's not just irresponsible, it's plain stupid.

"Fine." Peter takes a deep breath and holds up his hands in defeat. "I just wanted to help. Forget about it then."

Although I'm still trembling with all sorts of emotions, I do my best to swallow it all. He was just trying to help, I can see that. It's just so frustrating that with him, *helping out* quickly turns into trying to push me into seeing things his way. I need a new car, that much is certain, but I can't buy it like this.

"Fine." I ignore the salesman who is eyeing us curiously from across the lot as we return to Peter's car.

"Can I at least take you out for dinner tonight, to make up for all this?" Peter asks, while pulling out of the parking lot and joining the main road.

"Sure. That would be nice," I say, but my tone doesn't reflect my words.

We drive around aimlessly for a little while longer, before making a quick stop at his new place. Always the efficient one, he somehow managed to get some of his post forwarded already so there are a few letters for him to pick up. Rather than head to my place, we go for a short walk around Windsor town centre, which despite the chill in the air is busy as ever.

Now that office hours are over, the town is full of tourists and locals alike, most of whom are congregating around the castle. Looking at the imposing facade which towers over the little shops next to it, I can't blame them. It looks magnificent against the dramatic cloud cover behind it.

Sensing the change in my demeanor, Peter takes my hand as we stand there, opposite the massive stone structure, just staring at it.

"Beautiful, isn't it. So much history in those walls," I remark.

He nods, then pulls me closer against him with his arm around me.

"I'm sorry about earlier, Claudia. I should've known to ask you first."

"That's okay. I'm sorry for overreacting." I tiptoe slightly and give him a peck on the cheek. "Ever since yesterday, I just don't have my head on straight."

"What do you say, we have a pint at The King and Castle, then think about dinner. I know a great little Italian just a short walk from here," he suggests.

I shoot him a smile, keen to shake off the negativity from before. "That sounds great."

CHAPTER SEVENTEEN

The next day, I wake up bright and early despite having nowhere to go and nothing to do. No job, and still no prospects. Peter is already up by the looks of it so I put on a warm robe and head to the kitchen, seeing what he's up to.

As usual, he's made a pot of tea and is settled on the couch with the paper.

"Morning." He looks up and smiles at me as I enter. "Tea?"

"Yes please." I plop down next to him and watch as he pours it for me in the extra mug he's already put out. I'm going to miss this when he moves into his new place.

I lift the cup to my lips, about to take the first sip when I notice a pad with some notes on the table.

"Working on something?" I ask.

Peter shrugs, and smiles mysteriously. "Just a few ideas. For my *new and exciting life.*"

"I see." I settle back into the cushions, waiting for further clarifications, but he keeps quiet. Perhaps he's not ready to share his conclusions yet.

"What did you have planned for today?" he asks finally, after scribbling down one last thought and putting the pad into his laptop bag.

"Nothing. I don't know." Even though I've had time

to let my new circumstances sink in a little bit, as well as a good night's rest, it still hurts. I'm not ready to start the job hunt yet, the thought makes my stomach turn.

"Well, it's no use to sit around wallowing in self-pity all day. How about we go do something. A walk, maybe? It's unseasonably warm today."

I know he's right. Despite the rocky start we got off to yesterday, it was nice to get out of the house.

"Walk where?" I ask, adding up the local options in my head. It's too late in the year to visit gardens, but there are plenty of parks to choose from.

"What's nearest?"

"Virginia Water? The parking is practically opposite where we first met."

"Brilliant. I'll be ready when you are."

Within half an hour, I'm showered and dressed for the occasion in sturdy leather boots and warm clothes. It may be a sunny day and warm for the time of year, but it's still November. Peter is indeed ready as well, though his attire is a lot less cautious.

"You sure you're not going to get cold?" I ask, pointing at the light jacket he plans on carrying.

"I was thinking we could go for a little jog, in which case no, this should be more than sufficient."

A jog. That prospect makes our little outing a lot less exciting, but I don't argue. If that's what he wants, I'll give it a go. I guess jogging is how he stays in shape, and I certainly can't argue with the end result of all that hard work. My gentle curves do not require that kind of maintenance.

The drive is predictably short, and the parking lot is empty, as one would expect from a weekday in late autumn. Soon after we park up, Peter starts stretching his arms and legs, preparing for that jog, and I just clumsily stand around watching him.

"Let's start slow, so you can keep up," he suggests.

I shrug. "I guess. Let's see how it goes."

My non-committal response makes him smile. I'm sure he won't have much to smile about once he realizes that I'm about as fit as a sloth. Jogging is so not my thing.

We start at a very slow pace up the pathway leading away from the parking and towards the lake shore. It's quiet, almost desolately empty, allowing me to really take in the understated beauty of the place. I love Virginia Water because it looks deceptively natural despite being man-made centuries ago.

While I'm distracted looking at the reflections of the turned leaves in the calm waters of the lake, I slow, while Peter keeps up the same pace as before, the gap between us widening with every step.

I try to catch up, but am held back by my ever intensifying breaths. *Ugh, I hate jogging.* Why can't we just go for a walk, so at least we have the opportunity to look at the place without risking falling over our own feet.

"Wait up," I say, waving at him when he finally looks back at where I am.

I run up to him and lean with both hands on my knees.

"This is a lovely place, I'm glad you suggested it," Peter says.

"Yeah…" I gasp for air a few times, unable to finish my sentence.

"How about we walk slowly for a bit, and then continue?" he suggests.

I want to suggest that we just walk throughout, but keep quiet, opting instead to conserve my breath.

After a few minutes, he asks if I'm ready and I nod, ignoring my better judgment. We start off again, and I make it about three hundred yards, before I'm totally shattered. Peter has barely broken a sweat.

"Go on without me!" I exclaim dramatically.

"No way, what's the fun in that?"

"Really. I'll only slow you down." I shake out my cramped limbs and open up my warm coat, which is making me feel like I'm suffocating.

"Just a little more, we've hardly covered any distance yet!"

I look back at the path we've just come off, noting that the turn off to the parking has long since disappeared in the distance. It looks bloody far away enough for me!

"That's like half a mile right there!" I protest.

"So?"

"Enough jogging, honestly. Let's just walk, what do you say?"

"You give up too easily," Peter says, playfully patting me on my arm.

What is meant as encouragement only pisses me off

though.

"Just like with my painting, huh?" I remark, yesterday's arguments still ringing in my ears.

"Right." He pauses, scrutinizing me for a moment. "If you don't push past your comfort zone, you'll stagnate."

"What if I'm content? If it's not broken, don't fix it?" My face is burning up, partially from the jogging just now, but mainly because I'm angry again.

"You don't look content." Peter's face has tensed up too. This isn't just about jogging anymore.

"That's because I hate jogging. I only agreed to it to do you a favor, but I fucking hate it."

"Whatever. If you want to walk, let's walk." He turns away from me, heading further up the path around the lake.

"No. Let's have it out here once and for all." I put my hands on my hips and wait. "Best we sort this out now."

"Fine. What is it you want to say?" he asks, pausing again with his head turned back my way.

"You tell me? You're the one who seems to disapprove of everything I do, from my career choices to what kind of car I want to drive."

"You have so much potential, so much talent. Instead you'd much rather waste away in a job you hate because it feels safe. Well, it wasn't. They threw you out. And still you want to keep your head in the sand and go right back and replace it with another dead end job."

His words hurt. They did throw me out, like I'm

worthless. Way to go rubbing that in.

"It's a job. You go there to earn money, that's the only use it has. Life isn't all unicorns and rainbows, you know!"

"Believe me, I know. And I've seen more of it than you have."

Great, now he deals the age card. *I know better because I'm older than you.* How fucking original.

"You don't seem to act like it. You've gone and quit a well-paying job in order to *'figure out what you want to do with your life'.*Puh-lease! You know what that sort of thing is called in the real world? A midlife crisis!"

Although he had sort of kept his composure so far, my last remark sends him over the edge too.

"Oh yeah? I've paid my dues, made my fair share of mistakes; fifteen years' worth. But rather than listening to my advice, you're stubbornly on your way to doing the same thing. Take it from me, you waste the opportunities you have when you're still young, while you don't yet have anyone depending on you, you will regret it eventually!"

"At least I will be responsible for doing something I regret, rather than jumping head first into a stupid fantasy on somebody else's say-so!"

We're both breathing heavily from our shouting match, and still glaring at one another.

"I don't think this is going to work. Best I go home," I say through gritted teeth, and look back where we had just come from.

"If that's what you want."

"Yeah, it's what I want. You go and jog all you want, I'll walk."

"Right. Your choice." He turns as well but doesn't move.

Still fuming, I don't see a way out except through. There is no backing down now. This isn't working for me. *We* are not going to work. After walking a few steps, I pause and look back once.

"Move out your stuff as soon as possible. I'm going to need the space."

For a split second, our eyes meet, and I think I see surprise in his expression. Whatever. I'm done with being told what to do and how to think. It's been nice believing in our little romance, but I'm not ready to jump down his crazy rabbit holes with him.

I want a stable new job, a sensible new-to-me car, and a predictable, organized life. My days of impulsively leaving the real world behind to go off on some adventure are over. If he can't understand that then it's his loss.

I march back towards the car, out of the parking lot and down the main road that leads to my house. It takes me twenty minutes at the determined pace I'm going at, by the end of which I'm again out of breath and feeling more lost than I had been before.

Had I really meant it? Yes. We're too different, too set on our different paths.

With shaking fingers, I turn on the kettle and deposit a teabag in my mug. No need to make a pot full, not if it's just me drinking it. As the water starts to boil, silent tears start to run down my cheeks.

In the heat of the moment, I'd finally snapped and let my doubts run rampant. That whole debacle at the racecourse should have taught me something. I should have known then that it wouldn't work. One the one hand he seems to think money can buy happiness, on the other hand he recklessly wants to spend it until there is none left.

Just liking someone isn't enough. Compatibility in the bedroom means nothing outside of it. Not when you're going in opposite directions.

Peter reaches my place about an hour after me, letting himself in with the key I'd given him. I'd just finished packing his things into a large overnight bag five minutes earlier. My house is once more my own.

"Can we talk?" he calls out, knocking on my bedroom where I've hidden myself away as soon as I heard the car enter the drive.

"What's the point?" I sigh, turning over and pressing my tear-stained faced into the other pillow on my bed. It has his scent in it, causing a fresh lump in my throat. Lurking around in here while he leaves is no way to end things, I know that. It would be hypocritical to accuse him of being immature and then refuse to face him in the end. And so I fight all my instincts and get out of bed, drying my face and smoothing my hair down until I feel halfway presentable.

He's waiting right outside when I open the bedroom door.

"Are you sure this is what you want?" he asks, his

face hard and eyes stone cold.

I nod, while biting my lip, glancing at the floor. It's what's right. What's best for both of us.

"I can't change on a dime, neither should you. I hope you find what you're looking for." My words sound forced, that's how much effort it takes for me to speak quietly rather than scream out, releasing all the heartache I feel.

"Your keys." He hands me the spare bunch, his fingers brushing past my palm, making me flinch. My heart is telling me to ask him to stay, but I don't give in.

Although I fear the look in his eyes, I force myself to look into them one last time.

"Goodbye, Peter."

He nods and turns on his heel. "I'll empty the shed tomorrow. Unless you change your mind."

Somehow, I don't think I will.

CHAPTER EIGHTEEN

Every day I wake up, and for a moment I expect that the bed next to me will still be slightly warm, but it's not. It's cold. The pillow is unused. There is no pot of tea waiting for me in the living room. All I have to look forward to is an empty house and the occasional phone call from Mom, or Alice, calling to check how I am.

I've lost track of the amount of tears I've shed, before reaching the kind of blank emptiness I find myself in now. The pain has dulled, though it hasn't gone away. I miss him, desperately so.

When Peter packed up all his things last week I felt like it was goodbye forever. I would never see him again. Every day I'm fighting the urge to phone him, to ask him to come back. So far I haven't caved.

It's for the best. We're not compatible. Mom was right, I do have a strange talent for dating irresponsible men. Peter was supposed to be different, more mature. As it turns out, looks deceive. He was just like all the others: impulsive, irrational and reckless with his finances. And rather than listen to reason, he wanted me to jump into the deep end with him.

It would have never worked out. He wanted to go off and travel the world, while I try to make it as an artist. In the real world that's just not feasible.

People need jobs to pay bills. Jobs that have nothing

to do with what we dreamed of doing when we were kids. Real jobs aren't fun, they're so dull nobody would ever do them if it wasn't for the pay check. Anyone who thinks otherwise is deluding themselves.

Over the past few days, I'd worked out the bare minimum I would need a month for my daily expenses, I've also calculated I can afford to spend about a grand on a new car if I want to keep a three-month buffer. It's time I took my job hunt more seriously. Three months of living on savings is not a safety net, it's panic-inducing.

Once out of bed, I reluctantly go into the kitchen. So empty. While I haven't sorted out my car troubles, I'll need to have groceries delivered. Even the one pound ninety-nine they charge for delivery hurts, so I've been putting off my first order. My cupboards and fridge are getting empty pretty fast, while I do my best and eat my way through forgotten cans of soup and other random pantry staples everyone inevitably collects over the years.

I'll order groceries when I've exhausted all other options, I tell myself while pouring boiling water over a teabag containing some strange herbal concoction I found in the back of a cupboard when my normal tea had finished. Luckily it doesn't require milk, because I'm out of that too.

At least twenty applications today. That's my goal. Then I'll head into the shed and finish my latest work-in-progress as a reward. It's amazing how productive I've been these last few days, despite everything.

ONE NIGHT STAND

Just when I've finished my first cup and am debating whether I can face the laptop without a second one, I hear the post drop through the front door. More bills, no doubt… Might as well check that first before starting on my first of many applications.

The collection of envelopes on my welcome mat looks mostly predictable. Brown envelope: Council Tax, white envelope with bar code: credit card bill. However, underneath it all there is one which doesn't look familiar at all. Thick, expensive-looking paper with a gold logo on top which I do not recognize. *Galleria Eclectica* written in an ornate font. My first thought is that it must be an ad for something, though unusually it's addressed rather formally to me; *Ms. De Wit*, no first name.

I open it and start reading.

Dear Ms. De Wit,

We are excited to announce the grand opening of our new venue in Windsor on Saturday, the 10th of December, 3 pm onwards; address below. You are cordially invited to attend, though we hope for more involvement from your side.

As you may imagine, a lot of planning has gone into the launch of a brand new art gallery, including booking an impressive line-up of artists for our first showcase, 'Visions of Berkshire'. Unfortunately due to unforeseen events, we still find ourselves with a few open spots. Having had the pleasure of inspecting one of your works in person, as well as seeing photographs of your portfolio, we feel that you would be a perfect fit for our event.

The exhibition is a showcase as well as a sales opportunity for up and coming artists in the Windsor region, and we are confident it will be a great opportunity for your work to gain more exposure. We hope that you will consider this chance—despite the short notice—and get in touch by the 1st of December with a shortlist of five possible exhibits (large canvases, spec enclosed), if you wish to participate.

Our terms are very attractive—20% commission for any sales inspired by our event—no hidden charges and complimentary appraisal service.

Yours faithfully,
Lauren Clackton
Proprietor Galleria Eclectica

What the hell? This Lauren person has seen my work in person as well as some photographs? But I haven't displayed it anywhere, nor have I ever catalogued my old paintings… *Peter!* He said he'd taken a look inside my studio-cum-shed. It's the only explanation. Plus he's the only person who actually has one of my paintings, Mom excluded.

I'm not sure whether to feel flattered, or as if my privacy has been invaded. Still conflicted, I fold the letter and pop it back in its envelope. How do I even know this is a respectable gallery? And their terms… twenty per cent does sound reasonable, but how do I know whether that's attractive without knowing the market rates?

And then there's the matter of whether I *want* a bunch of random strangers to critique my paintings over bubbly and finger food?

Forget it, I don't have time for this nonsense. I throw the letter back on the pile of bills on the side table in the hall and settle down with the laptop, fully committed to not letting anything drag me off task. I have jobs to apply for, which will make me actual money. Letters promising me eighty per cent of some fictional amount in case someone, somewhere likes something I painted are just not going to do the trick.

Scrolling through ad after ad, from telesales to phone surveys, I can almost feel my will to live escape me. These are all easy jobs, things I'm more than qualified for, but every single one of them already has fifty or so applicants fighting over it, making it seem like I'll never be able to compete.

Still, I soldier on and manage ten applications with custom-written cover notes by lunchtime. That's when the doorbell rings.

I get up, rubbing my aching shoulders on the way to check who it could be, only to be greeted by Mom's face, peeking in through the little window in the front door.

"Hey, darling, how are you doing?" she exclaims when I open up. "I thought I'd check in on you…"

She gives me a warm hug and invites herself in.

"Hi, Mom."

"Wow, it's cold outside. Let's make a cup of coffee, what do you say?" She seems to talk mainly to herself while unraveling herself from layers of warm clothes, mufflers, even earmuffs. As usual for this season, Mom is dressed to survive an Arctic storm, rather than the mildly wintery temperatures we're seeing today.

"I'm out of coffee," I remark, as she piles the discarded garments into my arms.

"A cup of coffee is just what I need right now. Wait, what?"

I give her an apologetic look which does nothing to soothe her disappointment.

"Herbal tea?" I suggest.

"Claudia! That's no way to greet your mother. No coffee, at all?"

She shakes her head as she opens my kitchen cupboards, rifling through their sparse contents.

"Really, it's a good thing I came by, you seem to be starving yourself."

"Just haven't had the chance to shop while I don't have a car…" I try to justify myself, though I know she's right. I should have ordered food by now. One can only eat so many lunches and dinners consisting of random cans of oxtail soup.

"Anyway, this won't do. Let's go out, my treat." One by one, she picks up her warm clothes and puts them back on. "Go on, get dressed! We're going out for lunch."

I look down at my shabby old pajama pants and paint-splattered fluffy slippers. Ugh.

"I don't really feel like—"

"Nonsense! Look at you, you're turning into a recluse all by yourself!"

Funny, I've been by myself long enough but she's never had this complaint before. I swallow my protests and head into the bedroom to find something to wear. Laundry is also well overdue so my choices are severely limited. Finally I settle on a Fair Isle pattern knitted sweater and some jeans, the only ones that are still somewhat clean.

"Come on, let's go," she commands, while clapping her hands as if I'm ten years old, attempting to herd me out the door and into her car. I grudgingly do as she says.

On the way out, she pauses a few steps behind me.

"Claudia, what's this?" I turn to find her waving the envelope with the gold lettering at me. Damn, I'd totally forgotten about that.

"Nothing. Just some bullshit letter."

"No really, what is it? The logo looks familiar." She opens it and peeks inside, before fishing the letter out with her carefully manicured fingers.

"Don't," I sigh, knowing it's impossible to discourage her when she's set her mind on something. She wants to know what it is, and she's hell-bent on finding out.

"This…" She points at the paper, her eyes flitting back and forth as she's reading through more of it. "This is wonderful, Claudia! Congratulations!"

"I suppose."

"You *are* going to do it, right? It would be wonderful

for your work to be seen by more people."

"I hadn't quite thought about it." As soon as I finish my sentence, Mom gives me a disapproving look.

"Whatever. We're going for lunch now and you can tell me all about it on the way."

After more initial prodding and probing, I finally tell her the whole story. About the painting I'd given Peter, and my educated guess that he's behind all this. By the time I finish, we've reached the restaurant and are stationary in the parking lot.

"Remind me why you two broke up?" she asks after listening to everything.

"Because he's just like all the others. Irresponsible. It couldn't have worked out, we're way too different."

"Oh, Claudia." She reaches over and squeezes my hand while giving me a wry smile. "Sometimes different is just what you need."

"I disagree." I fold my arms and stare straight out the windscreen at the white wall surrounding the parking lot. "Plus, isn't this exactly the thing that drove you and Dad apart? Him living in his dream world, fantasizing about breaking out as an artist, and you stuck in reality trying to make ends meet?"

"Darling, there's nothing wrong with dreaming."

"But, Dad…"

"Your dad knew what he wanted, I must give him credit for that. The issue wasn't with his career choice, it was that he was so absorbed by his work that there was no space for *my* dreams, my goals in our marriage."

I consider her words for a moment, trying to apply

them to my own situation.

"What are you trying to say?" I ask.

"This man, Peter, he was trying to support *you*. Help you achieve *your* goals. That's a rare quality in men. Most of them only have eyes for what they want to achieve themselves."

"But what about money? What if I'm not good enough?"

Tears are prickling in my eyes now, after days of trying to swallow my hurt.

"Only one way of finding out. You can always look for a job later, can't you?"

"I made a mistake, haven't I?" I whisper.

She puts her arm around my shoulder, letting me rest my head against her.

"Only you can decide that. All I'm saying is, you could do a lot worse than having a man who would go this far to help you reach your goals."

"So you think I should exhibit at that gallery opening thing?"

"Opportunities like that don't come along every day."

"I don't know they're even legit," I argue.

"They've been in the paper, apparently it's quite a prestigious thing and that Clackton woman used to curate at the Tate Modern." She gives me a pat on my shoulder, before opening her door. "Let's go now, I really need a coffee before lunch."

No wonder she was so excited about the letter. The Tate Modern, wow. This new bit of information has the potential to change everything. Could it be that Peter's comments about my paintings were more than just flattery? Could his remarks have been more educated and sensible than I'd given him credit for?

Throughout lunch, I try to make sense of all she's said, and whatever my heart is trying to tell me. I *have* made a massive mistake. I just hope it's not too late to set things right.

CHAPTER NINETEEN

After having lunch, Mom insists we buy groceries as well and so she drops me off back home with enough food to feed an army. While I wave her goodbye, I keep eyeing the letter on the side table in the hall.

I'd never really thought about exhibiting my work, I've always lacked the confidence. Could I have been selling myself short like Peter said?

Peter… Clearly he must have set this up before our big fight, so would it be rude to accept the offer anyway? Mom didn't seem to think so, but then she probably thinks I still have a chance to make things right with him.

I'm not so sure now, I've said some pretty mean things and done a brilliant job of convincing myself I'd made the right call. Now, a week later, what if he's moved on? *Only one way to find out,* as Mom said.

Staring at his picture on my phone, I hover over his number. I should call him. Apologize. Talk things through.

Or should I call that gallery place first to set up a meeting? They wanted five large paintings, I have maybe three or four which I'm proud of, the rest are too old, too small, too crappy… No, I shouldn't meet with them until I'm prepared.

I hit dial before my better sense prevails and wait

with bated breath for the dial tone. It rings, once, twice, then clicks and I forget to breathe when I hear his voice.

"Hello?"

My heart is hammering in my throat, and I don't know what to say. He must hate me, he absolutely must.

"Claudia?"

Shit, shit, shit!

"Hi," my voice trembles. "I'm so very sorry." Before I can catch myself, tears start to flow and I'm sobbing on the phone. It occurs to me I'm embarrassing myself, but I don't care.

"Calm down, what happened?" Peter says. So calm, so warm. Like he genuinely cares.

"Nothing! Nothing happened. I'm an idiot, I made a mistake and I'm so sorry," I cry.

"Let's talk in person, what do you say? I can be at your place in fifteen minutes."

I nod, forgetting he can't see me, then swallow hard, so at least I can get a proper response out.

"Okay. Thanks."

He hangs up, and I'm left holding the phone, wondering if I am actually losing my mind and imagining everything that just happened. Surely, after I've been so horrible to him, essentially kicking him out of my house, he didn't just agree to come over at the drop of a hat, just because I called? That makes no sense at all.

Minute after minute passes while I continue try to work it out in my head. What am I going to say when he gets here? And the place looks like a war zone, I should probably clean up. Just when I get up to put the groceries away, his car pulls up outside and I leave everything exactly where it is to open the door.

"Hi!" I wipe my face with the back of my hand, and shuffle back and forth from one leg to the other while he walks up.

"Hi." He looks into my eyes, making my knees tremble uncontrollably.

His expression is calm, like he's unaffected at all by the turmoil I'm feeling.

"I wanted to say…" I stammer, then realize we're still standing in the doorway, so I step aside to let him in.

"Yes?"

"I wanted to apologize for being so horrible to you. I'll understand if you don't forgive me, but I had to say sorry." I blink a few times, trying to ward off further tears, but my eyes well up again anyway.

"I must say, it was rather unexpected."

I avert my gaze, staring at my feet. Mismatched socks? Really? Oh my God, this is getting worse and worse.

"Love what you've done with the place," Peter remarks dryly, as he walks through to the living room. There are papers, sketches, half-finished drawings and random magazine clippings everywhere. I really should have thought this through and tidied up.

"I guess despite all my protests, I've done what you said. Painted."

He turns to face me, the beginnings of a smile on his

face.

"And?"

"I got that letter this morning."

"Ah yes, the letter. Of course." He picks up the nearest sketch from the coffee table and sits down on the couch, studying it carefully. It's another concept for a landscape/human figure mash-up similar to the painting I'd given him for his new place.

"I realize nothing I can say will justify what I did, but…" I pause when he picks up another scrap of paper, a drawing I'd shaded in with watercolor pencil.

"Go on," he says.

"Losing my job was pretty much the worst thing that's ever happened to me, except for when I got the news about Dad, of course."

"I understand that."

"And then the car, and everything, and I wasn't ready to hear what you—or anyone for that matter—said to me. I've only ever shown my work to family before, because I didn't think it was good enough. But you're right. I should at least give it a shot."

"I shouldn't have pushed you, but given you time to get used to your new situation first. I tried to rush you, and for that I'm sorry."

"And this past week has been hell. I've missed you so much."

"Evidently." He gestures at the chaos surrounding us.

"But if it's too late, I totally understand."

"Too late? Claudia, I waited fifteen years to finally

meet someone like you, someone who would challenge me rather than just take my credit card and ignore my very existence otherwise. It's never too late." He turns to me, his eyes burning into mine so intensely it takes my breath away again.

"I'm sorry for all the things I said."

"You weren't all wrong. I'm sorry I tried to force my opinions on you."

We share a smile.

"I missed you too, Claudia. More than I can express. If we can get past our differences, I promise I'll do better."

"Me too." I scoot closer to him, sighing deeply when his arms finally surround me. This is exactly what I needed. "I think I love you."

"I love you too."

We gaze into each other's eyes for a blissful few seconds. Both at ease, both reassured by what we see.

"I'm still not going to let you buy me a car though!" I remark.

"We're going to have to work on that," he jokes.

He leans into me, our lips connecting finally in a kiss so intense it feels like fireworks are ready to erupt from my chest. I can't suppress a sob, making him pause.

"I thought I'd lost you," I explain.

"I'd been waiting for you," he responds.

"Why didn't you call me? Try to make me change my mind?"

"If there's one thing I learned in the past, it's that you can't *make* women do anything, least of all change their minds, unless that's what they want themselves."

He talks sense. I had to get to this conclusion myself or I would have just pushed him away all over again.

I'm overcome with a grave need for him, for his affection, his love. But before we get too distracted, there's something else that needs clearing up.

"That letter, how did you manage it?" I ask, though suddenly uncertain I want the answer.

"Lauren is an old friend, from university. After nosing around in your shed, I couldn't help myself and asked for her opinion. Whether it would be commercially viable. She was so taken with what I'd shown her that she wanted to invite you to join the exhibition. Actually, I had very little to do with it."

His modesty makes me smile. Sure, *very little*, except he orchestrated the whole thing.

"I should mention that I do also have a stake in her business, just as a silent partner. I don't have any decision-making powers, and she wouldn't listen to me even if I did."

I pull back, and stare at him with my mouth half open in surprise.

"You're what?"

"She approached me last year, when she was just drawing up the plans for her business, so I put her in contact with the venture capital division at the firm. Then when we got talking about your work she mentioned her investor wanted out, so I bought his share. After ensuring it was a sound investment, of course. Just because I don't want to work at an investment bank anymore doesn't mean I can't use my experience and knowledge for some personal investments." Peter smiles.

No way! Not only is he friends with a seemingly influential figure in the modern art world, he's also part owner of a chain of galleries? How much money *does* he have exactly? I suspect I don't really want to know the answer to that, it would only freak me out.

"Why didn't you say something?"

"We only finalized the paperwork this past week, there was nothing to tell yet."

The way he's looking at me, with such tenderness in his eyes, convinces me. I believe him. I guess that's what all the mysterious note-taking was all about last week. The whole thing is strangely funny. I panic because he wants to buy me a car, when at the same time he thinks nothing of buying part of a business to help out a friend.

"What's funny?"

I shake my head, but can't wipe the grin off my face. Oh my God, this whole situation is too surreal. "Nothing. Kiss me again."

He smiles back at me and gives me a wink. "That, I can do."

Before I know it, I'm on my back and he's on all fours above me, his lips pressed tightly into mine. Our tongues dance around one another, not to tease but to seduce. We're hungry, starved for affection, as our rushed movements clearly demonstrate.

He peels my clothes off in a hurry, while I struggle

with his until he helps out. My hands once again roam his perfect body, the sculpted muscles which I know to hold so much strength. He's already hard, has been probably since the first make-up kiss. I love the effect my body seems to have on him.

With his elbows resting either side of my head, he lowers himself onto me, our bodies pressed together impatiently, aching to merge fully.

Then, without warning, he lifts himself and takes my hand, pulling me up with him. He rushes into the bedroom, his hand still clutching my wrist so I can do nothing but run along behind him. Not that I had other plans, no. The bedroom will be just fine.

We all but tear the remainder of our clothes off and leave them dumped on the carpet. He lies down on his back, gesturing at me to climb on top.

"Ride me," he demands.

I bite my lip in anticipation as I straddle him, guiding his length towards my entrance in a feverish attempt to find sweet salvation. The way he looks at me makes me forget myself. There's so much need in his eyes, yet so much tenderness as well. I don't doubt he truly cares about me, he truly wants to see me succeed at whatever I choose to do. Why didn't I see that before?

He bucks his hips, dragging me out of my trance. When I lower myself onto him, a gasp escapes my lips and my eyes snap shut. It feels so good, so right to be so close to him. To once again let our bodies become one.

As I start to move my hips, grinding into him for more pleasure, he does too and soon our bodies find a common rhythm. Like waves in the sea, we rock forward, tensions mounting until the end is almost in sight, then pulling back to make the moment last longer.

Things feel different, this time around. There is still that undeniable passion we feel for one another, that desperate yearning to give pleasure as well as receive. But there's also a deeper connection that I don't think was there before.

He reaches out for my hands, wrapping his fingers around mine, allowing me to lean on him while speeding up. I continue to ride him, while staying completely focused on his face. I missed falling asleep next to him, his arm protectively around me, making me feel safe. And I missed this expression so much, the calm before his release.

Time seems to slow while I speed up. A slow burn develops in my thigh muscles, but I'm not so easily discouraged. Underneath me, his muscular body starts to glisten in the dim ambient light. He's so beautiful, so perfect, groans of pleasure escaping his lips with every thrust.

Unlike other times we've made love, gone is the illusion of control from his movements, his eyes are shut now, their brilliant depths hidden for the time being as I push him towards the limits of control.

I know now that although things might not always be easy, it's worth fighting for. In one last ditch effort, I push on, focused entirely on him, every slight change in expression, the subtle tremble of his lower lip that signals I'm on the right track.

As he erupts, so do I. Our bodies come to a halt when we're at our closest. His arms wrap around me, forcing me into a tight embrace.

We stay put, me on top of him cradled in his arms, until our breaths slow down to normal and even the last trace of stickiness evaporates off our skin.

"Will you stay the night?" I ask.

"One condition," Peter responds.

"What's that?"

"Tomorrow we stay at my place. I even have a bed now."

I smile into his chest before kissing him right in the centre of it. "Fair enough."

EPILOGUE

My heart is beating so hard, I feel like it might try to burst through my chest. What if people don't like my work? What if it turns out to be a huge failure?

Sure, Lauren seemed to like what she saw when I brought my five canvases in last week, but what if she's wrong?

"Don't look so scared, it's going to all work out," Mom says, gently prodding me with her elbow.

"But what if…" I rub my hands together, trying to get rid of the clamminess.

"Drinks?" Peter steps up with two glasses of champagne and hands them to us.

"Thanks, that's very kind," Mom says, shooting him and me a smile. "I'm so glad you two managed to work things out. She was always a stubborn child, my Claudia."

"Mom!" I protest, my hands still shaking as I hold onto the champagne flute.

"So I've noticed," Peter jokes, placing his arm around my shoulder.

"It's about to start!" Mom remarks, after checking her watch. "I'm so proud of you, Claudia. I'm sure it will be a great success." She beams at me, her eyes sparkling with excitement.

I'm not so sure, so I just stand there, focused on

breathing in and out, propping myself up against Peter's chest.

"Ladies and gentlemen, thank you so much for coming to our grand opening!" Lauren steps up in front of the crowd that has started collecting all around us. The beginning of her speech is met with polite applause. Towards my left, Mom takes my hand, squeezing it excitedly.

"For this landmark occasion, I'm very excited to announce a brand new addition to our line-up for tonight. Due to the last minute addition, she's not mentioned in the brochure. A fresh entrant into the local art scene, Claudia de Wit!"

Mom lets go of me, and applauds excitedly, causing a few bystanders to turn around and look at us. "Love you, sweetheart!" she whispers while I try to resist the urge to run.

"Of course we welcome familiar names as well tonight, including Tess Burgundy, and…" Lauren continues, pausing for the occasional applause when appropriate, introducing the rest of the artists included in the exhibit. I'm in amazing company, having seen some of the works earlier when they were still being set up.

As soon as the speech is over, everyone gets the chance to mingle and look around at the displays. I'm not sure at all what to do or where to go, so I just awkwardly stand around until Peter practically forces me to talk to some of the other exhibitors. Networking, he says. Awkwardness is more like it.

BEAUTIFUL STRANGER

Just when I'm doing my best to strike up a conversation with a rather nice lady old enough to be my grandmother who paints still lifes, Lauren comes up towards me with a big grin on her face.

"Wonderful news, Claudia. You've made your first sale already!" She holds out her hand, which I shake in a daze.

"Which canvas?"

"*Summer Moon.*"

I'm speechless. That's the one they valued the highest at more than two grand! More than what I'd make in a month in my old job even after deducting tax.

"Congratulations. We'll get the paperwork drawn up as soon as possible as well as a check when the buyer finalizes everything."

"Who bought it?" I stammer, preparing myself for it to be Peter, in which case I'm going to go nuts.

"You see the man over there, in the pinstriped suit?" Lauren asks, gesturing subtly towards the far end of the gallery towards a small cluster of people. "His name is Callum Byrne."

I nod, still skeptical that some stranger is actually happy to shell out that kind of money for a creation of mine. The man turns around, and raises his champagne glass in our direction. He looks vaguely familiar, but I can't place him. Could it be one of Peter's colleagues whom I met at the race event? No, that doesn't seem right...

"He said it will be the perfect centerpiece for a new restaurant he's planning on opening next year." Lauren gives him a little wave, which the man acknowledges before turning back to chat to his elegant female companion. "A good, regular customer of ours. I'm so pleased he's taken a liking to your work." She smiles at me and turns around to mingle some more.

I'm still shocked. He owns a restaurant? Where have I seen his face before?

"What did I miss?" Peter asks, offering me a new glass of champagne.

"That guy over there bought the moon painting. To hang in his restaurant apparently." I can't work out where I know him from.

"Wonderful! I'll drink to that." He holds up his glass, clinking it to mine. "I'd hate to say *I told you so...*"

"Oh, you!" I give him a playful slap on his arm, but I have to admit that for a change it's nice not to be right.

By the time the event is over, another two canvases have sold, and I'm about to be a lot richer than I was only hours ago. We say our goodbyes to Mom, then make our way back to Peter's flat, arm in arm.

"That went surprisingly well," I remark.

He winks at me while unlocking his front door.

"I never doubted that it would."

"That makes one of us. I love you, Peter." I tiptoe and give him a kiss right on the lips.

"Love you too." He returns my kiss. "So, any idea what you're going to spend your newfound riches on?"

I just grin in response, knowing very well what I plan to do with at least some of the money while keeping a sensible amount for the inevitable rainy day. I sure hope he still wants to travel, because I hear Egypt is lovely this time of year and I've always wanted to see the Great Pyramids…

If all this success is just temporary, I can always restart the job hunt when we get back.

***

Thanks so much for reading *Beautiful Stranger!*

This story holds a special place in my heart, because my entire writing career started with what is now the beginning of this novella. Back in October 2012, I took a deep breath, closed my eyes, crossed my fingers and even my toes, and clicked 'Publish' on a short story called *Ladies' Day*. Although I've made a few changes and additions, and unpublished the original, the same story is still present in Chapters 1 to 5 of this book you're reading now. It was the first thing I ever finished and offered for sale, and as such, the biggest milestone I have to show for as an author.

A lot has changed in the past few years. I like to think I've grown as a writer, and with it, my stories have developed. What started as a fun little encounter between a down-to-earth twenty-something girl, Claudia, and a middle class man fifteen years her senior has grown into something a lot more serious. Their relationship developed into something I couldn't have foreseen at the time.

We all want different things out of life, and it's so difficult to reconcile these hopes and dreams with those of another person. When Peter and Claudia first meet, they're both adrift, especially Peter. Claudia isn't quite as focused as she would want herself to believe, just going with the flow and hoping her job keeps providing the steady pay she so desperately craves. Towards the end of the story, obviously this is no longer the case and they're both in need of different future plans.

They complement each other. Claudia's backpacking experiences give Peter an idea for what he wants to spend his life doing more of: exploring the world. And Peter's encouragements finally get through to Claudia until she's willing to try out something she hadn't considered viable before: attempt to make a living from her art. She learns that one doesn't always have to be completely sensible and safe. Taking risks is OK, as long as it's not recklessly done.

I can relate to her fear that she isn't good enough to sell her paintings, and that she'll struggle to make a living selling the odd canvas here and there. It's not easy taking something you've created and expose it to other people, risking rejection and judgement. That's how I felt when I published that first story: uncertain whether it was up to scratch, and incredibly grateful when people actually bought and enjoyed it. Hopefully you, the reader, could relate to her as well.

BEAUTIFUL STRANGER

Beautiful Stranger could have easily become a fairy tale story, about an ordinary girl swept off her feet by a handsome older guy who showers her with gifts and ensures she never has to worry about money ever again. Of course, not everyone can accept that kind of thing, least of all Claudia who has always fended for herself. And would such an arrangement necessarily work long term? Would Peter never have wondered if perhaps she only liked him for his money? I think he might have, so they had to find another way...

Enough of all these rambling thoughts. I hope you enjoyed the story as much as I did while writing it, and if you're interested in reading more of my work, perhaps you'll consider signing up for my newsletter. I'll even give you a free book of your choice when you sign up!

x, Lorelei

- ❖ LMoone.com
- ❖ Lorelei Moone on Facebook

ONLY A

TASTE

CHAPTER ONE

All my belongings are neatly packed into cardboard boxes, but all I feel is chaos inside.

I don't want to go. I don't want to leave this little student flat which I've been sharing with Sarah for the past three years. But with no money or prospects, I don't have a choice.

I let out a deep sigh and sink down on the edge of the sofa.

"You alright, Mandi?" Sarah asks, handing me a cup of tea. Strong yet milky, just how I like it.

I just shrug.

"This sucks, hey." She puts her hand on my shoulder.

"Life's a bitch, especially when your family can't accept that in this country, things work a little differently," I respond.

"At least you won't have to worry about laundry. Or rent." Sarah is only half joking. Moving back home to act like the perfect Punjabi daughter to my parents will have some—admittedly small—benefits. Mostly it's a big, fat negative though.

"Yeah, I get to relive my childhood. Yay." I rest my head in my hands and try not to panic.

No more pretending to be a grown-up at twenty-three. No more staying out with Sarah—or anyone else for that matter—until the clubs close and our feet stop cooperating. No more freedom to hang out with anyone of the opposite gender, and forget about inviting a guy home with me.

Sure, I'll have a job to go to, with Mr. Gupta—Dad's friend, but that's hardly a pleasing prospect

"I'll miss you, you know." Sarah plops down next to me and puts her arm around me.

"Yeah, I'll miss you too."

"OK, this is bullshit." Sarah lets go of me and sits upright. "It's sad you have to move back in with your folks, but it's not like anyone died. They're not expecting you until tomorrow. Let's go do something!"

"Like what?" I ask, while still feeling way too sorry for myself to really care.

"I dunno. It's a nice, sunny day, I don't have anything on, neither do you. Let's just drive down to Brighton or something." *She's lost her mind.*

"And then what? I'm broke, remember? That's why I'm moving back in the first place."

"How much do you have exactly?" She grins at me expectantly.

"I dunno, about a tenner in cash, plus perhaps fifty in the bank?"

"Great! Get dressed." Sarah jumps up, visibly excited.

I stare at her in disbelief but once she's set on something, Sarah cannot be deterred. She grabs my hand and starts dragging me off the sofa and towards the large suitcase that contains all my clothes.

"What's the plan exactly?" I wonder out loud. Does she even have a plan?

"We drive down, hang out at the beach, eat fish and chips, get a bit of a tan." She looks over at me; my skin is already pre-bronzed of course. "OK, so I'll get a bit of a tan—head to the nearest pub or whatever, get sloshed. Dance, enjoy ourselves, have a proper farewell party for you. What do you say?"

"You did hear me when I said I have literally *no money?*"

Sarah shrugs. "Since when do we have to pay for our own drinks when we go out?"

She makes a fair point. *But when we're done partying, then what?* "I'm sure even the cheapest guest house down there would wipe me out though."

"Who said anything about a guest house? I'm not planning on sleeping! Plus, we can always crash in the car."

Sometimes she has the craziest ideas. But I have to admit that the prospect of being all but grounded with my parents breathing down my neck every day is a powerful motivator to go along with her spontaneity. What have I got to lose?

"Fine. You win."

She winks at me. "Admit it, we both win."

For all my earlier grumpiness, I can't suppress a smile now. Within minutes we've thrown on colorful summer dresses—bikini underneath of course—and shoved a random collection of supplies into a pair of beach-ready canvas bags. Towel, sunscreen, sunglasses, plus a couple of books—check.

Before I have the chance to change my mind, she's herded me into her piece-of-shit car which sounds so rattly I'm surprised nothing of note has fallen off it yet. The stereo—possibly the best part of the entire car—does its best to drown out the traffic noises and creaks with loud music. I don't care what happens anymore, today I still get to be me, not who my folks expect me to be.

***

The traffic has been horrendous, and the parking situation is worse. But at last, at just after four—three hours after setting off—we finally make it to Brighton beach.

As I take my sandals off and try to follow her towards an empty spot among the sunbathing crowds, I remember why I fucking hate Brighton as a beach. Who the hell decided it's a good idea to sunbathe on rough gravel? The stones cut into my feet with every step, causing me to swear under my breath.

"What's that?" Sarah turns and asks.

"Nothing. Bloody stones." I try to tiptoe ahead, but it doesn't help. In the end I decide to put my shoes back on.

"No pain no gain, darling."

Whatever.

We manage to find a spot between some giggly

teenagers and a family with a crying toddler. Not how I had wanted to spend my last afternoon of freedom, but choices are limited when the entire south of England seems to have congregated on the same stretch of stony coastline.

"Put sunscreen on me?" Sarah asks, handing me a bottle.

I do my best coating her pale back, not leaving any spots, but I already know it's hopeless. She'll be bright red within an hour, or two at the most. I would put money on it.

"Me too, please," I request when I'm done doing her.

"You sure you need it?"

"Hey, just because I have darker skin than you, doesn't mean I'm immune to cancer." I push the bottle into her hand and turn around, lifting my hair up to give her room.

"Fair point."

Soon we're both sticky, but reasonably protected against the rays. I lie down on my towel, keeping my beach bag behind my head as sort of a pillow while I decide to make a start on the novel I brought. Sarah has other ideas though.

"Don't you want to go in the water?" she asks.

Not really, no. I shake my head and open my book to the first page.

"Come on!"

"I can't swim!" I protest.

"We won't go that far."

I put the paperback down and observe the waves,

rolling in and crashing against the stones up ahead.

"Don't be a spoilsport!" Sarah insists.

"Fine. Fine! But if it's cold, I'm not doing it."

The sun is burning down onto the beach, if it wasn't for the light breeze, we'd be getting cooked. Still, the idea of cooling my toes in the water isn't so bad. Almost attractive, if it wasn't for the hellish walk to get there. Once again, I seem to have an uncanny ability to place my feet onto the sharpest rocks I can find. I'm surprised I'm not bleeding yet.

Sarah meanwhile is about ten feet ahead of me, rushing towards the sea much more eagerly, as if she's impervious to the pain of walking on hot, pokey stones.

"Oh my God, it's lovely! Not cold at all," Sarah exclaims as she takes the first steps into the water.

I soon follow, finding a definite chill travelling up my spine when I take the first dip. Then, I must admit it's pleasantly cooling.

As soon as I'm knee-deep in the water, a wave comes and wets most of the rest of me too. I squeal, trying to regain my balance, while Sarah's laugh rings loudly in my ear. It takes all sorts of inelegant acrobatics for me not to fall over. I can just imagine the spectacle that must have been; me trying to balance my rather solidly built frame in the waves.

"Very funny," I remark dryly, while Sarah continues to giggle at me.

"It was. You should've seen yourself."

Emboldened by a desire for revenge, I take a few steps in her direction and try to splash water at her. She promptly dives down under the water, evading me and wetting the rest of her body in the process, ruining my plans. *No matter, I'll get you sooner or later!*

When she pops up again, she gives me a wide smile. "See? It's fun!"

Another wave rolls in and she paddles along with it effortlessly, while I'm again almost thrown off my feet. But I refuse to go in further where the waves are less intense. Just because I'm grumpy about moving back home doesn't mean I'm ready to drown myself.

Five, maybe ten minutes pass while we continue to soak ourselves. It occurs to me that our stuff is sitting unguarded in a crowd of strangers, and I decide to head back.

"You enjoy yourself. I'm going to read now," I call out to Sarah, who has gotten distracted by a stray volleyball, thrown in her direction by a group of guys also enjoying the waves.

"Fine, see ya!" She waves at me, then throws the ball back to one of them. Well, I guess she's not going to get bored at this rate.

I'm in the process of limping back to my towel, when my stomach starts to growl. Of course, in our hurry to get out of the house, neither of us bothered with lunch, nor packed any snacks. A quick scan of the surrounding area reveals that the only thing somewhat nearby is a food truck close to where we left the boulevard. That's one hell of a walk.

Needs must, so I grudgingly take my wallet and phone out of my bag and go on limping over the hot stones. Why couldn't we have gone to a sandy beach instead?

CHAPTER TWO: CALLUM

"Mr. Byrne, I can assure you that you won't find a better location for your new restaurant in all of Brighton." The estate agent flashes his extra-white teeth. He looks almost like a shark, readying himself to tear his prey to pieces—me in this case.

"The rent is too high; it won't be viable," I argue, while looking around the empty building again. A lot of decorating would be needed as well. It's too much.

"Think of the footfall!" He points out the window which is currently partially obscured by white paint. Still, masses of day-trippers can be seen from where we stand.

"How about you speak to the owners again and let me know if the lease is negotiable? It will take a lot of investment to bring this property up to scratch." I offer him my hand, signaling the end of the viewing, as well as the discussion. If he comes down enough, I may consider this property, otherwise, it's back to the drawing board.

"Very well. Thank you very much for your time." The estate agent shakes my hand slightly less enthusiastically than at the beginning of the meeting.

After leaving the empty shop, we say our goodbyes and go our separate ways.

It's a beautiful day, deep blue skies with not a cloud in sight. Warm too, the surging temperatures of our current summer heat wave evident in the amount of exposed skin outside. Apparently, I'm overdressed. Swimming trunks and bikinis, that's Brighton's dress code in the summer. I stand out like a sore thumb in my jeans and button-up shirt.

The footfall would be good here, though I'd expect my new restaurant to quickly become bookings-only once the new show airs. Perhaps I should consider a location that's a little further away from the madding crowds, and hopefully more affordable. I don't want to have to shutter up the place as soon as I'm no longer on TV.

Enough work for one day though. Today is too lovely to waste.

The beach is crowded. So much so, I'm not at all tempted to go near it. Perhaps if I walk further out towards the western side of town I'll find some peace and quiet. But not without sampling some of the local refreshments. The only establishment not selling fish and chips around here seems to be the ice cream truck parked up on the pavement. There's a queue of people already waiting, but I can't help myself. Gelato will do that to a person.

I join one of the two queues and wait my turn. It takes a while, but it'll be worth it.

"One scoop of rum and raisin, please," I say, shocked to find that the young woman to my left has word-for-word ordered the exact same thing. The two guys behind the counter look at each other and pause.

"Okay, you're going to have to sort this out between yourselves," my guy says. "We've only got one scoop left."

Looking over at my competition, I'm struck by her striking feminine beauty. Big brown eyes gaze up at me, a mixture of disappointment and hope. Her full lips half-parted as if she's about to say something, but something interrupted her. I find myself uncharacteristically reluctant to speak up first, but it looks like I have no choice.

"Let's flip a coin for it," I attempt a joke.

Her stare tells me I failed. My eyes are quickly drawn to her hand, clutching a purple leather wallet. No ring, no tan line where one might have been. She looks pretty young, but not inappropriately so.

"I can just get something else," she whispers at last. Her eyes are still glued to me. Did she recognize me and that's why she's staring? Or is it something else? Have I got something stuck in my teeth?

"I hope you won't take this the wrong way." I pause, while she raises an eyebrow.

My guy, who decided to serve the customer behind me instead of waiting for us to resolve our gelato stand-off, pauses mid-conversation. He's clearly listening in to our exchange.

The black-haired beauty patiently waits for me to finish, but something in her body language has changed. I'm sure she gets this all the time. Fuck, I feel like a creep for even trying.

"You have it." I turn to face the chalkboard again, ready to pick another flavor. "I'll have tiramisu," I tell the guy behind the counter, who just shrugs. I guess he was looking forward to watching me get shot down, had I actually made a move.

Meanwhile, the younger guy hands the woman her scoop of rum and raisin in a cone, which she accepts with a smile. God, what a radiant smile. She takes her change and turns, walking off towards the beach. I quickly take my cup and impossibly tiny spoon and rush after her.

"Excuse me, miss," I say, when I catch up with her a few steps ahead.

She turns and stares at me again. How the hell do I do this without coming across like a total douche bag? Funnily enough, coming across like a douche has never been much of a concern. You win some you lose some, and ever since the first season of my show aired years ago, I haven't really had to work hard to get female attention. But there's something different about this one. I wonder if much of my interest in her is caused by how hard she's making things?

"Yes?" she asks, sounding stand-offish. Her rich amber-colored eyes are too distracting, I almost forget what I was about to say.

"I was wondering if I could take you out to dinner?" I ask at last.

She scrutinizes me from head to toe, as she considers the question. Perhaps she's wondering if it's worth the sacrifice to stick the ice cream in my face.

"Do I know you from somewhere?" she says finally.

Normally, I may have been more than happy to explain, but not this time. *Oh yeah, I'm on TV*, seems way too tacky. So I shrug. "Maybe I just have one of those faces?"

My answer makes her pause as she cocks her head and looks me right in the eye. Shit, she can tell I'm bullshitting her.

"Where would you take me?" She has a lick of ice cream, rescuing some droplets that were about to dribble off the side of the cone.

I hadn't thought that far ahead. What is it about this woman that she throws me off so much?

"That entirely depends on what type of food you like."

A hint of a smile plays on her lips.

"I'm here with a friend. Is she invited for dinner as well?"

Crap .

Finally a full grin does appear on her face. "No need to look so shocked, I'm only joking."

I smile back at her, relieved to have not made a complete ass of myself. Yet.

"But I'd better let her know anyway." She turns to scan the beach stretching out ahead of us, before facing me again. "So. What time and where?"

"Nine? Here? Unless you have a better idea."

"Bear in mind I'm only here for the day, so I don't have a change of clothes with me. What you see is what you get, I'm afraid." She glances down at herself, smoothing down the multi-colored cotton summer dress that covers what appears to be a bikini. And curves; ample curves as far as the eye can see. I shouldn't stare. No matter how tempting. God, she's beautiful.

"No matter, same here." I suddenly realize I don't even know her name. "I'm Callum, by the way." In the absence of a better idea of what to do, I stretch out my hand towards her.

She accepts the handshake, though the slight curl of the corners of her mouth suggests I did indeed just make an ass of myself at last.

"Mandi. *Lovely* to meet you." Yep, her tone confirms it. *Ouch.*

I try to think of something else to say to break the tension, or at least to distract me from the instant reaction I feel upon touching her hand. What is it about her? You'd think I'd never interacted with a beautiful woman before. How is it that she makes me feel more like an awkward teenager than a grown-ass and dare I say successful man in his thirties?

"Perhaps we should exchange phone numbers, so we don't miss each other in the crowds here," I mumble, while quickly pulling my hand back and fishing my mobile out of my pocket.

"Sure," she says, before giving me her number. When we say our goodbyes immediately after, I can't help wondering if I'll ever see her again, or she'll decide she'd much rather vanish with her supposed friend. Only time will tell.

CHAPTER THREE

"Oh, you're done swimming," I remark, as I lower myself onto my towel.

Sarah looks up from her phone, her expression brightening immediately when she notices the half-eaten cone in my hand. "Ice cream! Where?"

I point back towards where I had just come from, the truck. "Up there. Anyway, so listen. The funniest thing just happened." I proceed to tell a severely distracted Sarah all about the guy, Callum.

"Seriously hot though. Like *seriously*," I finish. His dreamy blue eyes and weather-ruffled blond hair are hard to forget, as was the obviously toned body which his fitted white shirt didn't obscure as much as emphasize. Although he looked a few years older than me, there was something boyish and innocent about him.

Sarah looks like I've got her attention again and she's over her gelato craving, at least for the moment.

"And you think you know him from somewhere?" she asks.

I nod slowly, still unable to place him. "Yeah, it's driving me crazy. And he was no help whatsoever."

"Oh well, maybe you'll figure it out on your date."

"I guess that means I have to actually turn up, eh?"

"What, you planned not to?" Sarah's eyes are close to popping out as she stares at me.

"Well, it doesn't seem fair for you to be on your own." I shrug, trying to rid myself of the feeling that I really would like to see this guy again.

"Bitch, please! This is your farewell party of sorts. You think your folks will let you go on dates with hot strangers when you move back?"

Her remark hurts, because it's true. No. I don't expect they'd let me go on dates, and especially not if the guy in question is *white.*

"So that settles it then." Sarah rests her hand on my shoulder. "You go have fun, I'm sure I can entertain myself. In fact, did you see the guys who were swimming at the same time as us?" A mysterious smile forms on her lips.

"Yeah?"

"One of them seemed quite, you know... interested. They asked if I wanted to join them at some local club tonight. I was planning on asking you, but I'm sure it'll be fun even if I tag along on my own." Sarah lets go of me and lies back on her towel, putting her sunglasses over her face, still smiling to herself.

"If you're absolutely sure..." I say.

She waves away my remark. "I can take care of myself. And if not, I totally intend to let the guy in the red and black swimming trunks have a go at taking care of me. Plus, you can always join us if the date bombs."

I let out a giggle and she joins in too.

"Slut."

"Whore."

She raises her hand and I give her a high five before lying back on my own towel as well. Tonight is going to be awesome. I can't wait until nine o'clock. Let's hope this book is interesting enough to make the time pass quickly.

***

"So, I'll see you when I see you," I say, while waving at Sarah, who is staying behind at the beach until the group she's joining for the evening is going to leave.

"Have a great one. Make it count!" She winks at me, making me smile. Yes, I intend to make it count indeed. This could be the last time in a long while I'll get to enjoy myself. Let's hope the guy, Callum, doesn't turn out to be a freak.

When I walk up the steps towards the boulevard, it's three minutes past nine. Hopefully that's late enough not to seem desperate, and punctual enough for him to actually be there waiting for me. Assuming he's punctual.

It's busy, as it has been all day, and it takes me a moment to find him in the crowd. His face lights up in a smile when he spots me.

"Hey!" I say, smiling back at him. Oh God, this is going to be awkward, isn't it?

"You made it," he responds, hesitating for a moment, before leaning in and giving me a peck on the cheek.

Good job, much better than the weird handshake earlier.

"Said I would, didn't I?" Ignoring the fact that he's got Sarah's insistence to thank for my presence.

"Your friend, she's okay being on her own tonight?" The slight lilt in his accent is endearing, I wonder where he's from originally? He doesn't sound English.

"Oh, Sarah. She has a knack for finding company wherever she goes." I look around at the busy street leading off from the coastline, wondering if that's where we're headed. "So where are you taking me?"

"I've got a few options. What sort of food do you like?" Callum asks. How very attentive of him to ask.

"Anything is fine, I'm not picky. Surprise me."

I don't know why I don't just say the first food that pops into my head: Italian. Part of me wants to see what he'll come up with when it's purely down to him. He seems to want to impress me, so I let him.

He nods, then offers me his arm which I accept. A nice, gentlemanly gesture. I glance over at him. That face. I know his face from somewhere and I still can't remember from where. It's infuriating.

"I love Brighton," he remarks, as we start on our walk up the narrow streets. "It's just so colorful."

"Yeah, it's not bad. Too many people, though."

A lot of the shops have already shut, leaving only the eateries and bars open. Still, the sun is burning down brightly, sunset is still some time away, which always makes summers seem surreal to me. It looks like it's daytime, when in fact it's almost time for the nightlife to start.

My stomach growls painfully, reminding me of the fact that I've had nothing but a gelato for lunch today, as Callum pauses outside a rather cozy looking bistro. That was quick!

"Outside or in?" he asks, eyeing the tables that line the pavement beside us.

"Outside, obviously."

He pulls out a chair for me, before seating himself. Almost immediately, a waitress arrives with two menus.

"Here you go, sir." She hands him the leather-bound folder, and then stares. And stares. And continues to stare even as she gives me the other one.

"Thank you." Callum starts leafing through the pages, and it's only then that the waitress catches herself, blushes a deep red and rushes off back inside.

"That was weird." I turn around to watch her almost run into the 'Staff Only' door at the back of the small restaurant.

"What?"

"Oh, the waitress. She looked like she'd seen a ghost."

Callum chuckles, then goes back to inspecting the offerings.

Wonder what all that was about? And he didn't seem all that surprised either, which is bizarre. Where the hell do I know his face from?

The menu is simple, mostly French-inspired with hints of Mediterranean cuisine here and there. There aren't a lot of options, four main courses, six starters, and yet it all looks tempting and I can't decide.

"What are you having?"

"I've read that the lamb is great here." Callum hovers his finger over the page, then looks up at me. "You?"

"I guess the fish, since we're at the seaside?"

"Good choice. Wine?"

"Oh, you pick. I don't know much about wine." I close the menu and look over at Callum. He *is* gorgeous. Let's hope we get past the initial weirdness soon.

"Now that that's out of the way..." Callum sits back and we make eye contact for the first time since reaching our destination. I can't deny that there's something there, a promising spark. "Tell me about yourself? What do you do?"

"Oh..." I think for a moment, wondering whether to be honest or not. "I *was* a student, but I've got my degree now and have been looking for work. Unsuccessfully, I might add."

"Okay, what did you study?" His eyes are fixed on mine, and I dare not look away.

"Business administration, specializing in finance."

"That sounds pretty serious." He smiles briefly.

I wonder if I've intimidated him. A lot of guys hate it when they think you're smarter than they are.

"I guess so. Not that it helped me find work. This is actually sort of a historic night for me." I avert my gaze, kicking myself that I'm even bringing this up. I'm supposed to be enjoying myself, not venting to a complete stranger! Rule No. 1 of one night stands: don't bring your baggage into it.

"How's that?"

Shall I steer the conversation in another direction? Make something up? I look up again, noting the concern in his eyes. He seems to really want to know...

"I'm actually moving back in with my folks tomorrow. One of Dad's friends is offering me a bookkeeping job in his company. Not quite what I had hoped for, but better than nothing."

He frowns. "I see. Perhaps it's just temporary, until you find something else."

I smile at his attempt to comfort me, but I already know the only way I'll get to move on is if I get married first, and that's something I'm really not ready for.

"Anyway, enough of that. I'm sure you didn't ask me out here to listen to me whine about my life." I nod thanks at the waitress, who has just arrived with two glasses and a bottle of whatever wine Callum picked out. She's fucking staring at him again and it's starting to get on my nerves.

"Are you ready to order?" she finally says, while fumbling with her notepad and pen.

I'm too pissed off to say anything, so Callum steps in to order for the both of us. She blushes again, thanks him and vanishes.

Seriously? Am I fucking invisible? What is her problem? I get that he's hot, but hey, he's here with *me*, isn't he?

"So, how about you? What do you do?" I ask, hoping to rid myself of any lingering annoyance now that we're alone again.

CHAPTER FOUR: CALLUM

"What do you do?" Mandi's voice sounds a little choked, perhaps she's feeling much more down about moving in with her parents than she let on initially. She seems bright, well educated. Surely she'll get her break, even if it doesn't seem like it right now.

Anyway, what did she ask? Oh shit, what do I do?

"I'm a chef," I finally say.

She stares at me for a moment, her eyebrows pulled together into a half-frown.

"A chef..." Then her eyes widen. Oh dear, there it is. The moment of recognition.

"Oh fuck!" she exclaims, covering her mouth with her hand as soon as she catches herself.

"Sorry, I'm just... Okay, now I get why that waitress kept staring at you. Callum... Of course. God, I feel pretty silly now."

I grin at her, hoping that the awkwardness will wear off soon enough. "Sorry about that, I should have been upfront when you asked earlier—"

"Where I'd seen you before. It's been driving me crazy, I couldn't figure it out! I kept thinking have we met somewhere and I just didn't remember it properly? TV didn't even come into it." She picks up her glass and takes a generous sip of wine to deflect.

"I didn't want to be all 'so, I'm on TV' and come across like a total dick."

Thankfully, my remark has the desired effect. She bursts out laughing and sets the glass down again.

"Yeah, that would have been weird. Point taken."

Encouraged by her reaction, I decide to take the humor to the next level. "Anyway, it was refreshing, having to work for this dinner date. Thanks for that."

In a fraction of a second, her smile vanishes and she just stares at me. Shit, that went too far, didn't it? "What do you mean, ' *work for it'?*"

"Uhm... You know... You didn't make it easy, that's all," I explain, certain I've just dug a deeper hole for myself.

Then she grins again, brushing her hand past mine in the centre of the table.

"Oh God, you're so easy to wind up!" She takes another sip of wine and leans back into her chair, her eyes completely relaxed now.

"Well, you're impossible." I smile back at her. This one is something else. Hilarious, if only I wasn't so damn off my game with her.

"Your food." The flustered waitress is back, setting down our cold starters ahead of us. "Umm... If you don't mind me asking..."

I look up only to find her staring at me with a look of adoration on her face. That's what Mandi meant. She's clearly a fan and I'm too used to it to realize how weird this must be for everyone involved.

"Yes?" I ask.

The waitress looks down at her hands, then quickly retrieves the notepad from the pocket of her apron. "Could I have your autograph? It would mean a lot. I watch your show all the time..."

I smile at her, then glance at Mandi, who is just observing the scene with an incredulous look on her face.

"Sure." I take the pad and pen and start. "What's your name?"

"Maria."

'To Maria, lovely to meet you. Callum Byrne'

"Here." I hand her the completed note.

"Thanks so much!" She grabs the pad and rushes back inside.

"I get it now, but that's still so bizarre," Mandi remarks.

"Sorry about that." I smile, then lean forward, admiring the presentation of the food in front of me. Not bad. This place truly is a hidden gem.

"Full marks for being all nice about it, I would find it hard. Especially if it happens a lot."

"It was a learning curve at first, but I'm getting better at dealing with being recognized. Still very refreshing not to be though. Kudos to you." I wink at Mandi, then pick up a fork, ready to attack the food. "Bon appétit."

"Likewise." From the corner of my eye, I see her hesitating to start on her own food. "You know, I'm sorry for commenting."

"Not at all."*Lovely.* The fresh flavor of coriander makes this salad stand out. The reviews were right about this place.

"No, I feel I must be totally honest. I was a bit annoyed earlier, before, you know. She was just staring at you, like... It makes sense now." I look up, finding Mandi looking just a little bit flustered herself.

"Sounds like you were jealous," I blurt out before catching myself.

"I wouldn't say jealous *per se*." Mandi looks away for a moment, brushing a lock of her thick blackish brown hair behind her ear.

"Yeah, you were!" I say, emboldened when I notice the slight curl in the corner of her lip. She's all about the subtle cues which most guys would never notice.

"Okay! Jeez. I give up." She throws her hands in the air in defeat, then looks straight at me again and I know my gamble has paid off.

It makes sense now, I know what to do. Games won't work on her, neither will self-censorship and false niceties. No, with her somehow I have to let the real me out for a change. Uncensored. Anything less won't do the job.

Rather than feel out of my depth like before, I'm relieved. It's time to take off the mask and let her see the Callum Byrne they'd never air on TV.

"This food is lovely," Mandi remarks, as she takes another bite. "I probably shouldn't be so surprised."

"They don't just keep me around for my charming personality and good looks, you know. I do know my food."

"I wouldn't know, I don't really like cooking shows." *Ouch,* her honesty is refreshing to the point of bluntness and I like it. What a change from the women I usually end up meeting, who are already fawning before I even say a word. It takes a lot more than cheap fame to impress Mandi, yet I'm not discouraged. Far from it.

She glances at me through her full black lashes, her gaze lingering on me just a little bit longer than before. My eyes are drawn to the curvature of her full lips, before I catch myself.

"Fair enough." I take a sip of wine, then return to her lingering eyes again. "What *do* you like? What do you do for fun?"

"This is going to sound really stupid." She plucks off a piece of bread, before dipping it into the juices left on her plate and putting it in her mouth, chewing thoughtfully. Again, those inviting lips, how they beg to be kissed. It takes a lot for me stop staring and continue the conversation.

"Try me."

"Crochet."

My glass is halfway between the table and me, when I put it back down again without taking a second sip. "Wait, what?"

"Told you it's stupid. But I really enjoy it. It's creative as well as useful and it relaxes me." *Is she joking?* She looks completely serious this time.

"Not stupid at all when you put it like that, but just not something I imagined someone like you would enjoy. My grandma used to crochet."

She shrugs, then smiles widely at me. "I'm only kidding."

"Really? You totally had me."

"I don't think crochet is stupid. Funnily it was *my* grandma who taught me, actually. We're very close." She grins at me, clearly unapologetic about her unusual hobby. Though she is undeniably beautiful, it's her confidence that makes the biggest impression on me. She seems completely comfortable with who she is. And that smile... I can't get enough of her smile.

Yep, she's completely unlike the women I usually end up dating. In every possible way. She's real in a way that most people around me are not.

"Oh well, I have no right to talk. Growing up, I was the boy who would rather lock himself in the kitchen than go out and play football with other kids."

"So uncool," she teases.

"Oh yeah. Very. Luckily for me, it turned out okay."

"A toast. To us, being really uncool."Mandi raises her glass, and I follow her lead. Refreshing, indeed.

"I'll drink to that. How was the wine anyway? Ready for another bottle?"

She nods. I feel like I'm getting better at reading her, or perhaps that's just the wine deceiving me. Either way, she looks like she's enjoying herself, which is a relief.

I'm not used to worrying about what people think of me. Tonight though, I not only want to be my uncensored self, I want her to like me for it.

"So you and your grandma were close, then?" I ask,

for lack of a better question.

"Still are. Mom and Dad are always busy working."

"If you don't mind me asking," I start, hoping she won't take my question the wrong way. Her inquisitive eyes encourage me to continue. "Where are you from?"

"Langley, near Slough. Born and raised."

I nod, I'd spent a short while living in Slough after coming over from Ireland, so I know the area. "And your family?"

"Punjab, India." She looks away for a brief moment, making me wonder whether she did find my question uncomfortable.

"Beautiful country," I remark, remembering mainly the food I'd sampled on my various trips to India.

She just shrugs, then looks me in the eye again. "I wouldn't know."

"Don't tell me you've never been?" I exclaim, almost offended on her behalf.

"Well—" Mandi starts, but we are interrupted by the presence of the same waitress from before, along with a man dressed in a chef's uniform, one looking even more flustered than the other.

"I'm sorry to interrupt," the chef starts, while wiping his hands nervously on his apron.

"Not at all," I say.

"I was just wondering if the food was to your liking, Mr. Byrne?"

"Very nice. I enjoyed it very much, how about you, Mandi?" I ask, noting she's again very subtly showing signs of disbelief or frustration, I can't quite tell yet which, perhaps both.

"Amazing," she says, while folding her hands and looking up at the two intruders.

"Thank you, thank you, I'm glad to hear it. I was just wondering something else... Ehh..." He scratches his forehead, then fidgets with both of his hands. "This is just a small family business, you see, and I was wondering if Maria here would be permitted to take your picture? We have a whole wall inside with photographs of previous guests, and we would love to capture this moment right here, with you... and your lovely companion."

I smile patiently and nod. It's not the first time, neither will it be the last. Whenever I visit any eatery not directly affiliated to me, it's very common to be asked for a photograph by the staff.

"Wonderful, please smile!" the chef says, while the waitress takes out her smart phone and awkwardly takes a shot of Mandi and me. As I look over, she's not only not smiling as requested, she looks like someone's about to pull a tooth or worse. Shit, this is uncomfortable, dragging her into the weirdness of my everyday life.

CHAPTER FIVE

Well, this is bizarre. The whole thing, with just the waitress at first, then even the chef who especially came out of the kitchen to talk to Callum... I don't know how he deals with it on a regular basis, because I'd be hopeless.

I look over at him as he first gives the chef, then Maria the waitress a friendly handshake. He smiles at me apologetically when they finally leave again. I admire how patient he is about all this.

"Sorry about that."

"The price of fame, eh?" I remark, while playing around with the last bit of purple frilly lettuce on my otherwise empty plate.

"Yep."

"This sort of thing happens all the time?" I ask, wondering why otherwise sane and rational grown-ups would act like blushing teenagers around someone, simply because they've been on TV. While he's gorgeous and probably cooks well enough, he seems to be just a regular guy. Why go all gaga in his presence, then?

And then I remember how Sarah gets when some big-time writer or blogger comments on one of her articles, and I wonder if perhaps I'm the odd one out for being too utterly dry to become anyone's fan. The obligatory boy band obsession from my teenage years I'll conveniently ignore. It doesn't count. Teenagers *aren't* sane.

"All the time," he confirms, looking away at nothing in particular.

Our meal is interrupted by a few more moments of awkwardness with Maria the waitress when she brings us our wine refill and main courses. In the meantime Callum tells me all about the new restaurant he's planning to open here in Brighton.

As he enthusiastically lays out his plans, it becomes clear that his new venue will be a very different affair from the little takeaway Mom and Dad run, with the help of my brother, Jai.

Callum's passion shows though in his words. It's obvious he really does love what he does in a way that I'll probably never know for myself. I've never met anyone who was even half as passionate about finance. Even for my classmates at university, it always seemed like the subjects we studied were a means to a greater end: finding a highly paid job.

I hesitate to mention Mom and Dad's takeaway at all, considering I've never really been into the whole catering thing and don't want to give the impression that I'm only bringing it up in order to keep up appearances. The truth is, I might as well be a complete layman when it comes to the restaurant business, and that's fine by me.

After some pressing from his side, I do at last let my guard down and tell Callum all about what I really wanted to do with my life: become an interior designer. If it wasn't for my parents disagreeing with those plans, and strongly steering me towards something more serious, that is.

Although I hadn't planned to share so much about myself, the way he seems to hang on every word of mine makes me reconsider. It's strange, how after chatting for just an hour, you can feel closer to someone who is actually still a total stranger. The way our conversation flows, it's almost as if we've become friends already. Friends who are hopefully heading for some *benefits*.

"Say, what were your plans for after the meal?" I ask, wishing desperately for him to get over with the small talk and get his flirt on properly. I'm eager to celebrate my last night of freedom in every way possible.

"I'm going to assume that there's nowhere you have to be for a while?" he asks.

"Free as a bird. Just for tonight."

He considers my words, hopefully catching their hidden meaning.

"We best make the most of that then." He gives me a stare that suggests he did get my drift. Nice. Perhaps now we can get over the *date* part of the evening and onto that tasty stuff you only get to when a date goes well, or when you didn't really have long-term intentions at all.

Shit, I hope he doesn't think this is a proper first date?!

"I just want to make something clear," I start.

He nods once while rubbing his chin, yet never

breaks eye contact. It's putting me on edge but I try not to let it show.

"I've touched upon how things are a bit complicated for me right now. So I'm not *looking* for anything, all right? I just want to have fun tonight."

He presses his lips together tighter, as if trying to prevent himself from making a smart-ass remark.

"I can live with that, on one condition."

"Yes?" I ask.

"Let's see where the night goes and keep an open mind."

I open my mouth in protest, I know exactly where this can go: beyond hopefully a shared bed for a few hours, it can't go anywhere else.

"Shh... That's my condition, and I'm sticking to it."

I sigh in defeat, realizing he's probably not going to back down. "Fine. I'll keep an open mind." Not that it'll do me much good. From tomorrow, no matter what my supposedly open mind has decided about Callum, my folks will make the decision for me.

"I feel like I owe you a gelato, or some other dessert," I tease, while pushing my creaky chair back.

He scrutinizes me, looking for the subtext in my words. "I'm sure we can work something out." Callum leaves a generous tip on the table, before offering me his arm.

We walk for a while, through the streets which have gone from crowded to quieter to crowded again now that the day trippers have turned into partygoers. We pass by pub after pub, resisting live music trying to invite us inside. It's an easy choice—at least for me—I'd rather have alone time with him than be surrounded by drunken revelers.

By the time night sets in, we're back at the boulevard, Callum's arm protectively around my shoulders as we enjoy the view. Now that it's dark, the sea is mostly invisible. The one thing left to light it up are the twinkling lights of Brighton pier, jutting out from the coast and into the calm waters. Of course his hand resting on top of my arm is distracting me. His body next to mine is begging to be the sole focus of my attention.

It's there, with a backdrop of city lights to my right and the dark waters of the English Channel to my left, that he makes his move. He takes both my hands as we stand face to face, his features barely lit up by the streetlights, though I can see him well enough to understand the intention in his eyes.

I raise myself slightly, and he wraps one arm around my waist, supporting me, drawing me closer. His cologne smells fresh and inviting. His eyes linger on my lips for a painfully long moment, until he moves in for the kill.

Usually, I'm never this involved, this overwhelmed by the presence of a guy I've only just met. My eyes shut when his lips touch mine, and my heart seems to somersault in my chest. For just a moment, I forget what lies ahead tomorrow, and just feel privileged to have this moment with him.

"Shall we call it a night?" I ask, once I've regained my

composure. It's odd, the imbalance I feel. I could float away if it wasn't for Callum holding on to me.

"Already?" He never once breaks eye contact. Why the question, though? I figured the kiss meant he's interested.

"Assuming you want to take things further, I figured it would be best not to have an audience," I remark, while nodding over to the side at the group of teenagers hanging around a couple of scooters shooting looks in our direction.

"What about dessert?" His previously brilliant blue eyes have turned a deep, dark black in this light.

"Exactly." I couldn't look away if I wanted to; he captivates me.

"I have an idea, follow me." Callum breaks the spell and takes my hand, leading me through the narrow streets once more. With anyone else I might question where we're headed, or what the plan is. Somehow, with Callum, I don't feel the need to be in control. We pass through the busiest part of town into a quieter alleyway and pause in front of an unassuming restaurant.

"Wait here." Before I get the chance to respond, he disappears inside, leaving me wondering what he's up to. Through the window I can see that the place is mostly empty, possibly they're planning to close up soon.

He's talking to a middle-aged man whose black hair and olive skin hint at a Mediterranean heritage. After some back and forth, the man nods and heads into what I presume must be the kitchen. Callum, meanwhile, gets his phone out and makes a call.

What is he doing? If only I could read lips.

By the time he's finished with the phone, the man—who I'm guessing is in charge of the restaurant—comes back carrying a cardboard bag.

Callum fishes his wallet out of the back pocket of his jeans, and a friendly argument ensues, ending when Callum finally tucks a few notes into the restaurant owner's shirt pocket. They shake hands and out he comes.

"Sorry, hope you didn't get bored waiting."

I shoot him a suspicious smile and eye the fancy bag with the gold printed logo in his hand. It looks a lot less like a takeaway bag than something one might get at an expensive boutique.

"Do I get to ask?"

Callum smiles and shakes his head. "It's a surprise."

"Now where to?" I ask.

He gestures back to where we had just come from. "Not much further now."

Again, he takes my hand, and we walk for another five minutes until the sea comes back into view further up ahead and we pause in front of a charming Victorian villa that's been converted into a hotel.

"After you," Callum says, holding the door open for me. I'm impressed that the reception is still open, even more impressed that a place like this would even have a vacancy on what has got to be one of the busiest times of the year in Brighton.

I step inside and am greeted by a proper-looking gentleman who looks to be in his seventies. Like a throwback to another era, he's wearing an old fashioned three-piece suit, including a golden pocket watch. The interior of the hotel seems to match, with period-correct wallpaper and a huge crystal chandelier lighting up the lobby.

"Welcome! Your room has been prepared. If there's anything else I can assist you with, don't hesitate to ring the bell."

"Thank you, Cecil. Good night." Callum takes the key from the old man's outstretched hand and leads me up the ornate wooden staircase that winds around the back of the reception desk. Another few flights of stairs later—thankfully I'm wearing sensible sandals today—and we stop in front of what I assume to be our room.

He slips the key into a teak wood door, and steps back, leaving it slightly ajar.

"Go on," he says.

I push the door wide open and am speechless. The room isn't very big, but the decor more than makes up for that. And the view, oh my, the view. The four-poster bed in the centre of the room is perfectly positioned in front of a balcony which overlooks the coastline.

"Wow." It's all I can say. I've never thought of myself as the romantic type, but I can't deny I'm impressed.

"Beautiful, isn't it?" Callum says, pulling the door shut behind him. That accent; is my mind playing tricks on me or has his accent become more pronounced compared to earlier tonight?

"Breathtaking."

I awkwardly wait by the bed for him to join me, trying desperately to regain my composure. It's no use though, my heart is hammering in my throat and I don't know where to look anymore.

"As are you," he says, placing his hand on the side of my neck, drawing me closer for a kiss which reduces the remainder of my defenses to rubble.

CHAPTER SIX : CALLUM

"Breathtaking," Mandi says. She can hardly take her eyes off the view.

"As are you." Her reaction is clear, the most guarded person I've ever met is impressed, in her own way.

The look of wonder and amazement in her eyes is almost better than all the smiles I managed to inspire this evening.

I can't take it anymore and move in for another kiss. The first one at the beach side had left me wanting throughout our walk to get here.

She sighs into my lips, and her body seems to give in to me completely.

I want her, my God, I want her so badly it makes my skin ache. I leave the bag containing our desserts on the bedside table and reach out for her.

Our lips fuse hungrily, both of us equally eager for things to progress. She and I are on the same page now, desperate for the night to claim us.

Finally, after holding back before, I sense the time has come to leave words behind and express ourselves by touch. I run my hands over her back, exploring her elegant shoulders, the curvature of her spine, down towards her generous buttocks. She doesn't stop me, rather she melts against me, pressing her body into mine, as her hands start on their own little journey of discovery.

Every touch of hers sets me alight, almost singeing my skin as well as soothing it. Looking into her endless eyes, I see a reflection of my own lust.

"I want you," I hear myself say with a voice so raw it's almost unrecognizable as my own.

She doesn't respond, at least not using words, instead she hooks her fingers into the belt loops of my jeans and tugs at it. She yearns for more closeness, as do I.

I run my fingertips over her naked shoulders, teasing the straps of her dress downward, then kissing the freshly exposed skin left behind. She shivers, then starts unbuttoning my shirt slowly, one button at a time, as if trying to make the moment last longer.

It's my favorite too, that brief period before you've seen everything, felt everything another person has to offer. How everything is so fragile, like the mood could get spoilt with one wrong move or word, and your body is a mess of hormones and adrenaline.

Soon though, she's done, and with a last tug on my sleeves, the shirt falls to the floor. She places her palm flat onto my chest, then curls her fingers, running her nails over my skin. Exquisite, slow, torture.

I close my eyes and thread my fingers through her long hair, kissing her deeply, until her breaths pause along with my own. How sweet her lips taste, how fragrant her skin is. Both overwhelm me, and yet I fight with all I've got to maintain pace.

Her reactions suggest she likes it that way: slow.

ONLY A TASTE

Then, something about her changes, she pushes against me, guiding me backwards to the bed until I can go no further but down. She doesn't let up, and I find myself on my back, with her straddling me.

Her eyes are a soulful black which consume me, I can barely muster the discipline to look away. She pulls the dress over her head, revealing a red halter bikini, the straps of which had been teasing me with their presence all evening. Beautiful bronzed skin as far as the eye can see; almost spilling out of the tight confines of her top.

I reach out for her, grabbing her wrist and pulling her down against me. Her hair smells of flowers, her soft locks tickle me as they cascade over my bare chest and shoulders.

As I lie there, with this gorgeous voluptuous woman on top of me, kissing my chest, I can't help thinking that I've just made the most wonderful discovery. Like nobody has ever felt this way before. I certainly haven't. *Lust* I understand, and Mandi certainly inspires that in me as well, but all the other stuff is new. All evening I've felt this inexplicable drive to make her smile, to crack the surface and reach her core somehow.

The fact that she seemed so guarded made me even more determined.

This creature I see above me, staring down as she starts to unbutton my jeans is no longer out of reach though. She's present as present can be, and entirely focused on me as I am on her.

There's no pretence about her. No undeserved adulation, like I'd gotten from the waitress at the restaurant. No wonder Mandi had felt weird about it. There are two types of people in the world: leaders and followers. Mandi clearly is the former. Powerful and confident in herself, so she doesn't need to look to any outsider for direction

She lifts herself off me, letting me rid myself of the jeans at last. Meanwhile she reaches around and undoes the knots of her bikini top, revealing the rest of her exquisite body. Full-figured feminine perfection.

Some might mistake the dips and valleys of her flesh for flaws, but they're not. She's perfect just as she is. A Rubenesque goddess, who deserves my complete adoration.

Her eyes show not a hint of nerves, no doubts or concerns, like she's completely in tune with herself. It's a self-assurance that some with a lesser understanding of who she is might mistake for arrogance. I know better though.

We are one.

I lean up and wrap my arm around her, almost cradling her as I turn things upside-down. With her on her back, I'm free to reach over to retrieve the bag containing dessert. A selection of items, their sole purpose is to bring her pleasure.

"Close your eyes," I say.

She looks at me defiantly for just a moment before seemingly changing her mind and doing as I say.

Inside the bag, I'm spoilt for choice. Remembering her choice in gelato earlier today, I'd picked up some chocolate truffles with a hint of Cuban dark rum, rose-scented Turkish Delight as well as an old classic: chocolate covered strawberries. The fig and vanilla custard tart Chef Arnaud added on the house just because it's a new addition to his menu. Best to leave that for later, since it requires the use of a spoon and patience. Two things neither of us have right now.

I pick up a piece of Turkish Delight, careful not to spill any of the fine sugar onto the bed. The crinkle of the heavy paper bag seems to echo around the room.

"Open up," I whisper in Mandi's ear.

Her nose twitches, she's desperate to know what's coming. Soon though, she opens her mouth so I can feed her the treat. I dive down into her invitingly full cleavage, allowing myself a taste of her aroused nipple which had received a light dusting of sugar as I fed her.

She moans softly as she chews, encouraging me to stimulate her other breast with my hand.

I pause only to pick up another sweet, this one chosen blindly by touch. A truffle. I hold it between my teeth, offering it to her from my lips while slipping one hand between us for a first, most intimate touch. She arches upwards, gasping when I find her clit in between soft, inviting curls. I kiss her half-open lips, tempting me with the taste of rich chocolate.

With every bite I alternate the flavors I feed her, while continuing to lavish her body with affection, aiming to increase the intensity of her pleasure each time. It works, judging from her reactions, which have grown more pronounced after every mouthful.

Finally she can take it no longer, opening her eyes

and focusing on the last truffle, which instead of feeding her, I finally deposit inside her belly button. I lick at it, tasting the bitter cocoa powder covering the lusciously rich chocolate inside.

Then I carefully pick it up with my teeth, and tickle her with its slightly bumpy texture, until it finally starts to melt against the heat of her skin. All the way down her lower abdomen I go, coming to a stop just above her mound. She leans up, her eyes wide with expectation and surprise as she observes me. I let go of the half-molten truffle, leaving it in her belly button again, then start to lick the trail of chocolate off her.

She writhes underneath me with every touch of my tongue. When she's clean, save for her bellybutton, I slip my fingers between her moist folds and into her at last, and just watch for a moment. She reacts sharply, crying out in pleasure. Her whole body moves under the gentle manipulations of my fingers, so I dive in for one last, chocolaty taste, taking my time on her bellybutton until no trace of truffle remains.

Finally her patience reaches its limits and she lifts herself until she can reach me. Her hands close around my cock, making me shudder with delight. It's almost too much, too intense. Just watching her enjoy herself brought me painfully close to my own release. It didn't help that I've been fighting these dark urges all evening, a primal lust so persistent I only barely managed to conceal it throughout our dinner date.

She looks me in the eye, no words are needed for me to know what she wants. It's not a pleading glance, but a command. Time for me to answer it.

I hurriedly find a condom in the drawer—this is one hotel I know to be well stocked at all times—and rush to put it on as she watches.

She spreads her beautifully voluptuous thighs, all the while continuing to hypnotize me with her eyes. The time for teasing is over, I couldn't do it even if I wanted to. I push into her, aiming to claim her just with that first move. Her lips open, but her moan sounds choked, as if she's trying to fight her release.

I am too, I don't want this first time to be over so soon.

But then she can't hold back any longer and starts to move underneath me. Her hips buck upwards, setting the pace she needs, and I follow along on her rhythm. I've picked up women before, and I've *fucked* plenty of them, but this... it's different. *She's different.* I hesitate to think of it as *making love*, but that's the only term that seems to fit.

Can you fall in love with someone you've only just met? This and many more confused thoughts enter my mind, before they are wiped out by the perfection of our union. The relentless rhythm she's chosen for us makes me blank out, until nothing matters anymore. Not the worry of whether she feels the same, not my curiosity at why tonight is so different than any other intimate encounter in my past.

She matters. Her eyes, which stare back at me, until they close involuntarily into a frown. Her soft feminine body, as it thrusts up at me every time I push deeply into her. Her gasps and moans that match my own.

She's *all* that matters.

I force myself back in control, but I'm desperately close to losing it. Her eyes are permanently shut now, and her moans quicken until there's almost no pause in between. I speed up along with her, feverishly focused on lasting long enough to take her over the edge. Then there's silence as she bites down hard on her bottom lip, and her body freezes underneath me. Every muscle of hers tightens, seemingly keen to keep me exactly where I am.

It's too much. Too intense. Too beautiful.

My own orgasm washes over me instantly. An explosion of energy originating deep inside my lower abdomen overwhelms me, until everything from my toes to my fingertips is filled with a mind numbing heat.

She opens her eyes, suddenly aware of what's happening, and starts to move again. I can't fight it, can't cooperate, I'm helplessly locked in place as she draws out our first release. Our moment of togetherness. Until we're both out of breath and paralyzed in exhaustion.

I force myself partially off her, struggling to make my muscles cooperate. Then I wrap my arm around her, and rest my head against hers. Her hair smells so nice, it intoxicates me all over again.

"Now I owe you two desserts," she says, her voice trailing off towards the end.

ONLY A TASTE

I smile, but the heavy feeling in my limbs and eyelids prevents me from responding.

After years of wandering, I feel like I've finally come home.

CHAPTER SEVEN

I lie awake, staring at the chandelier which glistens in the faintest beginnings of daylight filtering through the French windows. Beside me, Callum's deep, even breaths suggest he's still sleeping, so I take care not to move much so I don't disturb him.

There's a horrible, heavy feeling in my chest, like a weight holding me down under water. I'm drowning, desperate for air, but relief seems so impossibly out of reach, I don't know how to get it.

This has been the best night of my life, and with it, it's the worst. What if I just didn't go home today? What if I ran away with him; wouldn't that solve everything?

I know it would not. The guilt of leaving behind my family would eat me up.

But don't I deserve to be happy too? Do I have to do without, just so Mom and Dad can be proud of who I am? Even if it is a lie? Why does it have to be one or the other?

I turn onto my side, facing Callum's sleeping form. He looks so peaceful, like an angel—as stupid as that sounds. At dinner, he insisted I keep an open mind tonight, suggesting he's after something more than just a one-nighter. Could this beautiful man actually be *that* interested in me? He's successful, famous even, whereas I'm a failure professionally and not even a nice person most of the time. Sarcastic: definitely. Nice: not so much.

Neither am I that special to look at. I'm the girl who's been told her entire life that she'd be *so* pretty if only she lost a few pounds.

And then there's the baggage: not just one or two issues, but a whole collection the size and shape of a conservative extended family.

Whatever this is between Callum and me, it can't work out. There's no happy ending to be found here. And he couldn't possibly be wishing for one either.

Tears sting in my eyes, and I'm annoyed at myself for letting it get so far. Sarah was right: this was supposed to be my farewell party. A last celebration before I'd have to forget myself and fit in with whatever is expected of me. It was never meant to be a beginning of anything, just an ending.

I didn't think this could happen; that I'd go to bed with someone and get tangled up in complicated emotions afterwards. It certainly never happened to be me before. But for some reason now that I'm here, looking at him, I'm not thinking of escaping before he wakes up, or whether I'll need to block his number if he calls me too often afterwards.

It's the opposite. I wonder how long I can stay here with him, before real life catches up with me. I'm terrified that he won't *want* to call. All the while, I have nothing to offer him at all.

The more I think about it, the more certain I am

about what I must do. I need to be really clear with him, tell him that as nice as our time together has been, this is it. The end. Tonight will become a nice memory for us to keep, perhaps to think back to as *that crazy night in Brighton.* Nothing more.

It hurts to look at him now, knowing I'll probably never see him again after this, except on the damn TV. I lie back down on my pillow and cover my eyes with the back of my hand, doing everything possible to swallow my tears.

What the hell? I've never been the emotional type, why start now?

He's just a guy. We just had sex. No big deal. So why is my heart trying to make it into something more meaningful?

"Morning, beautiful."Callum's voice pierces through the silence. "You're up early."

"How did you know I was?" I ask, hoping my voice doesn't betray my innermost feelings.

"Your breathing. You sounded different when you were asleep."

It's time. The moment of truth. I have to tell him now, before he manages to distract me with his boyishly handsome looks and ruffled bed hair. Before he says something to make me reconsider.

I lean up on my elbows and look over at him. *Shit.* Just seeing his half-naked form as he sits up, ready to get out of bed, is making my heart beat faster again. I don't know if I can do this! If only I had another choice...

"I had a lovely time last night..." I start.

He turns, his blue eyes piercing me and peeling back my defenses layer by layer. "Me too."

"But..." Even my voice sounds breathless now, that's how uncharacteristically nervous I am.

"But things are very complicated right now and you're not looking for anything," he repeats my words from last night almost verbatim.

I press my lips together, again fighting the sting of tears and nod.

His expression is no longer carefree, but has hardened as he continues to look back at me. I wonder what he's thinking. I wonder if I really want to know.

"Look, it's not you, okay," I try to justify myself. "Things at home... My parents are very traditional."

"I see."

"They'll never let me date, especially not outside our community."

"How old are you again?"

I bite my tongue. He'll never understand. I'm not even sure *I* understand. It's so unfair that I have to choose between their happiness and my own. But crying about it isn't going to change anything.

"I really like you, Callum. I wish things were different."

"So do I." He turns around again, leaning forward to pick up his clothes off the floor.

There's nothing more to say, so I just watch him as he gathers his things and heads to the bathroom. The door shuts behind him with a painfully loud click. I fall back into my pillow, and focus on deep, even breaths. *Stay calm. This awful moment will pass.*

I stay like that for about five minutes, until the bathroom door opens again, revealing a fully dressed Callum. If it wasn't for the slight stubble on his chin—which could be justified as fashion—nobody could tell this overnight stay was unplanned.

"I have to get back into London for a meeting this morning," he says, while picking up his wallet, phone, and other items still on the antique-looking chest of drawers opposite the bed. Then he turns to face me, his expression is firm, almost neutral, although his eyes still betray the fiery passion that had made last night so special.

One, two steps forward, and he's at my bedside. He leans down, his face just an inch from mine, sending my self-control into a tailspin.

"I've heard what you said, and I understand," he says, while running his forefinger over my chin.

The tickle of his breath against my lips is almost too much, forcing my eyes to flutter shut a few times while he speaks.

"But don't think I'll give up that easily. This isn't goodbye." He emphasizes his statement with a kiss that knocks the wind out of me, then lets go and leaves me panting in bed as he makes his exit.

"Just leave the key in the room whenever you're done, it's all paid for. See you later, Mandi." The door clicks into place behind him, and the silence that remains overwhelms me.

ONLY A TASTE

After what feels like forever, I finally lean up and retrieve my phone from the bedside table and dial.

"Hey," Sarah's groggy voice answers. "What time is it?"

"Dunno. Hey, can you come and get me whenever you're ready? I'll text you the location," I say, doing my utmost to disguise the disillusionment in my tone.

There's a pause, and something sounding like a yawn on the other end. "Dude, you have to tell me all about last night, how was it? I'm assuming the date went well since I didn't hear from you..."

"Get ready, come pick me up, I'll tell you all about it on the drive home." I hang up before she has the chance to say anything else. Hopefully by the time we get together, I won't feel so raw and vulnerable. I'll tell Sarah what she wants to know, minus his identity and the part where I wished he wouldn't leave me behind. Even after I explicitly told him to.

This is all an impossible dream, isn't it? He can't be serious about planning to pursue me, after everything I tried to tell him? He can't possibly!

And yet, against my better judgment, I desperately hope to see Callum Byrne again.

CHAPTER EIGHT

"I'm home!" I announce myself as I close the front door of the house I grew up in behind me. It's four minutes past three. Not a bad time, considering we only got back from Brighton at eleven.

Bye, bye, outside world. You shall be missed.

"Mandeep!" Dadi—Dad's mom, who has lived with us for as long as I can recall—appears in the doorway leading to the living room, shuffling in my direction as quickly as she can manage with the help of her walking stick.

I put my bags down and rush towards her, giving her a warm hug. She's the one I missed the most when I moved away for college and it's so good to see her now that I'm back.

"Look at you! So skinny. Have you been eating properly?" She scrutinizes me up and down and pinches my cheek with her trembling fingers.

She looks frailer than when I last saw her and everyone else at my graduation ceremony. The lines on her face seem to have deepened, and her skin seems just that little bit more fragile than before. I should have visited, but the job hunt had taken up so much of my time, I didn't get the chance to.

"Don't worry, I've been taking care of myself."

"If you say so. You're just skin and bones, girl!" The quasi-strict expression on her face makes me smile and I hug her again. Even if she's obviously lying. Skin and bones; hah!

"Where is everyone?" I ask, upon letting her go again.

"The shop, of course. Where they always are."

Of course. It's the weekend, the busiest time of the week for a takeaway restaurant. Dad will be manning the phone, while Mom's in the kitchen, supervising the cooks. And ever since my little brother Jai got his license, he's been doing the deliveries.

I drag my two suitcases of clothes further into the hallway and dump them by the stairs. Sarah will drop the rest of the stuff in her car next weekend.

"Have you had lunch? Come eat something," Dadi waves at me as she turns to head back into the dining room.

"I had something on the way. Just going to put my stuff in my room, then I'm coming," I call after her.

Nothing has changed I see. Food still is the main social glue holding this family together. But before I feel like eating anything at all, I need a moment to myself to find my bearings.

I carry both my suitcases up to my old room. Everything, from the purple organza curtains, to the Moroccan style steel and glass lampshade, are a throwback to another era, one I don't belong to anymore. It's overwhelming, looking at it all. But it isn't nostalgia that hits me; it's despair.

Fighting back tears, I take a deep breath. If I'm going to stay here, things are going to have to change. I'll start with the bookcase full of old textbooks. What am I, back in school?

I dump one of my suitcases, the bigger pink one, onto the bed and start rummaging through the clothes I'd packed. All of it goes straight into the closet, without much thought. Make-up goes onto the dresser, underwear and socks into the drawer.

All the old junk I left behind when I moved out years ago, I simply brush aside. I'll sort it out later.

When I take my toiletry bag into the family bathroom across the hall, I realize that I've left my toothbrush and deodorant behind at Sarah's. Brilliant. I'll have to head to the shops as soon as possible.

By the time everything is sort of unpacked and I'm back downstairs, I'm exhausted, physically as well as mentally.

"I've made you some tea." Dadi points at the cup on the heavy wooden dining table in front of her, covered with an up-side-down saucer to keep it hot. "Sit, girl, you must be tired."

She slides a tray towards me featuring multiple bowls of nibbles, peanuts and other spicy treats. My stomach growls at the sight of it. I gratefully serve myself as I take a first sip of the strong, milky tea she's made. Nobody makes *chai* like Dadi does.

Sitting back in the chair, I close my eyes and try to relax.

"Thanks. It's been a long day," I mumble. Mainly it's

the long night with little sleep leading up to today that's having an effect on me, but I keep that detail to myself.

She smiles at me, but doesn't say a word. There's always something in the way she looks at me that suggests she knows exactly what's going on in my head. Often, that has been reassuring. To feel understood by at least one person at home.But today, I can't help feeling uneasy about it.

What if she guesses what I was up to yesterday? I had a shower before setting off, and I'm obviously no longer wearing the same bikini and summer dress anymore. But, I can't help wondering if she has an inkling that I've been with a man last night. Glimpses of our escapades keep coming back to me when I least expect them to. What if it's written on my face?

"Your father tells me Mr. Gupta is very eager for you to start work," she says at last.

Mr. Gupta. Ugh. He and Dad have been friends for as long as we've lived in this neighborhood—pretty much forever. Of course he was happy to offer me a job. My inner cynic wants to believe it's because I'll be so ridiculously overqualified for it, that we're doing *him* a favor. In truth, I think it's going to be torture.

But, everyone has to start at the bottom, as Dad likes to say. I just never thought my completed degree would have me heading for a bookkeeping job where my main activity would consist of data entry for a shop selling cheap underwear imported from China.

"Yeah, I'm so excited too," I respond, while taking another sip of hot tea in an attempt to drown out the continuing sense of loss that's been hanging over me ever since I left Sarah this morning.

"You'll find something else in a while. You're smart, I've always said that you're smart. Give it a few months at least, though," Dadi tries to reassure me.

I smile bleakly at her, grateful she's latching on to my job concerns as the main source of my mood today. I'd feel horrible if she thought I was sad to be back home with her. And if she found out about Callum, well that's just a whole other bucketful of awkward right there.

We sit quietly while I finish my tea. Remembering my missing toiletries, I ask Dadi if we need anything else from the shops, to which she responds with a smile and a nod. I know exactly what she's after.

"Oh, Mandeep," Dadi reaches for my arm just as I'm about to leave and gives me a serious look. "As usual, no need to mention the gin to your father."

I wink at her. Our understanding still stands. "Of course not. No need to mention to him that I'm not looking forward to the new job either."

"My lips are sealed, child. See you later."

I grab my handbag and I'm out the door.

The shopping centre is only a short walk away, and the blue, cloudless skies overhead suggest I'm safe to leave without an umbrella. While I'm already out, I might as well show my face at the takeaway too, give the impression that I'm happy to be back, etcetera.

The warm summer air carries with it the heavy floral scents of our neighbor's, Mrs. Singh's, colorful front garden. Other neighbors must have been mowing their lawns, adding the aroma of cut grass as their contribution to today's summery atmosphere.

The contrast between yesterday and today couldn't be bigger. From the city, followed by the hustle and bustle of Brighton beach, I'm back in suburbia. Back in our old street, where I know every single person who lives here—mainly because nobody ever seems to move away—and more unnervingly, everyone knows me too.

"Mandi!" a voice drags me out of my bittersweet thoughts. "So it's true, you're back."

I look up to find Leila from five houses down standing there looking down her nose at me with her arms propped up against her hips.

A casual bystander may have mistaken her smile for genuine, but I know better. Leila is the mean girl of the neighborhood after all.

"Leila. Nice to see you," I remark, returning a fake grin of my own. *With neighbors like her, who needs enemies?*

"Your parents must be thrilled."

"I'm sure they are."

She stands in silence for a moment while really looking me up and down. As if she's tallying up new ways to insult me. A few years ago, I would have felt embarrassed; even humiliated. But now, it's just irritating. I have bigger fish to fry.

"So I hear Mr. Gupta has a job lined up for you," she says finally. "Exciting. You know, I applied for that one too, but I guess he owed your dad, or something." As if she needed even more reason to hate me, now she thinks I stole her job away from her too. Great.

"Just chance, I'm sure."

"Yeah..." She pauses for a few awkward seconds. "Well anyway, good luck with that."

"Thanks. See you around." I shoot one last glance in her direction, only to find she's whipped her phone out of her pocket already to spread the news that I'm back. I roll my eyes and wonder how many more uncomfortable conversations with people from my past lie ahead...

Thankfully the rest of the walk, as well as my short visit to the small supermarket across from our takeaway, passes without further interruptions. The bored-looking middle-aged bleached blonde with the dangerously long red fingernails scans my meager purchases—toothbrush, deodorant, bottle of gin—without comment. Thank God I don't know her, or she'd no doubt start grilling me about the booze.

Shit, the takeaway! I can't very well walk in there carrying a bottle of gin!

"Umm, sorry, mind if I leave this here for just a minute? I'll be right back," I ask, pointing at the bag.

She nods in such a disinterested manner, I wonder if she's even heard me properly, but breathe a sigh of relief when she accepts it when I hand her my shopping across the counter.

Moments later, I cross the threshold of *'Passage to India'*, which has looked and smelled exactly like it has done for the past twenty years at least. The aroma of mixed spices brings back a whole lot of memories.

"Dad, I'm back!" I call out at the empty wooden

counter. Dad appears from the back within seconds, a wide smile on his face.

"Good. Your mother is in the kitchen," he says, before turning around "Kamal, come out here for a moment?"

"What is it?" Mom shouts back, before popping her head around the doorway. "Mandeep! Sweetheart!" She rushes towards me and gives me an awkward hug, trying not to touch her flour-covered hands on my clothes. "How lovely that you're back. Did you go home yet? Of course you did, you wouldn't have just come straight here, would you?"

"I've left my stuff in my room. Just needed a few toiletries," I explain.

"Right... Right..." She takes a step back and smiles at me for a moment. "It's so wonderful you've come. Finally the family is complete again. Now everything can get back to normal."

"Yes. Wonderful," I repeat. "Well I just popped in to say hello, but I'm kind of tired after lugging my suitcases around on and off the train, so perhaps I'll rest a bit. See you at night?"

"Sure thing, darling." Mom gives me a wave and turns to head back into the kitchen.

"Bye, Mandeep," Dad says.

I wave back at them and head across the street again to collect my shopping. While it's nice to see everyone again, I can't help feeling just a little bit resentful.

I'm back. And now I'm stuck here.

CHAPTER NINE: CALLUM

"So if you're keeping the lamb as a main, you'll have to rethink the starters. It doesn't gel together," Jack Cleary remarks, while looking up from the print-out with suggested dishes.

"Right you are," I say, though I'm only half listening to him.

"Also, you're quite thin on salads. That may fly for a winter menu, but in the summer, you're going to turn people off, son." Jack leans out of his leather armchair and picks up his scotch, clinking the ice in it together while he brings it to his lips.

"Mhm."

"Well that does it. Why so distracted? Are my insights boring you?" He gives me a strict stare, just like back in the day when I was training under him. He's always had an air of authority about him; ruling his kitchen with an iron fist.

"It's not that, I'm just finding it hard to concentrate. Didn't sleep well."

"I recall a time when you didn't need a mundane thing such as sleep."

"Well we're not getting any younger, are we?" I attempt a joke, but it falls on deaf ears. What am I saying; Jack has at least ten years on me.

"There's more to it than that. I'd be willing to put money on it," Jack says. "This isn't so much a sleep issue as a... It's a woman, isn't it?"

I sit back into the creaky leather and let my thoughts wander back to Brighton. Back to Mandi.

"That obvious, is it?" I ask, while picking up my own glass for a sip.

The Scotch is smooth. Expensive. Exactly to Jack's taste. It's quite early in the day to be drinking, but I decide that I don't care.

"In some cultures—say in Hull—our friendship would be old enough to have children of its own. Of course, it's bloody obvious."

I let out a chuckle. He's right. We've known each other coming up to fifteen—maybe sixteen years now, when I first joined his restaurant as a fresh-faced dishwasher with grand ambitions.

"Fine. It's a woman."

"Well don't be so mysterious!"

I take a deep breath, sighing all the air back out again. Where to begin...

"I may not have found the perfect location for my Brighton restaurant, but I did find something else there."

"Oh?" Jack folds his hands together, waiting for me to continue.

"Her name is Mandi, and she's..." *Beautiful, magnificent, perfect in every way.* "Probably unavailable."

"That's never stopped you before," Jack remarks.

"It's not so simple. There are family issues."

"Well you certainly work quickly if you already know all about her family. You were only in Brighton for a day, weren't you?"

"One night."

"One night..." he sounds thoughtful. "So, tell me more."

"We both ordered the same flavor gelato, but they only had one scoop left."

He laughs out loud. "That sounds like the beginning of a girly movie."

It does, he's right, but I'm in no mood to laugh about it. "Then I asked her to dinner, and that was that."

"That's all the detail I'm going to get out of you, isn't it?" he teases.

"Use your imagination, you old pervert."

I take another sip, savoring the burn of the Scotch on my tongue. I've got to get in touch with her.

"Hey, Callum," a cheerful voice greets me from behind. I turn to find Carrie, Jack's assistant, standing in the doorway, waving at me. "I thought I heard your voice in here. How's it going?"

I exchange a quick look with Jack, who looks thoroughly amused. Carrie has always had a thing for me, and there have been times—one time—she managed to tempt me into something more than just idle small talk. She has nothing on Mandi though. I don't know what I was thinking.

"Just working on my new menu. In fact, we ought to get back to that, if you don't mind." I shoot Carrie a quick business-like nod and turn to face Jack who still has a smug smile plastered on his face.

"No problem, you boys get back to it," she says, presumably while leaving.

"I see. You're thoroughly screwed, mate," Jack remarks.

"Bugger off. Now what were you saying about the lamb and the starters?"

***

By late afternoon, Jack and I finally manage to put something together we're both reasonably happy with. A menu with something for everyone, which won't tax the kitchen too much even during the busy periods. Perfect for a new restaurant. We can always switch things up once the staff are properly settled in.

After saying our goodbyes, I find myself wandering through Waterloo Station on my own. As insanely busy and chaotic a place it is, somehow walking through the crowds alone has a calming effect on me. The ambient noise of a thousand people rushing through the main hall and to and from platforms, is almost hypnotic. Whenever I have something to mull over, this is where my feet seem to take me.

What do I know about Mandi?

The quick glance I managed to steal at the expired student ID card in her wallet gave me her full name: Mandeep Grewal. I know her parents live in Langley, and she's just moving back in with them. How many Grewal families who run a takeaway could there be in

Langley? It's not that big of a place, is it?

Although she insisted that we have no future together because her folks would disapprove, I know I can't just let this go. I meant it when I told her this morning wasn't goodbye. Within just a few hours, she's embedded herself in my thoughts permanently.

When I close my eyes, I can still see her smile; her eyes full of warmth when she lets her guard down. I can still smell her sweet scent and imagine the taste of her lips against mine.

I've had relationships before, though arguably not many serious ones, but this connection I felt with her was unlike anything I'd experienced with anyone else. It's all new, yet I instinctively know it's not a fad that will just pass in time.

I decide to head home to think things over and perhaps do a bit of research on her. Perhaps I can find out more about her family, or look her up online somehow.

Of course I could just call the number she gave me, but what if she doesn't answer? When she gave me her number, it was before we'd even talked properly. What if it's not actually hers? What if her plan was always to ditch me, so she purposefully gave out a fake number to avoid complications?

In this day and age, you can find a person's whole life on the internet. In case the number turns out to be a fake, there has got to be a way I can get in touch with her. Otherwise I might have to resort to going door-to-door in Langley until I find the right house.

That would make things a lot more awkward than they need to be. But I'll do it if I have to. She's worth it.

"Excuse me?" a voice interrupts.

"Yes?" I respond, almost on autopilot. The expression on the professional-looking woman in the trouser suit is one I know all too well. She's recognized me.

"Are you...?"

"The one."

"Would you be able to..."

"Sign that?" I ask, pointing at the magazine she's holding with my face on the cover. "Sure."

She smiles gratefully while I go through the motions of giving her my autograph. This sort of thing happens so often, I'm well beyond thinking about it. But Mandi... it was weird for her last night with the waitress. Could she ever get used to this?

What if I find her? What if her supposed family issues aren't that big of a deal after all, but she can't deal with the constant spotlight on my life; and by extension on hers? Now I'm really getting ahead of myself.

I nod at the woman, shake her hand, and leave her standing in the middle of the crowds in Waterloo's main hall, clutching onto her newly signed magazine. I head out into the street with the beginnings of a plan developing in my head. First, I'll try to find Mandi online. Then we'll see what happens.

"Taxi!" I wave at a black cab approaching from the left.

"Where to?" the cabbie asks.

I give him my home address and gaze out the window at the world passing us by. As soon as I get home, I'll see if I can get in touch with her somehow. I owe it to us both to at least try.

I reach my place fifteen minutes later, and I'm still determined. Ignoring the long To Do list on the notepad on the coffee table, I open my laptop instead, and start searching for Mandi. It seems she shares her name with thousands of others, so I change strategy and search for more details on the takeaway in Langley instead.

Bingo.

Old articles pop up about her and her family, the sort of quaint news you get in local papers. *Local takeaway wins Best Curry of Slough award.* A short quote from Mr. Grewal, presumably her dad, in a longer article about the redevelopment of a park. *Langley girl comes second in Craft Fair competition;* that sort of thing.

The photograph with the latter article catches my attention instantly. It's her, a few years younger of course, and at the same time so very different. The hip length hair worn in a thick braid made her look a lot more ethnic than she does now. But the sparkle in her eyes and smile are unmistakably her own.

An hour passes as I continue my stalkerish behavior. None of what I find reveals a subtler way of contacting her, though. I'm going to have to rely on the phone number she gave me yesterday. I guess I'll find out soon enough whether it works.

I hover over the 'call' button for a while, then put my

phone back down in my lap again. Too soon. I'm going to give it at least another day or so.

As if by magic, my phone starts ringing in my hand. Unlisted number.

"Hello?" I answer, dreading as well as hoping Mandi was having the exact same thoughts as me and actually made the call herself.

"Callum, it's Trisha. You have a moment?"

I close my eyes and breathe a sigh of relief or disappointment; I'm not sure which. Trisha is the new PR contact for the TV network that airs my show.

"Yeah, sure, what's going on?"

"We're going to push the new season hard. Media appearances, interviews, the whole lot," she says

"Go on..." I grab my notepad and pen from the table and settle back into my chair while she runs me through the various promotional events she wants me to do. Looks like I have a busy few weeks ahead of me.

I start my job with Mr. Gupta sharp at nine on Monday morning. Although the first day is intense because I don't know what I'm doing yet, it soon turns into the drudgery I expected it to be. Tuesday, Wednesday and even Thursday pass without incident or excitement. I go to work in the morning, and try to survive the day without having any existential crises. In the evenings I head home to help out with dinner while trying not to think too much.

It's only at night, and during those moments before fully waking up early in the morning, that Callum stalks my thoughts. And boy, is it hard to banish those dreams from my imagination for the rest of the day.

My approach to fitting in back at home almost works, until finally on Friday evening, I arrive home to quite the spectacle in our living room.

Mom, Dad, Dadi and even Jai are dressed as if they're about to attend a wedding. Opposite them on the other sofa, there's another set of well-polished parents and a guy, who looks completely and utterly terrified.

"Mandeep, come sit with us. We'd like you to meet the Sandhus."

My heart sinks. Considering I've never seen these

people before, and the state the guy—roughly my age—is in, this can only mean one thing: our parents have collectively decided to play matchmaker. *Fuck.*

In an effort to hide my annoyance, I bow my head and mumble a greeting at the visitors, before sitting down next to Dadi with my hands folded and my eyes fixed straight ahead.

"So lovely to meet you. What a lovely girl," the woman—Mrs. Sandhu—remarks, while exchanging an approving look with her husband. Their son barely even looks up from the floor.

"She's just completed her Bachelor's in Business Administration," my dad says proudly.

"Very bright. And she cooks well too," Mom adds.

I can hear Jai chuckle under his breath, but sadly he's too far away for me to kick in the shin. *Just you wait 'til it's your turn, dipshit.*

" So, what does your son do?" Dad asks.

"Oh, Diljeet is working with a multinational in the city. He's just been promoted to team leader," Mr. Sandhu beams.

Next thing I know, our parents are comparing salaries, both current as well as projected. I wish for the ground to just open up and swallow me whole.

"Anyway, what do you say we let the kids get to know each other a little? How about a drink, Mr. Sandhu?" Dad suggests, gesturing at me to get up and take the Sandhus' man-child somewhere for a private chat. As if this meeting couldn't get any worse.

I sigh, then head for the kitchen area to pick up a

bottle of Coke and two glasses. Then, out the door and into the hallway and up the stairs I go. Diljeet is a whole bunch of steps back. I can hear his folks encouraging him behind me.

I don't even check what he's doing behind me, it's enough that I hear footsteps.

"Want some?" I ask once inside my room, holding up a glass with my back still turned to him.

"Uhh... Sure." He clears his throat, but is unable to disguise the nerves in his voice.

I pour two glasses, then turn, handing him his. He doesn't even look directly at me.

"So... I guess we're supposed to get to know each other," I say, while checking the clock above my old desk. Five minutes alone with this guy would be too long, but I don't think I could get away with less.

"Yeah..."

Silence.

I look at him, as he stares at his shoes. I bet he's a virgin.

"So?"

"So?" he repeats.

"Who are you?"

"Diljeet. From Staines."

I decide to give him a chance to continue this very meaningful exchange, but he's not exactly a sparkling conversationalist. In fact, now he's quiet again. Without my intervention, the silence lasts a whole minute. I know this because I'm timing it on the wall clock.

"So have your parents met with a lot of girls yet?" I

ask at last.

If brown skin could blush properly, he'd be red by now. He shakes his head.

"How do you think it's going so far?"

He shrugs. *Yeah. Whatever.*

"Whenever you're done, let's go back inside before they wonder what we're up to." I put my empty glass down on the desk and head straight for the door without giving him the chance to reply.

Once I make it back inside the living room, Jai can barely contain his amusement, much to Mom and Dad's displeasure. Dadi gives me a look of understanding and pats on the sofa beside her.

"Well?" Mom asks, though I instinctively realize it's a rhetorical question.

"It's been wonderful meeting you, Mr. and Mrs. Sandhu. And Diljeet, of course." Dad nods at the lot of them, just as *His Shyness* shuts the living room door behind him, looking even more terrified than he did when we were alone in my room. "We'll be in touch."

As his parents get up to say their goodbyes to my parents, I don't have the energy to keep up appearances anymore. All I can do is sit next to Dadi, who is gently patting the top of my hand as if to tell me everything is going to be all right.

The second everyone makes it out the front door, and Mom and Dad come back into the lounge, they both pounce.

"He's a handsome boy, isn't he?" Mom asks.

"Very well settled. Good family," Dad adds.

"I'll be in my room," I say, and bolt out the door and up the stairs. What the actual fuck? They couldn't wait at least a week to let me get used to being back home before parading me around like cattle at an auction? Well settled, bah! I slam my door and turn the key.

"Hey, Mandi," Jai's voice filters through my bedroom door moments later. "Awesome guy, innit?"

"Leave me alone!" I shout.

He bursts out laughing on the other side, requiring me to turn on the radio to drown him out. The irritating little shit can drop dead for all I care.

It's at that moment, to the raw and vulnerable vocals of Tom Odell's *Another Love* that the first tears start to form. If I stand my ground, I can probably steer my folks in the direction of someone a bit more compatible, but what would be the point? I already know nobody could ever match up to Callum!

Being honest with my folks just isn't going to work either. If they found out about Callum at all, they'd just dig in further about Diljeet or whoever else comes along. They'd never let me date on my own; and certainly not a white guy.

On top of that, I don't even know if Callum is even interested at all. We haven't been in touch since that one night, obviously. Perhaps he's been a lot more successful forgetting me, than I have been at forgetting him.

It's hopeless. All of it.

I hide my face in my pillow and let the floodgates open until my pillowcase is soaked with tears. There's no way out of this. Either I take a stand for me, *my happiness*, and destroy theirs in the process, or I need to accept the fact that I just cannot get what I so desperately want.

"Mandeep?" Dadi's voice calls out from beyond my door, followed by a subtle knock.

I sniffle loudly, hoping to contain all the wetness and goo that is still dripping from several of my facial orifices.

"Open up, talk to me."

Pressing the pillow on my face one final time in the hopes it'll dry me off a bit, I drag myself up and open the door.

"Yes, Dadi?" I whimper a bit too miserably.

"Child, tell me what's wrong." She shuffles inside, then closes the door behind her, almost dropping her walking stick in the process.

I sit back down on the bed with my hands folded and wait for her to reach me. She puts her hand on my shoulder, squeezing it encouragingly.

"I wasn't impressed either, I'll have you know," she says, before sitting down with a loud sigh.

Her remark makes me smile despite myself, but the tears are still coming, just more silently than before.

"I... He... Oh God, what do I do?" I complain.

"Your father is a very stubborn man, has been ever since he was little."

"Yeah..."

"I remember when he was eight years old, some older boys from the neighborhood told him he was too little to play football with them. And he played and played on his own, every day after school, practicing so that he would be good enough. It was so hot outside that he fainted. We had to take him to the doctor because he'd gotten dehydrated. Still, he refused to give up and just went back to practicing as soon as I let him out of my sights. That's how stubborn your father was."

This story, which I've heard probably a hundred times before, does nothing to make me feel better. If anything, it's further proof that everything is lost. I hide my face in my hands.

"How many times can I say 'no' before Dad loses patience, you think?" I ask, hoping that if I can get away with refusing a whole bunch of matches, perhaps someone or other will come along who will make me reconsider everything. Someone I could actually accept. Though I doubt that's even possible.

"You know when I was to marry your grandfather, I wasn't thrilled either. Back in those days, you didn't even meet until the day of the wedding. I thought he was too skinny, too awkward when I first saw him at the ceremony. But in time, I grew to love him. That's what happens in arranged marriages. The start is never easy, even if you think you know each other well. Marriage is never easy." She looks down at her hands, gripping the knob on her stick tightly.

"Mhm," I respond, lacking the words for a proper reply.

A strange, extra quiet silence follows.

"Who is he?" Dadi's words cut through my defenses

like a hot knife through butter.

I look up, shocked at her question. *Did I hear that right?*

"What?" I ask.

"Don't you play with me, young lady. I wasn't born yesterday."

I sigh and lie back on the bed, covering my eyes with my arm.

"Just. A guy." Just the most amazing guy I've ever met, who's always in the back of my mind, no matter how hard I try to forget him.

"And? Is he ready to marry you?" she asks.

"No! It's... I don't know. We haven't talked about it." He couldn't possibly be. He doesn't seem the type anyway, plus we haven't spoken. What do I even know about him? Practically nothing. For all I know he's gone straight from me to someone else, without looking back even once.

"I suggest that you do, before your father gets in one of his moods and puts his foot down." She pats my leg, then heaves herself up with the help of her stick and shuffles back to the door.

"Consider it. If you can get this boy to meet your father, perhaps something can be done."

I'm still in shock that she could see through me so easily, when the door clicks back into place behind her. Of course there's no way I could ever consider her advice. Despite his insistence that last week's one-nighter was more than that, he hasn't been in touch.

And Dadi doesn't know he's white, or she wouldn't

even have suggested any of this.

From the corner of my eye I notice that the little light in the top corner of my phone is blinking. I must have forgotten it on silent when I left work earlier. Perhaps it's Sarah. I could use a good talk with her right now; or rather, a good cry.

I unlock the screen and find that it's not Sarah at all. It's a message from Callum. I open it with shaky fingers.

This is a sign, isn't it? After wondering whether he even thinks about me at all? It's as if he could read my mind and knew I'm in trouble.

'Mandi. Sorry I've not been in touch, work has been crazy this past week. I really would like to see you again though, can't stop thinking about you. Call me when you can? Callum'

After reading and re-reading the message a few times, I decide not to call. Not that I don't appreciate him reaching out, I just wouldn't know what to say, plus I'm all stuffed up after crying earlier. The last thing I want right now is to have to explain why. Instead, I type out a quick response:

'Been thinking about you too, but things are really complicated at home right now. I'll call you tomorrow. Mandi'

The moment I've hit 'send', I pull up Sarah's number instead.

CHAPTER ELEVEN

After being plagued by confusing as well as explicit dreams featuring one—and only one—perfect subject all night, Saturday morning has crept up on me rather suddenly. I rush to get up, splash water on my face and head for the stairs. Sarah is coming in a short while with the rest of my stuff, and it would be nice to at least be showered and ready beforehand.

After living together for years, it's been weird not having her around at all. It's only been a week, but I've really missed her.

As is typical for weekends in our house, everyone else has been up for hours when I make it downstairs at ten. The living/dining areas are abuzz with activity. Dadi is sitting in her usual seat at the head of the table, with Dad towards her right. Mom, meanwhile, is rushing back and forth between the open plan kitchen and the table, bringing in breakfast.

Off in the lounge area, the large flat screen TV is on, but nobody seems to be paying attention to it.

"Mandi, finally, you're awake. Make some tea, will you?" Mom says, the moment she spies me standing in the doorway.

I suppress a yawn and start making myself useful. Cups. Kettle. Tea bags.

"Jai, what time is your game?" Dad asks. I turn around to observe the exchange.

Jai mumbles something about eleven, before stuffing way too much omelet into his mouth.

I turn back when the kettle's click lets me know the water is boiling and ready.

"Shush... My program is coming," Dadi says to no one in particular, while picking up the remote and dramatically increasing the volume.

Right in the middle of pouring the third and fourth cup, watching the near boiling water create swirls of dark brown originating from the tea bag, I hear something from the living area that stops me in my tracks. A familiar voice.

I accidentally spill some of the hot water over the counter, then quickly recover and put the kettle down to avoid further accidents. When I turn around, despite being as far away from the TV as I possibly could be, I instantly recognize Callum's handsome face.

Fuck. Of course. I had forgotten all about Dadi's love for a BBC weekend morning staple: 'Saturday Kitchen'. Next to the smiling host of the program, Callum is animatedly explaining something or other, but I can't seem to concentrate on his words.

This show. It's hosted live, isn't it? That means I'm literally looking at him in real-time. Almost as if he's literally standing here in our family living room!

"Mandeep? Oi!" Mom snaps her finger, startling me. "How about that tea? What's wrong with you? You look like you've seen a ghost."

"Tea. Of course." I turn around again, force a couple of deep breaths to get rid of the tightness in my chest, and pour hot water into the remaining cups. My hands still shake when I add milk and place the cups on a tray ready to deliver to the table.

"Perhaps she's just distracted because she can't stop thinking about Diljeet Sandhu," Jai remarks, chuckling to himself. "Mandi and Diljeet, sitting in a tree..."

"Shut up!" I shoot him a nasty look. The worst part is that he's hit the truth on the head without realizing, except it's Callum, not Diljeet, who's on my mind as well as on our bloody TV this morning. Must avoid looking at him. *Shit.* This is really bad.

"Are you okay, darling? You look pale," Mom asks again, touching my forehead with the back of her hand while I put the tea down.

"Yeah, fine. Had some trouble sleeping," I mumble, while making my way to the other side of the table. Even though I sit down with my back towards the TV, Callum's voice is still throwing me off balance.

To think he actually messaged me last night. And I said I'd call him! What the hell will I say? I like him, of course I do, but I have nothing whatsoever to offer him. He's not going to be content with the occasional phone call and message. I wouldn't be either, in his place.

I should ignore him. I should tell him to go away and delete my number. I should...

"Mandeep!" Dad almost shouts. His expression suggests he's been trying to get my attention for a bit too long already.

"Uhh... yes?"

"The salt."

I look over at the salt shaker right in front of my plate and almost knock it over while picking it up to hand it to Dad.

"She really doesn't look well. Are you sure you don't need to see a doctor?" Mom asks.

I just shake my head and start poking around in my food. Ugh. At this rate, I'm going to make all of them suspicious.

"Shh... I can't hear the TV," Dadi says, while increasing the volume yet again.

While everyone else is quietly eating, I rush to clean my plate as much as I can before excusing myself and heading back upstairs. That was bizarre. Let's hope Callum doesn't turn up in more unexpected places or I might just have a meltdown.

A quick shower later, the doorbell rings as I've just finished drying my hair. That'll be Sarah! And she couldn't have arrived at a better time.

I race downstairs, but Mom has beaten me to the door.

"Morning, Mrs. Grewal." Sarah shoots me a wide smile as she nods at Mom.

"Oh there you are, Mandi, your friend is here. Let me know if you need anything." She turns and heads back into the living area, giving us some much needed privacy.

"Oh my God, I'm so glad to see you," I say, while giving her a hug.

"Me too," she responds.

"How about we quickly unload your car and then head out somewhere for coffee?" I suggest. I can't wait to get out of here and tell her all about the mess I've found myself in. Yesterday's set-up orchestrated by my folks was awkward enough, but I think it's time to spill the beans about Callum. There's only so much confusion I can deal with on my own, and it would be good to get her insights before I call him and accidentally muck things up further.

She nods, then cocks her head to the side. "You look tired, are you okay? You're not getting sick, are you?"

"God, why does everyone keep asking me that this morning?" I complain.

"Because it's obvious."

I shake my head. "Later. Let's get this over with first."

She shrugs and heads out towards her car while I follow. There are only about half a dozen boxes, so it doesn't take long for us to get everything out of her rust bucket vehicle and into my room.

I sit down on the bed and rub my eyes. I really am exhausted this morning.

"So, you want to tell me what's going on now?" Sarah asks.

After taking a moment to figure out where to start, I decide it's best not to beat around the bush.

"You know the guy I met in Brighton?" I begin.

"Yeah."

"He wants to keep in touch."

"So? Tell him to leave you alone." Sarah squints at me suspiciously, but then her eyes widen when she realizes what I'm trying to tell her. "Holy shit, you *like* him!"

I sigh. "Yeah. I do like him. It's a massive pain in my ass."

"So now what? Are you going to tell your parents?"

"My parents? They seem to be intent on marrying me off to whichever candidate has the best possible career prospects. It's like a bloody job interview. Whether I like the guy or not doesn't seem to be much of a priority." I let my shoulders hang down in defeat as I tell her in exacting detail about yesterday's post-work ambush and Diljeet Sandhu, the shy virgin.

"But, they're your *parents*! Surely they want you to be happy in life, don't they?" Sarah's shocked expression emphasizes that she hadn't taken much of what I'd told her about my background seriously.

"Of course they do, but they think that's what they're doing! They think in the long term that's what'll keep me happy," I explain. "I should just tell him to leave me alone, you're right." Just the thought hurts more than anticipated. I'm not sure I have the strength to do that.

"No! You can't! What if the both of you are totally right for one another? What if you're meant to be?"

I always knew Sarah was a romantic at heart, but what she's telling me now is next level. And unhelpful to boot.

"But what's the point, when my parents will never agree to let us be together?"

Sarah sighs deeply, then places her hand on top of mine. "I can't advise you about that. But there will come a time when you have to choose between your family and your own happiness."

Even though she can't fully relate to my situation, she's right about that. I will have to choose.

But perhaps, I just need some time to figure this thing out. Maybe my fascination with Callum is just a phase I'll grow out of. I should keep in touch with him behind everyone's back and see if things between us fizzle out naturally. And then, I won't have to tell a soul about it. Indeed, perhaps everything will find a way of working itself out.

"Anyway, how about that coffee?" Sarah asks.

I sigh deeply, reassured in the knowledge that now I have at least some semblance of a plan. Even if it relies almost completely on apathy.

"Yes. Let's go."

"I also have a bit of news I wanted to share with you, actually," Sarah tells me while we make our way out of my room and down the stairs.

"Oh yeah? Spill."

"Yeah, so, I got a job!" Sarah says.

"You already had a job." Unlike me.

She counters with a dismissive wave.

"Just freelancing; nothing stable. But this, this will be a *proper* job."

I grab my handbag on the way out of the house, then pat her on the shoulder with my free hand. "That's great, congratulations!"

"Yeah, so you remember that classmate of mine, Megan?"Sarah carries on.

"Uh-huh."

"She works for this website, *'Celeb Roundup'*, doing the lifestyle column. She put in a good word for me with her boss. I start in two weeks."

I frown. A gossip website? She sounds so excited though, bless her.

"It's actually perfect timing that we're meeting up this weekend, because I'm planning to move closer to the office to avoid the monster commute. I start house hunting next week!"

"Wow, this is all happening pretty quickly, huh?" I say, unsure what to think about all this. A couple of weeks back we were living in a tiny flat in the city together, and now I'm back home and even she's moving away. Things are changing a bit too quickly for my taste.

One thing is for sure, though. I was right to hide Callum's identity from her. She must never know who he is.

***

In the afternoon, after Sarah as well as mostly everyone else has left the house, I'm back in my room to try and build myself up for that all important first phone call.

It's strange, how we've done so many things in person, and yet simply dialing Callum's number to talk to him seems like such a big step. What if I'm interrupting something? What if he's busy?

Only one way to find out.

I dial his number before I get the chance to chicken out. It rings once, twice, thrice, and then he picks up.

"Mandi, hi!" He sounds genuinely pleased to hear from me, which helps some ways towards making me less nervous.

"Callum. How are you?" I ask.

"Not bad, but busy. If trying to open a new restaurant wasn't enough, now the network is after my life to promote the new season of my show as well. I just did a promo appearance this morning, actually."

I'm reminded of the sheer awkwardness of having him pop up on our TV earlier today. I close my eyes and breathe deeply. It's good to hear his voice. Comforting.

"Oh yeah, I actually saw that. To my own detriment," I blurt out.

"Was it that bad?" he teases, making me chuckle.

I counter by telling him all about this morning, when I nearly spilled everyone's tea hearing his voice behind me. Thankfully this retold version actually is a lot funnier than how it felt when it happened, and we share a good laugh.

"... I almost had a heart attack," I chuckle.

"I must say I was a bit worried, messaging you last night," Callum remarks after a short pause.

"Why?"

"Call me paranoid, but part of me was convinced you'd given me a fake number."

"Is it?" I'm doing my best not to burst out laughing,

mainly because I almost did.

"Yeah... I think it was the 'I'm here with a friend, can she come too?' response to me asking you out that threw me."

"That seemed like a funny thing to say at the time," I remark dryly, to which he laughs again.

"Funny, yes. I guess I can see that."

Just like that, a couple of laughs and nonsensical exchanges later, things are fine again. I lie back on my bed, mobile phone in hand and close my eyes, just focusing on our conversation. It's almost like he's here with me, lying next to me. Of course if that were the case, we wouldn't be *just talking*.

CHAPTER TWELVE:
CALLUM

I haven't seen Mandi in weeks. The occasional phone conversation and back and forth messaging has been frightfully dissatisfying. She feels the same, or so I assume, based on how she tends to sound over the phone.

My decision to make the trip to Langley didn't actually involve her directly, though. She would have said no, and tried to dissuade me. But, her folks work pretty much constantly through the weekends and she told me that her grandmother has some neighborhood bingo event to go to today.

So, today is the perfect day to give Mandi a little surprise. And meeting in person will give us the chance to find out if whatever we feel for one another is real, or just a desperate yearning to get back the memories of that one perfect night together.

I pull into her street, and the SatNav confirms her house should be up ahead on the right. Number seven.

My heart is racing, and I run my hands through my hair in an attempt to calm my nerves. It doesn't work.

Why am I even nervous? She liked me, right? She could have told me to bugger off on the phone if she didn't want to keep in touch. Instead, we've been in touch daily since that first phone call. And most of the time, she's initiated it.

It occurs to me that coming here in my Aston Martin was quite dumb, though. People will see it and talk. I should have rented a car: something more normal like a modest hatchback.

I find a parking spot a little ways up the road, far enough from her house, and leave the car there. Hopefully this will be enough to divert suspicions.

Crap, I should have brought flowers. No, that would be hard to explain to her folks. Chocolates. I should have brought chocolates. *Damn.*

As I consider back and forth whether I'm making a huge mistake, I see the curtains of the house I'm parked in front of twitch. Nosy neighbors. Brilliant.

I quickly get out of the car and head for her place, while scanning the otherwise empty street. It seems to be a rather typical neighborhood. Terraced houses with perfectly manicured front gardens. Hatchback cars and station wagons in all shades of grey line the street.

What am I going to say to her? What if she's upset that I came here?

I decide to just go for it. It's too late to back out now.

I ring the bell and almost instantly come face-to-face with what looks like a younger, male version of Mandi. Their eyes are the same color, the same shape even. His face resembles hers quite a lot, except for the carefully trimmed edging of beard, and the ultra-short buzz cut you often see on youths living in the inner city.

"Yeah?" the guy, presumably Mandi's brother, says. "Who are you?"

"Is Mandi home?" I ask.

He scrutinizes me for a moment, then pauses in the doorway, as if he's still deciding what to do.

"Jai, who is it? Is it a courier? I'm expecting a parcel," Mandi's voice calls out from inside the house.

"I dunno, he don't look like a courier," Jai shouts back.

Footsteps come down the stairs, until she appears in the hall behind her brother. Breathtaking. Even simple jeans and a fitted plain black t-shirt can make her look radiant somehow.

"Oh shit," she blurts out.

Well, this is awkward.

"Hi, Mandi," I say.

"Jai, weren't you heading out?" She turns to her brother.

"I'm wondering if I should maybe stay home." He folds his arms and gives her a suspicious look.

"Don't be a dick, Jai," she says.

All I can do is stand by as they stare each other down.

"Explain why I shouldn't call Mom and Dad right now and tell them you've got a guy visiting you at home?"

Bollocks, this whole surprise visit thing isn't going as well as I'd hoped.

"Firstly, because that would be really shitty of you,

secondly, because maybe one day there will be a time when you need me on your side, and then you'll kick yourself for not being more cooperative right now." She props her arms up on her hips and gives him a dirty look.

"Fine! Jeez. I guess I gotta go then." Mandi's brother shrugs at me, grabs a bundle of keys from the shelf beside the door and heads outside.

Before I get the chance to feel somewhat relieved, Mandi's expression reminds me that I'm still in trouble.

"What the hell were you thinking just turning up here?" she complains under her breath.

"I had to see you." I shrug apologetically. "But it's obvious we can't stay here. Get ready, let's go for a drive. Then you'll be free to tell me all about how I'm a terrible person for visiting you."

She pauses for a moment, then turns back to pick up a handbag from the coat rack on the wall. "Okay. I'm ready."

We walk back to my car in silence—I sure hope the same nosy neighbor isn't still spying on us now—and get in. That's when I notice how her body language has changed. Although she started off tense; even a bit hostile, now, sitting in the passenger seat of my car, she seems vulnerable. The way she's fidgeting with the hem of her t-shirt suggests she's nervous too. Thank God, it's not just me then.

"Where are we going?" she asks when I turn the key and check my mirrors for non-existent traffic coming up the road from behind.

ONLY A TASTE

I hadn't thought of that yet and quickly rack my brain for nice places in the area.

"Iver Heath?" I suggest at last. "We could, uhh... have a picnic?" At least it'll be quiet there. And a reasonable distance from Langley.

She settles back into the plush leather of the seat and rests her hands on her knees as if forcing herself to relax. "I suppose that *would* be nice."

And so that's exactly what we do: head to Iver Heath, only stopping on the way for a few snacks to carry along. It's not much of a drive, and after we've found a suitable place to park, we head into the lush green of the park area, looking for just the right spot.

Any benches near the parking are already occupied. There are families who've had the same idea as us, and the odd couple or single person, taking a rest from walking their dogs.

Finally, beyond the next bend in the walking path, there's an empty spot. Perfect. We sit down and start unpacking the food between us. It's not much, but it's better than nothing. I should've planned for something like this, prepared something special and carried it along, but it's too late for regrets now.

"I'm sorry to just drop in unannounced. I couldn't take it anymore." I look into Mandi's eyes, hoping to see recognition and a reflection of my own desires in there.

She'd been acting weirdly tense throughout our drive, as well as the little walk to get to this bench, but finally, something in her gaze softens. She takes a deep breath, and at last a smile appears on her lips too.

"I know the feeling, it's just... difficult. What if Jai tells on us?" Her eyebrows are pulled together in concern. Being found out is clearly a very big deal to her.

"You were very convincing. About him needing a favor from you in future. I doubt he will rat you out."

"You don't know Jai. We fight a lot."

"He's still your brother." I smile at her. Her frown evens out as she continues to stare back in silence.

Those eyes, those beautiful amber colored eyes, and how the emotions they hold manage to make the hairs on my arm stand up. If we weren't out in a park surrounded by families with small children, I would have been sorely tempted to lift her over my shoulder and have my way with her right here in the bushes behind this bench. But I restrain myself, with difficulty.

"I've really missed you a lot," she whispers at last.

That's what I was waiting for.

"Me too. Talking on the phone doesn't quite do the trick," I say.

She presses her lips together, and scans our surroundings before letting her gaze settle on me again. I love how she looks at me, how she seems to see me for who I am, without showing the slightest interest in all the superficial crap other women I've been with seem to care so much about.

My eyes are drawn to her shapely lips. I so want to taste her lips again.

Mandi subtly leans forward, like she doesn't even realize she's doing it. I can't resist and dive in to steal a kiss. Her arms wrap around my neck and she melts into me. I clear the space between us, causing various little plastic snack containers to end up on the ground.

It doesn't matter. None of it matters. The picnic was just an excuse to be here. I'm not even hungry, not for food, anyway.

I cradle her in my arms, noting how soft and feminine she feels in my embrace. Much more so than in Brighton even. She's curvier than any of my previous flings. I never knew what I was missing.

"Every night I close my eyes and I can't get you out of my head. In the mornings, just before I wake up, I'm back in Brighton, next to you," I mumble.

The words coming out of my mouth seem all jumbled up and senseless now that I've said them out loud, but her gentle moan against my lips suggests they made perfect sense to her.

"I know," she whispers, in between kisses. "Me too."

Our tongues devour each other with an intensity I've never sensed before.

My whole body seems to ache for her attention. I want her to touch me, to soothe me, even if I know that even the slightest caress will set me on fire. Never once have I wanted something—someone—so badly. What a cruel joke that she's been so far away and out of reach ever since that first time.

I wondered earlier today if the weeks we've been apart made me rely on false memories. If seeing her again would disappoint in any way, because the fantasy is better than the reality ever was. There's nothing disappointing about the elegant creature melting against my lips, though. Nothing.

For most of my life—at least ever since I've been able to afford it—I've been all about instant gratification. I've never repressed a single impulse of mine: good food, fine wine, fast cars, and beautiful women. Whatever I desired, I always pursued it until I had it. With her, I find myself ridiculously out of control.

I can't just take her home with me, rip her clothes off and keep her around for my pleasure. Part of me wants just that. Another part of me, one that makes even less sense, threatens to overwhelm me with guilt. I've brought her here today, against her better judgment. If someone she knows spots us and tells her family, she'll be in a whole lot of trouble. And yet, I couldn't stay away any longer. Because I'm selfish.

"Not here," I say, as she slips her hand under my shirt. *Oh God, don't stop.*

"You're right." She sounds breathless as she pulls away, then presses herself against me again for one last kiss. I shouldn't have suggested a picnic at all. Why the hell didn't I take her to a hotel, or somewhere— anywhere—more private? What an idiot I am.

Next time.

"Next time, I'll make sure we're alone," I say.

Her eyes understand, even if our bodies still refuse to step in line and realize that restraint is required. Finally, shrill laughter interrupts us, forcing us to behave ourselves just before the child it belongs to stumbles into view. Shortly after, the little girl's parents follow her on the footpath leading right past our bench.

We awkwardly start picking up the still closed food containers, placing them between us to maintain a safe enough distance. It's time for our so-called picnic.

The food we'd bought in a hurry is tasteless, but the company and innuendo-filled conversation more than make up for it.

CHAPTER THIRTEEN

"Mandeep, open the door!" Dad shouts, his fist banging against the wood.

I jerk up in bed, my heart racing. *Where am I? What's going on?*

"Right now, young lady! Your mother and I want to see you downstairs."

I try to blink the last remnants of drowsiness away and get out of bed. Wonder what's got them all excited so early on a Sunday morning?

Shit, did someone see Callum and me yesterday? That's got to be it. Some nosy neighbor must have seen him around and told on us. Shit, I hate this gossipy neighborhood.

After putting on a robe and heading into the bathroom to splash water on my face, I reluctantly head downstairs. Jai is waiting for me in the hall, shaking his head. Yet, he's not laughing at me for a change. Oh balls, if he can't muster his usual Schadenfreude, things must be serious.

I push open the door, to find Mom, Dad, and Dadi sitting around our impossibly big and chunky dining table. In the center, a glossy magazine.

"Explain yourself!" Dad snaps, tapping his forefinger impatiently on top of its cover.

That's not mine. And plus, since when are tabloids banned from the house?

I squint and lean ahead to take a better look at it when I see the problem: the cover photo. I choke on my own breath.

The background is familiar, the park where we had our picnic. In the center of the photograph, on the bench, there's Callum with his arm around me. Unlike most tabloid photographs, this one isn't grainy, out of focus, or in any way ambiguous. It's definitely me, smiling up at him. And then there's the headline: *Player both in and out of the kitchen? Notorious bachelor, TV Chef Callum Byrne sighted with mystery squeeze*. Fuck. Fuck! Thank fuck they didn't get a shot of when we made out shortly before this particular shot was taken, but still. FUCK!

"I..."

"You're so screwed," Jai whispers behind me. Thanks. I'd noticed.

"You stay out of it, Jai," Mom scolds him, then turns to face me "What were you thinking, Mandeep? Mrs. Singh just brought this over. Everyone in town talking about it!"

I'm speechless. Of all the ways for them to find out about Callum, with the exception of a leaked sex tape from our night in Brighton, this right here has got to be the worst. I had considered that people from our neighborhood might have seen us. Jai could have ratted us out when Callum first turned up. Maybe I would have been able to explain both of those accusations away, or flat out refuse them.

Not once did I consider the possibility of someone taking our picture and publishing it in a bloody magazine. Can't argue with photographic evidence like this.

"And at a time when we're trying to find you a match? Honestly, I had no idea you hated us this much!" Mom complains.

"Hang on, wait a minute!" I blurt out as my temper gets the better of me. "I never asked for a match! Nobody even thought to ask if I want to get married!"

"Did you hear that, Harry?" Mom turns to face Dad, who looks so furious, little droplets of sweat have collected on his brow. "She doesn't want to get married even! I told you that school was a mistake. We should have sent her to an all-girls school instead, where they teach the kids proper values!"

I roll my eyes and half-turn.

"Not so fast, young lady!" Dad's voice echoes through the room. "Sit down, right bloody now!" He points at the empty chair across from him.

I hesitate, but finally decide to give in. The cat's out of the bag, we might as well have the whole argument right now in one go. Get it over with. Not that I suspect this is something that we will easily resolve.

"How long have you been lying to us? Well?" Dad balls his fist and slams it onto the table, making Mom and me flinch.

"I didn't... I mean..." I stammer.

"How long?" he insists.

"We only just met recently."

"Good, so you can break things off and pray that word hasn't spread too much. Perhaps the Sandhus are still willing to consider the match. Let's hope they don't have a subscription to *Heat* magazine." Mom sits back and folds her arms.

Shuddering at the memory of Diljeet Sandhu, the pathetic guy who couldn't even get a sensible word out with me, I can't hold my tongue. "I'm not marrying that loser!"

"You may not have much of a choice! Your actions will have seriously limited our options! How are we supposed to convince anyone of your suitability as a bride when your face is in all the gossip magazines? They might as well have written right there 'Mandeep Grewal is easy, don't consider her as a bride for your son'!" Mom rants.

Though still in shock, I muster the courage to look around at everyone. Dad looks constipated with rage which is just begging for further release. Mom's part hysterical, part disillusioned.

Dadi is just sitting quietly with her hands folded together. She's present, but not really involved at this moment. No matter how hard I stare in her direction, she won't look me in the eye. Great, now I've lost my only ally in this house.

"What I don't understand is, what did we do to you to deserve this? You've never wanted for anything: toys, clothes, education. And you repay us like this?!"

"I'm not doing this *to you*!" I sigh and hide my face in

my hands. God, this is a disaster.

"Oh yeah?" Mom says, crossing her arms. The angry tears that had collected in her eyes are starting to flow over. Let the guilt trip begin. "We're working our hands to the bone every day to give you and your brother everything we never had, and you turn around and spit in our faces. All the effort we've gone through to find someone nice for you to settle down with. But none of it is good enough. I blame this place. Kids here are so self-entitled!"

"I didn't ask to *settle down* and marry some random stranger I don't even like!"

"If you wanted to find someone for yourself you could have said so. We might have considered that option. But couldn't it at least have been a nice, Punjabi boy?! Someone from our own community?" Mom rants.

As if. When I tried my best to dissuade them from parading more husband candidates in front of me, they brushed away my concerns like they didn't matter.

"We'll give it a couple of days for things to blow over," Dad says. He still looks furious, and his voice still has that edge to it as well, but he's trying his best to stay calm now. "Then I'll speak to Mr. Sandhu. You can apologize and assure them it was all a misunderstanding and you're not actually... dating... that man."

"What?!" I say.

"You heard me! You'll apologize. Perhaps we can still salvage things."

"Is nobody listening to me? I am *not* marrying that..."

"And you're grounded!"

"Dad, I'm twenty-three!" I complain.

"You should have thought of that before acting out!" Mom butts in.

Why won't they understand that this is nothing to do with them! Why does everything have to be about *them!*

"I mean it. You'll go to work, then come straight home. No more frolicking around the countryside with strange men. As long as you live under this roof, there will be rules to follow," Dad says.

"What are you going to do, throw me out?" My last response passes my lips before I get the chance to reconsider it. Mom's eyes betray shock, while Dad's stare might as well be lethal.

"Enough." Dadi's voice cuts through our continued bickering. "Harpreet. Mandeep. Everyone, enough!"

She hasn't raised her voice much, but it's enough for us to take notice and swallow whatever we were about to say next.

"I'm parched. Let's have some tea." She pushes the chair back. The creak of the wood against the tiled floor makes the hair on the back of my neck stand up.

"I'll get it," I say, jumping up while gesturing at her to sit back down. I rush into the kitchen area and put the kettle on, then line up five cups on the counter. With my back towards everyone, I take a moment to collect myself, dabbing at the tears stuck in my eyelashes with a corner of my t-shirt.

Dad tries to say something but is immediately shushed by Dadi. The exact details of the muffled exchange are drowned out by the gradually increasing hisses from the electric kettle.

To think that only fifteen minutes ago I was blissfully asleep, unaware of the storm brewing downstairs. I stifle a yawn and lean against the counter, letting my head hang down. It's all fucked now. My secret is out.

And there isn't anyone I can talk to about it. Sarah might have been sympathetic, but I did keep Callum's identity from her all this time. That's bound to piss her off; I know I'd be furious. Shit. It seems I'm doomed to suffer through this disaster on my own.

As I pour the hot water into the cups, my vision blurs again. Everything is screwed up. I should have known Callum turning up here was too much of a risk to take. I should have sent him away, but somehow I can't muster the energy to blame him either. This whole thing is my fault, not his.

I should have ignored his first message from a couple of weeks ago. Instead I'd given in to temptation, and now we both have to pay the price.

As soon as it's ready, I carry the cups towards the table, where everyone is avoiding eye contact with me as well as each other. The only person who looks halfway normal is Dadi, who even shoots me a sympathetic smile as she accepts her cup.

"Whatever is going on between you and that man, it's over now," Dad says, while ignoring a disapproving glance from Dadi. "And that's the end of this discussion." He takes a sip of tea and resolutely puts his mug back down, spilling a few drops over the edge.

ONLY A TASTE

I guess he's right. Unless I'm willing to choose Callum over them, this is the end for us. Tears start to roll down my cheeks in full force again.

By the time I've somehow made it through my cup of watered down slightly salty tea, the tempers have calmed sufficiently for me to be excused. I head straight up to find my phone blinking with at least a dozen missed calls from Callum, and one solitary message:

'I'm so sorry. Are you OK? C'

I shakily hit 'call' on his number, and nearly choke on my own breath when he answers just moments later.

The conversation that follows passes in a blur of sadness and despair. In between sobs and apologies of my own, I tell him what happened and that I can't do this anymore. We're done.

CHAPTER FOURTEEN

Ever since the whole thing with Callum came out last week, I've tried my best to keep my head down. I've stuck to my decision not to keep in touch with him, no matter how difficult it's been. And I've tried to mend my relationship with Sarah, but it's been a hard slog. In the end, the hopeless romantic in her won out, and she's stopped dodging my calls long enough to tell me to not to give up on true love too quickly... Whatever that means.

What's true love anyway? How many people get together with the best of intentions, only to get a divorce a few years down the line? And that's without the added complications of a very vocal disapproving family. If I choose Callum over them, who is to say I won't regret it and take out my resentment on him later? Plus, I would have to cut off an integral part of my identity and trust that the phantom pain stops after a while. People recover from broken hearts all the time, right? How many people recover from cutting their family out of their lives?

Friends and lovers can come and go. You only get one family in this life.

All that has been going through my mind during

those dark hours when the ticking clock on my bedroom wall is my only companion.

All that, and I don't know if he's actually that serious about me. I don't want to know, because it'll hurt either way.

Every day has been the same. I've tried to just get out of bed in the mornings, go to work, come home, eat, work on a never-ending crochet project I've started just to keep my hands busy, go to bed again. Rinse and repeat, without thinking too much. Only late at night, or at times when I have nothing else to distract me, do I start to wonder *what if.*

It's taken a toll too, the lack of sleep has started to get to me, causing me to just switch off every so often, usually at work. All the numbers on the bills I'm supposed to enter into the accounting system seem to blur and swim on the page. I've taken up drinking multiple cups of coffee every day, instead of tea.

And so about a week passes. I can hardly stand talking to Sarah anymore, because every time I do, she tries to convince me of something or other I should be doing to rescue my relationship with Callum.

Neither do I talk much at home, because every conversation leads to the same place: an interrogation on whether or not I've stopped seeing him.

Thankfully at work, there's no one to talk to.

I idly hover over the 'save' button with my mouse. What else am I supposed to do today after this spreadsheet? I can't remember.

"Mandi, dear?" Mr. Gupta comes up behind me,

dragging me out of my late morning vegetative state.

"Yes, Mr. Gupta?"

"I've got to go to the bank this morning and Erica has taken a sick day. Would you be able to keep an eye on the shop for me? Take the laptop down with you if you like."

Fine. Might be an interesting change from being confined to the office.

"Anything in particular I should be doing?"

"I won't be long. If any customer does come in, just do your best to bill them. You do know how the register works, yes?"

I nod. Mom and Dad have one just like it. "No problem."

I lean down underneath my desk to unplug the laptop's charger and gather everything, including the stack of invoices I'd been entering, up in my arms, then follow Mr. Gupta down the narrow staircase to the shop.

"I'll be right back," Mr. Gupta says as he heads out the door.

After a quick look around, I decide to make myself comfortable behind the counter. I'm about to sit back and relax when the bell on the shop door goes off. Is he back already? Did he forget something? I lean forward to get a better look and see that it's not Mr. Gupta at all, but my arch nemesis, Leila, with her best friend Yasmin in tow. Great.

I'm about to duck back and out of view when they notice me.

"Mandi, fancy seeing you here," Leila remarks while flicking her long black hair over her shoulder.

"Leila. Yasmin." I can muster barely a nod. God, please make them go away now.

"So, you're quite the topic of conversation lately..." Yasmin remarks, while folding her arms.

"Oh?" I don't have the energy to pretend, meaning my tone must be dripping in sarcasm.

"Yeah. I've never watched the Good Food channel personally, but somehow it seems a lot more interesting now," Leila says.

I don't respond, meanwhile Yasmin leans over and prods Leila in the side, mumbles something about Callum and 'fat girls', then giggles profusely.

"What was that?" I snap. My patience is running dangerously thin these days. Thanks, sleep deprivation.

They give me a blank stare. Guess they're too chicken to body shame me directly.

"Look, are you actually going to buy something, or are you just here to laugh at me? Because if it's the latter, get it over with quickly, so I can get back to work. Thank you." I fold my arms and glare in their direction.

"Just browsing," Yasmin says, while making a show of herself sifting through one of the racks of sheer baby dolls with lace trim.

"U-huh." I look down at my laptop, and pretend to type something. These people are like vultures, circling around, looking for signs of weakness. When they see you're at your lowest ever, that's when they pounce.

"Actually," Leila says, "what I wanted to say was,

good for you."

I can't believe my ears, and look up at the both of them again.

"Hope it works out for you, though I can imagine your parents will have given you quite a bit of shit when those gossip magazines came out." Leila awkwardly shifts her weight from one stiletto-heeled foot to another, then waves at Yasmin and turns to leave the store.

"Uhh, thanks, I guess?" I call out after them.

Wow, that was unexpected.

***

"Hi, Dadi." I give her a quick hug as I enter the living area, then am about to head out and up to my room when she stops me.

"Sit with me." She pats the empty space next to her on the large, brown leather sofa.

I pause, then decide to just do as she says, plopping down beside her with a loud sigh.

"How was your day?" she asks.

"Fine," I respond out of habit. Under normal circumstances I might have told her about Leila coming to the shop, but today I don't have the energy.

"Mhm." She lifts the remote, then switches the channel from the news over to some early evening soap opera.

"You don't look fine."

"Just tired. Had a lot to do at work," I lie. I *am* tired, but I didn't do much all day.

"Well, why don't you have a shower, and wear something nice..." she suggests.

I turn to give her a questioning look. Wear something nice? What a strange thing to say to someone planning to veg out in front of the TV. "Why? What's going on?"

"I tried to talk to him out of it, but your dad had this idea he could not be dissuaded from..."

My heart sinks. *God, now what?* "And?"

"You have a date." Dadi looks straight ahead at the TV, prompting me to do the same.

This doesn't make any sense.

"A date. With whom?" Please, let it not be that useless boy they were so keen on. Anyone but him.

"His name is Karan, and he does something with electronics, I'm not quite sure."

"But..." I turn to face her again.

"We've been concerned about you, Mandeep. Ever since... you know... you've just withered away. Finally your father has come to the conclusion that he can't just make you marry someone, just because our families are compatible. You have to really like the boy. And apparently that's how these things work here, isn't it? By dating?" Her eyes meet mine, and indeed all I see is concern. She *is* worried about me.

"Yeah, but—" The whole situation is just so outlandish, I can't find the words to argue. They want me to go on a date with some guy they themselves picked out in order to get me to agree to a match? How does that help?

"So tonight it's this boy, Karan. Tomorrow night another one. I've forgotten his name."

I just shake my head. *Unbelievable.*

"That's not how dating works."

"I told you, I tried, but your father has always been extremely stubborn."

Since I don't have the energy to argue, I decide to just do as I'm told. It's not ideal, but what are the chances of this guy being as hopeless as the last one? Low, right?

"Think of it this way, at least you get to go to the movies for free," Dadi calls after me as I head out the living room.

Ugh. This whole plan is ridiculous. And so typical that Dad decided everything and then left it up to Dadi to tell me at the last minute. I can't even argue with her.

Within half an hour, I make sure I'm showered and dressed in a pretty pale blue chiffon dress and heels. I decide not to go overboard with make-up and hair. I don't have time either, because the doorbell rings shortly after I'm somewhat done. *Already?*

Within minutes, Dadi has presumably made it to the door and calls out for me to come down. I reluctantly do so, until she makes a quick escape and I'm face-to-face with a guy who can only be described as *pretty*. Metro-sexual would work too, but mainly just pretty.

"Hi, I'm Mandi." I offer my hand, but he just dives in for a hug and a kiss on each cheek.

"Karan. Nice to meet you."

He smiles widely at me. His cheerfulness is almost contagious.

"Ready to go?" he asks.

I nod and pick up my bag to leave when he pauses in our doorway.

"One thing, just so we're clear." He looks at me a lot more seriously than before.

"Yes?"

"This whole date thing was my mom's idea. Like, she gave me some money even, so I'm like 'OK, great, so we'll go see a movie, have a nice dinner, etc.', but I'm not interested in finding a *girl* to marry." His tone, as well as his exaggerated gesturing makes me smile again. He doesn't need to spell it out, his emphasis on the word 'girl' explains everything.

"I think we're going to get along brilliantly." I instinctively slip my arm into his, just because it seems like the right thing to do somehow, and we're off.

Just like that, and completely unintentionally, Dad's idea has completely paid off for me. For a few hours, I actually feel normal again. By the end of the RomCom we'd decided to see, and after oodles of dinner conversation comparing 'arranged marriage' disaster stories, we agree to tell our folks that our date went horribly.

If nothing else, I may have got a friend out of it though.

CHAPTER FIFTEEN:
CALLUM

"Callum, focus!" Trisha pleads with me.

I look up from the notes she's given me, but nothing is sticking.

"Would it help if we took a break?" she asks, her expression somewhere between dejection and sympathy.

"Yeah, let's." I drop the sheet of paper onto the coffee table and get up, heading straight for the kitchen. Chocolate. There should be some chocolate in here somewhere, preferably to be ingested in combination with some caffeine. I press a few buttons and wait as the espresso maker whirs into action, then find an unopened bar of *Lindt* in one of the nearby cupboards.

Today is a new low. Not only am I unable to remember the smallest details Trisha is trying to drill into my head for the upcoming interviews, every time I do try to concentrate, all I can think about is Mandi.

I should have known. I should have expected some bastard paparazzo to come across us sooner or later.

Of course now they're going to ask me about my love life in every upcoming interview too. Trisha has suggested a few phrases for me to fall back on when I feel like telling the interviewer to fuck off and mind their own business. But, I just know my patience will run out and I'll snap sooner or later and resort to more direct language. I feel like cancelling everything, but I'm contractually obligated to follow through with whatever Trisha and the network suggest.

As perfect as everything was when we were together—Mandi and I—our worlds have fallen apart. With her, I could see myself leaving my bachelor days behind me. Now, that hope is gone.

I know she must be hurting a lot too, and that makes it all worse. I know she has feelings for me too, but she's made her choice. I ought to respect that, right? No matter how much it hurts.

"Callum," Trisha calls out for me.

I realize I've just spent the best part of ten minutes staring at my espresso machine, even after it had long finished making my drink.

"Yeah," I respond.

"How about we call it a day, huh? You're clearly distracted. We could just pick this up again tomorrow."

"Fine." I don't even turn around to say goodbye, just continue to stare at the foam-topped black liquid in my cup.

Mandi made her choice, and I should respect it.

But then again, her decision to call it quits wasn't made voluntarily. *What if...*

I break off a square of dark chocolate and put it in my mouth. It's wonderfully bitter, just like my mood.

What if somehow things could change in our favor... What if her parents could be convinced to give us a chance? What if all it takes is the right approach, the right *gesture*?

Mandi isn't religious, though her family might be. I can relate to the moral restrictions religious people impose on their relationships, I grew up around enough strict Catholics to be able to understand the thought process. We're all sinners in their eyes, so a *real* commitment is required to validate a couple's love in the eyes of God.

Assuming they want what any other parents want—what's best for their child—what could be the reason for them to reject our relationship? Tradition? Culture? *Incompatibility?*

That's got to be it: they want her to settle down with someone with a similar background, because they assume it would make them compatible. But Mandi and I *are* compatible, though. Aren't we? How could I convince them of that?

I think back to my various trips to India. To the people I'd met during my travels, the smells and sights and most importantly, the tastes I'd encountered.

Food tends to be synonymous to culture. This will apply doubly so in the case of Mandi's parents, since they're in the restaurant business as well, and ambitious enough to enter their recipes into various local competitions. *What if I can use that...*

Putting the chocolate back down, as well as the now empty espresso cup, I pick up a notepad and pen and head back to the coffee table to turn on the laptop. Before everything unraveled, I'd made a promise to myself as well as her: that morning in Brighton wasn't goodbye. I was going to pursue her, because I couldn't let go of how she made me feel. To give up now would mean to throw away my last chance to turn things around.

The road ahead might be difficult as well as uncomfortable, but I don't have any other choice. I need her in my life, and I'm willing to fight for the privilege.

***

It takes a couple of days to put my plan into action, but finally, I find myself driving down the same quiet residential road in Langley again. It's a Wednesday, late afternoon, and the clear summer skies of the last time I was here have made way for the cloud cover this damp country is better known for.

There are plenty of empty parking spaces everywhere, but I decide to take a gamble and park up right outside her front garden. Number seven.

To pretend I'm not nervous at all would be a lie, I'm terrified of what's going to happen. The food aspect I'm not so worried about, I'm confident it's spot on. But there's no way of predicting how everyone will react. The trunk of my car contains a number of gift options, depending on how things go. The most important, as well as the smallest, is safely tucked into my shirt pocket.

Before it's time for any of that, I will need some

inside information though. If my assumptions are correct, at this time of day, Mandi's parents should be at the takeaway and she should be at work, leaving only two players at home. Mandi's brother and grandmother. I'll have to win over both of them eventually, or my plan fails.

I walk up the short path and ring the bell, tapping my finger against my thigh restlessly while I wait. It's a fifty-fifty chance as I see it, whether her brother or her grandmother opens up. I'm hoping for the former, to give me an easier way in.

The longer I wait, the less I like my chances.

Finally, as I'm about to turn and head back to the car, the net curtain next to the door stirs. A pair of suspicious eyes, a good foot lower than my eye height peers out. Crap. It's unlikely Mandi's grandmother will be swayed by the bribes I intended to tempt the brother with. I'll be forced to rely on charm instead.

I smile at her nervously, hoping against all hope that she'll actually open the door. The door lock clicks once and indeed, there she is. The old lady looks physically frail, but her eyes command respect. Her stance as well as expression stand in stark contrast with the soft, floral patterned fabric of her traditional clothes, and the wispy white hair that frames her face.

"Mrs. Grewal?" I ask, unnecessarily.

Remembering all my research had taught me, I bend down to touch her feet when she stops me with a pat on the back halfway through.

"Please get up," Mandi's grandmother says.

"My name is Callum B-" I start.

She raises her hand, cutting me short. "I know who you are."

"Although I understand I'm probably not welcome here, I was wondering if I might come in and speak with you."

Her stare could cut through steel, just like Mandi's can, and I instinctively avoid eye contact. The similarities between the two, despite the age difference, are striking.

She leans forward on her walking stick, as if to get a better look at me, then seems to relax just slightly.

"I probably shouldn't say this, but I really enjoy your show," she says.

Looking at her directly again, I see the same subtle cues that Mandi displays when she's amenable but trying not to let it show. *Whew*, she doesn't hate me. Perhaps all is not yet lost.

"Please come in, have some tea." She gestures at me with her free hand and steps aside to let me enter.

Although I try not to act too intrusive, I can't help myself from having a good look around. The decor is a throwback to the seventies, except for the open plan kitchen which looks like it has been renovated within the past few years. The heavy wooden furniture, along with the patterned rug in the living area and busy wallpaper all round remind me of when I moved in with my grandma after Mom and Dad had their accident. She favored a similar style.

"Can I help at all?" I ask, when I hear the electric

kettle start up in the kitchen.

"Please take a seat." She gestures at the dining table, rather than the sofa in the living area, so I pull out a chair and wait. My hands are damp with nervous sweat, so I make a few half-hearted attempts to dry them on my trousers. She's let me into the house, so far so good, and she likes my TV persona at least. But there's still a lot of scope for things to go horribly wrong from here.

Looking around the room, I notice the many framed pictures of the various members of the Grewal family. Mandi and her brother, from a few years ago. Another frame displays a couple—presumably Mandi's parents—at work in a small commercial kitchen. Yet another shows the same couple, a few decades younger: her in a traditional red bridal outfit, and him in an ornate suit type thing with a color coordinated turban. The one thing that strikes me is how little her dad has changed between the two photographs. It must be the beard and turban, which make him look fierce as well as ageless.

When Mandi's grandmother returns, I get up briefly to accept my tea. She sits opposite me with a cup of her own, wrapping her hands carefully around the hot porcelain.

"What is it you wanted to say—may I call you Callum?"

"Of course, yes. Well, I know that you don't approve of my relationship with Mandi."

"Our traditions differ quite a bit from the norm in this country when it comes to relationships."

"Indeed, and I completely understand. Which is why

I wanted to explain my intentions."

"I'm listening." She folds her hands and keeps her eyes completely focused on me.

"Despite what the papers may say about me, I'm very serious about your granddaughter. I care for her a great deal, and it is really unfortunate things had to come out the way they did." I take a sip of tea, while finding the right words for what I really want to say.

"What I really would like is a chance to prove myself to you, and Mandi's parents also. If you still disapprove, that's fine—I mean not fine, I'd be devastated—but at least I know that I will have done everything in my power to turn this situation around." I'm rambling. This isn't good.

Mrs. Grewal's expression is hard to read as she continues to keep me in her sights.

"What exactly did you have in mind?" she asks at last. The slight sparkle in her eye suggests I may just have at least one member of the Grewal family already on my side before I've even put the rest of my plan into action.

As I explain my ideas, she mostly nods in agreement, jumping in with the occasional suggestion.

There may just be a chance this works out.

Mandi will be home at five, and Mandi's grandmother will call her parents back from the takeaway around that time too. It would be ideal if they arrive at the same time, just so it doesn't feel like a complete ambush.

We'll have tea and snacks ready, and hope for the best.

CHAPTER SIXTEEN

When I walk home from work, the skies overhead signal a change. The unusually warm weather is about to make way for what an English summer is more known for: endless grey skies and regular showers. I speed up, in the hopes that I can beat the first drops.

The wind picks up as I turn into our street, encouraging me to walk even faster. But then, something stops me in my tracks. The spot outside our house where Dad normally parks is occupied by another car, a sports car. My heart skips a few beats.

What the fuck is Callum doing here? Did he not get the message? Does he not realize how much trouble I'm going to be in?

Walking past the silver grey coupe, I note that it's empty. Fuck. He didn't go inside, did he? At least Mom and Dad aren't home this time of day, but Dadi is!

I reluctantly approach the front door, key in hand, listening out for voices. Once I enter, I hear a muffled conversation coming from the living area. Shit. My heartbeat is going into overdrive and panic threatens to wash over me. Why didn't he just listen to me? Why come here?

When I open the door, I'm faced with a sight I never expected to see: Dadi and Callum sitting at our dinner table, having a seemingly pleasant chat over tea and sweets.

"Mandi!" Callum gets up to greet me, but I avoid eye contact with him.

"What's going on? Why are you here?" I wrap my arms around myself, as if to protect me from the inevitable fallout of his actions.

"Sit down, Mandeep." Dadi gestures at the chair next to Callum, then slides over an empty cup. There's a teapot in the center of the table. She nods at me to serve myself.

We never use that teapot except when we have guests Mom wants to impress...

"They'll be here any minute now," Dadi remarks while glancing at the wall clock behind me.

Oh God, please let this not mean what I think it means?

Sure enough, within moments, the front door clicks open and footsteps as well as voices enter the hallway, heading right for us.

The door swings open and in comes Dad, who can't hide his shock at seeing Callum sitting between me and Dadi at our table.

"What is the meaning of all this?" he booms.

"What? Oh my!" Mom exclaims as she enters the room just behind him.

"Harpreet, please take a seat, have some tea. Listen to what the boy has to say," Dadi speaks calmly.

"How dare you invite him here, after embarrassing us by having your picture taken together?" Dad rants at me.

I press my lips together tightly, unsure of what to say.

"She didn't know, she's only just come home from work as well," Dadi explains. "Sit down. Listen to him."

I steal a glance at Callum, who looks wooden and tense as he gets up off his chair.

"Mr. Grewal," he starts, stretching his right hand out in an attempted handshake.

Dad glares back and forth between Callum, me and Dadi, his eyes bulging. "You're not welcome in my house."

"Harpreet!" Dadi raises her voice, making all of us flinch. "This is my house too. Sit down!"

Mom takes the lead, walking around the table to take a seat opposite me. I dare not look directly at her. Not knowing what else to do, I pick up two empty cups that were already laid out on the table and pour the tea.

After staring all of us down, Dad finally follows, taking a seat beside Dadi. Callum sits down last.

"Mr. Grewal, I understand that we all started off on the wrong foot. And I do apologize for visiting your home unannounced."

Dad shoots me an angry look and shakes his head. I'm so done.

"Mandi- Mandeep did not know about any of this. We haven't spoken in a week."

Callum slides the tray of traditional Indian sweets over towards Mom and Dad. The selection of laddoos and burfis looks familiar as well as alien. They don't look like they came from any of the shops around here.

"Thank you," Mom whispers, while picking up a laddoo almost on autopilot. She's never been good at resisting temptation. I get my sweet tooth from her.

"I know you object to our relationship. I think I understand your reasons."

"Then why are you even here?" Dad says, while waving away the tray Callum is now holding in his direction.

"To show you that I have nothing but good intentions. To hopefully address some of your concerns."

"Right." The sarcasm in Dad's voice is obvious to me, I wonder if Callum hears it too.

I don't know what to expect, but I'm not holding out much hope. As Dadi has made it clear on numerous occasions, my Dad is the most stubborn person she knows. Some idle talk over tea and treats is not going to sway him. No way.

"I have great respect for your culture, your traditions."

"And what do you know of our culture?" Dad snaps, and is instantly met with a stern look from Dadi.

"I've travelled extensively in India, I've always been fascinated by the food anyway. The diversity. Then again, it's necessary to understand the people, the traditions, in order to make sense of the food."

"And?" Dad, who seems to have calmed down just slightly, sits back in his chair and finally takes a first sip from his cup.

"You're concerned about the happiness and well being of your daughter, that much is obvious. You want her to be with someone who will take care of her, understand her, provide for her and any future children, correct?"

"That's right."

"You are looking for someone who is compatible with her as well as your family. Someone who believes in keeping promises and commitments, who won't just run away when things get tough as they inevitably must in life."

"Yes."

"I love your daughter more than anything in the world." Callum's words seem to echo around the room.

I can't believe he just said that! And to my Dad, no less.

Shocked, I turn to stare at Callum. I've got to be hallucinating. This stuff doesn't happen in real life, just in movies.

"I can provide for her, take care of her. I think I understand her at least a little and I believe us to be compatible. The rest, I'm willing to learn. You see, I didn't tell her I was coming here today, because I knew she would have dissuaded me. We shouldn't have been hiding our relationship from you. That was wrong and disrespectful. I deeply apologize for that."

Dad scoffs, but then takes another sip of tea, seemingly relaxing just a little bit more. It's the calm before another storm, isn't it? It has to be just a matter of time before he loses his patience and kicks Callum out of the house once and for all.

"You see, where I grew up in Ireland, family is all-important. Family, and the church. I believe we share a lot of the same values, even if our religions and origins differ. My parents passed when I was quite young, and ever since then I really missed the feeling of being part of a close-knit family. I've had more professional success than I could ever dream of, but I never had that same feeling of belonging which you can only get from your family. Until I met Mandeep."

Although I knew about his parents, he'd told me about growing up with his grandmother, I never quite understood properly how that would have affected him. Having to speak about it so openly must be very difficult, especially when faced with someone like my dad. I reach over under the table, placing my hand on his thigh.

"I realized that that's why I was drawn to her in the first place. Because the warm loving relationship you all share has shaped her into the sort of person she is today."

I can't believe what I'm hearing.

"The tabloids may be full of nonsense about me, but deep down, we're not so different. From the moment Mandeep and I met, I knew that my search was over. That I'd never look at another woman. Never betray or abandon her. I knew that she's everything I'd been looking for my whole life."

Callum takes a deep breath, and straightens his back before continuing. "Mr. Grewal, with your blessing, I would like to start a family of our own with her." Callum glances at me for a short moment, I shoot him a subtle smile. Despite all the messages back and forth, and the way he reacted to me when we went on that ill-fated picnic, I had no idea he felt this deeply about me.

"I'm here to ask for your permission to marry your daughter. Which, in the Catholic tradition is considered to be life-long promise before God."

Callum's hand finds mine, cupping it protectively, but his gaze is firmly fixed on Dad's face. In fact everyone, including myself, is now staring at Dad. My heart is hammering in my throat. That was pretty convincing, wasn't it? But there's no accounting for Dad's stubbornness.

Mom places her hand on Dad's, which is resting beside his cup of tea. Meanwhile Dad is glaring back at Callum.

Minute after minute passes in silence.

Finally, it's Dadi who can't take it any longer. "I think he makes a good case. It takes courage to come here and make a stand like this," she says.

Dad stirs, but only to pick up his cup, emptying it with one last swig. "I think." He clears his throat. The suspense is killing me.

"At this point, it's clear that it no longer matters what *I* think," he grumbles.

I'm shocked. All that, and he's not even going to answer Callum?

"What do you think? Are *you* convinced?" Dad asks me.

I don't know what to say, I just stare at him with my mouth agape. The room starts to spin around me, and I'm not sure where to look or what to say.

Then Callum gets up next to me, diverting my attention away from Dad. With my hand still in his, Callum gets down on one knee on the ground and retrieves something from his shirt pocket. Holding it up closer to me, I can see that it's a little velvet box.

"Mandi, I know this is sudden, and probably not how you expected this would go, but I meant everything I just said. I love you, and I always will. Will you marry me? Whenever you're ready, of course."

I cover my mouth with my free hand, and stare down at the little box, which Callum opens up to reveal a very sparkly diamond ring. It's beautiful, with its intricate floral design in gold, and diamonds small and large mounted in the center. The whole scene gives me goose bumps.

From the corner of my eye, I notice Mom dabbing at the corners of her eye with her scarf. She's always been the emotional one. Dad is still being his stern self, but at least his eyes are no longer shooting daggers.

"Well, answer him!" Dadi urges.

Tears well up and my throat threatens to close, but I force myself to answer anyway.

"Yes," I whisper. "Yes!"

Callum lets go of my hand, then takes the ring out of its little holder. His hands tremble as he slides it onto my ring finger. Dadi claps her hands. I don't remember seeing her this happy in quite a while. Mom now has tears streaming down her face openly and has given up on trying to dry them. Even Dad, who rarely shows any emotion at all, seems affected. His eyes have softened, and in a strange twist of fate, I think I can even spy a little smile peeping through his thick beard.

I look down at the ring on my finger, and it strikes me that although I've spent the best part of this month fighting tooth and nail to avoid getting married, actually, it's not the idea of marriage that I took issue with. Just as long as I'm marrying the right man.

"Well then. Everyone have something sweet!" Dadi says. Can't argue with that.

"These laddoos are really lovely. Where did they come from anyway?" Mom asks, picking up another one of the spherical sweets.

I follow her example, wondering the same thing.

Callum, who takes a seat next to me again, says, "I took the liberty of trying out a recipe that was given to me during my last visit to India."

"Wow, you made these?" I ask.

"You do realize he's a chef, right?" Dadi teases me.

"Yeah, but..."

Before I get the chance to finish my thought, the door swings open dramatically.

"Hey, did you see the sweet-ass ride parked outside our house?" Jai asks, while wandering into the room, until he finally notices Callum and stops dead in his tracks. "Oh, shit."

"Language!" Dadi scolds him.

"Sit down," Dad says. "Have some tea."

"Okay..." Jai eyes Callum and me curiously while making his way to the other end of the table, towards the only empty chair. "What's going on?"

"We've agreed on a match for Mandeep," Mom says in the most matter-of-fact tone she can muster.

"Well I'll be da-" Jai swallows the end of his sentence and scrutinizes me with one eyebrow cocked. "I mean, congratulations, I guess?"

"Cheers," I remark dryly.

Although he's still in shock, I can see it in his eyes that Jai understands how huge this is. A massive step, that'll have implications for him, too, a few years down the line. Whenever it'll be his turn to settle down.

EPILOGUE

The wedding preparations had taken up the best part of two months.

We were in a hurry, Callum and I. Although my folks had finally agreed to see things my way, they weren't about to let their daughter go off and spend a lot of alone time with a man, even if he was her fiancé. *What would people say?*

But the wait is finally over. The actual wedding took place earlier today at the Sikh temple Mom and Dad regularly attend. Now the reception—to which Mom insisted on inviting the entire neighborhood—Callum and I have officially been announced as husband and wife.

Nobody can come between us anymore.

Looking across the room at Callum, I'm relieved that he seems in his element. Especially considering the entire thing—including catering—was totally planned out by my parents, according to our customs and traditions. He's been a very good sport about it all; he even grew a bit of a beard and agreed to wear a turban just for the ceremony earlier.

He really meant it when he said that family was important to him. So, considering he doesn't have one of his own, he's been solely focused on keeping mine happy.

Most of the guests have already gone, leaving only a select few relatives and close friends. One of whom, Sarah, comes up to me holding a gift bag.

"I wanted to give this to you now, rather than you know, in front of everyone." She winks at me when she hands me the present.

I smile at her. "Thanks."

Even though I'd told her she should wear whatever she was comfortable with, she insisted on buying herself a pale pink and silver saree just for tonight. It's strange, seeing her dressed like this, but she's managed to carry it off extremely well.

"Well, take a peek," she encourages me.

I push aside the tissue paper covering the top of the bag and reach inside until my fingertips touch what feels like soft, silky lace. A quick look reveals it's indeed lingerie. Very romantic, very bridal.

"Neither of us could get away with wearing white at our wedding, strictly speaking. But that doesn't mean we shouldn't make an effort." Sarah grins at me.

Good thinking. In all the rush to make it through the day, I hadn't planned or prepared anything for when it's all over and Callum and I are finally alone together.

"Thank you so much. I think we'll get some good use out of this," I remark.

"I know you will. Slut."

"Whore."

After all the weirdness our friendship went through lately, finally the air seems clear between us again. She might be a newly employed tabloid journalist now, but she vowed to keep today's festivities entirely off the record. And I trust that she will.

We share a final giggle, then she hugs me goodbye. Sarah turns around and waves one last time before finally leaving the banquet hall as well.

"What was that all about?" Callum asks, resting his hand on my shoulder.

"You'll soon find out." I smile at him naughtily. *And I can't wait to see your face when you do.*

"Well then, let's not delay things too much," Callum says, as his gaze lingers on my lips.

I survey the room, spotting Mom and Dad speaking to Mr. and Mrs. Gupta, who appear to be leaving as well. Dadi is sitting at a table just off the side of the two of them, looking content, if tired.

"Let's excuse ourselves." I take Callum's hand and we walk over towards them to say our goodbyes. They exchange a look of understanding, then Mom hugs the two of us, one after the other, and Dad shakes Callum's hand, before protectively resting his hand on the top of my head. It took a little time, but Callum's absolute persistence and tireless efforts to find common ground between himself and my folks has borne fruit. They've finally accepted him as part of the family. Something I never thought could really happen.

We agree to meet in the morning at the breakfast buffet, before it's time to check out and make our way back home. Only, of course, my home won't be in Langley anymore...

After a quick honeymoon, the destination of which has still been kept from me, I'll move into Callum's place in the city. And then, who knows? I'm definitely not going to be working for Mr. Gupta anymore, or do anything else that has been pre-decided for me by my parents. From here on out, I finally get to be an adult. With Callum by my side, I finally get to make my own choices. I can't wait.

As we walk out of the hall, and down the corridor leading to the stairs, I keep stealing glances at him. I can't believe this has actually happened. And without any further drama, too. Even Leila was on her best behavior when she came by with her parents earlier.

We make it to our room, and Callum uses his keycard to unlock the door. He releases my hand and in one swift move, scoops me up into his arms to carry me over the threshold. Shocked as well as impressed by his strength, I can't stop giggling. I wrap my arms around him, gift bag still in hand behind his back, and rest my head against his shoulder. He's quite something; my *husband.*

It's weird, thinking of Callum in those terms... I guess I have a few things to get used to as well going forward.

"You want to tell me what's in the bag now?" He asks me as he carries me through the spacious room and towards the huge four poster bed, which has been decorated with flowers and rose petals by the hotel staff.

I shake my head.

"You want to tell me where we're going tomorrow?"

I counter.

He lays me down on the covers, and takes a step back to admire the view. "You're going to have to wait and see. I want to surprise you."

"Mhm." I grin at him.

Before tiredness gets the chance to overwhelm me, I get up and head into the en-suite, still clutching Sarah's gift bag in my hand. I kick off my heels and do my best to quickly get out of the heavily embroidered red silk saree—the same my mom had worn on her big day—before folding it and carefully draping it over the bathtub.

Next I strip down the rest of the way, removing jewelry as well, and put on the white lace corset and panty set Sarah gifted me. A quick glance in the mirror confirms that everything about it is just perfect. She knows her lingerie, Sarah does. You can tell that she used to work at *Victoria's Secret* when we first met in college.

When I slowly push my way through the door and back into our room, I see Callum sitting on the edge of the bed already, waiting for me. I pose in the doorway, drawing the moment out as long as I can. He's significantly less patient than me, and manages to get up while removing his coat, as well as his trousers before he even reaches me.

What a fine specimen of a man he is. Of course I knew that much already, from the moment I first saw him on the promenade in Brighton. But in an effort to respect my parent's wishes, we haven't seen each other alone like this in months, and the anticipation is killing me. Now, though, he's *all mine.*

"You look beautiful," he whispers, while nuzzling my neck.

"You're not so bad yourself," I respond, doing my best not to whimper when he starts to kiss me in that spot where I'm most sensitive, just below my earlobe.

"Will you join me on the bed, dear wife?" he asks, taking a step back while holding onto my hand.

I can't suppress a laugh, despite or perhaps because he looks so serious calling me that. It sounds bizarre to my ears. Callum and I; husband and wife.

"Of course, beloved husband."

He grins back at me, and takes another step closer to the bed behind him. I follow.

When he sits down on the edge, I straddle him, wrapping my arms around his neck again like when he carried me over the threshold. We share a kiss, which doesn't relieve the tension building between us for the past two months, as much as heightens it even further.

I need him. He needs me.

His hands roam my body, reclaiming what had previously already been his. This time, all I feel is unadulterated pleasure, no longer hindered by the little voice of a guilty conscience, that never fully left me the first time we did this.

Not everyone may approve of our choices, as some of the cooler faces around the room at tonight's reception already made abundantly clear. But, it's official now. We will never need to hide our relationship ever again.

I give in to his embrace and we both fall back onto the bed. He cups my face and kisses me more deeply, his tongue devouring mine with the kind of passion I'd never encountered before meeting him. Our first time was already special, but tonight will be all the more so because it's no longer illicit and forbidden.

Everything about this moment feels *right*. And it doesn't need to end, ever. Tomorrow, when we wake up together, neither of us has to leave the other. Neither of us has to worry about being found out. Well, except by the tabloids perhaps.

We'd done our best to keep the venue a secret by keeping his name out of the booking. But, someone always talks, Callum said. They'll probably be here tomorrow, hoping to find out every last detail about our relationship and get some candid photos of the two of us together. We intend to sneak out early to avoid them, but you never know.

I make my way down his body, tasting skin as I go along. I've craved this moment with all my being ever since our first time three months ago. The longest and most difficult wait of my life.

He's fit, with well-toned abs and a beautifully sculpted chest that could inspire jealousy in a Greek god. Unlike me; my figure is a lot softer and more curvaceous. Plenty of people advised me to go on a crash diet; to trim down for my big day. I was right to ignore them. The way Callum looks at me wipes any last shred of doubt from my mind. He loves me unconditionally. Just how I am.

Lust takes over as I make it further down his body. Caressing, and tasting perfectly smooth skin as I go.

I gesture at him to lie down flat and put his legs up on the bed. He does. I sit beside him and enjoy how every touch of mine makes his body tremble ever so slightly. This tense anticipation feels delicious, for him as well as me. I love how he's already hard, and actually shudders when I close my fingers around his length. He doesn't say a word, just groans once when I lean down and take him between my lips.

Every thought left in my mind serves to give him pleasure.

How to lick his shaft and then close my lips around the tip of his cock becomes second nature. He tastes perfect: clean, with a hint of saltiness; like the fresh sea air in Brighton.

I speed up, taking more of him into my mouth with each stroke, and rejoice how his body tenses every time I suck. I'm just getting into a faster rhythm when only minutes later his hand finds the back of my neck and freezes there.

"Stop," he gasps.

"Mm?" I look up at him, his expression tells me I have him right where I want him now. Struggling for self-control.

"Not yet," he says.

I decide to give in to his request. Just this once.

As soon as I lie down on my back next to him, he takes over. He rolls onto his side, then on top of me, and kisses me yet again. It's a desperate kiss, so urgent it's almost painful, but in a good way. He takes my breath away when his hand infiltrates my most intimate folds, playing, manipulating me, turning the tables on me.

My eyes close involuntarily as I am taken over by pleasure. Soon, we'll be joined fully. I'll be his, and he'll be mine, unconditionally.

He spreads my legs and enters me unsheathed. We both want a family eventually, though we've agreed to wait for the right time. But because we'd wanted our wedding night to au naturel, I'd started taking the pill to prepare. Gone is the need for barriers; rubber or otherwise.

Despite being sopping wet already, his cock stretches me out until it burns a little. The pleasure is so intense, it makes me cry out. Funny, how different it feels without a condom. How different it feels when you're married.

"I'm not hurting you, am I?" he asks.

I just shake my head and smile, but am mute otherwise. It's too intense and sensitive; too beautiful for words.

He pushes into me deeper and deeper with every move. I don't know what else to do but claw at his back every time he withdraws. I want more; so much more of everything he has to offer. He can see it in my eyes and is intent on giving it to me.

The heavy bed creaks under the intensity of our movements, but neither of us pay it any mind.

My consciousness is reaching another plane, one where petty concerns about furniture lose all relevance. As he continues to claim me—the term 'making love' would be woefully inaccurate for what's going on right now—my vision starts to blur. I can't focus on anything else anymore, just the in and out, the relentless rhythm of his hips as they goad me towards my release.

A sweet, tingly feeling spreads through my body, projecting outward from my lower abdomen, and yet staying largely in that part of my body. Until... His gasps fill the room, along with my moans. If another guest hears us, so be it.

He fucks me harder yet again, flicking his hips upwards at the end of each thrust. A thin coat of sweat covers my body, not because I'm hot or even tired, but just because I'm so close I can almost taste it.

As he leans on one arm, the other hand reaches between us again, this time going for my nipple. He tweaks and teases me, starting softly and then growing more daring when I thrash about underneath him. I need his body closer to mine, and I can't control myself anymore, clawing at him again to get him into a tighter embrace.

With one final scream, my body signals it's time. I freeze, but he struggles on despite me keeping him almost in a stranglehold. The next two, three, four thrusts threaten to make me cry. My eyes do moisten at last, such is the intense pleasure I feel.

I don't want him to see, but I'm powerless over my own body.

"I love you," I gasp, but I'm not sure he even hears me.

He grinds to an abrupt halt himself, his body shuddering against me as he reaches his own peak. The formerly rock solid muscles in his arm soften, and he lowers himself onto me.

I keep him there, lying in my arms with his head on my shoulder, for as long as we need to calm our breaths.

"I love you too," he finally responds, minutes later.

He leans up, then wipes the wetness off my face with his thumb. I worried it would ruin this moment if he noticed my tears, but the smile on his lips tells me he understands. From now on, I'll be forever understood.

I smile back at him, but then remember the one thing that's still nagging at me, despite everything.

"Won't you please tell me where we're going in the morning? It's going to come out at the airport anyway..." I beg.

His gaze rests on mine for a moment, then on my lips. He kisses me once more, as if to silence me, but then he leans back up and reconsiders.

"You're assuming our honeymoon will involve an airport," he teases.

"Well... doesn't it?"

"Okay, fine. There really was only one choice."

"Which is?" I ask. *One choice? What is he talking about?*

"When you said back in Brighton after we'd just met, that you'd never been to India yourself... Well... As I said, no other choice."

Other girls might have hoped for Caribbean palm

trees and cocktails on the beach, but somehow, the fact that he remembered that little detail from when we first met means everything. I smile up at him, grateful for the surprise, even if I forced him to reveal it early.

"India. Wow. That's going to be amazing!"

"It's only the beginning."

I nod and let the beautiful blue depths of his eyes capture me. This *is* only the beginning.

The beginning of our adventures together. And, the beginning of our wedding night. After three months of forced celibacy, we still have a lot of catching up to do. The way he's staring at me now with renewed hunger in his gaze tells me we're exactly on the same page.

***

AUTHOR'S NOTE

Thanks so much for reading *Only a Taste!*

This, the third of the Chance Encounters series of stand-alone novellas is different from the other two, not just because it features the first multicultural pairing I've written about so far, but also for how it came into being. Both *One Night Stand* and *Beautiful Stranger* started ages ago as short stories, which I then developed into novellas. *Only a Taste* was conceived as a novella from the beginning. While I was writing *One Night Stand* (If you haven't read it yet, don't worry, I won't mention any spoilers), I came up with two minor characters: Jack Cleary who plays the role of Lucy's nightmare client, and his friend and colleague, Callum Byrne. They're both renowned chefs with their own restaurants. I couldn't wait to incorporate these people into stories of their own, but I wasn't quite sure how to go about it, because obviously in order for romance to occur, every hero needs a heroine...

Enter Mandi. I've been exposed to Indian (specifically Punjabi) culture quite a bit, so it was just a matter of time for me to include that in my writing. Although I'm not Indian myself, I can relate to the feeling of growing up as somewhat of an outsider, a second generation immigrant. My childhood was spent juggling two identities, including different languages: my family's origins, versus the local culture where we lived. It's not always easy to figure out where you belong, when your family and friends seek to pull you in differing directions. I can also relate to the difficulty one may face when marrying outside of one's own ethnicity or religion.

Since all the Chance Encounters books feature real places in South-East England, I started brainstorming areas that I was at least somewhat familiar with. That's how the pieces started to come together. I know Slough and the surrounding areas well enough, and it just so happens that a lot of people of Punjabi origins live around there. I like throwing opposites together, so why not Callum Byrne, the Irish TV Chef who managed to build up a nice little career for himself in the UK, and a second generation British Asian girl from Langley whose difficulties finding a job after University meant she's forced to move back in with her parents. It seemed like a great opportunity to tell a story of clashing cultures.

Obviously that's the main conflict of this story: the clash between Mandi's conservative family and her own identity as an independent and free-spirited British woman. In her mind, her self-worth doesn't depend on how soon (or how well) she marries, she's perfectly content being herself. Her family, though, don't quite agree and would rather see her settled as soon as possible. Because that's what good girls do.

In such situations it would be easy for an outsider to say 'well it's *your life,* so just do what *you* want'. In reality though, having to go against everything your parents believe in, effectively giving them the middle finger, would be extremely difficult and painful. It's a lot easier said than done. Mandi feels stuck initially, she wants nothing more than for everyone to just get along, or at least for her worlds to continue coexisting without much overlap like while she was still living on her own during her studies. I hope I was able to portray her struggle accurately, based on what I've seen other people go through when they tried to go against tradition in their love life.

Meanwhile, Callum, with his money and fame, has never really had to fight for attention. He sees Mandi as a challenge initially, but then realises that their attraction runs a lot deeper. Despite everything, he's a true romantic at heart, he just never found the right person to bring to light that aspect of himself. In Mandi, he finds the girl he wants to settle down with. His money and success don't impress her much, which helps keep their relationship interesting. There's nothing more boring in the long term than to be with someone who agrees with or loves everything you do.

So that's what makes him willing to change for her. To ignore the customs of dating and relationships in the western world which expect that you spend a long time figuring out whether you're right for one another. You might even live together before even considering popping the question. With Mandi, that's not an option, because her parents will never accept him if he approaches their relationship from that angle. So if you feel you're right for one another, why not make a big commitment? He stands to lose the one chance to create a family with the only girl that's ever interested him like that, if he doesn't at least try.

Anyway, so those were my inspirations and I hope you enjoyed the story as much as I did while writing it. If you're interested in reading more of my work, perhaps you'll consider signing up for my newsletter. I'll even give you a free book of your choice when you sign up!

x, Lorelei

- ❖ LMoone.com
- ❖ Lorelei Moone on Facebook
- ❖ AuthorLMoone on Instagram

I also write Paranormal Romance as Lorelei Moone. Check out LoreleiMoone.com for more information.

SPECIAL OFFER!

For a limited time, all new mailing list subscribers will receive a FREE short story, called At First Sight.

Claim your free copy here:

LMoone.com

Look for the newsletter sign-up form on the right hand side of the page.

OTHER PUBLICATIONS

<u>Big Boys Do It Better Series:</u>
Recipe for Passion
Paperback ISBN: 9781913930547
Best Friends Forever
Paperback ISBN: 9781913930554

<u>The Chance Encounters Series:</u>
One Night Stand
Paperback ISBN: 9781913930080
Beautiful Stranger
Paperback ISBN: 9781913930103
Only a Taste
Paperback ISBN: 9781913930127

<u>The Undateables Series:</u>
The Rebound List
Paperback ISBN: 9781913930042
Sally
Paperback ISBN: 9781913930066

<u>**As Lorelei Moone:**</u>
<u>**The Scottish Werebears Series:**</u>
An Unexpected Affair
Paperback ISBN: 9781913930165
A Dangerous Business
Paperback ISBN: 9781913930172
A Forbidden Love
Paperback ISBN: 9781913930189
A New Beginning
Paperback ISBN: 9781913930196
A Painful Dilemma
Paperback ISBN: 9781913930202
A Second Chance
Paperback ISBN: 9781913930219

<u>**The Alpha Squad Series:**</u>
Boot Camp
Paperback ISBN: 9781913930233
Friends & Foes
Paperback ISBN: 9781913930240
Infiltrator
Paperback ISBN: 9781913930257
Showdown
Paperback ISBN: 9781913930264

<u>**The Vampires of London Series:**</u>
Alexander's Blood Bride
Paperback ISBN: 9781913930288
Michael's Soul Mate
Paperback ISBN: 9781913930295
Lucille's Valentine
Paperback ISBN: 9781913930301

<u>**The Shifters of Black Isle Series:**</u>
Claimed by the King
Paperback ISBN: 9781913930325
The Soldier and the Siren
Paperback ISBN: 9781913930332
A Dragon's Treasure
Paperback ISBN: 9781913930349
The Warlock's Conquest
Paperback ISBN: 9781913930356